The Dead Soldier's Locket

Private Nelson Hunter Vaughan, C.S.A., gritted his teeth, burrowed deeper in the hole he'd dug in the sandy soil of Fort Walker, and swung his rifle toward a tall Yankee soldier leading the landing party up the beach.

Private Vaughan had no taste for killing—he'd seen enough of it this day. But he knew that he must kill this man, now just a hundred yards away, or be killed.

Nelson Vaughan raised his rifle and sighted on the man's chest. For a brief instant, he hesitated, knowing not why. He wondered where this man hailed from, whether he had a family who would grieve for him. Still, the Yankee came on.

Nelson pulled the trigger and the man staggered, then fell. Nelson ran forward and knelt beside him. He was dead.

Nelson Hunter Vaughan picked up the locket clutched in the dead man's hand. He stared down at a daguerreotype of the most beautiful woman he'd ever seen.

Inside him, the certainty built that, somehow, somewhere, he would find that woman . . .

The FREEDOM FIGHTER *Series*

Storm in the South

Jonathan Scofield

A DELL/BRYANS BOOK

Published by
Dell Publishing Co., Inc.
1 Dag Hammarskjold Plaza
New York, New York 10017

Dell ® TM 681510, Dell Publishing Co., Inc.

ISBN: 0-440-07685-4

Printed in the United States of America

First printing—August 1981

It may be that our career will be ushered in in the midst of a storm; it may be that as this morning opened with clouds, rain and mist, we shall have to encounter inconveniences at the beginning; but, as the sun rose and lifted the mist, it dispersed the clouds and left us the pure sunshine of heaven. So will progress the Southern Confederacy, and carry us safely into the harbor . . .

President Jefferson Davis
Montgomery, Alabama
February 16, 1861

BOOK I

The Gathering Storm

FORT SUMTER

1

"Y OU, SIR," Nelson Hunter Vaughan said, "are a lying bastard."

He swirled the brandy in his glass. "You claim to be a fire-eater, another Yancey Rhett. 'Attack Sumter,' you say, 'and overwhelm the damn Yankees, show the Black Republican in the White House that South Carolina is no more a part of the Union than Canada is.' That's what you say, sir, while all the time you're trembling in your boots, afraid the Old Colonel is right when he says the war, if it comes, will be long and bloody. You, sir, are a coward."

Nelson paused as though expecting a reply. None came.

"You fear for your life," he went on. "You're afraid of the Yankees, afraid of your father, afraid of your own fiancée. What did you say when Colleen told you to dampen your ardor until after the wedding?

You said nothing, nothing at all." Nelson's voice rose. "Isn't it time you faced the truth, sir?" he asked.

He flung the brandy from his glass, the liquor splashing on the mirror and streaming down its surface. The reflection of his face wavered, distorted by the brandy.

"Now look what you done."

Nelson glanced behind him and saw Melinda watching from the doorway. "I'll wipe it off," he said, taking his handkerchief from his sleeve.

The pretty young black woman shook her head vigorously. "What if somebody was to come in and see Massa Nelson cleaning a mirror? What would they say? 'What lazy niggers they got in that house,' that's what they'd say. Now you go to your mother, she been asking for you."

"If Mr. Lincoln has his way," Nelson said, "you'll be free and won't have to care what people say."

Melinda looked away from him, all expression leaving her face.

"I don't know nothing about that," she said.

"You know more than you let on."

Melinda shook her head. Nelson stepped to her, putting his hand on her arm.

"Linda," he began.

She stiffened and stared at his hand until he took it away.

"You go see your mother," she said, her voice husky. "She got one of her megrims and she's asking for you."

Nelson sighed, turned and walked into the hall. As he passed the drawing room he heard the Old Colonel's voice. "Who's there?" his grandfather called out.

"It's Nelson," he answered, walking on.

"Nelson," the Old Colonel said loudly. "I don't like it here in Charleston. The time has come to go back to Santee. Do you hear me, boy?"

"We'll go back, grandfather," Nelson said over his shoulder. "Soon."

"Times are bad," the Old Colonel said.

"They'll get worse," Nelson murmured to himself as he climbed the curving stairs, hearing the Old Colonel echo the words.

He knocked on his mother's door. "Come in," a faint voice told him.

Nelson paused just inside the room, bowing to his mother who was sitting propped up on pillows in her four-poster bed. She waved him to a chair and when he was seated she nodded to her bedside table. Nelson saw the folded sheets of a letter next to the water pitcher.

"Jared's coming home," his mother said. "He wrote from Washington where he stopped to resign his commission. He should be in Charleston within the week."

Nelson drew in his breath and stood up, turning so his back was to his mother. Jared Hunter was a distant cousin, but not, Nelson had often thought, distant enough.

"There was nothing between Jared and Colleen Hughes," Ida Vaughan said. "A harmless flirtation, nothing more. Besides, that was all years ago."

"I never thought—" Nelson began.

No, damn it, he told himself, there have been too many lies, too many evasions. It's time to face the truth.

"Jared Hunter's a bastard of the first rank," he said.

His mother gasped. Nelson turned quickly to see

her leaning back against the pillows with her hand clasped to her lace-edged bed jacket. Her face had paled.

"My heart," she said. "It felt as though it stopped and then began racing twice as fast as it should."

"I apologize for what I said," Nelson told her, "yet it's the truth. You and I both know it."

"I acknowledge no such thing. Three years in the army has undoubtedly changed Jared for the better." She nodded to the bedside table. "Please hand me my powders and a glass of water, Nels."

He poured the water and watched as she drank. She was a small woman, frail, her face pale, her eyes lusterless and shadowed, her hair a mousy brown. Nelson couldn't remember a time when she hadn't been bedridden.

"Ida's always been delicate," her father, the Old Colonel, had told him once. "She's a sick woman; I fear she'll get worse before she gets better."

"The Old Colonel," Nelson said, anxious to avoid discussing his cousin Jared, "wants to go home to Santee."

"We all want what we can't have these days. Mr. Lincoln wants to hold the Union together by force of arms, General Beauregard wants to capture Fort Sumter without a fight, I want to regain my health and see your father regain his." She looked up. "What is it *you* want, Nelson?"

"I don't know," he said, then stopped and began again. "That's not true. I want so many things I can't begin to list them."

"Why don't you and Colleen marry now?" his mother asked, watching him closely.

"She has her heart set on marrying in June. The arrangements are all made for the wedding and for our trip to Nassau."

"These are uncertain times. There's no telling what might happen between now and June even if it is only two months away."

"You mean because Jared's on his way home?"

"Jared? Did I mention Jared's name? I was referring to South Carolina's secession from the Union last year and the other Southern states following her lead."

"What did Mr. Petigru say about that? 'South Carolina's too small to be a republic and too large to be a madhouse,' I think it was."

"Mr. Petigru's a Unionist. There's no accounting for what *he* might have said." She pressed her fingers to her forehead. "You're trying to befuddle me, Nels. We were discussing you and Colleen Hughes, not secession. If you wish me to speak to her mother, I will."

"Good God, no. I'll speak to Colleen myself when I see her tonight."

"I'm only trying to be helpful." With a sigh she lay back on the pillows. "Before you leave the house, please look in on your father. He had another bad spell today."

"He's all right, isn't he?"

"He's been working too hard for too long and worrying too much, that's all. He needs a rest. I've asked Dr. Misdom to see him this evening."

Nelson nodded and bent over the bed, kissing his mother on the forehead.

"You smell of brandy," Ida Vaughan said. "I worry about you, Nels. You don't know how much I worry."

"You still treat me as a child, mother. I'm twenty years old. I'm a man."

"I'd been four years married by the time I was twenty," his mother said. She sighed again. "Remember to look in on your father."

Nelson tapped on his father's door at the far end of the upper hallway. When there was no answer, he went in and saw Alexander Vaughan sleeping with the covers thrown off to reveal the top of his nightshirt. The older man's face was flushed, but no more than usual; his breathing was deep and steady.

Nelson shrugged and left the room, quietly closing the door behind him. He tiptoed past the sitting room so the Old Colonel wouldn't hear him. On the street outside the Vaughan townhouse, he paused, debating whether to ride or walk. The late afternoon breeze brought the fresh tang of the ocean and he breathed deeply. He set off on foot for his club, his walking stick tapping on the stone pavement.

Palmettos, looking like tall fountains, grew on both sides of the street. Ivy, roses and jasmine twined over garden walls partially concealing lawns that led up to houses with long piazzas and slim white pillars.

Nelson climbed the steps and entered the Bachelors' Club, fully intending to eat dinner, but Richard Petigru, a cousin of the Unionist Petigru, clapped him on the shoulder and in a few minutes they were throwing dice for drinks.

"They say there's a Union expedition setting sail from New York to relieve Fort Sumter," Dick Petigru said. He was tall, thin, and sandy-haired, perhaps the wealthiest of all the Petigrus, one of Charlestons' original Huguenot families.

"Let the damn Yankees come," Nelson said. "Old Beauregard's ready for them. Last week I brought some slaves to the city from Santee to work at Fort Moultrie and the new guns were all in place. If Lincoln's heart is set on fighting, we're ready to accommodate him."

"I don't understand that gentleman," Dick Petigru said in his slow drawl. "I honestly do not. Maintaining we should free our slaves is one thing. I can comprehend a man feeling that way, wrong-headed though it may be. But to say South Carolina had no right to leave the Union . . ." He shook his head, at the same time signaling the waiter for another round.

"The Old Colonel's afraid a war will last for years and that the South hasn't a chance of winning. He claims it's a matter of simple arithmetic. Most of the population is in the North, along with the industry and the railroads."

"The Old Colonel's seen his day. How old is he, ninety?"

"Close to it," Nelson said. "Did you know what they called him when he went to Princeton? My mother was telling me just the other evening."

"I didn't even realize he went north for his schooling."

"They called him the Young Prince," Nelson said. "He was a handsome bastard. I've seen the portraits to prove it. Black hair and a smile that told you he thought he was as good or better than any man alive."

"A good description of you, Nelson, except for the black hair and the being handsome."

Nelson grimaced and said nothing. He had little vanity about his looks. He was tall and big-boned and would someday be as burly as his father, but now he was thin. He had a small brown moustache, hair of the same color, and a broad open face. His eyes, also brown, had a wedge of yellow in the iris. Nelson secretly liked people to notice how different they were from the ordinary run of eyes.

"In his day, the Old Colonel must have been one of the wealthiest men in the Carolinas after the Hamptons." Petigru stared into his drink. "I've been

hearing distressing talk, Nels," he said. "About Santee. They say you-all had to sell off some of your
best slaves."

"My father sold a few of our hands. He had to
after his loss on last year's cotton."

"Aaron was one of them, I heard. I was told your
father sold Aaron for fifteen hundred dollars to Jethro Hunter. Aaron was the darky you grew up with,
wasn't he?"

"We were like brothers." Nelson frowned. Too
much like brothers, his father thought. Associating
with whites had made Aaron uppity, or so Alexander
Vaughan claimed, and that's why he sold him, or
so he said. The true reason, Nelson believed, was
that his father had wanted to show Nelson who ran
Santee.

"I don't envy Aaron," Petigru was saying. "Not with
Jared Hunter coming home from Texas. Jared's a
right mean son-of-a-bitch. Cruel. I never could bring
myself to trust the man."

"If the slaves ever revolt, it's Jared's kind that'll
have forced them to it. I don't hold with treating
slaves like animals the way Jared does."

"That's where you're wrong," Petigru said. "You
mark my words, if the niggers ever rise up against
us, God forbid, it'll be the spoiled ones who'll be
burning and killing. You have to treat them like what
they are. Members of an inferior race. Children. The
surest way to turn a child nasty and spiteful is to
spoil him."

Petigru looked up as a red-haired, freckle-faced
young man approached. James Wilkes, smiling,
clapped the two men on the back and signaled the
waiter for a drink.

"Have you two bastards heard the latest?" Wilkes

asked. "Major Anderson's getting ready to evacuate Fort Sumter and turn it over to Governor Pickens."

"I heard just the opposite," Petigru said.

"And I don't give a good goddamn," Nelson said. "I just wish it was over. One way or the other, I wish it was over—that we'd either starve them out or storm the fort and send the Yankees packing or else let them stay in peace. I just wish it was all over."

The two men stared at him."

"His approaching marriage befuddles our friend," Petigru said. "Here all this time I've been praising Nels Vaughan as a fire-eater and now he sounds as though he's shying away from the fight."

"If I were the intended of Miss Colleen Hughes," Wilkes said, "I might be a mite anxious for the fateful day to arrive, the day I began my wedded bliss. I'd be wanting to save all my strength, too, without dissipating it in fighting. I notice I haven't seen you at Miss Lettie's of late, Nels. She has a new girl, a Creole calling herself Yvette who hails from New Orleans."

"Sir," Nelson said, suddenly feeling lightheaded, "I must ask you not to mention Miss Hughes's name in the same breath as that of a woman of the town."

"An unfortunate slip of the tongue, sir," Wilkes said. He raised his glass. "To Colleen Hughes," he said. "Charleston's finest flower, the belle of the great Palmetto State of South Carolina."

"The epitome of Southern womanhood," Petigru added.

Nelson looked from one of his friends to the other. The room whirled and he shook his head to clear it, realizing he should have eaten. "Are you saying more than I hear?" he asked. "Are you casting aspersions on Miss Hughes?"

"Not at all," Wilkes told him. "If you hear more in our words than we intend, it's our envy that's doing the talking. Miss Hughes must have turned down ten suitors before she accepted you, Nels—including, some say, a certain Richard Petigru."

"I have always been one of Miss Hughes's admirers." Petigru raised his glass. "We haven't toasted her. Colleen Hughes!"

The three men drank.

"Jared Hunter's on his way to Charleston," Petigru told Wilkes. "To Hunter Hill."

"I hadn't heard," Wilkes said. "It's men like Jared who'll lick the Yankees. He has courage, dash, and endurance; he's a patriot. Or is the word state-riot now? As long as we have our Hunters, the South is unbeatable. If war comes, we'll be in Washington City sitting down to dinner at the White House inside of a week." He glanced at Nelson. "Jared was one of the unfortunate ten, wasn't he?" he asked.

"The unfortunate ten?"

"He means one of Miss Hughes's many suitors," Petigru said. "That was years ago," he told Wilkes, "before he earned his army commission, before his brother Fremont went north to West Point."

"Many's the time I saw Jared sitting on the Hughes piazza," Wilkes said, "passing the time of day with Miss Colleen. If I were you, Nels, and now I'm speaking as a friend of many years' standing, I wouldn't wait till June to lead Miss Hughes to the altar."

Nelson stood up abruptly. "I don't intend to," he said. "Don't you-all be surprised if you're addressing Miss Hughes as Mrs. Nelson Hunter Vaughan before this week is out."

"Good for you, sir," James Wilkes said.

Nelson bowed then walked carefully across the room, confident that no one in the club could tell how unsteady he really felt. At the door he glanced back. Both Petigru and Wilkes were shaking their heads, smiling at each other. When they saw him looking their way they lifted their glasses, saluting him.

"Damn you both," Nelson muttered to himself.

He paused when he reached the street, surprised it was as late as it was. The gas lights hissed softly and a hack rolled by, its wheels clattering on the cobblestones. From an open window came the sound of a woman's laughter.

"And damn Colleen," he said aloud, setting out for the Hughes house.

He handed his card to Henry, the colored butler, and followed him across the entry hall to the front parlor. Colleen took the card from the butler's tray and Nelson saw her frown, but when she looked up and found him standing in the doorway she smiled brightly and rose to greet him.

Nelson felt his heart lurch. God, she was a beautiful woman. Her glossy black hair was piled high on her head, her green eyes flashed in the lamplight, the bodice of her pink and white taffeta dress molded her small breasts. She drifted gracefully toward him, her hoop skirt rustling, her hand extended. He took her hand in his and kissed it.

"I'd quite given you up," Colleen told him. "Not that I don't know how time must fly when gentlemen sit down over their cigars and brandy. As I was telling Dyan only a few minutes ago."

For the first time Nelson realized that Colleen wasn't alone in the parlor. Looking past her to the settee, he had an impression of blonde curls, a fair complexion, and a gown cut so deep it revealed not only the rounded tops of white breasts but hinted at the nipples below.

"This is my fiancé, Nelson Hunter Vaughan," Colleen said. "Nels, Dyan arrived unexpectedly today from Richmond. Her father's on General Beauregard's staff."

"His aide-de-camp," Dyan said. She raised blue eyes to stare at Nelson.

"I'm charmed," Nelson said. "Welcome to Charleston, Miss Dyan."

"Her father's Colonel Roger Raleigh-Beckwith," Colleen said.

"I always travel with Father," Dyan told him. "He says I'm all he has left."

"Her mother and two brothers died of the typhoid," Colleen put in.

"I'm sorry." Finding himself staring at her breasts, Nelson quickly looked away.

"That was years ago." Dyan smiled sadly. "I scarcely remember my mother. Father says she was the most beautiful woman he'd ever met or could ever hope to meet. Father says he'll never remarry because no one could ever take her place."

Nelson nodded, uncomfortable without knowing why. "It's hard to imagine she could have been more beautiful than yourself," he said.

Dyan stood up and made an elaborate curtsy. "Colleen told me you were a gallant gentleman and you truly are," she said. Nelson's gaze returned to her full, rounded breasts. Again he looked quickly away.

"You'll find that all of our Charleston gentlemen are gallant," Colleen said. "I'm giving a party here next week to introduce Dyan to a few friends," she told Nelson. "Please make it a point to come."

"I wouldn't miss the opportunity to see Miss Beckwith again," Nelson said.

"Now I'm sure you two will want to be alone."

Dyan smiled up at Nelson, then nodded to Colleen. She left the room with a rustle of her skirts.

"She's a lovely child," Colleen said coolly as soon as Dyan was gone. "Dyan's only sixteen."

"She looks older."

"Yet she acts so much younger, don't you think? Still, I'm sure she'll cut a wide swath in Charleston society, at least among the eligible bachelors. I'm particularly anxious to have her meet your friend James Wilkes. He's such a sincere young man and so worldly-wise."

"As I'm not?" Nelson asked.

Colleen looked closely at him. "Do sit down," she said. He sat on the settee, breathing in the odor of lilies-of-the-valley. Not Colleen's scent, he knew.

"You seem so altogether strange this evening, Nelson," she said, "not like yourself at all. First you keep me waiting, embarrassing me in front of my young guest, then you question me as though I were in the witness box. Is something troubling you? Is your father feeling poorly?"

"Father's fine. He was sleeping when I left the house."

"Your father's not a well man, Nelson."

"It's my mother who's the invalid."

"She'll outlive us all, you mark my words. There's iron in that woman. Besides, she's her father's daughter. By the by, Nels, how is the Old Colonel?"

"The same as always; he never changes. For as long as I can remember he's looked just as he does today. The same thick white hair, the same cane, and with Caesar at his side. No man ever had a more faithful slave."

"I'm afraid of Caesar."

"Of Caesar? I'll grant you he's a brute of a man. He's over six-two and must weigh two hundred and fifty pounds, but he's as gentle as a nanny. You must know that; you've seen him taking care of the Old Colonel."

"I tell you, Nels, I don't trust him. You haven't noticed the way he looks at me. As though I were about to sell him to the Hunters just as your father sold Aaron. Which, come to think of it, might not be such a bad idea."

"The Old Colonel couldn't live without him. Caesar will not be sold."

Colleen came to sit next to him. "Oh, Nels, I was only teasing. Of course he won't be sold. And it's certainly not my place to suggest such a thing. I was just recalling how angry you were when your father sold Aaron. I wouldn't have put up with that if I'd been in your place."

"It's really none of your concern." Nelson smiled to soften his words.

"Now, you see, you *are* acting differently." She put her hand on his sleeve. "You're scolding me. After all, I was just supposing. I *am* to be your wife. Or had you forgotten?"

His hand went to the nape of her neck and he drew her to him, kissing her on the lips. She drew away, putting her hands between them.

"You're so strong," she said, a hint of irony in her voice. "So domineering."

He grasped her by the upper arms and shook her.

"Nelson!" Her voice rose in surprise.

"Stop it, Colleen." He stood and walked to the window, looking out at the gas lamp's halo of light. "You know you're marrying me because you think I'm just the opposite of what you just said. Because you think that you'll be able to manage Santee just as you think you can manage me. Just as you run your mother's household when your father's at sea."

"What's wrong, Nels?" she asked. "Is it true about your father selling off his slaves? Has he lost as much money as they say he has?"

"I don't listen to idle gossip, and you shouldn't either."

"I'm waiting," Colleen said.

"For what?"

"For you to come out with whatever it is you came here to tell me. I know something's troubling you. Now turn around and look at me and tell me what it is."

He turned and saw that her face was flushed, her eyes glittering in the soft light, her hair shining like jet. "You've never been more beautiful," he said, "than you are now."

Colleen shook her head impatiently. "Tell me," she said.

"I've decided to stop lying to myself," he said. "It's about time I faced up to the truth."

"I really don't know what you're talking about. Are you pixilated, Nelson? I do believe you had too much to drink at your club."

"Whether I did or not has nothing to do with what I'm talking about. This state, this country is on the brink of war. I think it's time to end the deceit."

"Are you about to tell me that Mr. Lincoln was right all along? That the slaves should be freed?"

"No, I'm not talking about slaves. I'm talking about you and me and Jared Hunter."

"Jared Hunter? Lord! What has Jared to do with all this?"

"You know he's coming home, don't you?"

"Yes, I do believe I heard as much. Is that what you're saying, that you're worried about what you may have been told about Jared and me? That was all years ago. Even at the time it didn't amount to a hill of beans."

"I think we should be married as soon as possible," Nelson said. "Colleen, I love you, you know I do. There's going to be a war, if not over Fort Sumter, then over some other fort or some Federal arsenal in the South. Marry me now; don't make me wait until June."

"I was going to suggest a change in our wedding plans myself."

"You were? Why didn't you say so? Why have you been letting me go on this way?"

"I was about to suggest we postpone the wedding, Nelson. Because of the unsettled times."

"Not because Jared's coming home? Not because you found out my father had to sell Aaron?"

"Nels, what do you take me for? A gold-digging hussy? I promised to marry you and I fully intend to keep my promise. I love you, Nels. Didn't I turn down one proposal after another until you asked me?"

"I wondered about that. Why *did* you accept me, Colleen? The truth now, tell me the truth. Why do you want to marry me, Colleen?"

She stood up and walked to him, touching him lightly under the chin. "Because I love you, silly. Because you're the only one I ever wanted to marry."

"You're four years older than I am."

"Of course I can't deny my age. Oh, I see, you're afraid I really want to mother you." She put her hand to the nape of his neck and drew his mouth down on hers. As she kissed him, her mouth opened and he felt the tip of her tongue on his lips, felt it touch his own tongue. He took her in his arms and pulled her to him, feeling her soft body against his.

"Everyone and his cousin will see us," she whispered.

Nelson walked around the room, turning off the lamps.

"Leave one on," she said in a low voice. "Mother will notice if you don't."

Leaving the light on the table near the door turned low, Nelson crossed the room to where Colleen was sitting on the settee. When he sat next to her she opened her arms to him, kissing his lips, a long, lingering kiss.

"Does that feel as though I want to mother you?" she asked.

He shook his head, his lips still on hers. She drew away. "I should feel insulted when you tell me I want you because of Santee," she told him. "After all, my father's not exactly a pauper, as you very well know. He's in Nassau now, buying another ship."

He tried to kiss her, the excitement rising in him, but she held him away.

"I must admit," she said, "that we're not old money like the Vaughans and the Hunters, not one of the tidewater planters. My father didn't know General Washington like your grandfather, the Old Colonel, did."

"The Old Colonel only shook hands with Washington at a reception, nothing more."

"Even so." She stiffened. "Now, Nels," she said.

His hand had slid up along her slim waist to cup her breast beneath the slippery cloth of her dress. He silenced her protest with a kiss, his hand feeling the delicious softness of her. She relaxed and moaned softly, pressing against him, her hand covering his and holding his fingers to her breast as her mouth opened and once more her tongue met his.

Suddenly she tensed, pulled herself away and stood up.

"Colleen," he protested.

"No, I can't. I want to, you can see that I want to, but I can't. If I did, you'd think me no better than one of Miss Lettie's girls."

He drew in his breath, surprised that she'd speak of Miss Lettie's.

"You didn't think I knew about her, did you?" she asked. "Well, there's a great deal you don't know about me." Although she was turned from him with her hands clasped in front of her, he thought she was smiling.

"I want to know everything about you," he said. He walked up behind her, putting both hands on her waist and drawing her back against him, his lips nuzzling her ear.

"You will," Colleen said, "I promise you that. You will once we're married."

"Then it appears I might have to wait forever."

"No, I was teasing you when I said I wanted to postpone our wedding. We'll be married on the fourteenth of June as we said we would be, no later, no sooner."

"I love you," he said. "I need you. I want you."

He blew softly in her ear and she moaned, twisting against him. His hands rose to cup her breasts as he drew her back against him, trying to shift his body to one side so she wouldn't feel his hardness.

"I love you, Nels," she said. "That's the reason we'll wait. I will not have the gossips sitting on their piazzas talking about us, wondering why we're marrying early. I won't have them counting the months."

"If they do start counting now, at this rate they'll be old women before they're through."

"So be it then." She turned in his arms and kissed him gently on the lips. "Goodnight, Nels," she said. "It's very late."

He kissed her hungrily but Colleen backed away,

putting her forefinger on his lips. "It's only two months," she said. "We only have to wait two months."

"My God, it's going to seem like two years."

He turned from her and walked from the room. A single light burned in the hall, throwing his shadow onto the far wall. As he neared the front door a figure appeared from the shadows, inclined his head to Nelson, and opened the door.

"Good night, Massa Nelson," the butler said.

"Good night, Henry."

The door swung shut behind him and he heard the bolt slide home. A fog had crept in from the sea and the mist swirled about him as he went slowly down the steps to the sidewalk. He began to walk north, away from the harbor, letting his cane clatter along the iron posts of the fence at the side of the Hughes house.

Nelson shook his head. He'd meant to be decisive with Colleen, demand that they be married as soon as possible. Insist on it. Somehow nothing had gone the way he'd intended. Not that she wouldn't be worth waiting for; she was more than worth it. He was a lucky man; everyone told him so and he had to agree. She'd talked about his mother having a will of iron; Colleen, in her own way, was just as unyielding.

Admittedly her passion didn't match his but, after all, she was a woman, a genteel woman.

What would she be like in a few more years? Colleen was already twenty-four, four years older than he was, and even now she was convinced she could twist him around her little finger. Well, couldn't she? Wasn't that really why she was marrying him? She wanted to be mistress of Santee, to be the lady of the plantation. He shivered suddenly in the chill mist, shaking his head to banish this unwanted and, he told himself, unfair view of Colleen. They'd be partners; together they'd revitalize Santee, together they'd face the future, whether it be good or bad.

God, but he wanted her. He had never felt like this about any other woman. He couldn't imagine feeling this way about anyone else. Had any man ever desired a woman as he desired Colleen? He hadn't lied when he said he needed and wanted her. She was like a fever in his blood, a fever with no known cure. No, there was a cure. Having Colleen.

From behind him he heard the approaching clip-clop of a horse and the rattle of carriage wheels over the cobbles.

God, but he needed a drink. He'd have a nightcap with his father before he turned in, see how the old man was, find out if there was anything he could do for him tomorrow. He'd tell him the latest rumors about Fort Sumter.

The horse was beside him now and when he glanced toward the street he saw a cabriolet appear out of the mist.

"Mr. Vaughan?" a voice asked. A woman's voice.

Nelson took off his hat and peered through the enveloping fog. He made out a lone figure on the seat of the two-wheeled carriage.

"I'm afraid you have the advantage of me," he said.

Her laugh was almost a giggle. "It's Dyan," she said. "It just seems like I've been driving forever and ever and I've gone and got myself good and lost. And at this time of night, too. I'd feel ever so safe, though, if you would be kind enough to show me the way."

"Of course." Nelson climbed up onto the seat beside her. "Yes, I'd be delighted."

Dyan laughed again, leaning her head momentarily

on his shoulder. The scent of lilies-of-the-valley was all around him, her body was warm against his. He took the reins from her hands, flicked them, and they set off through the fog.

2

"Y<small>OU SHOULDN'T BE OUT</small> alone at night like this,"
Nelson said. "Especially not with all the soldiers
bivouacked around Charleston these days."

"Will there really be a war, Mr. Vaughan? My father says President Lincoln is bluffing and all the
South has to do to call his bluff is to stand firm."

"I hope to God he's right but I fear there'll be
war."

"It's not right, it's just not right. Mr. Lincoln should
let the South go its own way in peace."

"I agree. Which doesn't change the fact that you're
out late at night without an escort."

"But I do have an escort, Mr. Vaughan. The young,
gallant scion of one of the best families in South Carolina." She held to his arm with both hands. "Where
shall we drive?" she asked.

"I'm taking you to the Hughes house before they
miss you and sound an alarm."

"I won't be missed until morning. My father is staying overnight at Fort Moultrie and I bolted my door from the inside before I slipped out of the window. If Colleen comes to wish me a good night she'll think I've taken a sleeping draught and retired. The boy who harnessed my carriage won't say a word. Not if he expects to get the half dollar I promised him."

"You're a little she-devil, aren't you?"

"Those are my father's very words." All at once Dyan shivered and moved closer to Nelson, snuggling close to his side.

"You're cold," he said.

"No, it's not that. The night's warm, even with the sea mist, warmer than I'm used to in Richmond. I just thought of something, something unpleasant. It's really nothing, Mr. Vaughan."

"Nelson."

"And you, sir, may call me Dyan." She spelled her name. "It's the name of the Roman goddess of the hunt," she said. "Will you think me brazen, Nelson, if I tell you that the only hunt I've ever been interested in was the pursuit of women by men? And vice versa?"

"I'm afraid I will. Young ladies in Charleston aren't that frank, I'm sorry to say."

"I meant to shock you and I did." She laughed. "It's not true, anyway. I'm the most reserved and proper young lady you might ever hope to meet, reared in seclusion by a jealous father who refuses to let young men court me until I turn eighteen."

"I don't believe a word you're saying," Nelson told her. Through the swirls of fog he saw the lamp in front of the darkened Hughes house. "We're there. I'll escort you to the door."

"Won't you take me to the Battery first?" she asked.

"Please, I've heard so much about it, the live oaks, the bandstand, the view of the harbor with Fort Sumter sitting like a huge and terrible monster at the entrance."

By God, he *would* take her to the Battery. They wouldn't be able to see more than ten feet in the fog but this young wench wasn't interested in the view. She wanted to be kissed, he was sure, and he'd be happy to accommodate her. What Colleen Hughes didn't know need never hurt her.

"Are you sure you won't be missed?" he asked.

"Positive. And if I am I'll say I was kidnapped by a damn Yankee and spirited off to Fort Sumter where all the Union soldiers had their way with me."

Nelson said nothing, wondering if all Richmond girls were as forward as this one.

"We'll drive down Meeting Street to the harbor." They were already well beyond the Hughes house.

"I have a confession to make," Dyan said after a short silence. When he didn't answer, she went on, "I was in the next room knitting and couldn't help overhearing some of what Colleen said to you. I thought it was just terrible the way she was teasing you."

"Colleen is a very proper young lady," Nelson said stiffly, wondering if he should be listening to this young girl talking about his fiancée. And suddenly wondering what the hell he was doing driving to the Battery with her in the middle of the night.

"If it had been me," Dyan went on, "I would have agreed to marry you tomorrow. A tall, dashing man like yourself, not to mention your being brave and masterful, too."

"Miss Hughes doesn't always seem to think I am," he said sardonically.

"All she ever talks about is Santee, the big house and all those slaves and all that cotton. . . . I do hope

I'll be able to visit your plantation while I'm here in Charleston. You will invite me, won't you?" She went on without waiting for an answer. "How many slaves are there at Santee?"

"Two hundred, all told. A few years ago we had more."

"If you sold all of them you'd have . . ." She paused. "Numbers are my undoing," she said. "You'd have well over a hundred thousand dollars," Dyan concluded triumphantly.

Nelson shifted uncomfortably on the carriage seat, for talk of money made him uneasy. Men might be concerned with such matters, but women shouldn't be.

"Not nearly that much," he said finally. "More of our slaves than you'd think are children and old folks who can't work. That's something the Yankees don't seem to realize. They imagine that all slaves pick cotton in the fields while a cruel overseer stands behind them with a whip to make sure they gather their two hundred pounds a day. It's not like that at all, as you know. We have to care for the field hands and the house slaves and for their children and the old people, too. For as long as they live."

"That's just what Daddy says," Dyan told him. "He maintains that the men, and the women and children who work eighty hours a week in the mills in Massachusetts are the real slaves."

"He's right. The Yankees just don't understand what it's like here in the South."

Dyan was silent for a time. "I don't know," she said. "I think if I had my choice, I'd rather work in the mills. Because I'd know I wouldn't have to stay there all my life. I could marry the son of the mill owner and live happily ever after." She sat up straight.

"La, Nelson," she said, "why are we discussing such a depressing subject? Look, the mist's lifting. You can see the water."

The thinning fog blew past them in gray swirls, the mist haloing the street lamps along the way and turning them into lonely islands of soft yellow light. Ahead and to their left, water lapped on the shore. The night air was damp and tangy with the odors of the sea.

"Is this the Battery?" Dyan asked when Nelson brought the cabriolet to a halt. In the mist the twisted oaks garlanded with Spanish moss looked like gnarled old men risen from their tombs and trailing their winding sheets behind them.

"Yes," he told her. "Fort Sumter's dead ahead in the middle of the channel leading from the harbor into the Atlantic. To your left are our batteries on Mount Pleasant and Fort Moultrie and to your right is Fort Johnson and Cummings Point. If the Yankees refuse to evacuate Sumter they'll be hammered into submission by our cannon in no time."

"Why do they stay in Sumter then?"

"God knows. Why does a Yankee do anything?"

"Only to turn a dishonest dollar. At least that's what Daddy says."

"I suppose they're trying to prove a point. Pretending that South Carolina hasn't seceded after all, that we're actually still a part of the United States."

Dyan released his arm and before Nelson could stop her she stepped to the ground beside the carriage.

"Walk with me," she said.

"Now? Wouldn't you rather wait until tomorrow?"

"No, now. Listen to the waves on the rocks, Nelson. Listen to that ship's bell. Can't you just imagine you're about to sail for distant lands? The ocean has always meant something special to me. I can't explain the feeling I get when I'm at the seashore."

He climbed to the ground and, after tethering the horse, offered her his arm. She took it, walking close beside him, so close he could feel the tantalizing softness of her breast brushing against him. Dyan no longer wore hoop skirts, he noticed. She was dressed in a long dark gown that buttoned high at the neck and was wearing a shawl over her shoulders. He could see ringlets of her blonde hair curling on her forehead.

A man's voice called out ahead of them; another voice answered.

"Two of Beauregard's sentries," Nelson said. "He's taking no chances. The Yankees are said to have warships stationed outside the channel."

Dyan tightened her grip on his arm. "I'm not afraid of Yankees as long as I'm with you," she said. "If war comes, will you fight?"

"I'm a member of the Sons of the South. If we're needed, Governor Pickens will call on us."

"It's so thrilling, being here in Charleston and not knowing whether there'll be war or peace, not being able to tell from one day to the next what might happen. We might be bombarded from the sea or the Yankees might land soldiers and lay waste to the city."

"There's little danger of that. South Carolina has five thousand fighting men in and around Charleston with more arriving every day. There's only sixteen thousand men in the entire U. S. Army and most of them are in the West."

"And how many does Major Anderson have on Sumter?"

"About seventy troops and fifty workers."

"You see," she said. "I was right the first time when I said there's naught to fear."

As the fingers of her free hand slid up and down his sleeve, Nelson felt the stirrings of excitement, of ardor. He tamped down his feelings, thinking of Colleen, forcing his thoughts to focus on his fiancée.

"What's this mysterious cousin of yours like?" Dyan asked.

"My cousin? You mean Jared Hunter?"

"Yes, that's the one. He can't possibly be as handsome and dashing as Colleen says he is." She stopped walking. "Oh my," she said, putting her hand to her mouth. "I shouldn't have said that, should I? I really shouldn't."

"I don't know what he's like now. I haven't seen him for more than three years."

"Colleen told me he's been fighting Comanches in the West with the army. She says that when Colonel Robert E. Lee left Texas to resign his commission, Jared decided to do the same."

"He had no choice. Jared would never fight for the North. He and his brother are South Carolinians, born and bred. Hunter Hill has been in their family for years and they have another cotton plantation near Camden and a tobacco plantation in Virginia."

"You still haven't told me what Jared Hunter is like." They were walking slowly through the park between the harbor and the city.

"He's good-looking, I suppose. At least women always seemed to find him so. And he's a gentleman; he fought his first duel when he was seventeen. He's right courtly when he's around the ladies. And a good soldier, I'm sure, I'll give him that. He's always been brave, even to the point of being foolhardy."

"From the tone of your voice, I'd judge you don't like your cousin Jared very much."

"When I knew him he was a mean son-of-a-bitch." As soon as he'd spoken, Nelson regretted his words.

"I think I'd like to meet this Jared Hunter," Dyan said, smiling slyly.

"If you ever tell anyone what I said, I'll deny it."

"I never repeat confidences. In fact, I'm the soul of discretion. My lips are sealed for all time. A hundred Yankees wielding red hot irons couldn't force me to reveal your secret." She giggled. "Really," she said, "I won't say a word. But I understand how Colleen feels. Some women like men who are said to be dangerous and unpredictable. It makes them exciting. With most men, a woman waits to find out what they'll say. With the other kind, the kind Jared must be, a woman is always wondering what they'll do, not what they'll say."

Nelson stopped. He saw what she was playing at, but knew equally that there must be some truth in her words. Gripping her arm, he turned her so she faced him.

"Tell me what Colleen said."

"Said? Why, I don't rightly know what you mean, Nelson."

"You know damn well what I mean. What did she say about my cousin Jared?"

"She just mentioned he was coming home and that she was looking forward to seeing him again after all this time. That's all she *said*."

"And what do you mean by that?"

"It wasn't as much what she said as how she looked. We women know how other women feel about a man from the way their eyes glisten or by the tone of their voice. Of course it's harder to tell when it's an older woman, like Colleen, but I still knew. I do believe she's in love with him."

"She was never in love with Jared. I'm certain she wasn't." Nelson let his hands drop to his sides.

"You believe what you believe and I'll know what I know." Dyan smiled sympathetically. "I shouldn't have said what I did about Colleen. I just didn't think it was fair, your not knowing."

"I'll escort you home," Nelson told her.

"Now you're angry with me. It isn't my fault Jared Hunter's coming home. It isn't my fault that Colleen feels the way she does about him."

"Colleen's going to marry *me* in two months' time."

"Of course she is. I never said she wasn't. I understand she had her chance to marry Jared years ago and didn't. There must have been a reason. I wonder what it was."

Nelson walked in the direction of their carriage, his pace so fast that Dyan had to run to keep up. Ahead of them a building loomed darkly through the fog.

"What's that?" Dyan asked.

"The bandstand. Where they hold the Sunday concerts."

"I have to rest," she said. "You've made me run and run until I'm quite out of breath."

She walked to the cupola-roofed bandstand and sat on one of the wooden steps. Nelson stood looking down at her, his arms folded across his chest.

"Don't be so stern," Dyan said. "Here, sit beside me for a moment. The wind off the water is sending a chill into my very bones."

Nelson sat next to her. His head was clear now, the effects of the brandy long since gone, and he was angry, though not at Dyan. And not at Colleen. He knew Colleen—at least he thought he did—and she couldn't help being the way she was. Flirtatious, a collector of men's hearts. Not that he believed all that Dyan had told him. Still, there had been something between Colleen and Jared years ago. He was sure of it.

"Listen!" Dyan grasped his hand. "I hear footsteps. Someone's coming."

"Probably one of the sentries."

"We'll hide in the bandstand."

"There's no need . . ." he began but she was already leading him up the steps. The octagonal stand was some twenty feet across with a solid plank railing all the way around the outside. Dyan sat on the floor with her back to the railing and drew him down beside her.

The footsteps neared, paused a few feet away, and, despite himself, Nelson's pulse quickened. A man coughed, spat and the steps began once more, receding into the night until the only sound was the slap-slap of water on the shore.

"What if we had been Yankees?" Dyan asked. "What would he have done if he'd found us here? Would he have shot us?"

"I don't imagine so. Probably he'd have taken us to his commanding officer to be questioned."

"What if you were a Yankee and I didn't know it and you managed to lure me here? What would you do?" He could hear her rapid breathing.

"I suppose I'd kiss you." Leaning to her, he felt her breath on his cheek and he brought his lips down on hers. Her arms went around his neck as she kissed him hungrily. He moved his lips a few inches away. "Like that," he said.

"Is that all? Is that all you'd do?" Dyan asked huskily.

She moved away from him and he heard the soft rustle of her dress. He felt desire surge in him, a building, urgent need. No, he told himself. She's going to tease me, just as Colleen did.

Nelson stood up and walked away from her to the far side of the bandstand where, with both hands on the railing, he stared into the mist in the direction of the sea. In the distance he heard the roll of drums, the call to general quarters, and he pictured gun crews hastening to man their posts.

"Nelson."

He turned and saw Dyan's dark form a few feet from him, the scent of lilies-of-the valley drifting to him, luring him, exciting him.

Her fingers touched his sleeve and trailed downward until they reached his hand. Taking it in hers, she brought his hand to her so that he felt the soft fabric of her dress, the lace at the neckline. Her fingers led him onward until he touched her skin. Her fingers directed him downward so his hand rested on the upper curve of her breast. Nelson drew in his breath. Her breast was bared to his touch.

His hand closed over her breast and when he felt her nipple between his fingers he trembled uncontrollably, trembled with desire, with panic, with the urgency of his need. Dyan moaned, swayed toward him and she was in his arms with his hand, still beneath her dress, no longer on her breast but on her bare back.

He kissed her and her mouth opened to his, her tongue flicking along his lips and his teeth, meeting his tongue and twining with it as her mouth moved against his while her body pressed against him. All at once she stepped away.

"Kiss my breast," she whispered.

When he leaned to her, her hands went to the back of his neck, drawing his head down to the curve of her breast and, finally, to her nipple. His tongue circled the nipple, his teeth gently biting her flesh. She moaned again, leaning back against the railing, her hands gripping his head harder, her own head thrown back so her upper body was thrust toward him, her body naked to the waist. He realized that she had worn nothing beneath her riding costume. Her dress was kept from falling to the bandstand floor only because it was held between her body and the rail.

Pushing his head away from her breast, she murmured, "The other one. Kiss the other one."

With his tongue extended, he sought and found the warm yielding flesh of her right breast. As he gripped her nipple between his teeth she cried out with pleasure.

Drawing him after her, she knelt on the floor. She leaned forward to kiss him, gently at first, then with rising ardor. Suddenly she flung herself on him, toppling him to one side so he sprawled on the wooden planking. He reached for her, took her shoulders in his hands and, pulling her toward him, held her above him for a moment, their bodies not touching, before she squirmed free to fall on top of him, her bared breasts twisting against his chest, her mouth covering his face with kisses, her tongue trailing across him, her teeth nipping him, gently biting his cheeks, his earlobes, her lips nibbling at his ear. When she blew into his ear he felt a tingling and he heard her throaty laugh. She brought her face to his, with her lips covering his lips, her tongue slipping inside his mouth again as her fingers clawed at his clothing.

She stiffened and held still.

"What?" he asked.

"Shhh!" Her whisper was urgent. He groaned softly, more aroused than he had ever been in his life.

Footsteps approached them. The steps stopped, then came on again. Nelson looked over his head. He was lying against the rail of the bandstand on his back with Dyan on top of him, still naked to the waist. Above the blonde halo of her hair he saw shifting shadows as though a lantern bobbed up and down somewhere near the bandstand.

"He's coming," Dyan whispered, her mouth to his ear. "He heard us."

Again the steps paused, only a few feet away from them now.

"Who's there?" The man's voice was a mixture of caution and bravado. Again the lights and shadows shifted above their heads. Nelson heard a footfall on the wooden steps.

Good God, he thought. If he finds us like this the story will be all over Charleston by noon tomorrow. Dyan will never be able to hold her head up in the city. As for himself, he shuddered to think of the consequences. Colleen would never speak to him again. And with good reason.

More footsteps. The crunch of gravel.

"Paul? That you?" The voice came from some distance away.

"Nate? Thought I heard a scrabbling around here somewheres. Near the bandstand."

"Probably heard me taking a piss."

Nelson felt Dyan shaking. At first he thought she was afraid but then he realized she was trying to keep from laughing aloud.

The light disappeared as though the lantern had been shuttered. Nelson heard the first sentry sit on the steps of the bandstand. The butt of a musket thudded on dirt, a match scraped on wood. In a few moments the smell of tobacco smoke drifted to him and, looking past Dyan, he saw the glow of a cigar some ten feet away.

"Awful quiet," one of the sentries said.

"Too damn quiet. I been hearing noises that ain't there all night long."

"They say old Beauregard's giving the damn Yankees twenty-four hours to pack up and leave Sumter. If they don't he's going out after them."

"I heard them Yankees only got food enough to last another week. Beau's intending to starve them out, or so they say."

"A man can't believe nothing he hears these days. Nothing at all."

"Ain't that the truth?"

Nelson drew in his breath as Dyan's hand crept around his waist to the front of his pants. She slowly unfastened his leather belt and twisted open the top button beneath it.

While the sentries went on talking, Dyan shifted her body to one side, her weight leaving him, and he heard the soft rustle of clothing. Then silence. The sentries were speaking wistfully of home, oblivious to the couple only a few feet from them.

Dyan's fingers returned to his pants and quickly undid the rest of the buttons. Her fingers teased him, creeping across his flesh, leaving him and returning. Nelson felt himself harden, heard his breathing quicken until the sound was like a great bellows in his ears. Dyan's fingers touched his sex for the first time, her hand springing away as though burned.

Nelson felt her hand on his face and he realized she was putting one finger to his lips, bidding him to be quiet. Slowly, carefully, quietly, she raised herself so she was above him, kneeling over him with one leg on either side of his body, and when he reached up he found that she was naked, completely naked, her flesh soft and damp beneath his fingers.

Her hand found his sex once more and she stroked it, teasing him as her fingers fluttered to him and then left, only to return for a few more caresses before departing again. He strained up toward her, choking off a moan of desire.

Dyan positioned him beneath her and slid down on him. Before he realized what was happening he was inside her, the warmth and wetness of her encircling him, claiming him, pressing against him. Slowly she lowered her body onto his until the tips of her nipples touched the cloth of his shirt. A moment later the fullness of her breasts pressed down on his chest and her mouth closed over his, her lips parting as she kissed him deeply while she kept her body rigid, not a muscle stirring, only her mouth moving avidly on his, her teeth bruising his lips.

Her lips stilled and he felt her body tighten around his sex. Ever so slowly she raised her hips a fraction of an inch, then another fraction, sliding up over him, drawing him to her, raising herself another fraction of an inch until she was poised over him, barely touching him.

For a long minute she held herself above him and then with an almost inaudible sigh she relaxed and slid down onto him, letting him plunge within her.

"Well, I'll be goddamned."

Nelson stiffened at the sound of the sentry's voice, his eyes opening wide. He turned his head toward the two soldiers, saw the glow of the cigar and nothing more.

"It actually happened that way?" the second sentry asked.

"I swear to God, that was the way of it and no one the wiser except me and him." The sentry paused

significantly before he added, "And her, of course."
"That's a right good one! I never did hear its like."
The soldier guffawed loudly.

Under cover of the laughter, Dyan raised and
lowered her body, then raised and lowered it again
while Nelson clenched his hands at his sides, trying
to control himself. Dyan started to tremble. The
quivering seemed to begin in her legs, spreading and
gaining strength until her entire body shook.

Nelson put his arms around her and held her to
him. Her hands left his body and he felt them go
to her face and he imagined them clasped over her
mouth as she sought to keep from crying out. Slowly
her trembling ebbed and, finally, ceased altogether.
Dyan relaxed and lay on him, not moving.

A sound drew Nelson's attention back to the two
sentries. They were standing, their dim figures outlined darkly in the mist; now they were walking away
from the bandstand. When he heard them speak,
their words were too low to be audible. A few moments later their footsteps receded and they were
gone.

Nelson let out his breath. "Good God," he said.
"Good God," he repeated.

Dyan giggled. "Well, I never," she said.

He put his arms around her and rolled onto his
side, kept rolling until he was on top of her, his sex
still inside her. She gasped as he clasped her tightly
to him and thrust within her, slowly at first, then
faster and faster until he felt her trembling begin,
felt the trembling spread until her whole body shook
beneath him. Though his passion mounted higher
and higher, he held back, letting the fever engulf him
until at last he exploded within her, surging against
her time and time again.

Finally, sated, he stopped. Her legs were wrapped

about him, gripping him to her, and when he tried to ease away Dyan held him tighter, held him to her as her trembling began once more. She cried out, keeping him within her until she stilled and went limp in his arms. He knelt above her, then stood and walked away.

Without a word he straightened his clothes, hearing the whisper of her clothing in the darkness behind him. When he was done, he looked across the harbor. The fog had lifted enough for him to see the dark outline of the far shore.

"I'm ready," she said.

He nodded and went to her, taking her by the arm.

"Kiss me," she told him.

He leaned over her, his lips meeting hers, and she returned his kiss briefly before drawing away. They walked side by side along the path leading from the bandstand, not touching. When they came to the carriage, the horse still tied to the hitching post, Nelson wondered whether the sentries had seen it and what they had thought if they had. He helped Dyan to the seat and, after untying the horse, climbed up beside her. He clucked to the horse and, to the steady clip-clop of hoofbeats, they rode back into the city in the dim light of early morning.

Nelson, unable to find words, at least not the right ones, said nothing. He was vaguely uneasy about what had happened. He couldn't define his feelings toward Dyan. What kind of a girl was she to let him do what he had done? To lead him to do what he had done? Not so much what he had done, as what *they* had done.

"You don't have to worry," she said softly. "No one need ever know. Not unless you tell them."

"A gentleman doesn't talk of such things." He wondered if she thought him as stuffy as he sounded to himself.

"We don't have to again," she said. Her hand trailed along the side of his leg and away. "Unless you want to."

"Your father—"

"My father has nothing to do with it," she interrupted, her voice harsh. "If I told General Beauregard what I know, my father would be cashiered out of the army." She subsided. "My father will never find out about us," she said after a moment. "Never."

"We're almost to the Hughes place." He had circled the block so they'd approach from the rear and now he slowed as they neared the entrance to the stable.

"I'll drive the carriage in," she said, taking the reins. "The stableboy will see the horse is tended to."

"You'll be all right?" he asked.

"Yes," she said.

He climbed down and stood aside as she drove past him through the open gate into the yard. After waiting a few minutes, he turned and walked quickly along the street with the sky paling in the east. When he reached the Vaughan townhouse he took his key from his pocket and trotted up the front steps to the door. He started to whistle "The Bonnie Blue Flag" but stopped, afraid he might waken someone.

As he was about to insert his key in the lock the door opened and he saw Melinda, a candle in her hand, staring up at him.

"Where you been, Massa Nelson?" Her cheeks were tear-stained. "We been looking high and low but couldn't find hide nor hair of you."

"What's wrong?" He felt a flutter of panic. "Is mother all right?"

"It's not your mother, it's him. He took a bad turn just after you left. He's been asking after you. All night he's been calling your name."

"The Old Colonel?"

"No, your daddy. Your daddy's dying, Massa Nels."

He drew in his breath, felt his heart pound in his chest. His father. No, there was nothing wrong with his father. He was tired and overworked, that was all. He'd been worrying too much about Santee.

Nelson strode past Melinda and climbed the stairs three steps at a time. In the upper hall he turned right and hurried along the corridor to the open door of his father's room. Inside, a lamp burned on a table beside the bed. Dr. Misdom stood gazing down at his father; his mother knelt at the side of the bed; the Old Colonel slumped in a chair, asleep.

The doctor and his mother looked up when he entered the room. His father's face was pale, his eyes were closed.

Ida Vaughan rose from her knees and walked slowly to Nelson.

"He asked for you and we couldn't find you." Her eyes stared accusingly at Nelson. "He's dead. He passed on ten minutes ago."

3

JARED HUNTER left the cars at Charleston's North Eastern Station and stood on the train platform, hands clasped behind him, a calm island amidst the feverish ebb and flow of soldiers around him. He was a tall, lean man dressed in gray civilian clothes, his strikingly handsome face bronzed by the sun and wind of the Texas prairies. A faint three-inch scar slanted across his left cheek.

Jared smiled. His time had come.

He had served his apprenticeship. First at the Citadel—he had both loathed and loved the academy. If the school had done nothing else, it had drilled into him the value of discipline. Without discipline order became chaos, a winning campaign faltered, the center of the line sagged, the less-seasoned troops broke and ran and the rout was on.

A man needed discipline as much as an army did. Jared glanced about the station, looking for familiar faces but seeing none. Most of these soldiers were up-country men, a sullen, scrabbling lot. He despised them. For a moment he thought of Nelson Vaughan and again he smiled to himself. While he, Jared, had suffered through his years at the Citadel, Nelson had indulged himself with whist, Madeira, horses and cotillions. A soft life for a weak, vacillating and undisciplined man.

Nelson wouldn't have survived a month on the Texas frontier, the final part of Jared's apprenticeship. Either Nelson would have fallen with an arrow through his chest on one of the Comanche campaigns or the boredom of life on an army post would have driven him mad. As it had almost driven Jared mad. The only purpose of an army, he told himself, was to fight.

He had a feeling he'd get his share of fighting here. Good; he was ready. He'd faithfully served his apprenticeship, he'd resigned his captain's commission in the United States Army, and now he was home in South Carolina to fight for the Confederacy.

Jared hailed a hack outside the station. "The Charleston Hotel," he told the driver.

Arriving at the balconied hotel on the corner of Meeting and Pinckney, his luck, which had followed him ever since leaving San Antonio, which had, in fact, followed him all of his life, held again. Beauregard had driven up only minutes before, he was told. The general was glad to see him; effusive, in fact.

"We need as many of you spirited South Carolinian gentlemen as we can get," Beauregard told him. The short, dapper Creole from New Orleans, Jared knew, was a twice-wounded hero of the Mexican War. The general was an artillery man, just what was needed in Charleston.

When Jared requested a three days' leave to visit Hunter Hill, the general nodded. "Permission granted, Colonel Hunter," he said.

"Captain Hunter, sir," Jared corrected him.

"From this day forward you will be Colonel Hunter of the Confederate Army."

Jared saluted, refusing to let his exultation show, about-faced and left the room. In the hallway he almost collided with one of the prettiest girls he had ever seen.

He swept off his gray top hat and bowed. "Jared Hunter at your service, ma'am," he said.

The girl gasped, staring at him with deep blue eyes. Her blonde hair fell in curls to the shoulders of her pale green hooped dress, but Jared's attention had been caught neither by her eyes, hair, nor gown. He found himself staring at the scoop neckline revealing the white upper curves of her breasts.

"Dyan!"

Jared glanced along the corridor to where a colonel in Confederate gray was studying him with eyes as cold as any Yankee's heart. "The general is waiting for us," the colonel said to the blonde girl.

Dyan smiled up at Jared before hurrying away.

"Who are they?" Jared asked a passing lieutenant as soon as the general's door closed behind them.

"Colonel Roger Raleigh-Beckwith and his daughter. They're from Richmond."

Jared nodded. He'd make it his business to see more of Dyan Raleigh-Beckwith. There had been that gleam in her eyes, a look promising dimmed lights, soft music, a woman's laughter. And more.

He borrowed a horse from the Yanceys. The Yancey family had been beholden to the Hunters ever since Cleavon Yancey had been sent to Congress as a result of Jethro Hunter's backing. And still Jared's luck held, for he found S.R. Yancey preparing to journey up-country to the Yancey plantation at Moncks Corner.

"What was the mood in Washington?" S.R. asked Jared as the two young men rode past the marshes along the Ashley River.

"Dread. Excitement. Confusion. What can you expect now that we have a gorilla for president?"

"Not 've'," S.R. said. "*They* have a gorilla for president."

"I yield to the clarification of the gentleman from South Carolina. I was about to say they not only have Lincoln as president but a mulatto as vice president."

"Hannibal Hamlin a mulatto? I hadn't heard that.'"

"He's black as any nigger and he has a brother named Africa. Now you tell me true, S.R., how could anyone named Africa be a white man?"

"Hamlin has brothers named Asia, Europe and America, I'm told. They're a globe-girdling family. There's no accounting for what goes on in the minds of some men when the time comes to name their offspring." S.R. smiled. "As I well know."

Jared laughed. "I always think of you as S.R.," he said. "I keep forgetting your full Christian name. Not that I don't like and admire it. States Rights Yancey has a ring to it, damned if it don't."

"I'll be obliged to you if you'll keep calling me S.R."

"There's the fork," Jared said, pointing with his quirt to where the road divided at a large oak. "We're nearing home."

"Santee lies to the right and Hunter Hill to the left. Did I remember it a-right?"

"Correct." Jared reined in. "This bay I'm riding's borrowed and I know you're on your own horse, yet

I'll race you even. To the fork. We're a half-mile away."

"A ten-dollar wager?"

"Why don't you make it enough to interest a man? Say fifty."

"You're on," S.R. said.

Jared swung from his horse and picked up a fist-sized rock. Remounting, he said, "When the rock strikes the ground, we spur. Not a moment before, S.R."

"Just like the old days."

Jared tossed the rock high into the air. Both men watched its arc, tensed, and as it thudded to earth they spurred their mounts. Jared sprinted to the fore, held a slight lead for the first hundred yards and increased his advantage in the next hundred. When his bay began to falter he spurred him viciously and the horse surged forward only to falter once more. S.R.'s gelding gained with every stride, raced side by side with Jared's mount, then swept past to reach the fork well in the lead.

"God damn," Jared said, "God damn." He cantered up beside S.R. "You'll stay the night at Hunter Hill, hear," he said, telling S.R., in effect, that he would settle their debt at the Hill.

"If you and your father will be so kind as to have me."

They rode on along the left fork until Jared swung his horse from the road onto a trail leading through an oak grove toward the river. They heard the whistling trill of a mockingbird and saw the green and yellow flash of a parakeet.

"When I was a lad," Jared told S.R., "this was my secret trail from the main house to the Charleston road. From the looks of it, no one's used it since."

After riding a few hundred feet, Jared reined up. "Look there," he said softly, pointing to a recently used path leading through the brush. "Someone's been coming from that thicket to the river and back. That thicket used to be one of my favorite hiding places."

"Kids, more than like," S.R. said.

"Kids hell." Jared swung his bay from the pathway and walked him into the brush. S.R. followed.

"As I recall," Jared said in a low voice, "there's a glade on the far side of this brush and a fallen oak beyond that. Fremont and I used to camp in the woods on the far side of the oak."

They rode from the thicket into the sun-dappled glade. The oak lay across the path on the far side, the once giant tree now a rotting hulk.

"Stop!" Jared shouted.

Two men leaped from behind the fallen tree and ran into the woods. Jared spurred his horse, pulling his pistol from the holster on his belt.

"Stop or I shoot," Jared called. The men, both Negroes, both barefooted, ran on.

Jared fired, deliberately aiming high, and the sound of the shot echoed in the woods. The two men stopped and turned, raising their hands toward Jared, palms out. Jared reined his bay to a halt ten feet from them, his smoking Colt in his hand. Hooves beat on the soft earth behind him and S.R. joined him, pistol drawn.

"Looks like we caught us a couple of Brown's boys," Jared said. He looked down at the two blacks. "Is that right, were you meaning to run off to the North and join up with old John Brown? He was hanged by the neck till he was dead up in Virginia, though I reckon you didn't know that."

The two slaves stared sullenly up at him.

"You niggers got passes?" S.R. asked.

The two men stared stolidly ahead.

Jared cocked his pistol with his thumb. "When a white gentleman asks you a question," he said in a steely voice, "you had best answer it."

"We ain't got no passes," the taller and heavier of the two said. "We done lost them."

"Lost your passes," Jared said. "Now ain't that a shame, ain't that truly a crying shame." He fired, the shot missing the head of the taller black by inches. "That's to teach you respect for your betters," Jared said. "When you speak to a white man you will say 'sir.' What're your names?"

"I'm Spartacus," the taller slave said. "And this here's Dred." Again Jared cocked his pistol. "Sir," the slave added hastily.

"Spartacus?" Jared smiled. "Now you and me both know that no master is going to have a slave who's named after the man who led an uprising against the Romans. We know that, don't we, Spartacus? Now, tell us your name."

"I done give myself the name. I got the right to be called whatever I want to be called. Sir."

"Now will you just listen to that, S.R.," Jared said. "This here boy's been poisoned by listening to the ranting and raving of those Black Republicans. Those abolitionists. Pretty soon we'll have slaves calling themselves John Brown and Abe Lincoln and whatever unholy name suits their fancy. Isn't that right, Spartacus?"

The slave said nothing.

"Answer when I speak to you," Jared demanded.

"I reckon so. Sir."

"Who's your master, Spartacus?" Jared asked.

"Mr. Alexander Vaughan. I'm from Santee."

"You see," Jared said to S.R., "this is what happens when you spoil them. They become uppity, begin getting big ideas, thinking their black souls are as good as our white ones. I might have known anyone calling himself Spartacus hailed from Santee. Where are you from, Dred?"

Spartacus started to speak but Jared silenced him with a wave of his hand. "Let him speak for himself," Jared said.

"Five Oaks," Dred told them.

"Rhett's place. Well, S.R., I see we just got to teach these young bucks a lesson, one they'll never forget. A lesson none of the slaves round these parts will ever forget."

"What you meaning to do, Jared?" S.R. asked.

"You'll see." He took a length of rope from his saddle and threw it down to Dred. "You, Spartacus," Jared said, "hold out your hands and let Dred tie them. You'll tie them good, won't you, Dred?"

"Yes, massa," Dred said. He took the rope, winding it several times around Spartacus' wrists before knotting it.

"You got a rope, S.R.?" Jared asked.

When S.R. handed him a coil of rope, Jared dropped to the ground and tied it to the bindings on Spartacus' hands. Remounting, he looped it several times around the pommel of his saddle.

"I'll show you how the Comanches treat their prisoners," Jared told S.R.

He swung his horse around and started out at a walk with Spartacus following at the end of ten feet of rope. When Jared increased his horse's pace to a trot, Spartacus had to run to keep up. The slave stumbled and fell and was dragged forward on his stomach, his hands gripping the rope. Jared dug in his spurs so his horse galloped across the rough ground with Spartacus' body raising a cloud of dust behind him.

When Jared reached the road he went on until he came to the fork, where he stopped in the shade of the giant oak. Looking behind him, he saw that Spartacus, bleeding and with his clothes in shreds, lay unmoving on the ground. Jared smiled, took a cigar from his vest pocket, and lit it.

Several minutes later S.R. joined him, with Dred trudging along beside his horse. Dred knelt next to Spartacus, looking fearfully from the black's battered body to Jared.

"Is he alive, Dred?" Jared asked.

"Yes, sir." There was a tremor in Dred's voice.

"Good." Jared dropped to the ground, tossing his cigar to one side. "Help me lift him into the saddle," he told the black. The two men struggled with Spartacus' limp body, finally heaving him onto Jared's horse.

"What you meaning to do?" S.R. asked. "That there's not your slave, Jared. He belongs to the Vaughans."

"I know right well who he belongs to," Jared said. "Maybe I'll be able to teach old man Vaughan and his son Nelson a thing or two about dealing with slaves. While I'm teaching these niggers a lesson at the same time."

"I wouldn't do nothing rash, Jared," S.R. said. "There's bad blood between you and the Vaughans as it is."

Jared loosened the rope looped around his saddle and pulled it free. He climbed to a limb of the oak fifteen feet above the ground and tied the end of the rope to the branch, testing it before climbing from the tree. He formed the other end into a noose and, standing in one of his stirrups, looped it around Spartacus' neck.

Jared stepped to the ground and took his quirt in his hand.

"Good God," S.R. said, "that nigger's worth all of fifteen hundred dollars."

"He ain't now," Jared said, striking the horse's rump with the quirt.

The horse bolted ahead and Spartacus jerked free, his body first swaying at the end of the rope and then jouncing up and down again and again, the movement less pronounced with each stretching of the rope. His body spun, first one way and then the other. His eyes bulged and blood oozed from his mouth as his teeth bit into his tongue.

After retrieving his horse, Jared rode to the oak and looked up at the hanging man. "I reckon he'll be good and dead soon enough." Turning to Dred, he said, "Now you pay heed to what was done here this day. You understand?"

Dred nodded.

"This is what happens to niggers who try to run off to the North. This is what happens to Nat Turners and to John Browns. They're hanged by the neck till dead. Do you understand, nigger?"

Again Dred nodded.

"Answer me." Jared's voice was low and deadly.

"Yes, sir," Dred said. "I understands."

"Good. Now you just follow after me and Mr. Yancey to Hunter Hill and we'll see you're sent home." Jared and S.R. rode back onto the river path with the black man trotting after them.

"You know, S.R.," Jared said, "in a lot of ways that was like having a woman. Is some ways better than having a woman. If you know what I mean."

4

AFTER S.R. Yancey had been shown to his quarters, Jared walked idly from room to room while waiting for his father. His imagination had magnified Hunter Hill in the years he had been away and now, returning, the plantation seemed diminished.

The main building was a warren of mismatched rooms. The house had been added to through the years, with the original Hunter Home built by Douglas and Sarah Hunter in the previous century now being used for the kitchens and pantries. Visitors often called Hunter Hill a maze, and rightly so, because of its proliferation of corridors, sudden turnings, and small flights of stairs, some leading not to doors but to blank walls.

As a boy Jared had loved Hunter Hill, and now a man he found he loved it still. When he was master here, he wasn't sure if he would tear the old

place down and build the most magnificent house in
the South, surpassing even the Hampton mansions,
or leave it exactly as it was.

"Jared!"

His father stood in the doorway. Jethro Hunter, a
tall man, handsome still, looked older, grayer and
heavier yet undiminished.

Jared walked to his father, opened his arms, and
the two men embraced. When Jared stepped back
he saw tears in the older man's eyes.

"Three years," Jethro said. "You've been away only
three years. It seemed like ten."

"It's good to be home," Jared said.

"You left the Hill a boy and you've returned a
man. You've resigned your commission?"

"I'm now a colonel in the Confederate Army. Serv-
ing under General Beauregard."

"Good. The Hunters have always been the first to
answer their country's call to duty. I've half a mind
to raise a company myself."

"You're needed here. With three plantations to
see to, I'm sure even Jeff Davis would advise you to
stay where you are."

"Damn Jeff Davis. They should have picked a man
with a little fire in his blood as president. Someone
like Toombs or Rhett."

"I agree."

His father, Jared sensed, was hiding an excitement,
a fever that seemed to be burning within him. Happiness because his older son was home? No, more
than that. Jared wondered what it could be.

"S.R. Yancey rode from the city with me," Jared
went on. "I asked him to stay the night."

His father nodded distractedly. Going to a sideboard, he took two glasses from a shelf and poured

Madeira from a decanter. When Jethro handed Jared the glass, the older man's eyes were glittering.

"Damnation to the Yankees!" his father said and the two men drank.

Perhaps it was both his homecoming and the possibility of war that had roused his father. Jethro was, after all, a mercurial man, given to days of exultation followed by prolonged bouts of dark malaise.

"The people have never gained except by revolution," Jethro said. "First in 1776 and now in 1861. 'To dare!'" he quoted, "'and again to dare! and without end to dare!'"

Jared nodded absently, tired of rhetoric, wearied of having heard the same words over and over again in the last ten years. The time for words was past; the time for action was at hand.

When he glanced around the sitting room he saw new lace antimacassars on the chairs. A woman? Was it a woman? He looked closely at his father. After Jared's mother died eight years before, he had heard talk, speculation as to when his father would remarry, later whether he would at all. Jethro never had. If he visited the slave quarters, Jared never knew of it. What his father may have done on his frequent visits to Charleston, Jared had no idea; he didn't know and didn't care to know.

Jared walked to the window and looked past the oaks surrounding the house to the newly planted fields where slaves hoed between the rows of cotton.

"Is there something you want to tell me?" Jared asked.

"A thousand things."

"I mean something special. About Hunter Hill perhaps."

"I'm satisfied with the plantation. Cotton's twelve-

and-a-half cents a pound. The crops have been good three years running. Campbell is still overseer. I'll have a look at the books with you later."

"Fremont?"

"Your brother appears to like West Point." Jethro shrugged. "You can never be sure with Fremont. He's become a young man of plots and strategems. I never really understood him when he was a boy and I still don't."

"The slaves?"

"Quiet. Campbell makes them toe the mark. I don't think they're even aware of the storm that's brewing."

Jared frowned. The slaves know a lot more than we give them credit for, he thought. He considered telling his father about finding the two runaways near the river but decided against it.

"How long can you stay?" his father asked.

"Only until the day after tomorrow, when I have to report to General Beauregard in the city."

"Is there any news of Sumter?"

"No hard news, only rumors. Some say the fort's to be reinforced from the sea; others claim Major Anderson will surrender it without a fight."

"At least you'll be here for the funeral."

When Jared looked at his father in surprise, the older man went on, "You did come through Charleston? You did stop over at the Vaughans'?"

"Through Charleston, yes, but I didn't go to the Vaughans'. I'll have time enough to see them later. I expect to be stationed in the city."

"Alexander Vaughan is dead."

Jared placed his glass on the sideboard. So that's the reason his father was acting this way. Jared was surprised by the news, yet not overly so. Alexander Vaughan had been an old man, much older than his wife.

"He was sixty in January," Jethro said. "He died in bed at five in the morning. He'd been sickly off and on the last year or year-and-a-half. Had the gout, you know. Drank too much, ate too much, gambled too much. He was generous to a fault, I'll say that for him."

"I know you never liked him."

Jethro Hunter walked to the fireplace, where he paced back and forth on the stone hearth. "That's not altogether true. You couldn't help liking the man. I may have despised him but I never disliked him, if you see the distinction. He was wrong for her, that's the heart of the matter."

"Her?"

"Ida Buchanan. Who else?"

Ida Buchanan Vaughan. In Jared's memory, Ida Vaughan was a wraith, an insubstantial presence, a woman seldom mentioned and hardly ever seen. She had been an invalid for as long as he could recall, leaving her home at Santee bundled in a carriage robe for the ride to Charleston or, in the summer, making the journey to the Vaughan family home at Camden to escape the low country's heat, mosquitoes and sand flies. Jared had the impression of once having a fleeting glimpse of a pale, thin face, nothing more.

"I didn't know you knew her. Before she married Vaughan, that is."

"Of course I knew her. Didn't everyone in Charleston know Ida Buchanan? In the early thirties she was the belle of the city. At the Cecilia Balls she was always surrounded by the most dashing of the young blades. Lord, she was lively! How she loved to dance and flirt! Beautiful, that goes without saying. She was said to have had eleven suitors during one season alone but she accepted none of them."

Jared looked at his father with a new interest. "Were you one?"

"Of course I was. What red-blooded man wouldn't have been? It wasn't her beauty, though, or her gaiety, that attracted me. There was always something that made Ida different from all the other girls, an intelligence and the suggestion of a strong will beneath the glittering surface. After all, she is the Old Colonel's daughter."

"She must have changed after she married."

"Vaughan broke her spirit. Oh, he didn't mistreat her. He did worse—he pampered her. And squandered all the Buchanan money. And, of course, there were the four children within the span of six years."

"I didn't remember there were so many."

"Yes, four. All born healthy and each one dead within a year. It was enough to break any woman's heart. It's no wonder that Nelson's as spoiled as he is. What a blessing he must have been to Ida. After all, he lived."

"He's a weakling. There's no backbone to him."

"He may change now that his father's dead. He'll have to if he's to save Santee. Even with cotton at twelve-and-a-half cents, they're losing money. They have to retrench, sell the town house, sell off their unproductive slaves. Alexander was selling off some of their best ones. They need a firm hand at Santee, though it's probably already too late to save the plantation."

"Could the Old Colonel do it?"

"Once he could have; now he's in his dotage. His eyesight's failing as well. He's a magnificent relic, though, still a wonderful gentleman of the old school. Whenever he hears someone coming he asks, 'Who's there?' and if it's a woman he struggles to his feet, takes off his hat and holds it to his breast."

"I've always admired the Old Colonel."

"We all have." Jethro put his hand on his son's shoulder. "Jared," he said, "I have a gift for you. In honor of your homecoming. Wait here."

After his father left the room, Jared pondered what the gift might be. The sword? He'd always admired his father's sword, a weapon handed down from Hunter to Hunter since colonial times. When he heard the door open behind him, the door to the rear of the house, he turned and saw his father in the doorway motioning to someone behind him.

A Negro came into the room, a muscular young man of medium height, his hair short and kinky, his skin exceptionally dark, the color of sable. The slave stopped in the center of the room, his hands at his sides as he stared straight ahead, looking at neither of the white men.

"This is Aaron," Jethro said. "I bought him six months ago from Alexander Vaughan. He's yours if you want him. I admit I'll hate to lose him. He makes a good field hand though he was trained as a body servant."

Jared stood in front of Aaron, studying him. He circled the black man, then felt his arm muscles with his fingers.

"He's still a strong son-of-a-bitch," Jethro said. "Strong as any ox."

"I know Aaron," Jared said. "He was brought up with Nelson Vaughan. They treated him more like a member of the family than a slave." He stopped in front of the Negro. "Do you remember me, Aaron?" he asked.

"Yes, sir," Aaron said stolidly.

"Has he given you any trouble?" Jared asked his father.

"No, none."

"When we were boys," Jared said to Aaron, "who was the only one who could whip you?"

"You were, Massa Jared."

"You fought *him?*" Jethro asked. "Fought a nigger?"

"I fought him with my bare fists," Jared said, "and I whipped him. Not once, three times. I could whip his ass now if I had a mind to."

"If you think he'll be trouble, don't take him. There're others. Hannibal, for one."

"No, I'll take Aaron. I wouldn't want anyone else. Thank you, father. You couldn't have chosen a better gift."

"Not just because he belonged to the Vaughans?"

"Not only that. But I do want to see Nelson's face when he finds out." Jared smiled. "Aaron can drive us to the funeral at Santee tomorrow."

"The sword's yours as well," Jethro said. "Do it honor. It's gone to war with Hunter men since the Revolution."

"I'll wear it with pride." Jared turned to Aaron. "I want you in livery in the morning," he told him. "You'll take us to Mr. Vaughan's funeral."

"Yes, sir," Aaron said. Jared nodded in dismissal and the slave left the room.

"Did you notice he never once looked at us?" Jethro asked.

"I'll break him," Jared said. "Never fear, father, before we're through, Aaron and I, he'll have no doubts about who his master is."

The next morning they drove to Santee, the two Hunter men inside the phaeton, and Aaron, resplendent in a uniform of red and gold and wearing a black top hat, in the driver's seat in front. The April morning was warm, the air redolent with the sweet odors of spring. Ancient oaks grew on both sides of the drive leading to the Vaughan plantation, their branches interlacing above the carriage, and only when the phaeton clattered across the wooden planks of the bridge was the sun able to slant inside the carriage. On the circle in front of the house jasmine and climbing roses twined around every shrub, post and pillar, giving Santee an almost tropical luxuriance.

As they rounded the last curve in the drive Santee came into view, a large brick house, spacious yet unadorned, built by the Old Colonel when he was a young man. Steps led to a piazza that spread across the entire front, and its overhanging roof was supported by six square wooden pillars. Above the roof the windows of the second floor looked down on the new arrivals, their shutters open. On the sloping roof of the house Jared saw four dormer windows and three of the house's many chimneys.

A Negro opened the door of the phaeton and Jethro and Jared stepped down and walked slowly up the steps. The service was about to begin in the parlor and so, after chairs were found, they sat at the rear. Mourners crowded the room, for Alexander Vaughan had been well liked. There were few tidewater planters who had not sampled his hospitality.

"Well-liked he may have been," Jethro whispered to his son. "Highly regarded he wasn't."

Jared nodded as his eyes roved over the seated mourners. Nelson was at the front of the room with a short woman beside him, undoubtedly his mother. Colleen Hughes sat on the other side of Ida Vaughan. Jared frowned. Did that mean what it seemed to mean?

"Colleen Hughes?" he whispered to his father.

"She and Nelson are engaged to be married in June."

Jared shook his head. By marrying Nelson, Colleen was repeating Ida Buchanan's mistake, he thought. Next to Colleen was her mother and next to Mrs. Hughes was a girl with blonde hair curling from beneath her black hat to her shoulders. Jared recognized her from somewhere. When she half-turned he drew in his breath. Of course, Dyan whatever-her-name-was. He smiled to himself.

The last rites for Alexander Vaughan were short and solemn. The Reverend Nathaniel Williams of St. Dunstan's Episcopal Church eulogized the deceased by praising his many benefactions and mourning his untimely passing. Handkerchiefs fluttered, the congregation knelt in prayer, and the service was over.

Only the family accompanied the casket to the Vaughan burial ground on the hill beyond the oak grove, the other mourners either returning home or remaining at Santee for the dinner that was to follow. The Vaughans rode to the cemetery in a carriage behind the open hearse carrying the coffin which was covered by the funeral wreaths. Jethro and Jared, as distant cousins, followed, although they chose to go the short distance on foot.

The two Hunter men stood apart from the other mourners on the hillside, with the family gathered below them at the open grave and the household slaves clustered farther down the hill. The Reverend Williams prayed for the soul of the departed, scattered earth on the casket after it was lowered into the ground, and then raised his hand as he led them in prayer.

As soon as the minister finished, Jethro walked up to Ida Vaughan, took her hands in his and spoke quietly to her. Ida, dressed in a black alpaca gown, her face heavily veiled, nodded as she listened but Jared couldn't hear what was said.

When Jared glanced at Nelson and nodded stiffly, Nelson stared back, trying to catch and hold his eye, but Jared's glance moved on to Colleen's unveiled face. She dabbed at her eyes with a black handkerchief although he noted that no tears stained her cheeks. When she saw Jared her mouth opened slightly and he was surprised to see a smile that came and went in the blinking of an eye.

The mourners began walking slowly down the hill, Nelson and Jethro on either side of Ida, Caesar walking apart with the Old Colonel, the minister towering over Dyan, the slaves, in a group to one side, returning to the house on foot. Jared walked toward the open grave where he stood with bowed head, seeing, from the corner of his eye, two field hands standing a short distance away with spades in their hands.

Jared saw that the Alexander Vaughan plot was enclosed by stone posts connected by a low black metal railing. Inside the rail were four small headstones covered with garlands of spring flowers, Alexander's open grave and an empty grass-covered space next to it, presumably for Ida Vaughan. Jared waited, not sure what he expected, wondering why he had remained here. The cemetery, after all, depressed him.

He glanced down the hill and saw that Colleen had lingered behind the others, who were now standing and talking beside the carriages. Still, Jared waited. By God, she would come to him.

Colleen hesitated and then walked up the slope. "You might have come to me," she said.

"Did you really want me to?"

"No." She looked steadily at him, her green eyes glittering. "I heard you'd returned to Charleston," she said. "I hoped you'd be here."

"I only came on the off-chance of seeing you."

"You're lying. I can tell when you're lying. After all, I've had to listen to a great many of your lies."

"If you were a man I'd call you out for saying that."

"I know." She glanced behind her at Nelson, who was helping his mother to her seat in the carriage. "You've changed." Colleen touched the scar on Jared's cheek. "You were hurt," she said. "Did you heroically stand off an attack of red Indians?"

"Did you come back up the hill to flirt with me?" Jared asked.

"We went beyond flirting years ago."

"My father tells me you intend to marry Nelson in June. I wish you all the best. I assume I'll be invited to the wedding if I'm still in Charleston."

"No," she said, "I don't intend to invite you. And yes, I'm going to marry Nelson. He proposed for a year-and-a-half and I finally accepted him last Christmas."

"He's a fine example of South Carolinian manhood. From one of our first families. The wedding will surely be featured on the front page of the *Mercury*."

"You don't have to be sarcastic, Jared. I know what you think of Nelson—you've told me often enough." She frowned. "What did you mean when you said *if* you're still in Charleston?"

"Colleen!" Nelson's voice. They looked down the hill to where he stood beside the carriage, glaring up at them. "We're waiting for you," he said.

"Coming, Nelson," she called.

"I've been commissioned a colonel in the Confederate Army. Under General Beauregard. When war comes there's no telling where I'll be stationed."

"*If* war comes."

"When," he said. "Your fiancé's waiting for you,

Colleen. Hadn't you better join him? What will people think? What will they say?"

"I don't give a damn what people think or say."

"You've changed, Colleen. You would have cared three years ago. You would have cared a great deal."

"Perhaps I'm becoming more like you, Jared. You taught me more than you realize. You always said a person had to decide what he wanted in life and then had to fight for it with no holds barred. Remember?"

He nodded. By God, he thought, she *had* changed. She'd always been intense yet fearful, too ready to be swayed by others. And he'd suspected that a deep well of coldness lay hidden beneath her seeming passion. Now . . . ? He'd have to find out.

"Colleen!" Nelson started walking up the hill toward them.

She touched Jared's arm. "Come to see me," she said. "Soon."

When he didn't answer he saw her face flush and he thought she was about to strike out at him.

"You bastard," she whispered.

Colleen turned from him and, holding her skirts off the ground, ran down the hill. "Oh, Nels," he heard her say, "do forgive me. I haven't seen your cousin for three years and there was so much I wanted to ask him. About Texas and the West and all."

Nelson offered her his arm and escorted her to the carriage, where he helped her up into the seat beside her mother. The driver flicked the reins and the horses trotted toward the main house, leaving Nelson standing on the dirt roadway below the grave.

He looked up at Jared, shading his eyes from the sun. Jared thought he saw the other man's shoulders slump, then straighten as Nelson walked toward him, stepping over the iron railing and facing Jared across the open grave. Jared glanced again at the two Negroes. They had retreated down the hill, out of earshot, where they stood leaning on their spades, watching the two white men.

"Colleen says you were telling her about Texas." Nelson's face was flushed and Jared decided his younger cousin had been drinking. He wasn't surprised.

"No," Jared said, "you must have misheard her. I don't believe we said a word about Texas. We were recalling old times in Charleston, before I accepted my commission. Which reminds me. I must extend my congratulations on your engagement, sir. I've always been a great admirer of Miss Hughes. As you may know."

"I didn't come up here to talk about Miss Hughes."

"Oh? I thought you had." Jared looked in the direction of the main house. "Did you want to ask after Aaron? I've decided to take him with me as my body servant."

"No, not about Aaron, either. It's Joseph. Last night we found him hanged from a branch of the oak at the fork."

"Joseph? I never heard of him. Was he one of your slaves? Did he kill himself?"

"No, he'd been dragged behind a horse before he was hanged. He was one of our prime field hands. You murdered him, Jared."

Jared smiled coldly. "I wouldn't make accusations I couldn't back up if I were you," he said. "As I say, I never heard of Joseph. What makes you think I was involved? Why would I kill a nigger for no reason?"

"The slave that was with him, Dred from Five Oaks, said you hanged Joseph."

"You've been listening to nigger talk, Nels. Do you mean you'd take a nigger's word above mine?"

"Of course not, Jared." Nelson looked around him, confused. His face slowly reddened. "I didn't think—" he began. "It never occurred to me—"

"You actually thought I hanged that nigger from the oak, didn't you?" Jared asked, smiling. "Admit it, Nels, you thought I came home and on my first day at Hunter Hill after three years of being away I'd string up some nigger I found wandering along the road. That I'd hang him out of sheer spite or pure high spirits. You did think that, now didn't you, Nels?"

"I reckon I did, Jared," Nelson said slowly, apologetically. "That Dred sounded so sure of himself, said it was you, right enough, even described you. I never imagined he was lying to me . . ."

"Maybe this Dred hanged your nigger himself after he saw me on the road and thought to shift the blame around a bit." Jared shrugged. "Who knows what goes on in an African's mind? We could study them for the next hundred years and not know much more than we do now."

"I'm sorry for my suspicions, Jared. I apologize for accusing you."

"Not only do you have my word about the hanging but you can have the word of S.R. Yancey as well. He rode with me yesterday from Charleston to Hunter Hill. You could ask S.R. if you've a mind to."

"That won't be necessary, Jared, I take your word for it. I don't have to ask S.R."

"Course it would take a little doing to ask him; he rode on to Moncks Corner this morning. When next you see him, though, ask him if I hanged a nigger at the fork. He'll tell you the truth of the matter. Now I want you to do that, Nels. I definitely want you to ask S.R., hear?"

"It isn't necessary, Jared."

"Now aren't we a couple of damn fools," Jared said.

"Here I come home after three years on the western frontier, after fighting in the Comanche wilderness, and we stand over your father's grave arguing about some nigger talk."

"I should have known you wouldn't do such a thing," Nelson said, relieved that his prickly-natured cousin had chosen to dismiss his mistake so easily. "Joseph was a top hand, worth fifteen hundred dollars if he was worth a cent. I should have known you wouldn't have hanged him, not with him being property that valuable. No matter what he might have done."

"Hold on a minute, Nels. Now I didn't say the man shouldn't have been hung. I just said I didn't do it. What with the Black Republicans in power in Washington and the Southern states seceding and all, we got to keep our niggers in line. If they get restless, we got to teach them a lesson they'll never forget or one of these days we'll all be murdered in our sleep. We don't want South Carolina to become another Santo Domingo, now do we, Nels, with the blacks running wild, murdering and raping and burning? We don't want that, now do we?"

"Course we don't. I never said we did. We've got no quarrel, you and me."

"It's not seemly, quarreling over your father's grave. I always admired Alexander Vaughan, Nels, as my father did. The first thing he said to me yesterday when I arrived at the Hill was that your father was dead and that a more generous man never lived. Generous to a fault—those were Jethro's exact words. Generous to a fault."

"He was that. I don't think he had an enemy in the world. He'd give the shirt off his back to anyone who asked, black or white."

"A wonderful man. Unlucky with money, but that's often the hallmark of a true gentleman. You have to care overmuch for a dollar to handle it properly."

"Like the Yankees." Nelson paused. "You're aiming to fight under Beauregard?" he asked.

"He's offered me a colonelcy and I've accepted. I don't doubt but what I'll be on his personal staff. Except for the older men who were in the Mexican War I'm one of the few with campaign experience. Against the Comanches and the Cheyenne. And you, Nels?"

"I'm in the Sons of the South. A private. I didn't choose to accept a commission."

"You're making a big mistake. Gentlemen should be officers; planters should be officers. What has our experience running plantations fitted us for if not command? If you'd like, I'll be happy to speak to the general in your behalf."

"No, if war comes I'd rather be fighting in the ranks."

"War will come, make no mistake about that. Perhaps we'll find it started by the time we return to the city." He nodded in the direction taken by the carriages. "I hope you'll forgive my rudeness in detaining Miss Hughes. I was asking her about her friend. Is Dyan the young lady's name?"

"Dyan Raleigh-Beckwith," Nelson said. In spite of himself, the blood rushed to his face.

"You know the young lady, I see."

"Yes, I know her."

Jared laughed. "Perhaps better than Colleen realizes. How well *do* you know her, Nels? Perhaps you're the one I should have spoken to about her."

"I've only known her for a few days. I met her the night my father died."

"I thought you seemed almighty flustered when I mentioned her name, but I wasn't thinking. If it had been my father that died, if Spartacus had been my slave, I'd be feeling mighty flustered myself right now."

"This has been a difficult time. For all of us." Nelson looked up. "Spartacus? How did you know the name Joseph called himself?"

Jared smiled. "I listen to nigger talk, too, Nels. I couldn't avoid hearing it this morning at Hunter Hill."

"You're lying to me, Jared. You've been playing me along like you would a hooked fish, letting me have a run and then jerking the line taut. Just like you used to do when we were boys. You hanged him, didn't you? You killed Spartacus just like you kill everything you touch."

"Nels, you're letting your imagination make a fool of you. If it weren't for your father being dead only these few days, I'd have to call you for throwing the lie at me."

"You goddamned bastard," Nelson said, his voice low with anger.

Jared smiled.

"I'll wipe that smile off your face. I'll . . ." He swung at Jared, forgetting the open pit between them. Slipping on the loose earth, Nelson plunged forward, grasping at air, falling into the grave and landing with a thud on top of the coffin.

Jared leaned over and looked down as Nelson raised himself to his hands and knees. "Are you all right, cousin?" he asked. "Here, let me help you." Nelson stared at the proffered hand and turned his head away.

Jared shrugged. As he walked around the grave and down the hill in the direction of the house, he took a cigar from his pocket and lit it. Atfer a few moments he began to laugh, the laughter building as he pictured Nelson sprawled on top of the coffin.

"I'll be goddamned," he said aloud. "I will be goddamned."

5

WE MUST OWE everyone in Charleston." Nelson pushed the pile of bills away from him.

"Your father was a gentleman," the Old Colonel said. The two men were sitting in the front parlor with a single lamp burning on the table in front of Nelson. The last of the mourners had been gone only a half hour.

"A gentleman has obligations as well as responsibilities," the Old Colonel went on. "His house is always open to his friends, whether they wish to stay for the night or for a week. If a friend needs an advance of funds to avoid an embarrassment, a gentleman accommodates him."

"My father must have had a great many about-to-be-embarrassed friends."

"He had friends of all kinds and today they have honored his memory." The Old Colonel leaned forward in his straightbacked chair, folded his hands on top of his gold-headed cane and rested his chin on his hands. He closed his eyes for a moment and Nelson thought the old man had fallen asleep.

Suddenly the Old Colonel shook his head and opened his eyes, their pale blue clouded by cataracts. His face was creased and worn, like an old letter that has been folded and refolded many times over the years. His hair fell thick and white to his collar.

"At times my memory isn't as good as it once was," the Old Colonel said. "What were we discussing a moment ago?"

"My father."

"Of course, Alexander Vaughan. He had the unfortunate habit of always being slightly out of step. He'd sell cotton just before the price went up. He'd buy slaves at the top of the market. He even managed to die at precisely the wrong time."

"I don't know what we'll do if war comes," Nelson said. "According to the *Mercury,* Jeff Davis is talking of putting an embargo on our shipments of cotton. He thinks by keeping it off the market the English and the French will be forced to cast their lot with the Confederacy."

"War with the North is madness!" The Old Colonel thumped his cane on the floor. "Twenty million Yankees arrayed against our five million. Arithmetic is still the same today as when I went to school. Two and two still make four. There's no way to make five equal twenty."

"We're fighters, though. We're ready to fight and we want to fight. The Yankees don't."

"You can only goad a dog so long before he'll turn on you. The same with a man or a country. No, the Yankees won't fight, at least not with their hearts in it. But if Mr. Lincoln ever makes this a war to free the slaves, that's something Northern men *will* fight for, wrong though they may be."

"Negroes are better off as slaves."

"Of course they are. Even the Bible says there should be masters and slaves. It's our task to bring Christianity to the African heathen who were brought to our shores by the Yankee slave traders. Haven't I supported the Negro Mission Church all these years?"

"There's talk of planting corn instead of cotton," Nelson said, "so we can raise our own foodstuffs. I don't rightly know what we should do here at Santee. Wait till next year's sowing to decide, I suppose."

Nelson saw that the Old Colonel's eyes were closed once more. Nelson stood up, walked to a table near the glass-fronted bookcase and poured himself a glass of wine, raising the glass in the Old Colonel's direction before he drank.

"Colonel," he said softly, "if you were thirty years younger, if you had your eyesight back, you'd save Santee. Now there's no one, no one at all."

"That's not true."

Nelson swung around to face the doorway.

The Old Colonel shook his head and sat up. "Who's there?" he asked.

"It's Ida, father."

The Old Colonel rose slowly from his chair and stood leaning on his cane with his left hand while holding his right across his breast.

"Mother," Nelson said, "you shouldn't have come downstairs. You should be in bed."

Ida Vaughan stepped into the room. Though still dressed in black, she had changed into a gown with long pleated skirts, a high neckline and long sleeves. A dress from another era, Nelson realized, a style fashionable twenty years before.

"I feel much improved," she said. "I believe my illness has passed its crisis. I suspect Dr. Misdom was dosing me with too much medicine. I've stopped taking the laudanum and the rest of his tonics as well."

"Is that you, Ida?" the Old Colonel asked.

"Yes, father," she said in a louder voice.

"Are you certain you're well enough to be up?" Nelson asked. "I'll be glad to escort you to your room." He stepped toward her but she raised her hand and he stopped.

"I'm perfectly capable of climbing the stairs myself," she said. Ida glanced at the table with its pile of letters and accounts. "You've been going over the books."

"You don't have to worry about the books. I'll take care of all that."

"Are you all right, Ida?" the Old Colonel asked. "Are you feeling better today?"

"I feel perfectly fine, father." She looked at Nelson and, though her face was pale and her hair dull, she looked younger than he ever remembered seeing her. He had always thought of his mother as being of his father's generation, though he knew she was fifteen years his junior.

"What did you find when you went over the accounts?" Ida asked. "How much in debt are we?"

"I only glanced at the books, mother. Mr. Brady and I will review them in detail in the morning. I'll have him prepare a report for us."

"You don't have to worry, Ida," the Old Colonel said. "I'll look after you for as long as I live. You'll marry well, you're a pretty child, and then you'll have your husband to look after you. You'll never have a worry in the world, Ida."

"No, father, I'm sure I won't," she said. "Tell me how much we owe, Nelson. I insist on knowing."

Nelson sighed. "We may be as much as twenty thousand dollars in debt."

"Then I'll sell the town house. And I'll see to it that we retrench here at Santee. We'll just have to learn to make do or do without."

"Santee will always be here for you to come back to," the Old Colonel said. "You'll always be able to make your home at Santee with your mother and me. I built Santee for your mother before you were born."

"I'll never sell Santee, father. Now what about Joseph, Nelson? Jared Hunter did hang that unfortunate young man, didn't he?"

"I'm certain he did. Jared denies it but there's no doubt in my mind. He found Joseph hiding along the river and he hanged him."

"Then Mr. Hunter will have to recompense me for his full value. I'd say he was worth two thousand dollars, wouldn't you?"

"Fifteen hundred would be closer with the market down the way it is."

"He'll pay two thousand."

"I doubt if Jared will pay a cent. Even if it was to you and not to me."

"The Negroes are our obligation," the Old Colonel said. "Our burden given to us by God. It's God's will that we look after them."

"I don't intend to go to Jared," Ida said. "Jethro will pay. How can he refuse, considering?"

The image of his father's coffin, banked high with flowers, appeared in Nelson's mind.

"Considering everything," his mother concluded.

Nelson nodded. Jethro Hunter might pay two thousand Yes, he very well might. If the old man often chose to turn a blind eye to his son's true nature, it was because Jethro Hunter was a proud man. And a gentleman.

"I heard some talk of planting corn," Ida said.

Nelson nodded, realizing his mother must have overheard his conversation with the Old Colonel. "The government in Montgomery wants us to put in food crops," he told her.

"Then we will. The river valley fields are lying fallow this year. We can still plant a corn crop there. I'll speak to Mr. Brady in the morning."

"I say to hell with the government." The Old Colonel thumped his cane. "In '76 we fought to keep King George from telling us what to do. Now we should tell the Yankees to go to hell."

"It's not the Yankees, father," Ida said. "This is Jeff Davis and the Confederacy."

"It's still the government, isn't it? Whether it's Jeff Davis or King George. How in all logic can we have a states' rights government telling the states what to do? How can we? Answer me that?"

"We may be going to war, father."

"No, we mustn't have war. Two and two still make four, don't they?" The Old Colonel held out his hand. "Come to me, Ida," he said. "Come to your father."

Ida crossed the room, knelt beside the Old Colonel's chair and laid her head on his knee. As he put his arms around her his cane fell to the floor.

"Where's your mother, Ida?" he asked. "I was looking for her to tell her about Alexander dying and I couldn't find her."

"She passed away years ago. You remember that, don't you? She passed on in her sleep and we buried her on the hill."

The Old Colonel sat staring straight ahead. Nelson

saw that his cheeks were streaked with tears. "I remember now," the Old Colonel whispered. "My memory's not as good some days as others. When I forget something, Ida, I would appreciate it if you'd remind me."

"I will, father. I've forgotten a great deal over these last years myself. I've neglected my responsibilities to my family and to Santee. I'll appreciate it if you'll remind me of them."

The Old Colonel straightened and Ida rose to her feet.

"I seem to have mislaid my cane," he said.

Ida knelt, picked the cane from the floor and handed it to him.

The Old Colonel stood and, swinging his cane back and forth in front of him, walked to the door. "I'll make sure the house is locked," he said.

"We don't have to lock our doors."

"We do. We never did when I was young but we do now. Times are bad; they'll get worse."

"Father," Ida Vaughan said, "you're mistaken. You're seldom wrong but in this you are. Times are bad, yes, but they'll get better."

"They'll get worse," the Old Colonel muttered under his breath.

"Father," Ida said. "Look at me." The Old Colonel stood unmoving in the doorway. "I said look at me, father."

Her father turned slowly, leaning on his cane, and peered back into the room.

"Do you see me, father?" Ida asked.

"I think I do. Yes, I see."

"You've forgotten, father. Times will get better, here at Santee, in Charleston, in South Carolina, in the South. Say it father. Tell me."

"Times are bad," the Old Colonel said. "They'll get

—" He paused, then nodded. "They'll get better," he said. "Of course, I remember now."

"I love you, father," Ida told him.

"I love you, Ida. Your mother always said I loved you too much. Too much, too much, too much." He sobbed, swung about, his cane striking the side of the doorway, and he left the room.

Ida drew in a long shuddering breath and looked at her son.

"You said you were going to sell the town house," Nelson said. "Demand payment for Joseph, see that corn's planted. I'll do those things, mother. I'm running the plantation now."

"No, Nelson, you're not," Ida told him. "I am."

She met his gaze until his eyes fell from hers. Then she turned away and followed her father out of the room.

When Jared returned to Charleston the day after Alexander Vaughan's funeral, the atmosphere in the city was electric. Crowds thronged the streets, soldiers hurrying to newly assigned posts, drays and wagons hauling powder and provisions, men and women watching and wondering. The air was tense, gay, excited, and beneath it all ran a current of unease.

We're on the threshold of a new era, Jared thought. It must have been like this over a hundred years ago when a Hunter stood on the docks in England ready to take passage to the New World, waiting to embark on a voyage that would change not only his life but the lives of all the generations of Hunters to come. It must have been like this when the colonists at Lexington and Concord laid aside their plows to confront the column of redcoats marching out from Boston. It must have been like this when the first pioneers, seeing that the prairie grass was up, prepared to set out across the American desert to California.

After he ate supper, Jared heard singing and, walking back along Meeting Street to the hotel, found a crowd serenading a man on a second floor balcony by singing "Dixie" and "Oh, Isn't He a Darling?"

"It's the orator, Roger Pryor of Virginia," an old gentleman next to Jared told him. Virginia, Jared knew, had so far declined to secede from the Union.

Pryor held up his hand and the crowd quieted. "I thank you," the tall, black-haired secessionist said, for having at last annihilated this accursed Union."

"What about Virginia?" a voice called.

"Give the old lady time. She's a little rheumatic." There was laughter from the street below. "I assure you," he said, his voice rising, "that just as certain as tomorrow's sun will rise upon us, just so certain will Virginia be a member of the Southern Confederacy; and I will tell your governor what will put her in the Southern Confederacy in less than an hour by Shrewsbury clock." He paused as the crowd strained forward to catch his next words.

"Strike a blow," Pryor said, almost in a whisper.

"Strike a blow," he repeated in his normal voice.

"Strike a blow!" he shouted.

The crowd cheered.

Later that night, Jared was wakened by alarm guns fired from Citadel Square, a signal for the reserves to assemble, and all night his sleep was interrupted by the beating of drums and the tramping of feet as the companies formed up in the street and marched off to their posts. In the morning he heard a report that a United States fleet lay off the bar outside the harbor and that signal lights had been seen atop Fort Sumter.

The day, April 11, 1861, was bright and clear. Jared joined Colonel Raleigh-Beckwith, Roger Pryor, and several newly arrived officers at the Battery on the tip of Charleston's peninsula.

Captain Wigfall, a graying Confederate who had been with Beauregard since the general's arrival the month before, led them to a vantage point at the water's edge.

"Fort Sumter, gentlemen," Captain Wigfall said, gesturing across Charleston harbor. From where they stood, Sumter, three miles away, looked like a large warehouse with two levels of gun embrasures in place of windows. A U.S. flag fluttered over the brick and stone fort.

"As you can see," Wigfall said, "Sumter commands the harbor. All shipping, in or out, must pass under her guns. With the Yankees in the fort, Charleston is at the mercy of the North."

"On the other hand," Jared said, "the fort is virtually surrounded by our shore batteries."

"Quite true, Colonel Hunter. To your left we have five batteries, four of them on Sullivan Island. To your right we have two batteries on James Island and another at Cummings Point on Norris Island. We have a nine-inch Dahlgren, eight-inch columbiads, 32-pounders, 24-pounders, ten-inch mortars and several seacoast howitzers. All in all, we can bring more than thirty guns and eighteen mortars to bear on the fort from four different points of the compass."

"And the fort's defenses?" Raleigh-Beckwith asked.

"The Yankees are outgunned and outmanned. Their only hope is to be reinforced from the sea. And I can tell you confidentially that those reinforcements are on their way from New York this very moment."

"If fighting begins," Jared asked, "which of our batteries will fire first?"

"I understand that Captain James's battery on Fort Johnson will have that honor," the captain said.

Jared nodded.

"When the State of South Carolina seceded in December," Captain Wigfall went on, "Major Robert Anderson and his men were at Fort Moultrie on Sullivan Island to your left. Fort Moultrie is completely defenseless against a land attack. As Major Anderson well knew. A few days after Christmas he moved his men by stealth to Sumter. I'm sure it wasn't his doing; Major Anderson's a Southerner with no heart for this war. I suspect one of his subordinates had a hand in the transfer of the Yankee troops. Captain Abner Doubleday, perhaps. He's an abolitionist."

"Doubleday? Haven't I heard that name from somewhere?" Roger Pryor asked.

"You may have, sir," Wigfall said. "I understand that some years ago the captain contrived a game played by striking a small ball with a wooden stick. I believe it's known as baseball."

"Quite right," Pryor said. "When I visited Baltimore, I actually saw grown men playing at it."

"After Major Anderson shifted his troops," Wigfall said, "the North made one attempt to reinforce the garrison on Sumter. They sent a ship, *The Star of the West*, into the harbor but she was driven off by our guns. Anderson kept his own guns silent all the time the United States flag was being fired on."

"Do you expect Beauregard will attempt to take Fort Sumter in the next few days?" Raleigh-Beckwith asked.

"I wouldn't be surprised," the captain told them, "to learn that General Beauregard is preparing an ultimatum to Anderson at this very moment."

And I'll make damn sure, Jared told himself, that

I'm at Fort Johnson with Captain James when he does. If that's where this war's to begin, that's the place I want to be.

Captain Wigfall was right, for Beauregard prepared an ultimatum on the morning of the eleventh. Three days before, a message had been read to South Carolina Governor Pickens and General Beauregard at the Charleston Hotel, a message from the President of the United States:

". . . an attempt will be made to supply Fort Sumter with provisions only, and if such attempt be not resisted, no effort to throw in men, arms or ammunition will be made . . ."

The general telegraphed the message to the Confederate government in Montgomery, Alabama, and on April 10 Beauregard had his answer from War Secretary Walker. As far as Fort Sumter was concerned, he was ordered to "at once demand its evacuation, and if this is refused proceed, in such manner as you may determine, to reduce it."

By afternoon, Beauregard's ultimatum was ready and a small boat flying a white flag left Charleston. At the Fort Sumter wharf the Union officer of the day, Lieutenant Davis, met the boat and escorted Colonel Chesnut, Captain Stephen Lee and Colonel Chisolm to the guard room, where Major Anderson met them.

Colonel Chesnut handed Anderson the dispatch from General Beauregard and waited while he read the ultimatum. ". . . the Confederate States can no longer delay assuming actual possession of a fortification commanding the entrance to one of their harbors, and necessary to its defense and security. I am ordered by the Government of the Confederate States to demand the evacuation of Fort Sumter . . ."

Anderson called his officers together, read them the message, and listened to their comments. An hour later the major had a blunt reply for General Beauregard. He refused to surrender Fort Sumter.

After handing the written reply to the three Confederates, Anderson walked with them back to their boat. At the wharf, the major asked, "Will the general open fire at once?"

Colonel Chesnut hesitated. "No," he said, "I can say to you that he will not, not without giving you further notice."

Anderson said he would take no action until he was fired on. As the boat pulled away from the wharf, he added, "If you do not batter us to pieces we will be starved out in a few days."

When Chesnut reported to Beauregard, the general telegraphed Anderson's message and his comment about being starved out to the secretary of war. He closed the telegram with a single word: "Answer."

Walker told him that if Anderson would definitely evacuate, without conditions, he should be allowed to do so. Beauregard immediately sent his three emissaries back to Sumter. They reached the fort's wharf a little after midnight. It was now April 12, 1861.

The fort, as Major Anderson had said, was almost out of food. With fifteen officers, seventy-four enlisted men, and forty-four civilian employees to feed, the provisions would be exhausted by the fourteenth. Major Anderson wrote to General Beauregard telling him he would evacuate Sumter on the fifteenth but added some important if's—if the Confederates did not commit a hostile act and if the garrison didn't receive new instructions from their government in Washington.

Colonel Chesnut read the message and shook his

head. The major was committing himself to nothing. Chesnut dictated a reply on the spot. "By authority of Brigadier General Beauregard," he said, "we have the honor to notify you that he will open the fire of his batteries on Fort Sumter in one hour from this time."

It was then 3:20 in the morning.

Again Major Anderson walked to the wharf with the three Confederate officers. Shaking hands with them, he said, "If we never meet in this world again, God grant that we may meet in the next."

The boat moved off into the darkness, leaving Major Anderson and his officers rousing the fort's sleeping soldiers, warning them to prepare for action. All around the harbor, bonfires and torches blazed at the Confederate camps and batteries so that Hunter was almost completely ringed by flickering lights. Only to the east, the seaward side, was it dark.

As the three Confederates were rowed from the fort, clouds concealed the stars and brought a suggestion of rain to the air. In the distance they heard the roll of drums and the rumble of guns being trundled into position.

The three officers landed at Fort Johnson where a signal gun, a seacoast mortar, was in readiness to fire the shot that would tell the Confederate troops, the city of Charleston and the world that the bombardment had begun.

"You are to open fire at 4:20 A.M.," Colonel Chesnut told Captain James, the battery commander.

"Yes, sir," the captain said.

Roger Pryor, the Virginian who had called on the South Carolinians to strike a blow, was at the battery. Captain James turned to him and bowed.

"Would you, sir," he asked, "like to have the honor of firing the first gun?"

Pryor's voice shook as he answered. "I could not fire the first gun of the war," he said.

When Captain James ordered Lieutenant Farley to fire the signal gun, Jared Hunter stepped forward. "If I might, Captain," he said, "I would be proud to fire the shot that will be heard around the world."

Captain James nodded and turned to Colonel Chesnut. "Sir," he said, "your orders will be carried out."

The three officers, accompanied by Roger Pryor, returned to their boat and set off for Charleston. They were only a short distance from Fort Johnson when the colonel ordered the oarsmen to stop rowing and they sat in the gently rocking boat, waiting. For ten minutes there was silence from the fort, the only sound the lapping of the harbor waves.

At 4:30 there was a flash of light from Fort Johnson and a dull explosion as the mortar was fired. The glow of the shell's fuse arced high into the night, hung in the air, started down and exploded directly above Fort Sumter.

Nelson awoke slowly, his temples throbbing. He found that he was sitting in a chair with his head cradled on his arms, which were folded on a table in front of him. A candle on the table had burned low. Next to the candle was a half-full decanter and an empty glass.

He raised his head and groaned. Looking around him he saw he was at the Bachelors' Club at Charleston. The room was deserted. From outside he heard a rumbling, like thunder, yet the sound went on and on and he realized it was not a storm.

He stood up and walked slowly to a window. In the sky above the buildings across the street soaring red lines of shell fuses etched the darkness of the night. Vaguely he remembered men coming for him, ordering him to report to his company, men who finally left him to sleep off his drunken stupor.

Had someone said, "He'll do us more harm than good"?

All at once he realized that the Confederate forts ringing the harbor were firing on Sumter. This was no training exercise; he was witnessing an actual bombardment. Excitement raced through him. The war was beginning.

Taking the decanter in his hand, Nelson groped his way to the hall and climbed the stairs, intending to get a better view. On the second floor an elderly man carrying a lantern passed him and Nelson followed him up the stairs to the third floor and then up still another flight and onto the roof. He was surprised to find a crowd gathered there, women in hoopskirts, men dressed in glossy black and wearing broad-brimmed hats. The roofs of the other nearby buildings were also crowded with spectators in a gay holiday mood.

As Nelson took a step forward he stumbled and had to grasp the arm of a man near him to keep from falling.

"Watch where you're going," the man told him.

Nelson held up the decanter. "A toast," he said. "Damnation to the Yankees."

"The time for toasts is past," the man said.

Nelson shook his head, trying to clear it. The war has begun, he told himself, the war has actually begun. He remembered the past week—his father asking for him and his arrival home, too late; the way Jared had goaded him at his father's grave; his mother, not trusting him, leaving her sickbed to take charge of Santee. And now, called to arms, he had been left behind, drunk.

He knew a burning shame; his face flushed and he

dropped the decanter and watched the wine gurgle onto the roof. Across the harbor a shell exploded over Sumter. By God, he thought, it's not too late. In a few hours a new day would dawn for Charleston and for the South.

And for Nelson Vaughan as well, he told himself.

BOOK II

First Victory

MANASSAS

6

Fairfield, Connecticut

I THINK, Mrs. DeWitt," Thomas Niles said, "that you are admirably suited to write a novel about a young girl growing up in Virginia. I should very much like to see you try."

"But Mr. Niles," Margaret DeWitt said, "so little happened to me when I was a girl. I'd have little or no story to tell. I couldn't possibly write such a book."

Thomas Niles said nothing. In the ten minutes since he'd presented his card at the door and she'd invited him into the front parlor, Margaret had discovered he was a man of long pauses followed by carefully considered words. Nothing at all like what she'd expected the partner of Roberts Brothers Publishers to be.

"I believe I've read everything of yours that's in

print," Niles said. "All your stories of princes and battles and maidens languishing in towers."

"I started writing those stories when I was a little girl. I remember writing my first tale when I was nine, a fairy story about a street urchin who found a pair of boots. When he put them on he changed into a prince."

"You have an exotic imagination, Mrs. DeWitt."

"I've sold ever so many of my stories to the magazines. The editors seem to like them; at least they always ask for more. And still you want me to write a book about Virginia."

"Have you ever seen a castle, Mrs. DeWitt? Have you ever met a prince?"

"No, of course I haven't. I've lived all my life either in Virginia or here in Connecticut. I've always wanted to travel but I never have."

Mr. Niles busied himself smoothing the crown of his hat.

"I know what you're going to tell me," Margaret said. "That I should write about what I know. What I know is so uninteresting. I've lived twenty-seven years, I've been married almost twelve of those years and I have two boys. Everything that's ever happened to me could be put in one short chapter. In fact, I think my whole life would make little more than a dull prologue."

"There's a novel in everyone's life." Mr. Niles looked at Margaret and then away. He had yet to recover from his surprise when he met her, for he had expected Mrs. Margaret DeWitt to be petite, shy and wistful. Nothing in her tales had prepared him for this tall and beautiful redhaired woman.

"It's the manner of the telling," he went on after a pause. "I greatly admired those sketches you wrote about your father."

"I wrote them shortly after he died to honor his memory. I loved my father, Mr. Niles."

"I could tell that from your stories. They had deep feeling in them, Mrs. DeWitt. Your stories of earls and barons, of ladies-in-waiting . . ." He shrugged. "If you'll forgive my saying so, one reads such tales and an hour later they're forgotten. But not your stories about your father."

Mr. Niles shut his eyes. "I read them five years ago," he said, "and I can still see that young man knocking at a plantation door in Virginia, surrounded by a flock of colored children, by hound dogs and mastiffs who were supposed to guard the gate but had been disarmed by this peddlers' soft words. Just as the women of the house were charmed by his descriptions of the virtues of his ribbons and combs, his buttons and thread, his knives and tin plates. I can still see him eating with the family and afterward sitting late in the library with the master of the house, relating the news from Richmond and Washington, the two men talking of guns and fishing, of politics and planting."

"My father was a wonderful man," Margaret said. "He loved good books and good talk; he had friends beyond number. He had everything except the knack for making money. We children never noticed that lack, Mr. Niles, even when we didn't have new clothes for school, even when we seemed to exist for days on nothing but beans. There was always wood for the fireplaces and the stoves and there was always love enough for all of us."

"I envy you," Thomas Niles said.

"We lived in a big old house," she said, "with seven outside doors and at first, when we had just moved in, every time we heard the knock of a friend coming to call we couldn't tell which of the doors to open since there were so many possibilities. So each of us had a door of our own to run to. My life seemed like that then, Mr. Niles, as though I had so many doors I could open, so many possibilities."

"You say you couldn't write a novel of your youth, yet what you've just told me would make a delightful first paragraph. Every life contains all the great themes, birth and death, love and, yes, hate. When I read your stories about your father, you made me love him just as you loved him. You could do that when you write of your mother, your brothers, your husband and your children."

Margaret smiled ruefully. "I'm afraid Mr. DeWitt doesn't completely approve of my writing," she said.

"When you have a gift, as you have, you must nurture and use it. You have a knack for making others see and feel what you see and feel. Those who can knit shawls should do so; those who can write, must write. It should make no difference whether they're men or women, married or single."

"And yet I have responsibilities. Obligations to my family, to my children and my husband."

"Of course," Niles said, getting to his feet. "Although I'm a confirmed bachelor myself, I understand."

At the door, he bowed to Margaret. "Please remember my suggestion," he said, "and if you ever do write a novel about growing up in Virginia, I hope Roberts Brothers will have the opportunity to see it first."

"They will, Mr. Niles," she told him. "And thank you for coming. I can live for a week on the fact that you liked my tales enough to journey all the way from Boston to Fairfield to see me."

She closed the door and stood for a time watching him carefully skirting the April puddles as he made his way around the side of the house to his waiting buggy. After he rode from sight, Margaret walked slowly up the stairs, knowing that Miss Telford would keep the boys, Curtis and Alex, at her mother-in-law's for at least another hour.

In the room she had converted from a sewing room into her room for writing, she sat in the chair by the open window, savoring the scent of the lilacs blooming beside the house. The grass in the loop of the driveway was a fresh green and the elms and maples were in bud. Dark clouds threatened more rain.

It would be so easy to write of her childhood, she thought. Yet who would want to read of her growing up in Virginia, of the huge drafty house, her first ride on a horse, the dolls her mother made for her, the trees she had climbed? She remembered the many times she had longed to be a boy or, if she had to be a girl, wished she didn't tower over all the other girls and, worse still, over most of the boys as well.

Time's a-wasting, she told herself. She turned her back on the lure of the balmy spring breeze, took her writing board from the table and adjusted it on her lap. Dipping her pen into an inkwell, she began to write in a large, flowing hand.

It was perhaps a half hour later when she looked up from her writing board, emerging from the imaginary world she had created for her hero and heroine. Margaret put down her pen. A breeze billowed the white curtains and she stared out at a patch of startlingly blue sky between the clouds.

"If you see a patch of blue as big as a Dutchman's breeches," her mother had said, "you can be sure the rain's over."

"How big a Dutchman?" Margaret had asked.

"As big as your Uncle Henry, I would say." Her

mother spread her shawl on a bench and, taking her prayer book from her reticule, sat down and began to read.

"Now stay close," she warned Margaret, "and don't play near the pond."

Margaret nodded, skipping away. She loved to run, especially on windy days like this one, when she could climb hills and, with the wind at her back, race down them. At the top of a hill she knelt to pick blue myrtle. Then, clutching the flowers in her hand, she ran down the path into the woods and along the edge of the pond to the dam.

When she leaned over to look into the water, she saw her reflection staring back at her, the red hair, the hazel eyes. She made a face at the reflection and, picking up a rock, skimmed it across the water, the rock bouncing twice on the surface before sinking. She found a smoother rock and threw it as hard as she could.

Margaret lost her balance and fell with a splash into the water. She cried out as she felt herself sinking. She struggled to the surface, but her clothes weighted her down and she sank again, surfaced again, trying to swim and not knowing how. The dam was so far away, beyond her reach . . . and again she was under the water, going down, down, as she had seen the rock sink. She flailed her arms, trying to hold her breath but swallowing water, her panic giving way to a gentle sensation of floating, of drifting off into warmth and sunlight. . . .

A hand grasped her wrist and she felt herself pulled from the pond onto the dam. She lay on the smooth stones, gasping for air, wondering what her mother would say at the sight of her sopping wet dress. Margaret opened her eyes. A colored boy was standing over her, his eyes large, his mouth open as he stared down at her.

"You all right?" he asked.

She nodded. She saw the myrtles scattered on the dam beside her. She gathered them and handed the flowers to the boy. He took them, nodded, and turned and ran.

She never saw him again.

Looking from the window, she realized that the Dutchman's breeches had grown larger as the clouds scudded out to sea. Margaret picked up her manuscript, reading what she had written. Dissatisfied, she crossed out a word here, an entire line there. It was Mr. Niles's fault; he had set her to thinking, to remembering. She tried to concentrate, to expunge everything from her mind except the chapter she wanted to finish before first Peter and then the boys came home for their midday meal.

She had almost drowned in the pond. She was certain that she would have if the boy hadn't happened along and heard her cry out. A memory of terror. And salvation. The other never-to-be-forgotten memory from her childhood was also one of terror, though of a completely different kind. How old had she been? She could only remember she had been a little girl at the time. It had been in the big old house, the house with the seven outside doors and the great central chimney.

The brick oven was built next to that chimney, an oven where her mother made a sweet-smelling, savory bread the likes of which Margaret had never tasted since. She had heard a sound coming from the oven, a strange tapping when there should have been no sound at all.

Curious, she went to the oven and gingerly felt

its handle. The oven was cold. Pressing her ear to the door, she listened and heard nothing. Had she imagined the sound? She lifted the loop of the metal handle and swung the door open.

A face stared at her from the dark interior of the oven. A black, gaunt face, a terror-stricken face. She gasped, slammed the door shut and ran through the house and up the stairs. Flinging herself on her mother, she held to her legs as she buried her head in her skirts. Sobbing, she blurted out the story, told how she had opened the oven, told of the face that had stared out at her.

"You must never speak of this to anyone," her mother told her. "Never. Not a word."

When she stared, not understanding, her mother sat down, lifted Margaret onto her lap and told her why. The man in the oven was an escaped slave, she said, fleeing from his owners to seek freedom in Canada. If he was caught he'd be flogged and anyone who had helped him would be arrested and punished.

"Do you understand?" her mother asked.

Margaret nodded.

She had never spoken of what she had seen, but neither had she ever forgotten the fear-filled face staring out of the oven at her, her horror when she learned that this man belonged to some one with the power to take him south in chains and whip him.

Strange, she thought, that the two most vivid memories from her childhood involved Negroes, one a boy who had saved her life, the other a man who had frightened her, both seen for a fleeting moment and never seen again, and both never to be forgotten for as long as she lived.

She had happy memories of her childhood, too. Memories of her brothers pummeling her with pil-

lows, her mother sewing with the cat curled on the
floor at her feet while a fire crackled in the grate,
her father showing her his wares before he set out
on one of his trips through the Virginia countryside,
her mother telling her stories of her own childhood
and of her great-aunt who had married the first
signer of the Declaration of Independence. Memories of exploring their cavernous attic, of trying on
her mother's dresses and walking in her mother's
shoes, of sitting on top of a trunk reading letters
and journals from long ago.

"Who is he?"

Margaret's head jerked up. Peter stood a few feet
from her, holding a sheaf of papers in his hand. It
was a few moments before she realized the papers
were the manuscript of the story she had been writing.

"I don't know what you mean, Peter," she said,
getting to her feet.

"You know very well what I mean. Philip. Who
is he?"

"Philip? The hero of my story?" She shook her head,
genuinely puzzled.

"I've read all you've written about him. He's a real
person, I know he is. I feel I recognize him. You
couldn't have described the way you felt about him
if he wasn't."

"Philip is completely imaginary, Peter. Just like the
men in all my stories are."

"No, Philip's different. He's not one of your princes
who gallops about rescuing maidens. He's real, you've
based him on an actual person. It's a person you're
in love with, Maggie, and I mean to find out who
he is."

She stepped to him and put her hand on his arm. He
brushed it aside and she drew away. Peter's face was

flushed, his blond hair awry. He was a tall man, taller than she and, she knew, strong. Even so, she wasn't afraid of him. She was used to his jealous rages.

"I don't intend to discuss it further," she told him coldly. "If you don't believe me, there's nothing I can do. Philip is wholly imaginary."

She hesitated, her hand going to her mouth as she realized there was some truth to what her husband said, that she *had* used a living model in creating her latest hero.

Peter had been watching her closely. "You're lying, Maggie," he said. "I can tell you are. Now why don't you admit to the truth?" His voice dropped, became conciliatory. "Why don't you tell me who he is and then we'll go down to eat? I'm sure Mrs. Harvey must have the meal ready and on the table."

"Peter," she said, "you're being foolish. Yes, let's eat."

"After you tell me," he said stubbornly.

"Now you're sounding exactly like Buck." Buck was the nickname her husband had given Curtis, their older son.

"Do you think I act like an eleven-year-old? Is that what you're telling me, Maggie?"

Suddenly she flared out at him. "Yes. You're like a little boy. When you act like this, you are. There's no reasoning with you. I'm not lying. Why should I lie to you?"

"Was that fellow Niles here this morning?"

"You knew he was coming. I told you he'd written. Yes, Thomas Niles was here. He told me he liked the stories I wrote years ago about my father. He thinks I should write a novel about when I was a girl."

"Is this the first time he's been here?" Peter asked. "Perhaps he was here before and you conveniently forgot to tell me. Perhaps he's been visiting you on and off since last winter and you've never let on. Is he the man you had in mind when you started writing this latest story?"

"Peter, you *are* acting like a child. Stop it, I won't listen to any more." She turned and stared unseeing from the window.

"I notice," Peter said, "that you haven't answered my questions about this man Niles."

"Of course I haven't answered them. You know very well that Thomas Niles wrote last week saying he'd like to come to see me. That was the first I'd ever heard of him. I showed you the letter, let you read the letter—not that you wouldn't have read it anyway, with or without my permission. You know that Mr. Niles isn't Philip."

"Then you admit Philip is real. Perhaps Niles isn't Philip. I've made inquiries about the man and he seems harmless enough from all I can find out. Who is Philip? Tell me, now that you've admitted he is someone. Who is he?"

"Oh, Peter, stop. Stop before it's too late. Please, Peter."

"Tell me who he is. That's all you have to do."

Margaret swung around and faced him. "I admit I had someone in mind when I began writing the story. I always do have a person in mind, in a way, or two or three or more persons. I take parts of each and join them with what I imagine. So what comes out in the story isn't really one actual person at all."

"Who did you have in mind, Maggie?" he asked. "Tell me."

"You, Peter. I had you in mind. That's why I named him Philip, because of the same first initial. I was thinking about when we met, when you were visiting in Richmond and your mother was taken ill and was quarantined and you were left to stay with your cousins. I remembered how dashing you were then, how young and handsome with your blond hair and moustache and how elegant I thought you were when you came to call dressed in a top hat and carrying a cane. I remembered how much you needed someone, needed me, I thought, and how you quite swept me off my feet. And so when I wrote the story I tried to put how I felt then down on paper. Oh, I did an imperfect job—don't I always? I couldn't recapture the way I felt. It's gone now, buried in the past, and no matter how I try I can never bring the past to life again." She lowered her face into her hands. "Oh, how I loved you then, Peter," she said.

"You're not telling the truth. If you ever really loved me, which I doubt, you'd not be doing everything in your power to thwart me." He spoke slowly, calmly, with a deadly intensity.

"You know I never try to thwart you," she told him. "Not consciously."

He slapped her manuscript against the desk. "You hide up here every chance you get. You're too busy writing to go to the Howards' because you have a deadline to meet. You're not dressed for the Thompsons' dinner party in time because you have to finish a chapter."

"Writing's all I have that's truly mine," she said.

"And I'm nothing? This house is nothing? The boys mean nothing to you?"

"You know I love them."

"This is what I think of your writing."

He took her manuscript in both hands and tore it across. Putting the two halves together, he tried to rip them again but the paper was too thick. Instead, he held the pages a few at a time, tearing them into small fragments. She watched him, her hazel eyes glistening with tears. When he finished he took the shredded manuscript in both hands and threw it at her, the paper falling like confetti to cover her hair, cling to her dress, and scatter on the rug at her feet.

Peter stood watching her as though unsure what her reaction would be. She folded her arms under her breasts, her heart thudding, her breath coming in short bursts.

"I hate you, Peter," she said. Her voice rose. "I hate you, I hate you, I hate you."

Margaret ran from the room, crossed the hall and went into her bedroom, slamming the door behind her. She threw herself on the bed. A moment later she felt the coverlet move and when she looked up she saw Ching, her Persian cat. His tongue licked her face.

The bedroom door opened. "I wish you wouldn't scream like that, Maggie," Peter said. "What will Mrs. Harvey and Miss Telford think? I'm sure they heard you."

"I don't give a damn what they think. Just as you don't give a damn what I think."

"Using vulgar language won't raise my opinion of you."

Margaret sat up on the bed and saw him standing in the bedroom beside the open door. "Do you know what I think?" she asked. "I know you don't really care, don't give a—a fig for my feelings, but I'm going to tell you anyway. You don't like me, Peter. I'm not talking about love, I'm talking about whether you *like* me. You don't. You don't approve of anything I do."

"That's not true, Maggie. But go ahead, get all the bile out of your system, say all the things you've always wanted to say. I'm listening, Maggie. I won't say a word. I'll just listen."

"You don't approve of me. I think you married me

because your mother was ill and you had no one to look after you. No one to fix your meals, no one to wait on you hand and foot, no one to smile at you and tell you how wonderful you were. Even then, when you married me, I don't believe you really approved of me. You had some notion of me, some dream, some expectation in your mind that wasn't me, not the real me. That was some other woman, Peter, it wasn't me, not Margaret. That's who I am, Margaret. I'm the woman you're married to even though you don't approve of me, don't like me, don't love me."

"Are you quite through, Margaret?" he asked. His voice was cold and distant.

"No, I'm not."

She wanted to say something about the times he'd come to her in the night, come to her room and lain with her and tried to rouse himself, the times she'd tried to rouse him, to love him, and had failed. The times he had turned from her and she'd clenched her hands into fists and said nothing, not knowing what to say, not knowing how to help him or help herself as she'd lain awake through the long hours of the night with her body crying out to him.

What can I do? she'd wanted to ask. Tell me, she had wanted to plead, yet she knew she must not, and had assured herself that this would pass, that perhaps he was ill and would grow better. He had not. Failure seemed to feed on failure and now, for the last two months, he hadn't come to her at all.

She wanted to say this, but knew she could not, that this could not be mentioned, could not be discussed. And so instead she said, out of her frustration and bitterness, "You're weak, Peter, you don't know your own mind. You let Mother DeWitt tell you what to do. Advising you on business matters is one thing, but I don't want your mother telling me how to raise

my children. I will not have her doing that. I will not
have her in this house looking for dust. I will not have
her constantly tidying every room. I won't, Peter, I
won't, I won't, I won't."

"Now are you quite through?" he asked.

"Yes." She covered her face with her hands.

"You're never to write again," he told her. "If you
do, I'll tear up every story just as I tore up this one.
You're never to have Mr. Niles in this house again. Of
course, if you don't write, there'll be no reason for
him to come here, will there?"

"No, Peter," she said, "no reason at all."

"Shall I have Mrs. Harvey set a place for you?" he
asked.

"No, Peter," she said. "Tell her I'm indisposed."

He nodded and went out, shutting the door quietly
behind him. Margaret lay on the bed for a long time,
sitting up again only when the cat climbed over her
and jumped to the floor. From downstairs she heard
the slam of the front door and footsteps on the gravel
drive.

She was living in a house with very few doors, with
very few possibilities, and, she felt, those doors were
closing one by one. She got up and walked to the
window. No, she told herself, there'll be no prince on a
white stallion to rescue you, Margaret. You have only
yourself.

After a sleep of troubled dreams, dreams of phantom shapes rising darkly in front of her, of long corridors leading to locked and bolted doors, she woke to
the pealing of church bells. Pulling on her robe, she
went to the window and looked down. In the distance,
she heard shouts and the crack of a rifle.

Mrs. Harvey came trudging along the drive to the
house as she did every morning at this time. Margaret

pulled up the window and leaned out. "Mrs. Harvey," she called. "What is it? Why are the bells ringing?"

Mrs. Harvey stopped in the driveway, standing with hands on hips as she looked up at Margaret. "It's war, Mrs. DeWitt," she said. "Those Rebels have gone and fired on Fort Sumter. The war's begun."

War. Margaret shook her head. Why did those Southerners want war?

When she went downstairs she was relieved to find that Peter had made his own breakfast and left for the store. They hadn't exchanged a word since he'd walked out of her bedroom the day before.

After she ate she debated whether to write, deciding not to. Best to let Peter work out of his rage. She knew he would in a few days, especially with the distraction of the war. Then all would be calm until the next storm. Besides, how could she write a romance in times like these?

She spent the morning cleaning. Peter didn't return for the midday meal and, although this was unusual, Margaret merely shrugged. In all probability he was off sulking somewhere—perhaps at his mother's. He had been in the wrong, knew it, and didn't want to face her.

Since this was Friday, she spent the better part of the afternoon in the kitchen helping Mrs. Harvey with the cooking. Her mother-in-law always ate with them on Fridays. As did her own mother when she was in Fairfield and not, as she was this month, visiting in New Hampshire.

She heard the front door open and close shortly before five. This, too, was unusual, for Peter made a habit of staying at the store until six, when he locked up and walked through the town and then along Prospect Street to their home. Margaret left the kitchen and was crossing the dining room when he came through the archway from the front hall. They stood facing each other, neither speaking.

Peter broke the silence.

"Well," he told her, "I've done it."

"Done what? What have you done?"

"Remember what you said about me yesterday?" he asked. "It's not true, none of it is. Don't think, though, that I did it just because of what you said. I wanted to, it's what I had to do—and what my father would have expected of me. A DeWitt could do no less."

"For God's sake, tell me. What have you done?"

"I enlisted," he said. "I've joined the Seventh Connecticut. We'll probably leave for camp in a matter of weeks."

"Oh, Peter," she said. She went to him, standing in front of him without touching him, looking up at him, his blond hair, his blond moustache already touched with gray, his blue eyes. "Oh, Peter," she said again, and took him in her arms.

And for a few weeks, it was as it had been when they were first married. He came to her room each evening and they slept as man and wife. They came together when one of them wakened in the night, and if what they shared was not love, they did not seek another name for it.

The train carrying the first recruits to the camp in New Haven left on a Sunday afternoon in late April. A military band played at the depot, girls threw bouquets of lilacs to the departing men, the locomotive was decorated with red, white and blue bunting and, above the cowcatcher, someone had placed a sign reading "Death to Traitors." There were speeches, the band played the "Star Spangled Banner," and then the train whistle blew.

Margaret left her two boys with Mother DeWitt and ran along the platform, crying and waving. Peter

leaned from the train window and she reached up to
press a locket into his hand and then she was at the
end of the platform, where she stood waving her handkerchief as the train gathered speed, the smoke from
the engine billowing back around her. A cheer rose
from the crowd and the band started to play "The
Girl I Left Behind Me."

Dear God, she thought, don't let anything happen
to Peter. He's going to war because of me, because of
words I spoke in anger, no matter how much he
denies it. Dear God, don't let anything happen to him.

7

THE INITIAL CONFEDERATE bombardment of Fort
Sumter was heavy and, after the gun crews gained
experience, effective. General Beauregard had laid
down a routine and the gunners followed it, some
batteries sweeping the open parapet of the fort, others
exploding shells on the parade ground inside, still
others battering at the fort's brick walls.

At first Major Anderson refrained from returning
the Confederate fire. His priority, he believed, was to
protect his men. Dangerously undermanned, his only
hope for survival lay in keeping his soldiers in action
until he could be reinforced from the Yankee ships
offshore.

Sumter was a massive fort with five-foot-thick brick
walls rising forty feet above the water of the harbor.
Anderson had three tiers of guns, the lower two placed
in solidly constructed compartments from which they
fired through small embrasures. The third tier, con-

taining Sumter's heaviest guns, was on top of the fort, completely unprotected except for a low parapet.

Anderson opened fire from his lowest tier of guns on the morning of April twelfth. His bombardment of the shore batteries was ineffective for his guns could handle only solid cannonballs, not the more destructive explosive shells. During the day, though, two Federal sergeants crept up to the parapet and fired two heavy guns, 42-pounders, hitting the Moultrie House which was flying a hospital flag. No one was hurt—the Confederates had yet to suffer a casualty.

The Confederate shells soon tore Fort Sumter's southeast corner asunder and set fire to the wooden barracks on the parade ground. The flames were put out, in part by water cascading from holes in the water tanks on the roof. The fires were ignited again by the exploding Confederate shells and again they were quenched by the defenders.

The Yankee fleet, the liner *Baltic*, the revenue cutter *Harriet Lane* and the warship *Pawnee*, waited twelve miles off Charleston. Troops had been loaded on the *Baltic* in New York and now, although seasick, they practiced getting in and out of the boats on board the chartered ship.

The small fleet sailed in toward the bar outside the harbor where they saw wisps of smoke and heard the distant "thump, thump" of the big guns. The commanding officer, Captain Gustavus Fox, tall, stout and bearded, an old Navy man, wanted to go in with his ships to reinforce the fort but the seas ran too high. He could do nothing but wait for a change in the weather.

The night was an uneasy one on Sumter as the sentries watched for approaching boats, afraid they'd be unable to distinguish friend from foe, their nervousness heightened by a Confederate battery that, every ten minutes, lobbed a mortar shell into the fort. The heavy bombardment resumed the next day; the fort's flagstaff was shot away and dark clouds of smoke rose from the burning barracks.

General Beauregard sent Captain Lee to the fort in a small boat flying a white flag. Major Anderson's men were exhausted, his cartridges were almost gone, and there was danger, with the fires in the fort, that his magazine would explode.

He surrendered and the siege was over.

The next day, Sunday, the United States flag was raised for the last time at Sumter. The garrison saluted the Stars and Stripes by firing one of the big guns on the upper tier, the band played "Yankee Doodle," and, the seas having quieted, the troops marched to a waiting steamer. More than four thousand shells had been fired by both sides and only one man had been killed, a Federal gunner mortally wounded when his gun exploded after the fight was over.

Beauregard's troops took possession of Sumter, raising the Confederate and Palmetto flags. Batteries fired victory salvoes as small boats bringing sightseers to view the battered fort crowded the harbor.

Nelson Hunter Vaughan watched the spectacle from Fort Moultrie where he had joined his company. The Yankees were heading home with their tails between their legs. Now, perhaps, Mr. Lincoln would reconsider and let the South leave the Union in peace. This was what had been needed, an object lesson to show the North that South Carolina and the rest of the Confederacy would stop at nothing to be free.

Jared, at Fort Johnson, shook his head as he watched the gaily-dressed women in the small boats waving their handkerchiefs at the victorious Confederate troops. This was a charade, he told himself, not what war was like at all. They'd learn, in time. Let them have their orgy of exultation; there'd be precious few such moments between now and the final victory.

Already, Jared was thinking ahead. The war, he reasoned, would be fought not in South Carolina but in the north. When Virginia came into the Confederacy, and now she must, the line of battle would be along the Potomac. How far was Richmond from Washington? Less than two hundred miles. There, between the Virginia capital and the capital of the United States, the great battle, the decisive battle of the war, would be fought. And he, Jared Hunter, meant to play his part.

That evening Jared pushed his way through the jubilant, celebrating throngs to the Charleston Hotel where he had engaged rooms. The excitement of the day still coursed through him, heating his blood, and now, for the first time since the bombardment began, he thought of Colleen.

He hadn't seen her since Alexander Vaughan's funeral. She wanted him, he was sure of it, and he felt the same need for her that he had felt years before, the need that he had at first denied and then, when it became too strong, turned his back on when he enlisted in the army. He hadn't meant to marry then and he didn't intend to now. There would be a time for marriage but that time was far in the future. He had yet to meet the woman he would marry but he knew that woman wasn't Colleen Hughes.

Jared walked through the crowded hotel lobby and climbed the stairs to his room.

"Aaron!" he called as he threw his hat on the bed. Jared unbuckled his belt and draped both belt and sword on a chair.

"Aaron!" he called again, glancing to the door of the adjoining room as he sat down to pull off his boots.

As soon as he had the boots off he walked in stocking feet to the connecting door. Just as he was about to fling the door open, it swung back and Aaron stepped quickly into the room, closing the door behind him.

"Yes, sir." Aaron rubbed his eyes, then finished buttoning his shirt. His feet, Jared saw, were bare.

"I wanted you to help me get those damn boots off," Jared said, "but I did it myself while I was waiting on you."

"I was asleep when you called," Aaron said.

Jared shrugged. "Finish getting dressed," he told him. "I have a message for you to deliver."

While Aaron returned to his room, Jared sat at a desk, wrote a few lines on a sheet of paper and sealed it in an envelope. He printed "Miss Colleen Hughes" on the outside. Handing the message to a now fully clothed Aaron, he said, "I want this delivered into Miss Hughes's hands. Don't leave it with anyone else. Do you understand?"

"Yes, sir," Aaron said. He paused as though he meant to go on.

"If she's not at home," Jared told him, "wait for her." He stared at the still hesitating Aaron. "Well?" Jared asked.

Aaron nodded and, pocketing the message, left the room.

That nigger's acting almighty strange, Jared thought, frowning. He paced back and forth across the room, reviewing the siege of Sumter in his mind. What would I have done differently in Beauregard's place? he asked himself. He shook his head. He couldn't fault the Confederate general.

What if I had been Anderson? The Yankee had been in a tight spot, no mistake about it, yet he'd only defended the fort for a day and a half and hadn't lost a man until the fight was over. I'd have fired the big guns on the parapet, by God I would have, no matter what the cost. And I'd have held on until the seas quieted so troops could land on the islands around the harbor entrance.

Jared stopped next to the door to Aaron's room. What was wrong with the man? He acted as though . .

Does he have a woman in there? Jared flung the door open. The bed was made, the room ordered and austere. And empty. Jared went to Aaron's wardrobe, opened it, and saw the slave's few clothes hanging in a neat row. Jared nodded. He'd made the right decision when he accepted Aaron as a gift from his father.

He was about to return to his own room when he heard a tapping on the hall door. Surprised, Jared crossed the room and opened the door to find a young Negro woman standing in the corridor. She stared at Jared for a moment and then started to walk away.

"Where are you going?" Jared demanded.

"I—I must have come to the wrong room."

"Were you looking for Aaron?"

She caught her breath and he knew she had been. "What's your name?" he asked her.

"Melinda," she said, almost too softly for him to hear.

"One of the Vaughans' niggers?"

She nodded.

"This is Aaron's room," Jared said. "Come in and sit and wait for him."

She looked suspiciously at Jared for a moment before shaking her head.

"I said to come in and wait for him."

Again Melinda shook her head.

Jared stepped toward her, grasped her wrist and pulled her into the room, slamming the door shut. Still holding her, he crossed to the door and strode into his bedroom with Melinda stumbling behind him.

He pushed her down so she was sitting on the edge of the bed.

"Take off your clothes," he told her.

She looked up at him, wide-eyed.

"I don't intend to say everything twice. Take off your clothes and be quick about it."

"Aaron will . . ." she began, her voice quavering. "Massa Nelson will . . ."

"Aaron can do nothing. Master Nelson will do nothing." Jarded gripped her arm above the elbow and she winced. "You're a pretty one," he said, looking at her fine-boned face. "And you have more than a little white blood in you, from your looks. I wouldn't be surprised if cousin Nelson hasn't sampled your wares long before this." He released her and stood back. "Now take off your clothes."

Melinda sat huddled on the bed with her arms folded over her breasts.

"God damn it!" Jared reached down and pulled her up to stand in front of him. He grasped the high neck of her dress and tore down, the buttons popping off, the top of the dress falling open. Melinda drew in her breath but said nothing as she held the torn dress together.

"All right," Jared told her, "if you'd rather have me take them off, I'll be glad to oblige."

He grasped one of her wrists in each of his hands and lowered her arms to her sides. Gripping the torn bodice, he ripped it apart while pulling the sleeve down her arms. The top of the dress bunched at her waist, revealing her small, perfectly shaped breasts.

Jared nodded in approval. "Yes," he said, "I can understand what Massa Nelson sees in you." He slowly circled Melinda, smiling. "Let your hair down," he said. Melinda slowly reached up, removed the pins, and her black hair fell halfway down her back.

Jared knelt in front of her, took the dress in both hands and drew it down over her hips. He sat back on his heels, gazing up at her .She was naked beneath the dress, her skin a rich coffee-with-cream color, her body small and well-formed. Jared rose to his feet and pushed her back on the bed, where she curled her body, her hands clasping her knees.

Jared dropped his trousers to the floor and stepped out of them. Going to the bed, he spread her legs and lowered himself between them. Melinda lay inert beneath him.

"My God," he said, "isn't there any fire in you at all?" He grasped one of her breasts, cruelly twisting the nipple until he heard her sudden intake of breath. "Is that what you like?" he asked. "To be hurt?"

Melinda shook her head.

Jared knelt on the bed, grasped one of her arms and turned her over onto her stomach. He raised her hips until she was on her knees in front of him with her face still on the bed. Putting his hands around her thighs, he probed between her legs with his fingers until he touched her sex. Slowly he parted the lips, sliding his finger back and forth. Still she made no sound, her body tense and unresponsive.

He thrust his sex between her legs, guiding it with the tips of his fingers until he entered her. His hands slid along her stomach to her breasts, covering them as he thrust into her. His passion grew and, on his knees, eased back and then again thrust forward, beginning a steady rhythm that grew and grew until he exploded within her. For a moment he lay on her, sated. Then, cursing, he pushed himself away to stand beside the bed, staring down at her.

Melinda lay face down, her head turned from him, her hips still slightly raised Jared took one hip in his hand and pushed her onto her back.

"You're a cold bitch," he said. He struck her face with the flat of his palm, making her head snap away from him.

Melinda put her hands to her face and began to cry.

"Don't think I'm through with you," Jared said. "You'll stay here until you show some enthusiasm for your work. Do you understand?"

She said nothing.

Jared drew her hands from her face and yanked her up so she sat on the edge of the bed. He stood in front of her with his sex only a few inches from her face.

"Do you understand?" he demanded.

There was a knock at the door.

"For God's sake . . ." Jared turned from the bed. Aaron? Back so soon?

"Aaron?" he asked.

The door swung open.

Nelson pushed his way through the throngs on Meeting Street. In the distance he heard a band playing, guns being fired, and voices raised in song. The victory celebration was like a carnival in April, he thought.

He stopped in front of the Charleston Hotel to look up at the men and women on the balconies who waved handkerchiefs and cheered when Confederate soldiers passed by on the street below.

He would talk to Jared, Nelson decided. The South was at war, and this was no time for petty personal quarrels; he meant to make peace with his cousin so they could begin afresh. With Santee so near Hunter Hill, with his father dead, the Vaughans and Hunters would be fools not to work together. Not that he meant to concede an inch. That was his fear, that Jared would interpret his offer of peace as a sign of weakness rather than of strength. To hell with what Jared thought, Nelson told himself; he was doing right by coming to see him.

He made his way through the lobby to the desk.

"Yes, sir," the clerk told him. "Colonel Hunter's one of our guests. You'll find him in two-thirty-one."

Nelson nodded and climbed the stairs to the second floor, where gaslights flared in sconces on both walls of the long corridor. He found room two-thirty-one and knocked.

"Aaron?" Jared asked from inside.

Nelson lifted the latch and pushed. The door opened. "No," he said, stepping inside. "It's Nelson."

He stopped, staring. Jared, his lower body exposed, stood facing him. A dark-haired woman sat on the shadowed bed behind him. For a long terrible moment Nelson thought the woman was Colleen.

"Do you always come into rooms uninvited?" Jared asked, stooping to pick up his pants from the floor.

"Melinda," Nelson said, surprise and relief in his voice.

Melinda lowered her face into her hands.

"Here," Jared said, taking her dress and throwing it to her. "Take this into the other room and put it on."

"Why are you here?" Nelson asked the young girl, wondering if he sounded as foolish as he thought he did.

Sobbing, Melinda shook her head. Clutching the dress in front of her, she ran to the door and into Aaron's room.

"What was she doing here?" Nelson asked.

Jared buckled his belt. "Now what in the hell do you think she was doing? She read in the *Mercury* that women should be knitting socks for the Confederate soldiers so she came to the hotel to find out what size I wore."

"Aaron." Nelson nodded at the door Melinda had closed behind her. "She came here to see Aaron. They've been keeping company for some time."

"Of course she came to see Aaron," Jared said caustically. "When she found me here instead she decided to stay. Nigger bitches are all alike." He gestured toward a low, overstuffed chair. "Sit down, Nelson."

"I prefer to stand."

"May I pour you a drink, cousin? Madeira's your favorite, isn't it?"

Nelson shook his head. Finding Melinda with Jared had startled and angered him. He couldn't believe she had offered herself to his cousin; more than likely he'd forced her.

"Now that you know why your nigger was here," Jared said, "tell me why *you're* here. Did the bombardment change your mind? Did you decide to accept my help in becoming an officer?"

"No," Nelson said, "I came here to offer you a truce. I'd decided that with the war this was a good time to make our own private peace. I can see I was wrong. We can't. We'll never be able to."

Jared came to stand in front of him, his hands on his hips. "You're right," he said quietly, "we never can. It's not in the nature of things. We'll be enemies until one of us is dead."

"So be it." Nelson opened the door, then stopped and looked back. "Did you enjoy your seconds?" he asked.

"I thought you'd probably had her, a good-looking wench like that."

"I didn't mean you were second after me. You weren't. I meant after Aaron."

Jared drew in his breath, his eyes narrowing, and for a moment Nelson thought he would strike out at him. Jared relaxed and put his hand on Nelson's shoulder. "You son-of-a-bitch," he said, a hint of admiration in his voice.

Nelson looked at the hand on his shoulder and Jared let it fall to his side. "Goodnight, cousin," Nelson said, pulling the door shut.

He's changed, Jared thought once Nelson was gone. No, he told himself, no one changed that quickly, not in a few days' time. Yet Nelson had, or seemed to have. That gibe about his being second to Aaron smarted, there was no question about it. In fact, Jared decided, he couldn't have handled himself any better than Nelson had.

Which, coming from Jared Hunter, was high praise indeed.

The next evening Jared strolled from the hotel down Meeting Street to the Battery. He walked beneath the live oaks in the park, finally sitting on a bench near the water. The night was calm and clear and around the harbor he could see the fires of the troops still camped near the Confederate batteries.

A horse's hoofbeats thudded behind him. The horse came to a halt, there was silence and then footsteps approached. Jared didn't turn around. The steps slowed and stopped a few feet away.

Jared looked up. Colleen Hughes stood with her hands clasped in front of her, the veil on her large purple hat covering her face. She wore a lavender long-skirted gown, ornamented with black buttons down the front and black ribbons at the shoulders. Jared slowly stood and bowed.

"Shall we walk?" he asked, offering her his arm.

She nodded, slipping her hand beneath his arm.

"You knew I'd come, didn't you?" she asked after a moment.

"I thought you would. I hoped you would. With you, I'm never sure."

"Don't lie to me, Jared."

"I didn't think I was lying. I was attempting to be gallant."

"Gallantry doesn't suit you. It never did."

He stopped and turned her to face him. Lifting her veil, he draped it over her hat. Lowering his face to hers, Jared kissed her. his arms at his sides, only his lips touching her. He saw her close her eyes as she returned his kiss.

Jared stepped away, took her hand and put it on his arm.

"Wait," she said, taking her hand away. "Kiss me, Jared. Kiss me as though you meant it."

He took her in his arms, pulling her tightly against him as his lips found hers in a long, deep kiss, their bodies as well as their lips molded one to the other. When at last she drew away, Colleen sighed.

"It's going to be just as it was before," Jared told her.

"No, it's not. I had illusions about you then. I have none left."

"Illusions?"

"I thought you meant to marry me and carry me off as your bride to Hunter Hill. Now I know you won't. You never will. I don't know if you intend to marry anyone, but I've reconciled myself to the fact that if you do it won't be me."

"I expect to leave for Richmond inside of two weeks," Jared said. "The fighting's finished here, at least for the time being. The war will be decided in Virginia as soon as their secession convention takes the state out of the Union. General Beauregard's preparing to journey north and I mean to be with him when he goes. I want you to come with me to Richmond, Colleen."

"Haven't you forgotten I'm spoken for? Or do you believe I can just ignore the fact that I'm to marry Nelson Vaughan?"

"You'll have to break with him. After all, you agreed to marry him before you knew I was coming home."

"Glory be," Colleen said. "I keep thinking I've plumbed the depths of your arrogance and then you manage to surprise me all over again."

"I was merely stating a fact. I don't see any arrogance in that, Colleen."

"And what if I don't break with Nelson?"

He leaned to her, kissing her. When she drew away, she said, "Besides, I have no reason, no excuse."

"Do women need reasons?"

"I do, Jared."

"What about that girl who's staying with you? Dyan Raleigh-Beckwith."

"What of Dyan?" She stared at Jared. "Do you mean Nelson and Dyan? You're mad, Jared, he hardly knows her. She's only been in Charleston a little over a week."

"I don't know if there's anything between them," he said, "not for certain. It's a hunch on my part, nothing more. Why don't you ask her? She'll deny it, of course, but I suspect you'll be able to tell. I know I could in your place."

"Dyan and Nelson." Colleen shook her head. "Lord! I can't believe you're serious. You're suggesting it because you hate your cousin so."

"I don't hate him, though I suspect the reverse is true. I pity him."

"No," Colleen said, "there's more to it than that. What is there between you and Nelson, Jared? You're nothing alike and yet at times I think of you as two sides of the same coin. No matter how much you may hate each other, you seem drawn together by something stronger than either of you. By fate, perhaps. Yes, that's it, fate."

"Colleen, you're being melodramatic. If I had my way, I'd never set eyes on Nelson again for the rest of my life."

"And yet you will, you know you will. You and Nelson are like two brothers bound to disagree, like Cain and Abel."

"And I'm Cain, I suppose. Do you mean to tell me I'll kill him someday? That I'll end up murdering Nelson and as punishment the Lord will send me east of Eden? In my case, I suppose I'd be sent west, to the Dakota badlands or the Arizona desert."

Colleen shivered. "Don't speak of killing," she said. "I don't want to see either of you dead."

Again he kissed her. "I don't intend to die for a long while. And when I do, I suspect it will be in bed."

"Don't even speak of dying."

"At times," Jared said, "I think of Nelson as my conscience—a conscience I take delight in ignoring. I admit I goad him. I can't seem to help it. Some people are so naïve, so trusting, that you can't help leading them up the garden path to discover the limits of their credulity. I don't think I've found Nelson's limits yet. At least I hadn't until yesterday."

"What happened then?"

"Oh, we quarreled over his slave girl, Melinda. He seemed to take less than kindly to her visiting Aaron at the hotel. I couldn't see any reason for his objections and I told him so."

"She's a pretty little thing. For a Negro."

"Nelson appears to think so. Not that I believe there's anything between them—I don't." Jared took a cigar from the inner pocket of his jacket and lit it. "You don't mind if I smoke, do you?" he asked.

"Of course not."

"You haven't answered me yet," Jared said. "I want you to come to Richmond with me."

"I'll admit I'm tempted."

"Good. I thought you'd see it my way."

"I didn't say I'd come. Being tempted and succumbing to temptation are miles apart."

Jared smiled, flicking the ash from his cigar. "Now," he said, "there's another matter I want to ask you about." He waited until a strolling couple had passed out of earshot. "About your father. Has he returned from the Bahamas?"

"My father? Why, Jared, if I didn't know you better I'd think you were intending to ask for his permission to pay court to me."

"That wasn't exactly what I had in mind, as you well know. It wasn't his daughter's hand I was thinking of asking for. It was his ships."

"You leap about so fast I can't keep up with you," Colleen said. "But yes, I'm expecting my father at any time. He would have been here by now, I suspect, if the bombardment of Fort Sumter hadn't closed the harbor. He should be in Charleston by the weekend at the latest."

"Good. And how many ships does he own?"

"Three. Or four if he bought the one he was interested in. That's why he sailed for Nassau, to look her over. Why do you ask, Jared? You were never interested in father's ships before."

"The Confederacy has no navy, none at all. The Union will blockade our ports if they have half the brains God gave them. They'll try to starve us out while keeping our cotton off the world markets. We'll need small fast ships like your father's to slip in and out of the harbors along the coast. I mean to have dinner with your father and broach the idea."

"My father's every bit as staunch a secessionist as you are. He'll do whatever he can to help the cause."

"Of course he will, particularly when he'll have a chance to make a fortune, besides. Running the blockade will be risky, so there'll have to be reward enough to make the chance worth taking."

"And what will you get out of it, Jared?"

"After I talk to your father I plan to present the idea to Jefferson Davis himself. Through the proper channels, of course. He'll be gratified to learn he has a young officer in his army who's able to think farther ahead than the end of his nose. And when promotions are due, I believe he'll remember Jared Hunter. Don't you agree?"

When Nelson was ushered into the front parlor to wait for Colleen, he found Dyan on the settee in front of the fireplace with her knitting on her lap. The young blonde girl looked up in surprise, her hand going to her mouth and her knitting falling to the floor. Flustered, she rose and fled from the room.

I'll be damned, Nelson said to himself as he retrieved the yarn and put it on the settee. Now I wonder what made her do that?

He didn't have to wait long before he found out.

"I'm leaving for Richmond in the morning," Colleen told him a few minutes later.

"For a visit? Now?"

"I'll be staying with the Raleigh-Beckwiths. Dyan's people." She stressed Dyan's name.

"Aren't you forgetting we're to be married in June?"

"I don't really know how long I'll be in Richmond," Colleen said.

Nelson drew in his breath, suspecting the truth.

"Dyan told me everything," Colleen said. "I'm sure, that if your performance, yours and Dyan's, had taken place twelve hours later, in the early afternoon, you would have attracted more spectators than a concert featuring Jeff Davis and Abe Lincoln singing a duet."

"Ah." The color rose to Nelson's face. He slowly drew on his gloves and bowed. "I trust you'll have a pleasant journey," he said, turning on his heel and leaving the house. Once on the street he had an uncontrollable impulse to laugh, so he laughed. A couple stopped to stare at him. Nelson raised his hat to them and walked on.

"I'll be damned," he said.

Virginia seceded from the Union in May of 1861 and the Confederate capital was moved from Montgomery to Richmond. Nelson was assigned to a regiment defending the islands along the coast between Charleston and Savannah after rumors warned of the possibility of a sea-borne invasion from the north. General Beauregard was accompanied to Virginia by Colonels Roger Raleigh-Beckwith and Jared Hunter. Colleen Hughes had already left for Richmond after announcing her intention of visiting the Raleigh-Beckwiths.

And, as June gave way to July, Union General Irvin McDowell sent his army across the Potomac and marched on Richmond in a campaign designed to end the war.

8

JARED HUNTER lit up and leaned back in his seat, looking from the car window at Virginia's fields and wooded hills as the train rattled north toward Manassas Junction. He felt a keen edge of excitement for he knew a battle was brewing near Manassas between Beauregard's Army of the Potomac and McDowell's Federal forces. And he was more than satisfied with what he had accomplished these last three weeks as Beauregard's courier between Manassas and Richmond.

His luck was holding. Even the heavens seemed to agree, for during the first week of July a great comet had been visible in the northern sky near the Big Dipper. An omen, he was sure, heralding victory for the Confederacy.

And then there'd been his meeting with Jefferson Davis.

"I read your letter to the secretary of war with

interest," Davis said. The president was a tall man, slim, haggard with illness. "I congratulate you on your initiative."

"Thank you, sir," Jared said. "I believe that if the war lasts beyond this summer's campaign we'll need all the ships we can find to run the blockade."

"The war may last longer than any of us think. Have you spoken personally to this Amos Hughes?"

"I have, sir," Jared told the president. "He stands ready to use his ships as you direct. And he knows of many other ship-owners who will do the same."

"Excellent, Colonel Hunter. You may rest assured that the government will pursue the matter. We may even call upon you for help in the future."

"I'd be honored, General Davis." Jared saluted.

Davis stood behind his desk and extended his hand. "I envy you," he said. "I wish I were in the field with our armies instead of here."

Jared nodded as he recalled the conversation. Just then, the train slowed, jerking to a stop. No, this wasn't Manassas yet. He looked ahead at the locomotive and along the track beyond but could see nothing to explain the delay. The entire journey north from Richmond had been a series of starts and stops. No wonder the soldiers suspected the trainmen of being in league with the Yankees.

He sympathized with Jeff Davis. Certainly he, Jared, would rather be here in northern Virginia, for he was sure this was where the war would be decided in the next few days. The Confederates had two armies in the field, Joe Johnston's in the Shenandoah Valley to the west and Pierre Beauregard's between Richmond and Washington at Manassas. Facing them on the Federal side were Patterson's army in the Shenandoah Valley and McDowell's based in Washington. During the last few days McDowell had been cautiously advancing into Virginia from the Potomac, first to Fairfax Court House, then to Germantown, finally to Centreville. Beauregard had taken up defensive positions along a stream called Bull Run to protect Manassas Junction, where the only rail line from the Shenandoah Valley met the Orange and Alexandria, the north-south line.

Yes, Jared decided, Manassas was where he wanted to be. Though he couldn't help smiling to himself as he remembered waking that morning at the hotel. When he opened his eyes, knowing that something rubbing against his face had roused him, he looked up to see Colleen on her hands and knees on the bed, bending over him so that her bared breast touched his cheek. He turned his head, circling her nipple with his tongue.

She moaned, taking his head in her hands and holding him to her. Much later, when she lay in his arms, she said, "You're the only one, Jared, who ever made me want to—to do this."

He said nothing.

"I know it's wrong," she went on. "I know you'll hurt me again, just as you did three years ago. And yet . . ." Her voice trailed off.

"And yet?" he asked.

"When I'm not with you, not near you, nothing seems real. It's as though I'm play-acting. I know you don't feel as I do; I know I'm a fool. Yet there it is." She nestled her head against his shoulder.

Jared smiled, remembering. All at once the train jolted into motion again, the cars rattling along the uneven roadbed, and ten minutes later they arrived at Manassas Junction. Jared retrieved his horse and rode to the McLean house, where Beauregard had set up his headquarters.

Colonel Raleigh-Beckwith stopped Jared as he was

about to go in. "Not now," he said. "Joe Johnston's with him."

Jared looked at Beckwith in surprise. "Johnston's here? From the Shenandoah?"

"Just arrived. General Thomas Jackson rode in yesterday with some of the troops from the Valley. More are coming all the time, though it's slow work. They have to keep sending a locomotive back into the mountains for them."

"Patterson?" Jared asked, naming the Federal general who had been facing Johnstons' men in the Valley.

"We can only hope to God he doesn't get wind of what Johnston's up to. If he does he'll follow him over the mountains and link up with McDowell."

"That means Johnston's in command here," Jared said. "Beau's outranked."

"It seems incredible that the Napoleon of the Americas could be outranked," Beckwith said in a low voice. "But that's the size of it."

"What do you know of Johnston?" Jared asked. Beckwith was a prime source of off-the-record information. Though Jared listened to him, he didn't like the man.

"Well," Beckwith said, "I did hear a story about him in Richmond last month. It seems Johnston has a reputation for being a capital shot, just as he's supposed to be an aggressive general. Hearing of his shooting prowess, Wade Hampton took him to his estate to hunt.

"As far as Johnston was concerned, the birds either flew too high or too low, the dogs were too far away or too near. Things never exactly suited him, he was too hard to please, too cautious, too afraid to miss and risk his fine reputation as a crack shot. Hampton banged away right and left, happy-go-lucky, and bagged a fine take of birds. Johnston never shot at all."

"I see," Jared said. "The others came back with the birds and Johnston came back with his reputation intact."

"Exactly. Of course, shooting birds and running an army aren't the same. At least I hope they aren't."

"Colonel Hunter." An orderly had appeared at the door. "The general is ready to see you now."

Jared went in, handed his dispatches to one of Beauregard's aides and saluted the general. There was no sign of Johnston.

"Let me bring you up-to-date, Colonel," Beauregard said, strutting to a map pinned to the wall. "This is where General McDowell will meet his Waterloo tomorrow."

Jared nodded. He was used to the Louisiana Creole's flowery language and his penchant for comparing his military operations to Napoleon's campaigns.

Jared studied the map. Bull Run wound its tortuous course from the top to the bottom. There were only a few places where McDowell could get his army across the sluggish stream, at Sudley's Ford in the north, over the turnpike's stone bridge, or at one of the four fords in the south.

"McDowell will strike at our right flank," Beauregard said. "He probed there two days ago and we drove him back. He'll attack there again because the country isn't as wooded as in the north. He'll think he has a clear path to the rail line."

Jared nodded. He'd learned that Beauregard didn't appreciate argument; instead, he expected agreement. Jared decided he also had a sublime faith that opposing generals would do exactly what he expected them to do.

"I've concentrated the bulk of our 25,000 men on

the right," the general went on, "under Longstreet, Jackson, Bee, Early, Ewell and the others. In the morning, we'll strike first, advance on Centreville and write *finis* to McDowell's offensive. I'm about to prepare the battle orders now." He paused. "With General Johnston's approval, of course."

Again Jared nodded. Beauregard's disposition of troops almost ignored his left flank. There was the potential for disaster if McDowell decided to advance in strength along the turnpike or through the woods to the north.

"On the morrow," Beauregard said, "I want you to serve as my personal liaison with my commanders. I've had problems making them understand what I expect of them. You know my thinking, Hunter, and the thinking in Richmond."

"Yes, sir," Jared said.

"Rest well, Colonel," Beauregard said. "And good hunting tomorrow."

That night Jared lay in the open, waiting for sleep to come. It was a beautiful night, with the sky clear, the moon full and bright, the air still and warm. Moonlight cast the shadows of trees onto the field where he lay; dying campfires glowed nearby. The men were restless and keyed up.

The Confederate soldiers were terribly green, Jared knew. In the three months since the fall of Sumter they had been drilled, armed and outfitted, but they had yet to do battle. Their guns were a mixed lot, the majority muzzle-loaders, and their uniforms were motley, gray for the most part, though some wore blue and others wore brown buckskins. And then there were the Zouaves from Louisiana, dressed in baggy blue and white striped trousers, short brown jackets and small caps with long red tassels.

Of course McDowell's troops must be just as inexperienced, just as motley. When green troops met green troops, Jared had been taught at the Citadel, the defenders held the advantage. Dug in, protected, defending troops were much less likely to panic than men charging across an open field in the face of heavy fire.

Wondering whether, in Beauregard's place, he would be so anxious to attack, Jared fell asleep. He was wakened before dawn by the long roll of the drums and the call of a bugle. In the distance he could hear the desultory pop-pop of small arms fire as, he supposed, Union skirmishers came up against the pickets Beauregard had placed on the far side of Bull Run.

As Jared rode to report to headquarters, he noted that most of the shooting came from the north, where Beauregard's line was weakest. Was it a feint by the Federals or the prelude to an all-out assault? He saw the flare of a torch overhead and looked up at a soldier signaling from one of the towers Captain Alexander had built behind the Confederate lines.

"Colonel," Beckwith said as Jared dismounted at the McLean house, "will you take this dispatch to Ewell? He's covering the rail line a mile below McLean's ford."

Jared nodded, read the message, and put the leather dispatch case over his shoulder. As he spurred away, heading south, the sun rose above the trees, promising a hot day. When he reined in at Ewell's headquarters he saw a woman approach the bearded general. *What the hell's a woman doing here?* Jared wondered.

"The Federals are advancing from Centreville along the Warrenton Turnpike," he heard the woman tell Ewell.

General Ewell waved his forefinger at her. "There's going to be firing here soon," he said.

"I'm not afraid," she told him. "I was up before dawn watching the Federals assemble. I rode here as fast as I could."

"You'll get killed. You'll be a dead damsel in less than a minute." The general's voice rose to a roar. "Get away from here! Get away!"

The woman retreated to her horse, where she stood, arms folded, glaring at the general.

"Women," General Ewell said to Jared. "I tell you, sir, women would make a grand brigade—if it weren't for snakes and spiders! They don't mind bullets— women are not afraid of bullets; but one big black-snake would put a whole army of them to flight. Here, sir, give me that dispatch. I've been all morning waiting with no orders. No orders! Is that the proper way to run an army?"

He read the message, crumpled it and tossed the ball of paper into a fire. "And then when orders come, they make no sense. If I read this message correctly, Beauregard wants me to attack Jones on my left. I'd gladly attack Jones but for the fact he's as much of a Confederate as I am. Doesn't that Creole know which side Jones is on?"

"I'm sure he does, sir," Jared said calmly. "I believe the thrust of the order is that you and Jones are to ford Bull Run and advance on Centreville."

"You believe! You believe! Am I to advance my brigade because of what a colonel believes?"

Jared said nothing and Ewell's choler subsided as quickly as it had risen. "I expect you're right," he said. "Tell General Beauregard I understand and will comply at once." He wrote rapidly on a piece of paper and handed it to Jared, who saluted and remounted.

When he returned to headquarters he found officers bustling about, couriers arriving and departing, and wagons stirring the dust along the road.

"Go at once to General Evans at the bridge," Beckwith told him. "Inform him that Bee and Jackson will reinforce him as fast as humanly possible. He's to stand firm until they arrive."

"The attack's coming on our left then?" Jared asked. The weak left flank.

"Beau still believes it's only a Federal demonstration, that the brunt of McDowell's attack will fall on our right."

Jared nodded and sat out for the bridge, some two miles distant. As he rode he saw soldiers stopping along the way to pick blackberries and to fill their canteens. The tempo of gunfire increased in front of him and he heard the thump-thump-thump of the Federal batteries. When he neared the bridge men were trying to duck and dodge the shells screaming around them. Some sought cover behind trees, others behind saplings.

Jared, riding behind them, shook his head in disgust. "Keep cool," he called out. "There's no use ducking at the sound of a shell. By the time you hear it, it's already past you."

A cannonball crashed through the trees directly over Jared's head with a rushing whine. Instinctively, he grasped his horse's neck and pressed his face to its mane. When he raised his head, he swore, angry with himself. Looking around, he saw grinning faces staring up at him.

With an effort, Jared smiled. "Well, boys," he said, "you may dodge the big ones." He rode on with the sound of raucous cheers following him.

He was nearing the stone bridge over Bull Run

when a sentry stepped from behind a tree, rifle at the ready, and blocked his way. "The password!" the man shouted.

Jared hesitated, then placed his right hand over his breast and said, "Our homes!" The sentry used his bayoneted rifle to motion him ahead.

General Evans wasn't at the bridge.

"The Federals have crossed the Run at Sudley's Ford," a lieutenant told Jared. "We're holding the bridge while the general double-quicks the rest of the men down the road to stop them."

Jared rode back along the Warrenton Pike, the sounds of battle increasing in front and to his right, where a pall of dust and gunsmoke lay over the Virginia fields and hills. He felt sweat bead his face as the sun rose higher. A scorcher of a day, he thought.

Evans had advanced north of the turnpike to intercept the advancing Federals. Jared headed in that direction, riding into a woods, smelling the acrid odor of burnt powder, passing a few stragglers and wounded men making their way to the rear. He approached the far edge of the woods just as men in gray swarmed from cover ahead of him toward what appeared to be the center of the Federal line. Jared saw Major Wheat leading his Zouaves. Wheat's Tigers, they were called.

The men advanced, growling and screaming, their bayonets fixed. A few of them threw down their rifles and ran forward armed only with their extra-long bowie knives. Zouaves fell to Jared's right and left. He saw Major Wheat go down. The line of troops parted to pass around him as Wheat waved them on with his saber.

Jared dismounted and knelt beside the major. Blood coursed from Wheat's mouth; his tunic was red. As far as Jared could tell a bullet had entered his body beneath one armpit and passed through his chest to exit at the same spot on the other side.

Jared waved for help and two men ran forward and carried the major back to the lines with Jared following. The major was still conscious. "I don't feel like dying yet," he said to Jared.

Wheat would never live out the day, Jared was sure. Later he learned that doctors behind the front had told the major, "There's no instance on record of recovery from such a wound," for at least one of the major's lungs was perforated.

"There will be," the major had said confidently, "when I put my case upon the record."

By the time Jared located General Evans, the charge of Wheat's battalion was spent and the men were falling back to their original position in the woods.

"Reinforcements are on the way," Jared told Evans, glancing about and seeing the general's Prussian orderly carrying a wooden one-gallon drum on his back. Evans called it his "barrelita," and it was always filled with whiskey. He was known at headquarters as the best drinker, the most eloquent swearer and the biggest braggart in the Confederate army.

"Goddamn it," Evans said, "they'd best be speedy. I've got the whole Federal army coming down on me from Sudley's. Tell them to haul their asses up here pronto."

"They're coming," Jared told him. "Bee's coming. Jackson's on his way."

Evans nodded and then turned away to greet a courier, and Jared set out to return to headquarters. The firing seemed to be all around him now and when he looked down the hill he saw line after line of blue-coated Federals advancing. From the woods behind them, cannon flashed and rumbled and a horse near Jared screamed in fear and pain as it was hit. In the distance, across Bull Run, he saw the glint of sunlight on metal as more Federal troops marched toward the ford and the battlefield.

This was no mere demonstration, as Beauregard must have realized by now; this must be the main thrust of the Federal attack. As Jared rode on he saw Confederates ahead of him fire and then drop back a few feet before reloading for another volley.

Jared rode along behind them. "Stand your ground!" he shouted. "Stand your ground!"

The line stiffened. Below them and to their left, Federals advanced up the hillside.

"Where are your officers?" Jared asked one of the men.

"Dead. They're all dead."

Jared rode through the line of Confederates, brandishing his sword. "We'll take them on the flank!" he shouted. "We'll bayonet them." He spurred his horse up and down in front of the men, urging them forward.

They followed him in a ragged line. Bullets zinged around him. Smoke and dust stung Jared's throat and nostrils as he led the men across the field and down on the flank of the Federal line. The bluecoats faltered, a few ran, then more and more turned and fled into a woods. Jared glanced behind him. Men had fallen. Some lay unmoving, while others writhed on the ground. One called out in pain, bloody hands clutching his stomach.

Jared rode into the woods, hearing the thrashing of men tramping through the brush on all sides of him. Suddenly his horse plunged forward, falling, and Jared threw himself from the saddle, kicking free of the stirrups. He tumbled to the ground, bruising his shoulder.

Looking up, he saw three rifles pointed down at him.

"You're our prisoner," one of the three Federal enlisted men said. "Hand over your sword."

Jared got to his feet and took his time brushing himself off. "I'm an officer," he said, "and I'll only surrender to another officer. Those are the rules of war."

The men stared at him, their rifles wavering in indecision. Shots came from off to their left and the soldier who had demanded Jared's surrender suddenly drew in his breath and dropped his rifle, clutching his side. Blood trickled through his fingers and he pitched to the ground at Jared's feet. The other two men turned and bolted.

Jared ran into the undergrowth toward his own line. He came on a group of Confederates.

"The others with us turned tail," one said. The firing around them lessened. A cannon roared, a wounded man called for help.

"Back to the line on the hill," Jared ordered.

They retreated to the verge of the woods, where they turned and ran for the Southern lines. Sun glinted on bayonets ahead of them. One of the men with Jared put his hand to his breast. "Our homes, our homes," he shouted. A bullet tore at the cloth of Jared's collar. He put his hand to his neck and felt wetness, drew it away and looked at his fingers. Sweat.

They were inside their lines. "Jackson's on the hill," a lieutenant told Jared, "holding a position just behind the crest, waiting for the Federals. When they see the enemy top the hill, Jackson told them, the whole line should rise, move forward with a shout, and trust to their bayonets. He said he was tired of this long-range work."

Jared nodded. Jackson must be on Henry Hill, a low rise that dominated the area. He wondered how commanders on either side could tell what was happening as the fight pulsed back and forth amidst the swirling smoke and dust. The Federal attack followed a pattern, he noticed, with artillery bombarding the Confederate line, followed by swarms of advancing infantry and, finally, cavalry charges to demoralize and scatter the Southerners.

While Jared looked about him for a horse, he recalled what he'd heard of Jackson. Little that was favorable. The general had fought in the Mexican War but had resigned from the army in '52 to become a teacher at the Virginia Military Institute. He was a stickler for discipline; two cadets at VMI had challenged him to duels.

When they weren't damning him, the cadets were ridiculing him. Jackson sucked lemons constantly to ease a stomach disorder. He wouldn't use pepper, fearing it would make his legs ache. His voice was high-pitched. He rarely laughed—but when he did, his head fell back, his mouth opened wide, and no sound whatsoever issued forth.

Jared, despairing of finding a horse, watched men straggle back from the front lines, some wounded, others claiming to be. Two uninjured privates helped a comrade who was limping from a wound in his foot. God damn them, Jared thought.

They're green, he told himself, but that was no excuse. On the lines, Jared knew, the artillery had thundered around them, officers shouted, bullets and shells shrieked by, men and horses fell and cried out in pain. Men lost their reason, some shooting straight up into the air while others, frantic to reload and fire, forgot to put a musket cap in place and pulled the trigger without noticing the gun had not fired

and so loaded again and again. Some forgot to re-
move their ramrods after shoving a bullet home,
and when they pulled the triggers the rods shot like
arrows across the battlefield.

A man fleeing the field of battle staggered toward
Jared, carrying his rifle at his side. A tall man, his
face streaked with dirt and sweat, he reminded Jared
of someone. Nelson. Yes, he looked like Nelson
Vaughan. When Jared stepped forward to block his
way he noticed several more stragglers behind the
man.

"Get back in line, soldier," Jared said.

The man shook his head.

"Are you wounded?"

Again the man shook his head. He seemed dazed.
The other men, after stopping behind him, started
toward the rear once more.

Jared pulled his pistol from its holster. "You're de-
serting your comrades," he said. "Get back to the
line or I'll kill you on the spot. You have more to
fear from me than from the Yankees."

"I can't go back," the man muttered. The soldiers
behind him had stopped again, watching.

Jared waited. The man started toward him. Jared
fired, the shot striking the man's chest and hurling
him back onto the ground. Still alive, he stared up
at Jared in fear and disbelief. Ignoring him, Jared
looked across his body at the other men. They gazed
back at him until, one by one, they turned and made
for the line of battle on the hill.

Later—Jared didn't know how much time had
passed—he found a horse wandering free. He mounted and spurred the horse to the east side of Henry
Hill. Scattered troops formed up behind him, the
remnants of companies shattered in the fighting. Most
of these Confederates wore blue.

"Did you hear what General Bee said?" one of the men asked him.

Jared shook his head.

"Bee said Jackson was standing like a stone wall. 'Rally behind the Virginians,' he said just as he was struck in the stomach and knocked from his horse."

"Good for Stonewall Jackson," Jared said.

He rode ahead with two score or more men following him. Hot, dirty, thirsty, the stench of powder, men and horses in his nostrils, he'd lost almost all sense of direction. He wondered if the others, Union and Southern alike, were in the same state. Surprisingly, he felt no fear. He had a task to perform and he meant to do his best.

His rag-tag troop came around the side of a hill, passed through a woods and into a field. Off to their right, bodies in gray and blue lay scattered over a field. On the slope, some hundred rods away, Jared saw an abandoned battery of cannon. Dead horses lay nearby, gunners in Federal blue sprawled beside and against the wheels of the guns and caissons.

Coming from behind the cannons, a detachment of Federals marched up the slope, shooting and reloading as they advanced, aiming their fire higher on the hill. Jared saw they meant to retrieve the cannons. He waved his men forward, intending to hit the Federals on their flank.

"Don't fire," Jared ordered. The word was passed down the line of Confederates.

Through the smoke, Jared saw an officer on horseback behind the Federal foot soldiers. The man stared at the oncoming Southerners, obviously confused by the blue uniforms. Slowly, inexorably, Jared and his men closed on the enemy, the Confederate bayonets glinting in the sun. A cannonball whirred overhead.

A Confederate soldier dropped his rifle and grasped his arm. Dazed, he picked up his gun again and plodded on.

The enemy officer rode toward them, reining in his horse a hundred feet away. "Who are you?" he called.

"Not a word," Jared warned his men in a low voice.

"Identify yourselves," the Federal officer demanded as the Confederates came on.

Jared raised his pistol, fired, and the officer twisted in the saddle and fell to the ground. Jared's men fired a ragged volley, the Union soldiers falling, looking about them in surprise, returning the fire as they tried to make a stand. The Southerners charged, thrusting with their bayonets, grappling hand to hand. The lines locked together for a moment and then the Federals broke and ran for the woods with Jared's men following until heavy fire from among the trees drove them back to the shelter of a rise. The battery of cannon remained, as before, between the lines.

More troops came up on both sides and the tide of battle swung back and forth until finally the Southerners advanced and the Federals fell back in good order. Jared was on a knoll looking down at the forward sweep of the men in gray when he noticed, far off to his left, a cloud of dust on the Warrenton Pike as column after column of men approached from his rear.

Was it Patterson? Had the Union general followed Johnston's army along the rail line and over the mountains so that he was now about to fall on the rear of Beauregard's line and turn a Northern defeat into victory? Jared saw a flag near the head of the approaching columns, the flag furled in the quiet air so he couldn't tell whether it was the Confederate banner or the Stars and Stripes.

The advancing troops came nearer. A breeze raised dust on the road and the flag billowed. It was the Confederate banner—these were more of Johnston's troopers arriving from the Shenandoah. All around Jared, men raised their hats in the air and cheered.

The Federals counter-attacked only to meet a withering fire.

"Them Yankees," a sergeant near Jared said, spitting, "are just marching up and being shot to hell."

As the Federal line wavered and broke, the Southerners surged forward, the Union soldiers threw down their guns and ran, turning the retreat into a rout. Yells and cheers echoed along the Confederate line as the men ran forward, some staggering with exhaustion, all firing at the fleeing enemy.

Jared spurred his horse ahead, waving his saber. "Finish them," he shouted. "Don't let them cross the ford."

Soon, though, overwhelmed by the mass of Yankee prisoners and exhausted from the fighting and the heat, the Southern drive slowed and the Federals crossed the ford and poured away from the battlefield.

Later, riding near a field hospital, Jared saw Jefferson Davis, also on horseback, ride up to a throng of soldiers who were looking for their units.

"I'm President Davis!" he shouted. "Follow me back to the field!"

Jackson, nearby having a wound dressed, called to the president: "We have whipped them! They ran like sheep! Give me five thousand fresh men and I'll be in Washington City tomorrow!"

That night, satisfied, Jared waited for sleep, knowing that the South had won the battle, perhaps the war, and that the pursuit would continue in the morning. He had fought well, though he probably hadn't been noticed by any of the higher ranking officers. He wondered if he should request a command position rather than remain on Beauregard's staff.

According to officers at headquarters, Beauregard had lost control of the battle and only Johnston's steadiness in forwarding fresh men to the left flank had saved the day. Beauregard would probably be the hero of Manassas, but was his star already on the way down?

Jared wondered what had become of the Confederate straggler he'd shot. He hoped he'd recover. The South needed all the men they could muster and the man had probably learned his lesson, one he'd not soon forget. Just before he slept, Jared looked up to see clouds drifting across the sky.

It rained the next day and Johnston's pursuit of McDowell's troops faltered and slogged to a halt in the mud. Confederate soldiers, bone-weary, huddled under trees and in their tents, relating tales of the battle. Burial details worked among the bodies, carting the Southern fallen to the rear to be shipped home, interring the Federal dead where they had fallen.

The work was slow. In the hot days that followed, the bodies bloated, and men died with maggots infesting what had been only superficial wounds. A great stench of death and decay rose from the battlefield, from Sudley's Ford in the north to the woods and fields bordering the turnpike, to Henry's Hill, and along Bull Run past the other fords to the rail line leading to Manassas Junction in the south.

9

"A COTTON FIELD in season," Ida Vaughan said as she and Jethro Hunter rode side by side in a carriage driven by one of the Hunter slaves, "is the most beautiful sight in the world."

"I couldn't agree more," Jethro said. "We'll harvest another good crop this year."

"If only we could sell it."

"Our government is mindless, expecting the Europeans to war on the Yankees to obtain our cotton. If the Yankee blockade wasn't bad enough, this self-imposed embargo is madness."

"You sound like my father. I tell him the men representing us in Richmond know better than we do what's good for the Confederacy."

"And what does the Old Colonel say to that?"

" 'I'll be damned if they do!' were his exact words," Ida said.

"Good for him. How is the old man?"

"In wonderful health, considering. Except for his eyesight, he never seems to change. He looks and acts today much as he did thirty years ago when he was sixty."

The carriage was brought to a halt in front of Hunter Hill and Jethro leaped out to help Ida down, Offering her his arm, he led her to the front piazza where, as soon as they were seated, Sara appeared with a tray of sandwiches and a coffee urn. From behind the house came the sound of sawing and the pounding of hammers.

Jethro walked with Sara to the door and spoke quietly to her. The house slave nodded and hurried off, and after a few minutes the noise stopped abruptly.

"And how is Nelson?" Jethro asked. He seemed ill-at-ease, Ida thought, more uncomfortable today than he had ever been when he courted her more than twenty-five years before.

"He's still at Fort Walker," she told him. "Nelson's impatient. According to his letters he spends his time drilling, swimming in the ocean, riding and playing cards. Many of the men on Hilton Head are bored and drink too much. And certainly Beaufort isn't Charleston."

"Strong drink's a curse," Jethro said.

"Nelson has sworn off. He says he likes liquor too much, so he's never going to touch it again."

Jethro nodded. "Come with me, Ida," he said, getting to his feet. "There's something I want to show you."

Smiling uncertainly, she put her cup on the table.

"I didn't realize you weren't done," he said. "No, wait, finish your coffee. God knows when we'll be able to buy more."

When she finished she put down her cup and got

to her feet, watching him. Jethro cleared his throat, impatient yet wanting to please her.

"Damn it," he said, "I'm not used to having a woman about the place." His wife, Mary, had been dead more than eight years. "Here, take my arm," he said.

"Oh, Jethro, don't treat me as company. We've known each other ever so long. Can't we just be friends?"

He stopped and looked down at her. "No, Ida, we can't."

She felt the blood rising to her cheeks as he led her along a corridor. They went through a back door and past the kitchen garden to where two Negroes sat in the shade of a tree. Beyond them were sawhorses, a pile of lumber, and the frame of an addition to one of the ells of the house.

"I'm adding a room." Jethro smiled. "As you can readily see."

"What on earth will you do with still another room?"

"It's a guest room," he said. "With only the two boys at home I'm afraid I got out of the habit of entertaining. I mean to do more. At least that's my excuse for the addition. Actually, I just wanted to plan and build the room. I want Hunter Hill to grow and change just as I intend to grow and change."

"My father built Santee years ago, as you know, and it's much the same today as it was then. He'll have it no other way."

"I'm not the Old Colonel," Jethro said quietly. "I'm not your father."

She looked at him quickly, surprised, then nodded. He was telling her he was his own man and intended to remain so. Jethro seemed about to speak and she thought he was about to compliment her, to admire her hair—which she had fastened into a chignon after incessant brushing—or the brown and orange hoopskirted gown purchased only the month before in Charleston.

He remained silent, though, and she was both relieved and disappointed.

"Come with me," he said at last.

Jethro led her away from the house to an untended garden where red roses bloomed among weeds. Taking a jack-knife from his pocket, he began cutting long-stemmed roses, walking from bush to bush to select only those on the verge of blooming.

When he had a bouquet of six roses he returned to Ida with the flowers cradled on his left arm. He offered her his other arm and she was surprised again, for she had expected him to give her the flowers. She took his arm and let him escort her away from the main house.

After skirting the slave quarters, they climbed a low hill where the grass was high and golden on both sides of the path. In the fields below them Negroes worked the cotton rows, plucking the white blooms with the quickness of long practice and putting them into the large bags slung over their shoulders.

The day was warm and by the time they reached the top of the hill Ida's face glistened with perspiration. Jethro left the path, stopping in front of a lovingly tended burial plot. He knelt, removed faded roses from the grave and laid them to one side, then placed the six fresh blooms at the base of the headstone.

MARY GRAFTON HUNTER, the marker read. REST IN PEACE.

Ida glanced from the headstones to Jethro's impassive face. "I can still remember the day Alexander came and told me Mary had drowned in the river," she said. "Such a tragic accident."

Jethro, still kneeling, looked up at her. "It wasn't an accident, Ida," he said in a monotone. "She waded into the water until she was swept away."

"Mary a suicide?" Ida shook her head. "I don't believe it. How can you be sure? You weren't even at Hunter Hill and there was no note."

"There *was* a note, Ida. I found it, read it, and burned it. So no one would ever know. You're the first person I've told. Fremont doesn't know. Nor does Jared."

"But why? Why would Mary do such a thing?"

"I wish to God I knew. Her note asked my forgiveness and God's. All these years I've asked myself the same questions. Was it my fault? What could I have done differently? I don't know the answers, Ida, I just don't know."

"She was such a quiet woman," Ida said. "At times she seemed to live in a world of her own." And haven't I, these last years, done the same? Ida asked herself.

"There was bad blood in the Grafton family," Jethro said slowly. "Mary had a sister, Louisa, who lived with relatives in Ohio. I only found out about Louisa after Mary and I were married. She was . . . well, what the Graftons called 'mental.' Of course Mary had another sister and a brother who were perfectly all right." He shook his head. "I don't understand it, Ida, I just don't understand it."

She put her hand on his sleeve. "God moves in mysterious ways," she said.

Jethro sighed and stood up. As he walked with her to the house, he said, "I wanted you to know about Mary," and then he talked of the war, of the victory at Manassas and the gradual turn of fortune against the South as the border states were lost to the Union. He didn't mention his wife again.

Much later, back at Santee, Ida stood on the piazza, watching Jethro's carriage drive off. Before it reached the oaks, he turned and raised his hand in salute and she waved her handkerchief until he was out of sight.

He means to ask me to marry him, she told herself. Not now while I'm in mourning; to court me so soon after Alexander's death would be unseemly even in wartime. But he does mean to ask. How will I answer him? she wondered. I like Jethro; I don't love him. Yet I'm an old woman, over forty, and perhaps liking is enough at my age.

She went into the house and found her father sitting in his favorite chair in the parlor. When he said nothing as she came into the room, she felt a flutter of apprehension.

"It's Ida," she told him.

"Ida?" He stared straight ahead, not looking at her.

She ran to kneel in front of him, taking his hands in hers. She didn't see his cane. "What is it, father?" she asked.

"Ida?" he said again.

"It's Ida. Your daughter, Ida. Father, what is it? Tell me what happened."

"Ida?" he said. All at once he looked at her and began to struggle to get to his feet.

"No," she told him, "you don't have to stand up, father. It's all right."

"I was walking in the garden beside the house," he said, closing his eyes. "I meant to go up the hill to the burial ground. I must have lost my way. I was walking and then I was on the ground. I was lying on the ground and I don't remember how I got there. Why was I on the ground, Ida?"

"Where was Caesar? He should have been with you."

"Caesar? I don't know. Caesar was here earlier, when you left, and then he wasn't here. I meant to go up the hill to the burial ground. I must have lost my way. All at once I was on the ground."

"It's all right, father," she said, bringing his fingers to her lips and kissing them. "You weren't hurt, were you?"

"I don't think so. All at once I was on the ground."

"I'll find Caesar," she said. "I'll make sure he stays with you."

The old man nodded. "I seem to have misplaced my cane," he said.

She found the cane on the lawn beside the house. She stood holding it in front of her as she looked from the main house to the slave quarters to the fields. As the Negroes went about their duties they glanced at her, fell silent, then went on, talking amongst themselves. She had no one to turn to. She was alone in the midst of Negroes, living in a village of slaves.

She turned and slowly, with an outward show of unconcern, walked back to the house.

"Our sergeant is John Bell," Peter DeWitt wrote Maggie from his recruit camp near New Haven. "He's a man of about forty, a veteran of the Mexican War and of Bull Run. He says he'll teach us to be soldiers or know the reason why. His middle name, I begin to think, must be Drill, for the first thing in the morning it's drill, then drill, then drill again. Then drill, drill and a little more drill. Then drill, and lastly drill. Between drills, we drill and sometimes stop to eat a little and have a rollcall before we drill some more."

His life, Peter found, was governed by the call of bugles and the roll of drums. The day started with reveille at five, followed by rollcall and then what the men called "peas on a trencher"—breakfast. Those on guard duty reported at eight and, after four hours of drill, dinner "roast beef"—was ladled into the mess gear carried by the long lines of men.

Following afternoon drill, the companies were dismissed to prepare for the retreat parade and inspection. "Spit and polish," Peter discovered, was meant literally as the recruits blacked their leather and polished their brass. The men formed by company for the parade, each captain called "Parade Rest," and the regimental band marched back and forth in front of the troops, playing a slow march on the way down and a quick step as they returned.

The sergeants reported to the adjutant: "All men present or accounted for, sir," and the adjutant relayed the message to the colonel. After the men were put through the manual of arms, "Parade Rest" was ordered once more. The officers sheathed their swords and reported to the colonel for orders. When they returned to their commands, the sergeants marched each company separately to its quarters.

"All this time," Peter wrote, "we're carrying full gear, some forty pounds of knapsack, blanket, canteen, musket, haversack, and what have you. The routine is monotonous but I can say with all sincerity that when the band plays and the flag of the United States is lowered from the regimental flagstaff, I feel a pride in our country and a swelling of my heart because I know I'm a part of a great crusade to keep our freedoms."

A few weeks later, Peter wrote, "I have been promoted to corporal or will be as soon as the paperwork is completed. No longer will my pay be thirteen dollars a month. I believe a corporal receives a dollar more. I suspect the promotion came about because I'm older than most of the other men here. I call them men when, in all truth, they're boys.

"Most are fresh off the farm. When we had our first issue of clothing many of them didn't know what to make of the drawers we were given, never having worn them before. Some of the old soldiers told them they were an extra uniform to wear on parade and I think the farm boys half believed them.

"Tell Buck and Alex that they are ever in my thoughts. I'm gratified to hear that you and they are well. I hope and pray for a speedy conclusion to this conflict so I may be with you once more and we can begin our life anew. Being far removed from you in miles has, I believe, brought me closer to you in thought and understanding. I often find myself opening the locket you gave me at the depot and looking at your picture, recalling all the times when we were close, one to the other. I mean to see that those times come again when this war is over and you are united once more with your proud and affectionate husband, Peter DeWitt."

"I had a disquieting experience yesterday," Peter wrote in August. "Sergeant Bell led us into the countryside near the camp and, after arming us with blank cartridges, divided our company into two groups, one to represent the enemy, the other, including myself, to be the Union soldiers. We waited while the 'Rebels' marched off to take up their positions and we then followed to attack them. We had crossed a field and entered a woods when I heard the sound of shots and looked up to see the 'Rebels' firing down on us from roosts in the trees. If this skirmish had been real many of us would have been casualties. I've cautioned myself to take this lesson to heart and exercise greater care in the future."

The weeks passed. "Rumors are everywhere," Peter wrote. "Some say we're to board the cars to go south to Washington to join the Army of the Potomac. Others claim our destination is the West, the Mississippi Valley, where, I have heard, Sam Grant is a general. As you may know, Sam has long been a close friend of my cousins in Ohio. Because of his drinking, Grant isn't steady and can't always be relied on. Alcohol is a curse."

The destination of Peter DeWitt's company had already been decided. A board of naval officers had convened in June of 1861 to plan how the navy could help crush the Southern rebellion. A blockade was already in force but, along the Atlantic coast from Virginia to Florida, numerous islands and harbors offered refuge for blockade-running Confederate ships. The North, the officers agreed, should seize bases along this coastline.

Late in August, Federals occupied the Southern forts at Cape Hatteras off the North Carolina coast. Another base was needed farther south, for Union vessels patrolling off Charleston and Savannah were forced to return to Hampton Roads, Virginia, or even to New York for coal. So the navy decided to attack Port Royal Sound in South Carolina, a waterway guarded by Fort Beauregard and Fort Walker.

Peter DeWitt and twelve thousand other men boarded transports at Annapolis and steamed to Hampton Roads, where they lay at anchor watching the gathering of the war flotilla. It was the largest fleet ever assembled under the American flag, with transports ranging from ocean liners to harbor ferries, warships including powerful steam frigates and lighter steam sloops, merchantmen converted into warships, "90-day gunboats" built in three months' time, and twenty-five schooners laden with coal.

Captain DuPont, the naval commander, gave sealed orders to the ship masters and on October 29 the fleet weighed anchor and put out to sea. The ships formed a double line off Cape Henry and sailed down the coast into a rising sea and a stiff easterly wind.

Men on the transport *Watervliet* retched and heaved, their faces ashen. Peter, who wasn't afflicted, found himself eating almost alone at the stand-up table in the mess. Some of the soldiers who tried to force food down, gagged and clambered topside to vomit into the sea. Others threw up on the deck of the mess. Grimacing at the stench, Peter finished his meal before going on deck, where he stood feeling the sting of the spray from the waves breaking over the bow.

When the high winds became a gale, ropes were strung on the decks so the men could make their way forward to the mess. The next day, with the seas still rising, the soldiers were restricted to their pesthole-like belowdeck quarters.

Peter listened to the creaking and groaning of the ship and felt the *Watervliet* lurch and shudder as it slammed into the waves. He feared the timbers would part, and expected at any moment to see water cascading into the hold where he lay in his canvas hammock.

"We're sailing for Port Royal," the man in the hammock below him said. "The captain opened his orders today."

"Where the devil is Port Royal?" Peter asked. Since "devil" was the extent of his swearing, he found the language of most of the other men in his company abominable.

"Below Fort Sumter, they say."

Again the ship rolled and Peter gripped the sides of his hammock to keep from being hurled to the floor.

At last the winds subsided and the fleet reassembled off the bar at the entrance to Port Royal Sound. Two ships had been lost in the storm, with seven men killed. One of the men, caught between two ships, had been cut in half.

Peter and the other men went on deck to watch as the warships crossed the bar. Small boats were then sent ahead to buoy the channel, for the Rebels had removed all land and sea markings. On the morning of November 7, DuPont was ready and the warships steamed toward the Sound, with Fort Beauregard on their right and Fort Walker on Hilton Head Island to their left.

The ships sailed down the middle of the two-mile-wide channel, firing at both forts. Just inside the harbor entrance, DuPont swung his ships about and came back close inshore to Fort Walker, hurling heavy-duty shells at the fort six hundred yards away.

Inside the fort, Nelson Vaughan heard the shelling start.

"My God," the man next to him muttered.

The blasts of the exploding Federal shells shook the fort, one following another as fast as a galloping horse's hooves beat the ground. Great spouts of sand shot skyward as the shells exploded in the revetments, guns were blown asunder, and the fort's flagstaff splintered and crashed to the ground. Again and again the ships' guns roared and the fort, overmatched, weakly returned the fire.

"Aim for the ships' bridges," someone near Nelson shouted to the fort's gunnery crews. "Between the mainmast and the smokestack. Kill their officers."

Again the ships came around, their gunners working with professional precision, overshooting at first, with many shells falling far behind the fort, but soon correcting their aim and zeroing in on the fort itself.

"Damn," a gunner said to Nelson, "we get the range and then the ship's gone before we can fire."

A small Confederate flotilla of four converted river boats sailed from the inner harbor. The Union warships returned their fire and the Confederates retreated in haste.

"Vaughan," a lieutenant called. "Dr. Buist needs more litter bearers. You and Bigge lend a hand."

The two men climbed to the parapet, where Nelson saw a boy, a powder monkey, bringing explosives to a gun crew. A shell tore two of the men at the gun to bits and the boy went on to the next gun in line, stepping over the bleeding shards of bodies as though they were no more than fragments of a gun carriage.

Another shell exploded behind Nelson and he turned to see a gunner hopping forward, clothes and face blackened by the explosion, his left leg hanging by muscle and skin. Holding to a stone revetment, the man pulled out his knife and tried to cut his leg free, sawing at the skin without result. Nelson ran to him and he and Bigge forced him onto a litter and carried him below to the surgeon's hospital.

Nelson felt numb as he laid the man on a cot in one of the galleries under the parapet. Dr. Buist, a bandage in his hand, looked up and nodded at Nelson.

"Is there anything I can do?" Nelson asked.

The doctor shook his head. "You'd be more trouble than help here," he said, motioning Nelson away.

Again the bombardment increased. The ships must be coming around to make another run at the fort, Nelson thought as he climbed up and down the stone

stairs, bringing wounded men to the hospital. Fort
Walker's guns still responded, though their firing was
more sporadic now. Nelson felt helpless. He wanted
to man one of the big guns, but as a foot soldier
assigned to defend the fort from land attack, his
knowledge of gunnery, like his knowledge of medicine,
was minimal.

He walked onto the parade ground, the stench of
powder everywhere, men lying dead on the hard-
packed earth, the wounded moaning and screaming.
He stumbled and looked back to see a man's severed
leg laying on the ground behind him.

A bugler ran to the shattered flagstaff and sounded
a call Nelson didn't recognize.

"Private," a lieutenant shouted to him, "we're aban-
doning the fort. Assemble to the rear."

"But the wounded," Nelson protested.

"The Yankees can care for them better then we can.
Leave them."

Nelson retrieved his rifle and followed the officer.
The soldiers fell in and left the fort at double-quick
time, being careful to keep its ramparts between them
and the ships in the harbor. They climbed a small
rise and from the top Nelson looked back and drew
in his breath in awe.

Out to sea the Yankee transports and troop ships
lay to, the ships nearer the shore bare-rigged, the outer
ships showing canvas, white and black smoke rising
almost straight up from their stacks into the blue sky.
In the harbor entrance, beyond the pall of smoke
over the fort, some twelve warships circled, firing
broadsides as they sailed past Fort Walker, smoke
drifting up from their stacks and guns. As Nelson
watched, a shell landed near one of the ships—from
Fort Beauregard across the channel, he supposed—
and a spout of water shot into the air. He was struck

by the dread beauty of the scene, the great ships, the thundering of the guns and, behind them, the calm sea stretching to the far horizon.

"Vaughan," Sergeant Jacobs said, "you'll be part of our rear guard." Jacobs named other men, placing them athwart the trampled route of their retreat spaced some hundred yards apart. "You aren't expected to stop the bastards," the sergeant said. "Just give them pause, something to think about. Don't put yourselves at risk. Fire a few rounds then retreat to the cove beyond the camp."

Nelson nodded and trotted to the far right of the line of the rear guard, hunching down behind debris at the top of the beach. After a moment he knelt, scooped a hole in the sand and fitted his body into it. After laying his rifle on the sand at his side, he nodded, satisfied . . .

Peter DeWitt, one of the first Federal troops to come ashore, found that the defenders had deserted Fort Jackson. The smell of powder burned Peter's nostrils as he climbed the stone steps to the parapet, steps stained with the blood of dead and dying Confederates. The other men of the Seventh Connecticut, he noticed, were as shocked by what they saw as he was. They tended to walk carefully, almost tiptoeing, and they lowered their voices when they spoke.

Death was everywhere, the galleries bloodied, the guns shattered, arms, legs and torsos scattered haphazardly about. On the breech of a gun he saw the face of a man; the back of his head had been sheared away as he bent to peer into the sights.

Peter staggered down the steps and into the open, where he bent over, retching.

"Corporal! On the double!"

He looked up to see Sergeant Bell motioning to him. Peter hurried over to the sergeant.

"Looks like the Rebs have cleared out but I'm sending skirmishers to make sure. You go along the beach." He motioned to the others, ordering them onto the island behind the fort in a long, widely spaced line. The men advanced cautiously, slowed by the sand. The island was barren here; the trees, oaks trailing Spanish moss, began farther on. There was no sign of Rebels. . .

Nelson tensed. Far up the beach he saw a single Federal soldier, tall and clean-shaven. He wore a blue cap with a black visor, a dark blue jacket and light blue trousers, and he held a rifle at port arms and carried a knapsack on his back.

Nelson hunkered down deeper in the hole he had scooped in the sand. Go back, he said softly to the other man, go back before it's too late, before I have to kill you. He had seen enough of death. He didn't want to kill. Yet he must if the Yankee came on, and Nelson knew he would, knew it with a dread certainty.

The Federal soldier was two hundred yards away. Nelson waited. He heard the crack of a shot from inland and saw the solider on the beach look that way, pause, and come on. The day was warm, not hot but balmy, the kind of day, Nelson thought, to peel off your clothes and plunge into the Atlantic.

Small flies and gnats swarmed in front of him. The surf, low and gentle, broke in a line of white foam, the water running with a swoosh up onto the sand. The tide was out, leaving the beach broad and white.

The Yankee was a hundred yards away. Nelson raised his rifle and sighted on the man's chest. The cap was set, the cartridge had been rammed home. His finger tightened on the trigger. He relaxed, easing his finger away, waiting without knowing why he waited. The Yankee came slowly toward him.

Nelson could still smell the stench of burnt powder, could still hear the moans of the wounded who had been left behind at the fort. The sun warmed his hands and his back, a comforting, drowsy warmth. And still the Yankee came on.

Again Nelson raised his rifle and sighted, saw the man's two stripes. A corporal, then. Again his finger tightened on the trigger. For a brief instant he wondered where this Yankee hailed from, what his work had been, whether he had a family waiting for his return home.

He pulled the trigger. The rifle cracked, gunsmoke drifted upward. The Yankee staggered back, recovered for a moment, then pitched headfirst onto the sand. Nelson looked around him. They were alone, he and this man. He half rose from his shelter in the sand, reloaded, all the while watching the wounded man.

He saw the Yankee move, the other man's hand going to his belt. Nelson saw the glint of sunlight on metal and he fired again. The man jerked to one side and lay still. Nelson ran forward and knelt beside him. He was dead. Gold glittered between his fingers. Nelson lifted the man's hand and saw a locket. He picked it up, opened it, and stared down at a daguerreotype of the most beautiful woman he had ever seen.

10

MARGARET DEWITT walked slowly home along Reef Road. There had been no letter at the post office from Peter, nor had there been one for the last three days. Peter had written every day since leaving Wethersfield—though the lack of a letter wasn't surprising, for he had warned her he might be going into battle. He hadn't told her where.

On the bulletin board at the town hall she had read the notices of the Federal victory at Port Royal Sound in South Carolina. Surely Peter wasn't at Port Royal; his last letter had been posted from Maryland and South Carolina was far away from Maryland. Even with her sketchy knowledge of geography, she was sure of that.

As she turned onto Prospect Street she saw a strange black buggy in front of her house. Maggie's heart beat faster. Enough of your foolish notions, she told herself. Must your thoughts always be so melodramatic,

like your tales? Life isn't like a story in a magazine.
Peter's all right. He has to be.

She quickened her pace, ignoring the icy wind as
she walked swiftly along the sweep of the DeWitt
driveway under the arching elms, up the porch steps
and into the hall. She stopped just inside the door,
thankful for the heat of the house after the cold of
the November day. A clatter of pots came from the
kitchen; otherwise the house was still.

Removing her hat and gloves, she slipped off her
coat and hung it on the rack. She stepped through the
open door into the front parlor and stopped, her
hand flying to her mouth, her heart in her throat.
Across the room stood a Union officer, his back to her
as he gazed from the side window at the row of pines
bordering the yard.

Sensing her presence, he turned, solemn-faced. He
was an older man with a full graying beard and
receding gray hair.

"Mrs. DeWitt?" he asked. "Mrs. Peter DeWitt?"
His voice, deep and resonant, seemed to come from a
great distance.

She nodded, unable to speak. She knew why he was
here, what he had come to tell her. Do it as quickly
as you can. Tell me and leave, let me be alone with
the horror you've brought, the knowledge that Peter
is dead.

"Would you like to sit down, Mrs. DeWitt?" the
officer asked.

Numbly, she shook her head.

"I'm Captain Kenney of the United States Army."
He cleared his throat.

Tell me she willed him. The captain was nervous.
She should make his task as easy as she could. She
drew in her breath and all at once she was calm. When

she heard her voice it was as though a stranger were speaking.

"Yes, Captain Kenney," she said. "I'm Mrs. DeWitt. How may I help you?"

"I fear I bring bad news," he said. "Concerning your husband."

He was killed in the battle for Port Royal, she thought.

"Corporal Peter DeWitt died bravely while fighting for his country in the battle at Port Royal."

She stared at him. Before he spoke she had held to a small shred of hope. Now there was no hope, nothing. Peter was dead. The thought lay in her mind, real yet unexamined. The captain, she knew, was watching her. What did he expect her to do? Did he expect tears? Should she thank him, thank him for bringing her the news that her husband had been killed?

"If there's anything I can do," Captain Kenney said, "anything at all . . ."

"No, there's nothing you can do, Captain."

"Your husband's commanding officer will write you." He took a hesitant step toward her and she noticed he limped. "May I call someone? The lady who let me in?"

"No, thank you, Captain. I'm perfectly all right." While she talked she seemed to be standing outside herself, watching and weighing her actions, her words, her lack of tears, her calmness.

The captain clasped and unclasped his hands.

"This must be very trying for you," she heard herself say.

"If there's nothing I can do . . ."

"There's nothing."

She went into the front hall and he followed her. When he started to speak she shook her head and he nodded, opening the front door himself and going out. She closed the door after him, standing with her back to it, hearing his footsteps cross the porch and go down the steps. After a few minutes she heard hoofbeats and the clatter of the buggy on the frozen drive.

I must break the news to the boys, she told herself. Finding Mrs. Harvey in the dining room, she said, "Tell Alex to go to Curtis's room." Mrs. Harvey stared at her, a question in her eyes, but then the older woman nodded and went past Margaret to the stairs.

Curtis will be outside, Margaret thought. She looked first in the woodshed but he wasn't there. Next in the summerhouse; not there. She finally found him behind the stable, throwing his knife at the trunk of a tree.

"Curtis," she told him, "come with me, please."

She turned away without waiting for his answer, heard him ask, "Why?" and then heard his running feet behind her.

She had the boys sit side by side on the chest in Curtis's room. Alex was four years old, blond, small for his age, restless. Curtis, at eleven, was solemn, also blond and stocky, a quiet boy whose features reminded her of Peter and of the portraits she'd seen of earlier generations of DeWitts.

"Boys," she heard herself say, "you know your father enlisted in the army to fight for his country. To defend the Union against the Rebels." Her words sounded empty. "You know he was sent to the South. I read you his letters from Maryland."

"Is dad all right?" Curtis asked.

"Your father was in a great battle and he was hurt very badly," she told them.

Curtis stared at her. "You mean he's dead?" he asked.

"Yes," she said. "He fought bravely and he was killed."

"I'll never see daddy again?" Alex asked, staring up at her.

Margaret shook her head. Suddenly the realization that *she* would never see Peter again struck Margaret like a blow. She clenched her hands, her nails biting into her palms. She closed her eyes. Oh, Peter, she thought, why did this have to happen to you? To us?

Hearing a sound, she opened her eyes and saw that Alex was crying. Curtis was staring at her, his face pale, saying nothing. She dropped to her knees in front of them, opening her arms, and they threw themselves at her, burying their heads against her. She sobbed once, crying out as tears streaked her face, and then her body was wracked with sobs as she held her children to her.

"We'll be all right," she murmured. "We three will show them we can look after ourselves."

"Of course we can," Curtis said. "We're DeWitts."

"Thank you for coming yesterday to break the news," Frances DeWitt said. She and Margaret were sitting in the kitchen of the older Mrs. DeWitt's home.

"I hurried over as soon as I'd told the boys," Margaret said.

Frances DeWitt walked to the stove and returned with a coffee-pot. "You have to keep busy," she said as she filled their cups. "If there's one lesson I've learned in seventy-one years it's to keep busy. The devil finds work for idle hands, my mother always told me, and she was right."

"I still can't believe that Peter's dead," Margaret said. "I was numb when the captain told me."

"How are the boys taking the news?"

"As well as can be expected. Alex is too young to fully realize what's happened. Curtis hasn't said much. When I left he was in his room reading a book about the Revolution."

Her mother-in-law nodded. "We DeWitts have always been an army family," she said. "Hold your head high, Margaret. No matter what grief you feel, you mustn't let it show. The DeWitts don't let others see our feelings; death is a private matter, not a matter for public display."

"I don't know whether I can do that, Mother DeWitt."

"You can and you must." She put her coffee cup on the table. "It's what Peter would have expected of you."

"How can you be so sure what Peter would have expected?"

"Oh, my dear." The older woman's voice faltered, almost broke. "Wouldn't I know? I'm his mother, after all. I've known him ever so much longer than you have. I loved Peter."

"And I didn't? Is that what you're telling me?"

"Not at all, my dear." She took Margaret's hand in both of hers. "I mean no more than I say. I loved Peter, as I'm sure you did in your own way. A mother's love differs from a wife's."

"I'm sorry for what I said, Mother DeWitt."

"I know you don't particularly like me," Frances DeWitt said. "You've always thought I interfered."

"I respect you. I always have."

"Then listen to what I have to say." Frances DeWitt leaned forward. "Peter's death was not your doing. I want you to remember that. Peter didn't enlist in the army because of you. He enlisted because he's a De- Witt and a DeWitt has an obligation to serve under his country's flag in time of war. Do you understand me, Margaret?"

"I can't help feeling it was my fault. You know we quarreled just before he enlisted."

"If I had a nickel for every time Peter's father and I quarreled, I'd be a wealthy woman today. Don't always think of yourself first, Margaret. You're a selfish person and have been ever since you were a girl. You're being selfish now in blaming yourself for what wasn't your doing."

Margaret drew in her breath, prepared to deny the accusation, but she held her tongue. "Perhaps you're right, Mother DeWitt," she said quietly. "I hadn't thought of it that way."

"Of course you hadn't." Frances DeWitt pushed her cup away and stood up. "Now," she said, "I intend to do my baking. I'll bring you your two loaves tomorrow morning as usual. Your mother arrives Friday from Claremont, doesn't she?"

Margaret nodded.

"I advise you to go home and keep busy."

"Yes, Mother DeWitt."

As Margaret left the house she thought, no, I can never like that woman. She's so cold, so controlled. I couldn't bear it if one of my boys died. I wouldn't be able to go on.

She remembered that thought the following morning when Miss Telford discovered that Curtis was missing.

"I've looked high and low all through the house," the live-in, who took care of the boys, told Margaret. "I can't find him anywhere."

"He didn't eat breakfast, far's I can tell," Mrs. Harvey said. "I thought he was with you, mum."

"We'll look in the yard," Margaret said, fighting down her rising panic.

Starting at the road in front, the three women searched the grounds, looking in the sheds, the summerhouse, the stable, and the grove of trees where Margaret had found Curtis on the day the news of his father's death had come. There was no sign of him.

"You don't think he's down in the cellar?" Miss Telford asked.

"We'll look."

Margaret raised the trapdoor and, a candle in her hand, descended into the half-cellar. She found it empty.

"I'll just have another look through the house," Margaret said. She went from room to room, from first floor to attic. Curtis wasn't in the house.

"Now don't that beat all?" Mrs. Harvey said. "Where do you suppose the boy's got to?"

"Do you think he went to school," Margaret wondered, "even after I told him not to?"

"He may have," Miss Telford said.

"I'll ask after him there." Margaret glanced at Miss Telford. "Why don't you walk through the village? Mrs. Harvey can stay here with Alex so there'll be someone at home when he comes back. I'm sure he's all right."

"He's bound to turn up for dinner," Mrs. Harvey said.

Curtis DeWitt was not at the Fairfield Grammar School.

By the time Margaret returned home it was noon and dinner was ready but there was still no sign of Curtis.

"He may have gone to his grandmother's," Margaret said, trying to keep her voice calm.

Frances DeWitt shook her head when Margaret

asked her. "I haven't seen the boy since I was at your house last night," she said.

"I'm going to the town constable," Margaret said. "He may have heard something. He'll know how to go about organizing a search for Curtis."

"Do you really think that's necessary? After all, boys will be boys. He probably was playing with a friend and forgot the time."

"All his friends are in school. I'm afraid he may be hurt, might have broken his leg. He could be lying somewhere in the cold, not able to get home."

"I believe that going to the constable is quite inappropriate, Margaret. The man's very young—and an outsider, besides. He's from the west, Tennessee or Missouri or Kentucky, one of those places."

"He comes from Chicago."

"As I said, an outlander. I'll help you look for the boy, Margaret. We don't want outsiders involved."

"I'm going to the constable, Mother DeWitt," Margaret told her.

Dan Cunningham *was* young, she discovered when she arrived at his office. He didn't look more than twenty, though she knew he must be older.

"My heartfelt condolences, Mrs. DeWitt," the young redhead told her. "I read of the death of your husband in the paper."

"Thank you, Mr. Cunningham." She told him that Curtis had been missing since at least daybreak and that she and others had searched in all his usual haunts without success.

Cunningham nodded. "Tell me all you possibly can about him," he said. "What kind of boy is he, what does he like to do, who are his friends?"

"Is all that really necessary, Mr. Cunningham? Wouldn't it be simpler to just start looking for him?"

"I want to try to put myself in his place," Cunningham said. "That's what Mr. Pinkerton always told us to do. Forewarned is forearmed, he said."

"And who is Mr. Pinkerton?"

"He's what's known as a private investigator. When I worked for him in Chicago he assigned me the task of finding the persons responsible for desecrating the graves in one of the cemeteries. It turned out to be medical students collecting cadavers to practice on. The way I—" He stopped, glancing quickly at Margaret, his color rising. "Mr. Pinkerton's in Washington now," he said hastily. "He's the head of the secret service in charge of sending spies into the South to gather information for General McClellan and President Lincoln. Now if you'll just tell me all you can about your son, Mrs. DeWitt, I'll do everything in my power to help you."

Margaret described Curtis, told of his quiet nature, his intense interest in his father's letters from the recruit camp, his unexceptional school grades except in history, and named his friends. When she finished, Dan Cunningham leaned back in his chair and closed his eyes while Margaret folded her hands in her lap, determined to wait until he took action. When she found she was wringing her hands she clasped them tightly together.

Dan Cunningham unfolded himself from his chair and stood up. "I'll start my investigation at the depot," he said.

"I'll come with you," Margaret told him.

"Why don't you wait at home, Mrs. DeWitt? I'll let you know the minute I have word of the boy.'

"No, I'm coming with you," Margaret insisted.

Dan Cunningham shrugged and strode from the town hall with Margaret at his heels. He helped her into the carriage in front and drove off with a flip of the reins and a cluck to the horse.

At the depot, Cunningham held the waiting room door open for Margaret. They found Mr. Klevesahl, the stationmaster, sitting on a high stool behind the grill of the ticket window.

"The DeWitt boy?" he asked. "Funny you should ask, constable. I did see him around here early on, just before the morning train pulled in. She was fifteen minutes late. The boy didn't buy a ticket and I didn't see him board the cars, but he was here, sure enough."

Cunningham thanked him and crossed the room to the telegrapher's cage, where he took a form from the counter and printed a short message. Showing it to Margaret, he said, "I'll send it to these places," and wrote several names on the pad.

"Do you really think that's what he did?" she asked.

"I'm not certain, of course," he told her. "It's what I might have done in his place. In fact, what I might do soon. If he did, your son has lots of gumption, Mrs. DeWitt."

"I never thought he didn't," she said. Her voice lost its edge as she added, "I only hope to God you're right."

Margaret met the four o'clock train from Boston. The engine rumbled past the platform, smoke and steam billowing about her as the cars creaked and jounced to a stop. Curtis DeWitt, the first passenger to get off, stood on the platform looking uneasily around him.

"Curtis," Margaret called, running beside the cars toward him.

He saw his mother and ran to her, opening his arms and throwing himself onto her. She lifted him from the ground, hugging him as she laughed and cried.

"Oh, Curtis," she said.

"You're not angry?"

"I have every right to be," she said. "You didn't leave a note, you didn't tell anybody. I was so worried about what might have happened to you. You should have let me know what you were going to do."

"I thought if I did you'd come after me and bring me home."

"You should have anyway. But no, I'm not angry with you, I'm just thankful you're back. Promise me one thing, Curtis. Promise me you'll never, never run away again."

"I promise." He squirmed in her arms and she let him slide to the ground. "They said I'd have to wait four years. Three-and-a-half, actually. Until I'm fifteen."

"I'm proud of you, Curtis," Margaret said. "Your grandmother says you're a DeWitt through and through. We should have guessed where you were, she says."

"They told me I can be a drummer boy when I'm fifteen. I don't want to be a drummer boy. I want to fight the Rebs like my father did. I want to be a soldier."

Margaret put her hand on his shoulder and pressed him against her. I hope to God, she thought, that this terrible war will be over by the time you're old enough to fight.

"If I can't be a soldier," Curtis said, "who will be? None of the DeWitts are old enough to fight."

"You don't always have to be a soldier to help your country, Curtis," Margaret told him.

"Mother," he said, "I don't want to be called Curtis anymore. My name's Buck."

When they reached home, Margaret climbed the stairs to her writing room and gathered all of her manuscripts together and packed them in boxes. She tied the boxes with string, labeling each with the names of the tales inside and the dates she had written them. Opening the closet door, she lifted the boxes one by one to the shelf.

When she finished she nodded to herself and, leaving the room, searched in her jewelry drawer until she found the key to the writing room. She locked the room and returned the key to the jewelry box on her dresser.

There'll be time enough for writing stories when the war's over, she told herself. Mr. Niles will have to wait for the novel of my childhood, if I ever write it at all. She had more important matters to attend to. Tomorrow her mother would arrive and later in the day she'd talk to Mr. Von Wantoch at his law office and to Mr. Jamison at the bank. And to the Reverend Duryea about the services for Peter when his body was returned. After that she'd be ready to do what she must do.

"Sir," Bruce said, "the young lady insists on seeing you."

"I'm too damn busy." Alan Pinkerton tapped his pencil on the pile of papers on his desk. "These are the reports of our agents in Richmond, Wilmington and Charleston. I have to correlate them and have my analysis on General McClellan's desk by eight in the morning. This Confederate blockade-running must be stopped."

"Mrs. DeWitt's waited three hours today," Bruce said. "And she waited all day yesterday and most of the day before." The young man smiled sheepishly. "I think you'll find her to be most attractive," he added.

"Oh, God," Alan Pinkerton moaned. "In your eyes all young women are attractive."

"You *do* have your damsel drawer." Bruce said. "I'm sure you'll be able to discourage her with that in short order if it becomes necessary."

Alan Pinkerton opened the upper left hand drawer of his desk a few inches. He sighed. "All right," he said, "show the young lady in."

Shifting his papers to one side, Pinkerton stood up as Bruce escorted a tall red-haired young woman into the office. "Mrs. Margaret DeWitt," Bruce said, "this is Mr Pinkerton."

Pinkerton bowed. For once Bruce had been correct; she *was* extremely attractive, he thought. "Please sit down, Mrs.—" He groped for the name.

"DeWitt. Margaret DeWitt of Fairfield, Connecticut."

"And what may I do for you, madam?" Pinkerton, a short, bearded man with a marked English accent, indicated the papers on his desk. "As you can see, I'm frightfully busy."

"I understand," Margaret said, "and I appreciate your taking time to see me. I came to Washington to offer my services as a government agent. I know the South and the Southerners. You see, I was born in Virginia, so I think I can be of use to you."

Oh, God, Pinkerton thought. She wants to be a female spy.

"I have one female operative at this time," Pinkerton said stiffly. "She has many years of experience in the work I've assigned her. What qualifications do you bring other than having lived in the South?"

"I'm committed heart and soul to the Union cause." Margaret reached into her bag and brought out three envelopes. "This is a letter from Dan Cunningham, our constable in Fairfield who worked for you in Chicago. This one is from my husband's commanding officer. Mr. DeWitt was killed in the assault on Fort Jackson in South Carolina in November. And this . . ." Margaret paused. "This is a letter of recommendation from General Ulysses S. Grant. He's a friend of my husband's family."

"Yes, yes." Pinkerton stacked the three envelopes at the side of his desk. "I'll read your letters as soon as possible and give your request every consideration. Thank you for stopping to see me, Mrs. DeWitt."

"You mean," Margaret asked, "that that's all you want to know? When can I expect to hear from you?"

"Perhaps in one month or perhaps in two, although it may take longer. If the right opportunity comes along, I'll surely let you know."

"You mean you're not interested in my offer," Margaret said. "You're telling me I'm wasting my time and yours."

"It's been my experience, Mrs. DeWitt," Pinkerton said, "that young ladies of your genteel upbringing often want to offer their services to their government without realizing the perils the work entails. They have romantic notions of adventure, of encountering gallant officers, of secret messages carried on horseback rides in the moonlight. The work is nothing like that."

"I assure you I have no such notions, Mr. Pinkerton."

"Young ladies such as yourself are prone to faint at the sight of blood, to—"

"Are the nurses in the Washington hospitals examples of women who are afraid of blood?"

"To faint at the sight of spiders and reptiles," Pinkerton went on.

"I admit I have no great love for spiders or snakes," Margaret said. "On the other hand, I didn't think I was applying for a position as curator of a reptile house."

"I remember once," Pinkerton said, getting to his

feet, "when I was on a case, I was searching a gentleman's office for some papers and opened a desk drawer much like this one." He pulled open the upper left-hand drawer. "And there I found *a snake.*"

He threw the four-foot blacksnake across the desk at Margaret. She screamed, putting up her hands to ward off the reptile. The snake dropped to the floor at her feet. Margaret swayed and crumpled to the floor.

Alan Pinkerton walked around his desk and retrieved the papier-mache snake and put it on top of his desk. He knelt beside Margaret.

"Smelling salts," she whispered.

"Oh, God," Pinkerton said in exasperation. "Bruce! Bruce!" he shouted, getting to his feet and going to the door. Bruce met him in the hallway. "The smelling salts," Pinkerton said.

"I have them here, sir."

"Administer them to the young lady, if you please."

The two men re-entered the room and Bruce knelt beside Margaret, passing an open bottle back and forth under her nose. She shook her head and opened her eyes.

With Bruce's help she rose slowly to her feet. She stared at Alan Pinkerton but the investigator refused to meet her gaze. Clutching her bag in both hands in front of her, she swept from the room.

Bruce lifted the snake from the desk. "I see you had to rely on Jefferson Davis," he said.

"Unfortunately, Mrs. DeWitt was more persistent than most." He looked after her. "In fact, I was rather disappointed when she fainted. I was beginning to admire her determination." He sighed. "Ah well, to work."

Bruce left the room and Alan Pinkerton sat behind

his desk, returning Jefferson Davis to his drawer. Picking up a pencil, he stared down at his desk-top. He lifted a sheet of paper, then another and another, searching frantically. He stood up and looked on the floor, got down on his hands and knees to peer under the desk.

With a cry of anguish he scrambled to his feet and ran to the window, yanked it open and looked both ways along the street. Shaking his head, he crossed the room and hurried into the corridor.

"Bruce!" he called. "Stop her, she's a Confederate agent." Bruce appeared in a doorway along the hall.

"She's made off with the reports from our agents in the South," Pinkerton said. "You search in back, I'll take the front."

Pinkerton ran along the corridor into the front hall of the converted house and threw open the door. He ran down the steps to the sidewalk.

"Were you looking for me, Mr. Pinkerton?" a voice behind him asked.

He whirled to find Margaret DeWitt standing beside the building entrance.

"What have you done with my papers?" he demanded.

She threw her arms wide. "What papers?" she asked. "I have no papers."

"I'll have you searched."

"You see," Margaret said, "I had what you call a confederate. The papers from your desk are quite safe with her."

"A confederate? Then you admit you're a spy."

"My choice of words was unfortunate, Mr. Pinkerton. Perhaps an accomplice would be closer to the truth. No, I'm not a Southern sympathizer. I'm exactly what I told you I was. The only thing I didn't tell you was that before I came to see you I conducted an investigation of my own. I'm afraid I was forewarned about your make-believe snake."

"The papers," he said. "What do you mean to do with them?"

"Why," Margaret said, "I intend to return them to you. After I make sure that every newspaper in Washington hears the story of how a damsel outwitted the great Alan Pinkerton. I think people might be amused by the story, don't you? I've heard that President Lincoln, for one, has a wonderful sense of humor."

"I somehow doubt whether Mr. Lincoln will be amused. Perhaps we can come to some sort of an understanding, Mrs. DeWitt. What is it you want?"

"I want to be a spy, Mr. Pinkerton," Margaret said.

He offered her his arm, looking up at her with a reluctant smile. "Let's go inside and discuss the matter, Mrs. DeWitt," he said.

BOOK III

The Bloodletting

SHILOH

11

THE TRAIN BRINGING Jared and Colleen from Richmond arrived in Wilmington four hours late.

"Damn these railroads," Jared said as he paced back and forth beside their bags on the depot platform.

"I'm sure they're doing the best they can." Colleen pulled her shawl tighter about her face to ward off the blustery east wind.

"And damn Aaron as well. What's keeping that nigger?"

"He'll be back in a few minutes. We can always hire a cab and have Aaron meet us at the hotel if you don't want to wait."

"Why must you always find excuses for him? I've decided to have Aaron hire us a rig—and hire a rig he will, if we have to stand on this platform till midnight."

Colleen suppressed a sigh. "We'll do whatever you want, Jared. We always do."

"I have to see Captain Hendricks tonight." He lowered his voice. "After all, I sail on the *Celeste* in three days' time."

"I wish you'd change your mind and let me go with you. It's not as though I'm afraid of the Yankee blockade. And I would like to see my father."

"Damn it, woman, must you go everywhere I go? Taking passage on a ship running the blockade from Wilmington to Nassau and back is too dangerous when there's no good reason for it. And you have no reason. I'll be back here inside of two weeks."

"Other than seeing my father," Colleen said, "my only reason is to be with you."

She heard him draw in his breath and expected an angry retort but Jared kept his peace. From the street she heard the clop-clop of a horse and saw a rig approaching through the gathering dark of the February evening.

What a fool you are, Colleen Hughes, she told herself. You know Jared's not a man who can abide being tethered. A loose rein works best with the likes of Jared Hunter. Knowing that, you still try to bind him to you.

How can I help myself? I have only one excuse. I love him so, love him beyond caring. Let him do with me what he will, treat me as he pleases, and I'll accept it. I'll go anywhere for him, do anything he asks of me.

"Well?"

Colleen looked up to see Jared waiting to hand her into the carriage.

She smiled and climbed into the seat behind Aaron. Yes, she decided, you're a fool, Colleen. Shall I tell Jared my secret? she wondered. No, this is neither the time nor the place. Besides, if I tell him now he'll never let me sail with him. Whenever I tell him, though, he's bound to see it as just another of my stratagems.

They clattered along the cobbled streets of the port city to the Wilmington House. Once they were in their room, Colleen faced Jared, opening her arms to him.

"Hold me," she said.

He came to her and took her in his arms, kissing her quickly. She put her hand to the nape of his neck and drew his head down to her, kissing him. After a moment, he broke away.

"Damn it," he said. "I'm sorry, Colleen, but I have a great deal on my mind. Captain Hendricks has probably been waiting for me for the last hour."

"I understand," she told him.

" 'I understand.' 'Yes, Jared.' 'Whatever you say, Jared.' What's come over you, Colleen? You used to have some spunk; there was fire in you. Has this abominable winter weather dampened it?"

With tears glistening in her eyes, she turned from him and went to the dresser. Looking in the mirror, she took off her hat and began unbuttoning the front of her dress.

"Will you be late?" she asked.

"Why must you continually question me? Are you a timekeeper, recording my comings and goings?"

"I only asked if you'd be late." Colleen slipped her arms from the sleeves of her dress.

Seeing her standing with her bare shoulders glowing in the lamplight and seeing her breasts straining against her camisole, Jared felt a sudden flare of desire. He walked up behind her and put his hands on her shoulders, his eyes meeting hers in the mirror.

"I should be back at the hotel by nine," he said.

When she rested her head on his chest, he reached down, his hands cupping her breasts as he leaned forward and kissed her, his tongue finding hers. Abruptly, he released her and crossed the room to the door.

"Jared," she said pleadingly.

He stopped with the door partly open and she said, knowing all the while that she should remain silent, "I love you, Jared."

He stared at her for a moment and then went into the corridor, pulling the door shut. God, he thought, how cloying she'd become! How long had they been together? Nine months, give or take; ever since Sumter. At first all had gone well. All through the Richmond summer—before and after the battle at Manassas, and during the remainder of his time on Beauregard's staff—he'd looked forward to seeing her after his long weeks in the field.

The trouble started after he'd been put on special assignment with the Ordnance Department, the Confederate agency overseeing the four government-owned blockade-runners and coordinating, as best it could, the comings and goings of the privately owned ships sailing from Wilmington and Charleston to the islands of Bermuda and the Bahamas.

Little by little Colleen had started to build her own private stockade around him. At first able to see what she was doing, she had laughed at herself. Lately, though, she had been given to fits of crying whenever she felt sorry for herself and, worst of all, to making demands on him. As though she owned him. Because he lusted after her, she thought he must love her. Because she loved him, she thought he was duty-bound to love her in return.

Someone should tell her, Jared thought, that life isn't like that.

He found Aaron waiting outside the hotel in the driver's seat of the hired rig.

"The Neptune," Jared told him and Aaron nodded. They'd visited the tavern twice during their stay in Wilmington the December before.

Hendricks had best be waiting, Jared told himself as he settled back in the seat. These blockade-running captains were becoming a damn independent lot. They could afford to be after a few trips at their exorbitant rate of a thousand dollars a voyage plus a percentage of the profit on the contraband cargo.

Jared closed his eyes and his thoughts returned to Colleen. She was acting more and more like a wife, inquiring into his comings and goings as though he was beholden to her. Before he knew it, she'd be expecting him to marry her. She probably envisioned herself as the mistress of Hunter Hill, giving birth to a new generation of Hunters.

Jared sat up with a start, opening his eyes. Good God, how could he have been so blind? These fits of crying, her clinging docility, that "I have a secret soon to be revealed" look in her eyes . . . Colleen was pregnant. The bitch was with child and she meant to use her pregnancy to force him to marry her. Well, he'd see about that. He knew she'd never agree to abort the child. We'll see about that, too, he told himself.

The rig came to a stop and Jared saw that they had arrived at the Neptune. "Wait for me," he told Aaron.

The grogshop, murky with smoke, reeked of whiskey and unwashed men. And, more faintly, of the salt tang of the sea.

"Captain Hendricks?" Jared asked. The barman nodded to a door at the rear.

Hendricks, alone in the room, was slouched in a chair with a glass on the table in front of him. He was a young man, not more than thirty, with a full black beard. When Jared paused in the doorway, the captain looked up but made no move to rise.

"A whiskey for the colonel," he shouted. "Another ten minutes and you'd not have found me here," he said to Jared.

"The Wilmington and Weldon isn't famed for keeping to its schedules." Jared silently cursed himself for the apology he heard in his voice.

When the barman placed the whiskey in front of him, Jared drained the glass. "A refill," he said, "and another for the captain."

While waiting for the drinks, Jared glanced about the room, noting there was but the one door and that the windows were shuttered. When the barman left the second time, Jared asked, "When do we sail?"

"Wednesday night. The tide will be in and there'll be no moon."

Jared nodded, sensing Hendrick's hostility. The captain was a master seaman; that was really all that mattered to Jared. "You've on-loaded your cargo?" he asked.

"Aye, the cotton's all aboard." The Confederacy, Jared knew, had relaxed its embargo on cotton shipments so it could trade for the critically needed military supplies routed from Europe through the West Indies.

"I'll be sailing both ways with you," Jared told the captain. "There's a cargo of Enfield rifles that should be waiting on the dock at Nassau for us."

Hendricks nodded.

Jared took an envelope from his inside pocket and handed it to the captain. "The other half will be paid when we reach the islands," he said.

Hendricks slipped the envelope inside his jacket. He raised his glass and for a moment Jared thought he meant to propose a toast. Instead he put the glass to his lips and drank the last of the whiskey.

"You're to be the hare on the voyage out from Wilmington," Jared said. "The same as you were on the last run."

"The *Celeste* can outrace any ship in the Union fleet."

"That's the reason we pay you so generously, Captain."

"If you don't pay the going rate for the use of my ship, the contract merchants will. What with the Federals putting more ships on blockade duty every month, my price will be higher before spring."

"Another round, Captain?" Hendricks nodded and Jared went to the door. "Bring the bottle," he told the barman.

The two men drank, talking in fits and starts. Jared didn't like Hendricks but he understood and respected him. The captain had two passions, his ship and money, and as a blockade-runner he was able to satisfy both. He must be a happy man, Jared thought, though you couldn't tell it from his manner.

"Did the Empire House get its new girls?" Jared asked.

"They arrived aboard the *Phantom* the day before I sailed from Nassau. There were two French whores among them."

"I've never had a Frenchie," Jared said. "Are the French ones all they're claimed to be?"

Hendricks shrugged. "I wouldn't know. I'm a happily married man."

Jared blinked. All at once his head felt woozy. When he held the bottle up to the light of the lamp he saw it was empty. What had Hendricks said? That he was happily married? What the hell did that have to do with having a whore?

Jared looked up and saw that the captain was on his feet. "I'd best return to my ship," the other man said. "If our business is done."

Nodding, Jared took two Confederate notes from his billfold and on the way out tossed them on the bar. The two men stopped for a moment on the board-walk in front of the tavern, where the east wind brought the smell of the sea and the hint of rain.

"I mean to sample those Frenchies when we get to Nassau," Jared said. If the captain disliked the subject of whores, then that's what he'd talk about. "They're bound to be better than what we've got here in Wil-mington. Now in Charleston last year I had a nigger wench—Melinda, her name was. She was no better. Cold as ice, if you know what I mean."

"Be on board by three Wednesday afternoon," Cap-tain Hendricks said.

"I will, Captain," Jared told him. "You can count on me to be on time."

Hendricks turned without another word and made off down the street in the direction of the wharves, his footsteps on the plank walk echoing in the quiet of the night. The bastard, Jared thought. He thinks he's too good for the rest of us. Jared shook his head to clear it. Where was Aaron with that rig?

"Aaron!" he called.

"I'm here." Aaron's voice came from a few feet away, startling Jared.

"I didn't hear you."

Aaron must have heard what I said about Melinda, Jared thought. He'd decided the girl hadn't told Aaron about what had happened at the hotel in Charleston, for his body servant had never alluded to the incident.

"I been waiting like you told me."

Aaron stepped forward. Some instinct warned Jared and he threw his head back just before Aaron's fist struck his chin. Jared staggered away from the blow, almost falling.

"I'll whip you to within an inch of your life for that," he said quietly.

Aaron advanced on him, saying nothing.

"I've whipped your ass before," Jared said, "and I can do it again. Do you hear me, you black bastard?"

Aaron swung again. Jared warded off the blow with his forearm.

"I mean to kill you," Aaron said.

Jared's hand went to the hilt of the knife in his belt and then shook his head. He didn't need a knife to handle the Negro.

He backed away with Aaron stalking him. The street was dark, the only light coming from the windows of the Neptune and from another building some hundred feet farther along the street. Jared retreated, backing from the boardwalk onto the dirt street with Aaron following.

Jared lashed out and felt his fist strike Aaron in the gut. Once, twice. The black grunted and came on. Jared jabbed his left at Aaron's face, struck his cheek, the blow stinging his fist. The Negro crouched low and charged, his head ramming into Jared's stomach. Jared grunted and fell, twisting to one side and rolling along the ground as he heard Aaron leap after him. The Negro's hand caught and held the heel of his boot. Jared yanked his foot away.

Jared rose to his hands and knees. Holding his breath and listening, he heard the black's heavy breathing a few feet to his left. He saw Aaron's shadowed form and sprang at him, pummeling his body with short, vicious blows. Aaron grunted, swinging wildly, and backed away with Jared after him, his fists jabbing at the black's face.

Aaron stopped with his back to the wall of a building. Jared crouched just out of reach of the Negro's roundhouse swings, darting in to jab at his body with rights and lefts. With a growl, Aaron charged, again bulling into Jared, but this time Jared was ready for him. He stepped to one side and chopped his fist down with all his strength, striking the back of Aaron's neck. With a grunt, the Negro sprawled on the dirt road.

Jared leaped at him but Aaron raised his feet at the last second, catching Jared in the stomach and lifting him up and over his head. Jared twisted in mid-air, trying to land on his feet, his right leg slammed instead into something solid. He lay on the ground with pain lancing his leg. When he pushed himself up, the leg crumpled under him. He rolled to one side and lay in the darkness, feeling along the leg with his fingers until he came to a bone pushing against the skin just below his knee.

The bastard had broken his leg. He couldn't move without pain stabbing through him like a hot knife. Reaching behind him, Jared touched a large flat-sided stone. A mounting stone? He heard Aaron coming at him. Jared reached to his belt and unsheathed his knife. Pulling himself up by grasping the stone, he stood on one leg, holding the knife in front of him.

Aaron charged. Jared saw the knife blade glint in the light from the tavern window. Aaron tried to stop his rush. Too late. Jared thrust forward and felt the knife bite into cloth and flesh. He pulled the blade back and thrust again. Aaron cried out. Jared pulled the knife from the Negro's body and thrust forward

a third time. Nothing; he found only air. He heard
Aaron stumbling away, moaning all the while, his
cry sounding like a strange incantation.

I hope he finds a hole, crawls in and dies, Jared
thought.

He tried to walk and fell, slamming down on his
side. Sour whiskey rose in his throat as he retched and
vomited. When his stomach was empty he laboriously
pushed himself to his feet again and hopped forward.
He stepped into a mud hole and fell. On his hands
and knees, his leg dragging helplessly behind him, he
crawled across the street, onto the boardwalk and up
the tavern steps. He heard singing coming from inside.

Jared pounded on the door with his fist. There was
no answer. Pushing himself up, he grasped the handle.
The door swung open and he fell forward on the
floor. The singing stopped and footsteps crossed the
floor toward him.

"Colonel, what's wrong?" It was the barman.

"Broke my leg," Jared said. "I need a doctor."

"Find a blanket," he heard a voice say. "Make a
litter."

"Seamen's Hospital," the barman said. "There's
likely to be a doctor there. It's only three blocks."

Jared nodded. He knew he couldn't take the pain in
his leg much longer without blacking out.

He clenched his teeth as four men carried him along
the street to the hospital. He'd be damned if he'd give
them the satisfaction of so much as a groan. And he'd
not pass out, he vowed as he closed his eyes, all the
while willing himself to ignore the pain slicing up his
leg. The steps of his litter bearers thudded on planking, he heard a door open and close, and smiled the
sickly sweet odor of chloroform. A man moaned. Jared
opened his eyes and saw he was in a long, high-

ceilinged room with rows of cots on both sides of the aisle down which he was being carried. Men lay in some of the cots; most, though, were empty.

He could no longer see the cots. White, he saw white instead. A sheet, he realized, now separated him from the rest of the hospital ward. A man in a white coat bent over him.

"I'm Dr. Gaddis," he said. Jared had an impression of bushy white eyebrows and stale breath.

He felt a knife cutting away the leg of his pants. He winced in pain.

"Nurse!" Dr. Gaddis called. "Chloroform, if you please."

"I don't want chloroform," Jared said.

"You ought to be glad I've got it to give to you," the doctor said. "I don't want you conscious when I set your leg. Nurse!" he called again.

"Yes, doctor."

Jared noticed her skin first. She had the clearest, most beautiful skin he had ever seen, almost transluscent. Next he saw her hair. Even pulled back into a chignon with a white net over it, her hair was glorious. A stunning red, the color deep and glowing. Jared drew in his breath as he felt a lurch within him. She's a woman a man would risk everything for, he thought.

A gauze mask was pressed over his nose and mouth. He stared up into the nurse's hazel eyes. A pungent odor made his eyes water.

"Count to twenty," she ordered him.

He stared at her, starting to shake his head and pull away when he felt her warm and soothing hands on his face. He breathed in the chloroform and as he did his vision of her blurred and he sank into nothingness.

When he regained consciousness, Jared looked up into Colleen's green eyes, saw her black hair and was disappointed without, at first, being able to remember why. Of course, the red-haired beauty. He looked around him but didn't see her. Had he imagined her? Had she been a dream?

"I've been so worried about you," Colleen said.

Jared shook his head, trying to clear it. He swallowed, fighting nausea. He felt disembodied; the taste of chloroform was on his tongue. He drew in his breath and raised himself on one elbow and saw that his right leg below the knee was encased in plaster of paris. He remembered now. Aaron. The fight with the Negro. The redhead had been the nurse who'd given him chloroform. Again he looked about him but saw only Colleen and the white screen separating him from the rest of the ward.

"That bastard Aaron," Jared said. "Have they found him?"

Colleen shook her head. "No one seemed to know where he was," she said. "I waited till after ten and then came looking for you. At the tavern they said you were here. They didn't seem to know what had happened."

"It was Aaron. He's probably dead. If he's not, I'll see that he's hanged."

"I never trusted him," Colleen said. "I don't trust any Negroes. It's the ones you've been the nicest to who are the first to turn on you when they get the chance."

"Vaughan spoiled that one," Jared said. "I'd had enough of his sass and he knew it. He jumped me without warning outside the Neptune after Captain Hendricks left. I wounded him with my knife, might have killed him. I hope to hell I did."

Colleen nodded. "They'll find him in the morning," she said.

"Get me out of here," Jared told her. "Take me back to the hotel."

The curtain was drawn aside and the redhaired

nurse came to stand beside his bed, looking down at him. She was every bit as beautiful as he'd remembered, though he hadn't realized before how tall she was.

"The doctor left orders that you were to stay here," she said.

"I'm leaving, Miss—"

"Boyd. I'm Margaret Boyd, Colonel Hunter." Her hazel eyes met his and lingered. Finally she looked away. "The cast on your leg isn't fully dry," she said. "If you leave, Colonel, you do so at your own risk."

"I'm accustomed to taking risks," he said. "As I suspect you might be."

"I've taken risks on occasion," she said.

"And have you regretted them?"

"No, I try to look ahead, not back. You're changing the subject. The doctor gave orders that you're not to walk on that leg for at least a week. You're to return to him in six weeks' time to have the cast removed."

"I understand." He looked at Colleen, who had sat listening to them, glancing first at one and then the other. "Get someone to help take me out of here," he told her.

"I think we can manage him between us," Margaret said, looking at Colleen. "All right?"

Colleen nodded and together they helped Jared to his feet. With one arm over each of the women's shoulders, he hopped to the door, fighting off his wooziness while at the same time conscious every step of the way of the nearness of Margaret Boyd. He was acutely aware of her body brushing his as they made their way to the carriage waiting in the darkness outside.

"Thank you, Miss Boyd," he said when he was

seated. As Colleen went around the carriage to climb in the other side, Jared raised the nurse's hand to his lips. She made no attempt to either encourage or discourage him.

"You're completely welcome, Colonel Hunter," she said.

As soon as he was in the double bed at the hotel, Colleen said, "She's very beautiful, isn't she?"

"Who do you mean?" Jared asked.

"You know very well who I mean."

"Redheads don't appeal to me. Their temperaments too often match the color of their hair."

Colleen turned the lamp low and began undressing. After putting on a thin batiste nightgown, she sat in front of the mirror brushing her hair. Was she pregnant? Jared wondered. Her breasts looked fuller but there was no other sign of it. All at once he thought of Nelson. Nelson would marry her no matter whose baby she carried. Nelson was a romantic. He'd consider such a naive gesture to be chivalrous.

"Have you heard from Nelson?" Jared asked.

Colleen paused with the brush raised above her head. "Now what made you think of Nelson Vaughan after all this time?" she asked.

Seeing her eyes on him in the mirror, Jared shrugged.

"You read the letter I had from him," she said. "The one telling me he was asking for a transfer to the western army. Into a Georgia regiment, I believe. He wanted to be where the fighting was."

"He needs to prove himself, I suspect."

"I don't know where he is now," Colleen said. "Nor do I care."

"I think you do care."

"You're right, I do in a way. I like Nelson. I *love*

you." She turned in her chair to face him. "What are you going to do, Jared? You can't sail to Nassau with your leg broken."

"Like hell I can't."

She put her brush on the dresser and came to kneel beside the bed. "I have an idea," she said. "Let me go in your place. I want to go, Jared. I want to do it for you."

"Have you completely lost your senses? It's too dangerous."

"You yourself told me that Captain Hendricks has the fastest ship on the Atlantic coast. I remember my father saying the *Celeste* can make up to sixteen knots. Surely she'll be able to outrun the fastest of the blockaders."

"You sound as though you believe everything you're told. Fast as the *Celeste* is, there's always danger. Fast ships have been known to run aground; they've been surprised and disabled before they've had a chance to get their steam up. Some have been poorly handled."

"My father says Captain Hendricks is the best skipper in these waters."

"No matter how competent he is, you can't go and that's the end of it."

Colleen drew in her breath. She got up from the floor and returned to her chair, where she once more began to brush her hair.

Jared closed his eyes and pictured Margaret's red hair, her hazel eyes challenging his. By God, he thought, she'd be a prize worth having. He shivered. Reaching down, he pulled a blanket up over himself.

"Are you all right?" Colleen asked.

"There's a draft."

"The windows are closed," she said. "It's probably

the shock of being hurt and having the surgeon set your leg."

"Besides," Jared said, "I have to deliver the messages to our agent in Nassau myself."

Jared knew this was not true and he knew Colleen knew it was not true. Anyone could deliver them. In fact, he'd considered sending a courier and staying in Wilmington, only deciding against it when he realized he wanted to be rid of Colleen, at least for a time.

"I'm sure I'd make a reliable messenger," Colleen said.

If she made the trip in his stead, he thought, the end result would be the same. She'd be gone for ten days, perhaps longer. He partially closed his eyes, saw the golden glint of light from the lamp and smiled to himself as he thought of Margaret.

A hand touched his and he gave a start. Opening his eyes, he saw Colleen kneeling beside him again.

"I want to do it for you, Jared," she said. "I don't want you to think of me as helpless, a woman who can't do anything on her own. You know I've never been one for knitting or nursing or any of the other things women do in wartime. I can go to Nassau in your stead, though. Please, Jared, let me do this for you."

"If you do sail in my place," he said, seeing her sudden smile at his capitulation, "I wash my hands of all responsibility. It will be your doing, Colleen, not mine."

"Jared, I knew you'd say yes." She leaned over the bed and kissed him, her lips lingering on his.

Colleen rose and pulled her nightgown over her head and let it fall to the floor. Naked, she stood before him with her arms at her sides.

"What do you mean to do?" he asked.

"You'll see," she said. "Don't move. You won't have to move at all. Just lie where you are." She pulled the blanket aside and knelt over him on the bed.

When he felt her lips on him, her hair touching his bared flesh, he smiled, imagining that the hair was red and that the lips were the lips of Margaret Boyd.

12

I'M SURE you won't mind if I don't accompany you aboard," Jared said. They were sitting in the carriage that had brought them to the wharf.

Colleen leaned over him, kissing him tenderly on the lips. "Just take care of yourself," she said. "In less than six weeks your cast will be off."

"My damn leg itches and I can't do a thing about it." Jared frowned as he looked across the quay to the sleek-lined *Celeste*. The ship, a three-master with a single smokestack, was painted slate gray. "I still don't feel right about letting you sail in my stead. I should be the one taking the risk, not you."

"Jared, we've discussed this before. It's settled. You know I want to go. Look, there's Captain Hendricks waiting for me to board. He'll be doubly sure no harm befalls me. He's a good friend of my father."

Jared nodded to Hollister, his orderly-driver, who picked up Colleen's bag and carried it up the gangplank onto the ship. As soon as he was out of ear-shot, Colleen said, "Jared, there's something—"

Not knowing what to expect, he put his forefinger to her lips and she smiled wistfully at him. "Something I want you to know," she went on. "I love you, Jared."

He kissed her. "And I love you, Colleen," he said.

She stared at him. "That's the first time you've ever told me. All these months and you've never once said you loved me until now."

"Perhaps the thought of losing you, however briefly, made me realize the truth." Wondering if he sounded as insincere as he felt, Jared smoothed a strand of her black hair. "Hendricks is waiting," he said.

Colleen climbed from the carriage and hurried across the quay. He watched as she turned at the foot of the gangplank to wave and then boarded the ship. He saw Hendricks greet her. As the two walked forward along the deck, Colleen glanced once more at Jared, nodding to him. He casually saluted her.

When Hollister returned to the carriage, Jared said, "Drive to the Seamen's Hospital."

Five minutes later they stopped in front of the converted warehouse. "Help me down," Jared told his orderly.

With one hand gripping Hollister's shoulder, Jared climbed awkwardly to the ground. Supporting his weight on a cane, he hobbled to the hospital entrance. When Hollister started to follow him, Jared shook his head. "Wait here," he ordered.

He stopped just inside the ward, his nose wrinkling at the smells of sickness. Margaret Boyd was at the far end of the room, bathing a patient. Not moving, Jared watched her and after a time she looked up, saw him, and smiled before returning to her task.

Jared waited. When she was done she walked along the aisle toward him, pausing at the foot of each occupied bed, smiling at one man, asking a question of another, saying a few words to each of the patients.

"I don't believe I'd like being a patient of yours," Jared said when she joined him.

"And why is that, Colonel Hunter?"

"I'd have so many other men to be jealous of."

Her face reddened and once again he marveled at her beauty, the lustrous flame of her hair, the sparkling green-brown of her eyes, her glowing complexion, the full figure which her long gray dress couldn't hide.

He was about to tell her how lovely she was when she shook his head. This woman would make a fool of him if he wasn't careful, he warned himself. Patience was the best tactic. He was used to the ebb and flow of women's natures, their initial coquettishness, their deepening interest, their sudden, unexpected and unexplained withdrawals, and, finally, their rush to fulfillment as they threw aside all caution.

He must bide his time. In affairs of the heart as on the field of battle, discipline was the key to success.

Margaret was looking steadily at him. "I'm afraid Dr. Gaddis won't be here for another two hours," she said. "I don't expect him before five at the earliest."

"I didn't come to visit the good surgeon," Jared said.

"I'm very busy just now. As you can see, I'm the only one here. We're shorthanded as usual."

"I have a gift for you. If you'll come with me to my carriage, I'll give it to you. It will only take you a minute."

"Colonel Hunter, I can't possibly accept a gift from you. You must know that."

"How can you be so sure before you've seen what I have? Do you always leap to conclusions so swiftly? If I did the same in battle, I'd be a dead man by now. Or, at the least, one of your patients."

"Perhaps you actually are as rash as you accuse me of being. After all, you were one of my patients only two days ago."

"That damn—" Jared reined himself in and bowed as best he could while leaning on his cane. "Your point's well taken," he said. "My rashness did lead to the breaking of my leg."

"Has there been any word of your escaped slave?"

"None at all. I suspect he made for the Union lines if he's still alive. Aaron knows that if I ever catch him it will go hard with him." Jared shook his head. "Why are we talking of slaves? Come with me to my carriage. Please."

Margaret nodded and walked ahead to open the door for him. Jared looked at the waiting Hollister and said, "Bring the trunk from the boot."

Hollister manhandled the heavy black trunk from the back of the carriage, lifting and carrying it to the walkway in front of the hospital, where he placed it on the ground. "Shall I open it, Colonel?" he asked and, when Jared nodded, Hollister undid the latches and lifted the cover.

"For you, Miss Boyd," Jared said as Hollister stepped aside.

Margaret knelt in front of the trunk. "Where on earth did you get them?" She picked up a bottle and read the label. "Quinine." Holding another bottle in her hand, she said, "Laudanum." She looked up at him. "How did you know we were in such short supply?"

"All of our hospitals are in short supply."

She stood and impulsively seized his hand and pressed it. "God bless you," she said.

"Was I right?"

"About what?"

"Was I right when I told you a few moments ago that you'd accept my gift?"

"I can hardly refuse. After all, the gift is for the men, not for me. And you haven't answered my question, Colonel. Where did you come by these supplies? Every hospital in the South is crying out for medicines."

"That will have to be my secret, Miss Boyd," Jared said. "When one is in the importing and exporting business—and I am, in a sense—there are ways and means to procure almost anything. Hollister will carry the trunk into the hospital for you." He nodded to his orderly.

"If you'll just take it to the storeroom in the back," Margaret told him.

As soon as Hollister entered the hospital, Jared said, "May I offer you a ride to your boarding house when you go off duty at eight?"

"There's no end to your surprises, Colonel. You not only know our needs and where to go to satisfy them, you know the time our tour of duty ends as well." She smiled. "You're not sailing tonight on the *Celeste,* then. I'm glad. The ocean voyage would have done your leg no good."

"How did you know of the *Celeste?*" Jared demanded.

"Not only the *Celeste*," Margaret said. "I know of the other ships that have been awaiting a high tide and a moonless night."

"Is no secret safe?"

"When one is in the nursing profession as I am, Colonel, there are ways and means to learn almost anything." When he glared at her, she said, "I'm sorry, I shouldn't tease you but I couldn't help it. I suspect you have no sense of humor."

"Not about the *Celeste*."

"Our patients are mostly men who were injured when blockade-runners beached along the coast while fleeing from the Yankees. What I don't hear from the sailors, I hear from their mates when they come to visit them. I wouldn't be at all surprised to learn I know more about the sailings from Wilmington than you do, Colonel Hunter."

"Did you know the *Celeste* will leave by the southern channel while the other ships slip out past Cape Fear? Did you know that?"

"No, I didn't. I was mistaken; you do know more than I do."

Why did he feel such a need to impress this woman? Jared wondered. Damn, he'd have to be more careful about what he said. Though there was no harm done here, for he was a good judge of who could be trusted and who couldn't.

"You've yet to answer my question," he said. "I offered to escort you to your lodgings."

"After what you've given me—given the hospital, I should say—how can I refuse?" Margaret asked, smiling.

Again Jared bowed, watching Margaret until the hospital door closed behind her. God, I'm acting like a young boy, he thought. He shrugged. So be it, he told himself.

* * *

The night was dark. There was no moon and a bank of fog lay offshore beyond the nearer of the two blockading squadrons of Yankee ships.

A man crouched on the beach with a pocketwatch in his hand. For perhaps the fifth time he held it in the crack of light coming from his shielded lantern. It was one minute to six. Luck had been with him—the message from Pinkerton's agent at the hospital had reached him just in time. He waited and when the minute hand stood square on twelve, he unshielded his lantern, shielded it again, unshielded it.

The man waited five minutes before he signaled again. There was no answer from across the water; he expected none. The surf ran up on the beach below him as the tide came in. High tide would be in another two hours.

After repeating the signal a third time he turned down the lantern's wick and saw the flame go out. Standing, he walked slowly among the dunes away from the beach. His job was done and now he looked forward to a draft of ale, a warm fire, and bed.

"If I'm in your way, Captain," Colleen said, "you have only to tell me and I'll leave the bridge."

"The daughter of Amos Hughes is always welcome here," Captain Hendricks said. "I've never held to the theory that members of the fair sex bring ill fortune to ships at sea."

They had cast off an hour earlier than originally planned and now the *Celeste* was easing her way down the Cape Fear River as the sky darkened. A light blinked from shore.

"That's our all-clear from the signal station at Nine

Mile Battery," Captain Hendricks said. "We'll soon
see the guns at Fort Lamb."

"You must be proud of your ship. She seems to
handle well."

"The *Celeste* is all a man could ask for." Captain
Hendricks's voice glowed with satisfaction. "She was
built in Liverpool last year. She's ideal for blockade-
running. Her hull only shows five feet above the
water, her draft's but eight-and-a-half feet and she
can steam at sixteen or more knots. She's a beauty,
right enough."

"I wouldn't want to be a Yankee trying to spot
her," Colleen said.

"The *Celeste* is practically invisible at two hundred
yards. It's not only her low silhouette and her gray-
white paint; she burns only anthracite coal so she's
practically smokeless as well."

Crew members on the port side were hailing Confederate sentries on shore.

"Fort Buchanan," Captain Hendricks told Colleen.
"We sailed early to catch the high tide crossing the
bar. I don't want to chance running aground there
or on the shoals."

"Too early, if you ask me," Angus Williams said.
"The river's not fully flooded yet." The river pilot
stood between the captain and the quartermaster who
manned the wheel.

Captain Hendricks ignored the comment and for
a time the only sound was the gentle lapping of
water against the hull.

"I recall when I was glad to have coal other than
anthracite aboard one of my ships," Hendricks said.

Colleen smiled, knowing the captain couldn't see
her in the dark. She'd learned that skippers loved to
relate their adventures. "Tell me about it," she said.

"We were off Charleston making for Bermuda on

board the *Martha Washington* when a Union warship gave chase. She was silhouetted against the lowering sun. Just as the sun set I called for my chief engineer.

"'Do you have a quantity of coal dust?' I asked.

"'I have, sir,' he said.

"'Then be ready to feed it and have fuel that won't smoke at hand as well.'

"When the darkness thickened until I could barely make out the warship pursuing us, I gave the order to burn the dust. The northeast wind spread out the soot-laden smoke to the south and west. I waited a few minutes and then ordered the engineer to burn clean coal. The plume of black smoke above us thinned so I put the helm hard over to starboard and made off at right angles to the long cloud of smoke hanging in the fading light.

"I don't have to tell you," Hendricks said, "that we got clean away. Or perhaps I should say we got dirtily away."

"I hope you won't have to use a ruse tonight."

"If we're lucky, we'll have you at your father's house in Nassau inside of three days."

Both Captain Hendricks and the pilot tensed, Colleen noticed, when the *Celeste* rounded a bend in the narrow channel of the river and sailed slowly through New Inlet toward the open sea. The ship shuddered slightly and its wake turned brown with mud.

"The channel's narrow here and the bar's shallow," Captain Hendricks said. "Treacherous."

"Ahead two-thirds." The pilot glanced at the wheel and the dimly glowing binnacle before staring ahead into the night. "Steady as she goes," he told the quartermaster.

The *Celeste*'s screws churned ominously loud below

them. After a few minutes the sound again faded to normal.

"We're across the bar," Captain Hendricks said. He raised his night glasses to his eyes and, following the direction of his gaze, Colleen saw the silhouette of a ship farther out to sea. "Two of them," the captain said, "one at anchor and one under way."

"They'll see us," Colleen whispered, breaking a vow to herself to remain silent.

"No, to them we're no more than a smudge of haze on the horizon."

Colleen heard the propellers and the water rushing past the ship's iron hull. The men near her peered intently ahead into the darkness. To her right she saw the low outline of the North Carolina shore.

A shot rang out.

"Federal picket boat dead ahead," a voice called from the *Celeste*'s rigging.

"Hard-a-port," the pilot ordered.

The *Celeste* veered, sailing to intersect the smaller boat's path. Captain Hendricks was trying to run her down, Colleen saw. At the last minute the boat eluded them, slipping past on their port side. A trail of fire shot skyward from the picket boat's bow and a moment later a signal rocket burst in the air. Musket fire cracked from the Yankees aboard the boat.

"A full head of steam," the pilot of the *Celeste* ordered. The ship plowed ahead into the night.

Colleen saw a tongue of flame burst from the nearest Federal warship. Shells shrieked through the *Celeste*'s rigging while from astern she heard the rattle of rifle fire from the picket boat. The *Celeste* zigzagged as she tried to escape the converging Yankee ships. Colleen saw bursts of fire coming from at least three ships off their port side.

Captain Hendricks grasped her arm. "Get below!"

He shouted to make himself heard above the scream of the shells.

"Make more steam, blast you!" he called to his chief engineer.

Colleen hurried forward, pausing near the mainmast. The entire ship vibrated as her engines drove her ahead, her screws churning through the water. Again the *Celeste* changed course and for a time the firing lessened.

Colleen let out her breath. Had they made their way safely through the Yankee dragnet? All at once flames spurted from the warships and shells shrieked around the *Celeste*. Explosions reverberated beneath Colleen. Smoke billowed from the stern of the ship and she heard the crackle of flames and the thudding feet of running men.

The ship changed course once more. Through the haze off the *Celeste*'s bow, Colleen saw the looming shoreline. Was the captain trying to beach her? A shell burst in cotton stored on the port side, turning the bales into a mass of flame. Another shell hit the ship's funnel, shattering it. Men lay sprawled on the deck. Smoke engulfed Colleen and she gasped for air. She heard a sound like the rattle of hail on the deck around her. Turning, she saw one of the crew clutch his arm, blood oozing from between his fingers.

"Prepare to abandon ship!"

Colleen froze, remembering the messages in her cabin that Jared had entrusted to her. If the ship was beached this far from the Confederate forts, the Yankees would surely be the first to board her. She mustn't let Jared's messages fall into their hands.

She hurried aft to the hatch and climbed down the ladder into a passageway lighted by a single storm lamp. A seaman ran toward her.

"Get back on deck," he shouted as he passed.
"We're lowering the boats."

She nodded but didn't turn back. Instead she sloshed
ahead, the water rising to cover her shoes as she
looked inside one cabin and then another. Why hadn't
she paid more attention when she was shown to her
cabin? The water was higher already, soaking the
bottom of her skirt. She ignored it, tried another door
and recognized the outline of the valise on the bunk.
This was her cabin.

She crossed the small room and opened the bag,
rummaging beneath her clothing until her hands
closed on the dispatches hidden near the bottom.
Clutching them in her hand, she struggled across the
cabin, the water coming to her knees. She could
scarcely move against the pressure of the surging sea.

Luckily, the cabin door was open. She waded into
the passage outside but as she started toward the ladder she heard a crash and the ship shuddered. Colleen drew in her breath, holding the dispatch case to
her chest. The light in the passage snapped from its
hook and exploded in the water, leaving her in total
darkness.

Feet pounded along the deck over her head. Flames
crackled ahead of her. As she pushed her way ahead
against the weight of the water, the beat of the engines
stopped. The *Celeste* must be sitting in the water,
unmoving.

Colleen's shoulder struck a bulkhead. With her free
hand, she felt ahead of her. The way was blocked.
She reached to one side. Again she touched a bulkhead. The water was to her waist and still rising. Des-
perately, she turned and made her way to the right.

Her knee struck an obstruction; again her way was
blocked. She turned, no longer able to make her way
against the water swirling around her. She clutched

the dispatch case in both hands, feeling the cold sea water rise to her breasts and above. The water lapped around her chin and she lifted her head as she tasted the brine.

"Dear God," she prayed, "have mercy on my soul."

She screamed, the unheard sound changing after a moment to a gurgle as water entered her mouth. Jared, she thought. Jared, I'm going to have your baby. Jared.

Jared Hunter, waiting in the carriage, doffed his hat to Margaret as she walked from the hospital.

"Forgive me if I don't help you in," he said.

She nodded. When she was in the seat beside him, Jared flicked the reins and they rode slowly away from the harbor toward the center of Wilmington.

As they drove first over hard-packed dirt and then clattered onto cobbles, Jared told her of Hunter Hill, describing the house and the new room his father was adding. He talked of growing up and told her about his brother, Fremont.

"He's still at West Point?" she asked.

"He was the last I heard. Fremont is, well, different. There's no predicting what he might do at any given moment."

"And with you there is?"

"Well, perhaps we are somewhat alike, Fremont and I. Neither of us take after our father; were both our mother's sons. She died years ago when she drowned in the river near our plantation."

"How horrible. At the hospital I've seen men after they've drowned at sea. It must be a terrible death." After a moment, she said, "I'm sorry, I didn't think before I spoke."

"My mother died years ago. She's more like a dream to me than a real person."

As he talked, Margaret sat beside him with her hands clasped in her lap, hearing only a word here and there as she remembered the dead and dying men she had nursed. How can I do it? she wondered. How can I calmly send men to their deaths and then nurse those who survive?

She knew it was possible only because she had somehow managed to separate the two in her mind, the passing on of information and the men who were carried to the hospital after their ships were sunk or beached. Besides, how could she possibly tell what was her doing and what resulted from chance, a change of wind, the vigilance of the Yankee blockaders? She couldn't tell, not for sure. Her information might be completely useless, too little and too late. Many times she found herself hoping it was.

At other times she was tempted not to report what she had found out from the men at the hospital, for then she couldn't blame herself for what happened. When that temptation was greatest, though, she thought of Peter, remembered the train rumbling into the station at Fairfield and the honor guard carrying her husband's flag-draped coffin from the car to the platform.

The coffin was sealed and remained sealed as Peter DeWitt's body was laid to rest in the Beach Road Cemetery, next to Bensons, Burrs and other heroes of the Revolution and the War of 1812. She could still hear the volley of shots saluting her husband and the mournful echoing notes of the bugler sounding taps.

The memory steeled her heart. The Rebels had killed Peter and she would wreak her vengeance. Didn't the Bible command an eye for an eye and a tooth for a tooth?

"What did you say?" she asked, belatedly realizing that Jared was looking at her for a response.

"We're here." Smiling, he said, "I don't believe you heard a word I said during the entire drive."

"Yes, I did. You were telling me about Hunter Hill. It sounds lovely." She frowned. "Sometimes I can't stop thinking of the wounded boys until hours after I leave the hospital, and often not even then. There's so much suffering in the world."

"I understand how you feel," he said. "I only wish we had more time together, you and I. I'll only be here another few weeks and then I have to travel to Charleston. I hope you'll come there someday so I can show you the city and the plantation."

"I've never been to Charleston."

"It's a new Eden, the most beautiful city in the South, which means it's the most beautiful place in the world."

"I'm from Virginia," Margaret told him. "A small town near Harpers Ferry."

"You're almost a Yankee then. The only fault you have is that northern twang in your voice. Otherwise, you're perfect."

"Which goes to show how little you know of me. I've been told I can be quite a shrew. I've been called a bluestocking by some and selfish by others."

"Liars, all of them."

"Thank you for the drive home." When Jared started to rise, Margaret put her hand on his arm. "No," she said, "stay where you are. You shouldn't put any more strain on that leg than you can help."

He nodded, taking her hand and raising it to his lips.

"Goodnight," he said, climbing from the carriage and going up the steps of the rooming house. When she was inside, she turned to look from the window to watch him ride away. She was surprised he hadn't tried to kiss her; she'd rather thought he would try and had smiled to herself as she imagined his chagrin when she refused. He hadn't made the attempt and now she felt almost disappointed.

She shouldn't feel that way, she knew. Peter had been dead little more than three months and she was still in mourning. She knew she could never again care for another man as she had for Peter. Why, then, had her heart pounded just a bit when she saw Jared standing in the hospital ward that afternoon?

She didn't like Jared—she was fairly certain of that—and doubted whether she would ever grow to like him. Still, there was something about him that attracted her, that made her want to know him better. Perhaps it was his open admiration of her. She had sensed it from the first, when he'd looked up at her as he was being carried into the hospital with a broken leg. That woman who came for him had been aware of it as well. What was her name? Colleen. Colleen Hughes. Margaret wondered who she was and what she was to Jared. There had been no sign of her since that first night, so perhaps she was no longer in Wilmington. I hope she isn't, Margaret thought.

She left the hall window and walked quickly up the stairs. Enough of Jared Hunter, she told herself, all the while wondering when she would see him again.

Jared was awakened by a thumping on his hotel room door. He pushed himself from the bed and, after putting on a robe, clumped across the room leaning on his cane. He unbolted and threw open the door.

"Captain Hendricks!" Jared stepped back, surprised, and the captain walked past him into the room, appearing not to notice the cast on his leg.

"Turn up the lamp," Jared said.

The captain went to the table and the light flamed higher. Jared saw that Hendrick's dark blue trousers

were wet and his jacket was soiled and torn. His hair
was tousled; he wore no hat. When he turned, Jared
saw a red wound on the captain's cheek. Jared's hand
went to his own cheek to finger his scar.

"A drink, Captain?" Jared had recovered his com-
posure and was prepared to hear the worst.

"No thank you, sir." Captain Hendricks cleared his
throat. "I bring distressing news," he said.

"I assumed as much. Out with it, man, out with it.
What happened?"

"We were intercepted south of Cape Fear by a
picket boat. The boat signaled the blockading fleet
and we were set upon by three warships. I tried to
make a run for it but we were badly damaged in the
attack. I had to abandon ship."

"The *Celeste* is lost then." It was a statement rather
than a question.

"Aye, she went down in ten fathoms. The Yankees
will salvage none of her cargo, nor will we."

"All right, now that I've heard the worst of it, we'll
make plans for the future. You'll soon have a new
ship, Captain. I'm confident you did all you could."

"But you haven't heard the worst, Colonel Hunter.
I lost six men, four killed and two missing. And Miss
Hughes. I fear she was drowned."

"There's no doubt?"

"None, I'm afraid."

Jared clenched his hands. He turned away to the
window and stared into the darkness. Colleen was
dead. He mourned her loss, though he couldn't sup-
press a flicker of satisfaction at having the problem of
Colleen solved once and for all. He saw Captain
Hendricks watching him in the reflection in the window pane.

"We were to be married," Jared said.

The captain shook his head. After a time, he said, "I'm afraid your dispatches were lost as well."

"Damn the dispatches. The Yankees are welcome to them. They'll find little in them they don't already know."

13

NELSON HUNTER VAUGHAN plodded along the dirt road near the rear of a long column of Confederate soldiers.

"Lookee there," said Saul Trapp, who was marching beside him.

Nelson glanced up in time to see the brown flash of a deer in the thick woods beside the road.

"March, wait; march, wait." Floyd Swanson, on Nelson's other side, hadn't looked up. He was an older man wth grizzled whiskers and a crooked, once-broken nose. Swanson was a complainer, Nelson had found.

Nelson shifted the Enfield rifle-musket to a new position on his shoulder and tramped on. The men ahead of him slowed, stopped, and the column of troops stood waiting. No one seemed to know exactly where they were, only that they were headed north from Corinth, Mississippi, and were somewhere west of the Tennessee River.

Nelson breathed deeply of the warm April air. Birds sang in a meadow to the left of the road while to his right squirrels scampered along oak branches, stopping now and again to chatter down at the soldiers. Deeper in the woods, he knew, violets bloomed. Dogwoods were in bud and a mile back they had marched beneath the delicate pink blossoms of peach trees.

"March, wait; march, wait." Floyd shifted his chaw of tobacco from one side of his mouth to the other.

"Do you think you'll be scared?" Saul asked Nelson. "I'm afeared *I'm* going to be scared."

"I don't know," Nelson said. "I plan to take it as it comes."

"If you keep talking about being scared," Floyd said, "you sure as hell will be."

"How can I help talking about it," Saul said, "when it's all I think about? You might of been in battle before, Floyd Swanson, but I never have."

"What you ought to do," Floyd said, spitting, "is this. If you get scared, just run back to where General Albert Sidney Johnston or General Pierre Beauregard are directing operations from the rear and hand them your shotgun and your Bowie knife and tell them you've decided to go home to your Georgia farm and will they kindly find someone else to make use of your weapons." Floyd laughed, slapping his thigh with his palm.

"There's nothing funny about being scared," Nelson said. "I suspect that if we had the brains we were born with, we'd be scared, too."

"Are you saying I ain't got brains?" Floyd clapped Nelson on the shoulder. "You're right, though, I reckon. Being scared's human. It's the worrying it to death I object to. Talking makes being scared like a disease that spreads and spreads till there's no stopping it."

Floyd raised his .58 caliber Springfield to his shoulder and followed an imaginary target across the field beside the road. "I'm tired of retreating," he said. "It's time we showed them Yanks what real men are made of."

The soldiers ahead of them started forward again and soon the entire column was in motion. They marched to a fork and swung right, passing other roads leading into dense woods. They crossed creeks on narrow wooden bridges or, at times, by slogging through the muddied water. Again they halted.

"Wrong road. Back to the fork." The word was passed from man to man and, disgusted, they turned in place and marched to the crossing, where they regrouped to head left instead of right.

In the later afternoon a horseman from the south rode past them and dismounted to talk to Captain Baird. The men halted beside a field and the captain faced them, a sheet of paper in his hand.

"I have a message addressed to the army from General Johnston," Captain Baird told them.

"'The eyes and hopes of eight millions of people rest upon you,'" the captain read. "'You are expected to show yourselves worthy of your lineage, worthy of the women of the South, whose noble devotion in this war has never been exceeded in any time. With such incentives to brave deeds, and with the trust that God is with us, your generals will lead you confidently to the combat, assured of success.'"

The men cheered, the courier rode off, and the march north was resumed.

"It kind of makes a man feel good," Saul said. "Proud of being here with all of them generals counting on me."

Nelson nodded.

"Bullshit," Floyd said softly.

When Nelson turned to glare at him, Floyd spat on the road and trudged on. Nelson felt a drop of rain on his face and then another. "Damn," he said, hunkering down into his jacket.

They camped beside the road, where they huddled in their tents as the storm continued into the night. The rain came in a cloudburst, then eased off only to come again in torrents until the ground was soggy.

"We attack in the morning." The word was passed from regiment to regiment, from man to man.

The rain stopped before dawn. After they ate breakfast—each man had been given five days' rations in Corinth—the captain led them into a woods to take up their position in the line. When a rabbit raced away in front of them, soldiers fired at it but the rabbit zigzagged to safety.

"No shooting," the captain ordered.

"How the hell can I tell if my powder's dry?" a soldier asked.

"No shooting," the captain repeated. "You'll have Grant and Sherman and all the rest of them damn Yankees down on us."

"They say we're supposed to surprise them," Saul said.

"One hell of a surprise." Floyd spat. "What with all this racket we might as well go in with our bands playing 'Dixie.' "

At last they were in position. The men sat on the ground or stood leaning against trees, talking in nervous murmurs. Nelson heard horses approach from the rear, one of the riders spoke to the men off to his right, and there was the sound of subdued cheering.

"The Creole hisself," a soldier said.

"Beauregard exhorting his troops," Floyd muttered.

"I wish I could of heard what he said." Saul was whittling a piece of wood with his Bowie knife.

They waited. Later in the day Captain Baird led them forward and through the trees they saw other Confederate companies moving up on both sides of them. They advanced perhaps half a mile before they were halted. The order to attack didn't come. They waited through the long afternoon and into the night when, at last, they were told to sleep where they were, their arms at their sides.

"Tomorrow," the word came. "We attack the Yankees at dawn."

"Tomorrow's Sunday," Saul said. "It's not right, fighting on a Sunday."

"Johnston probably asked and got special permission from on high," Floyd told him. "You heard him say God was with us."

"Sometimes I think God doesn't care," Nelson said, looking ahead into the darkness. The Yankees must believe God is on their side, too, he thought.

"God does care," Saul said quietly. "We matter to Him, the least among us matters. He sees even the fall of the sparrow."

"There's a lot of us here," Floyd said, "that will only see the sun rise one more time."

Nelson fell asleep only to be wakened by the sound of drums. He looked into the darkness around him and when he again heard the drums he realized the tattoo came not from the Confederate lines but from the Yankee encampments. It sounded as if they were less than a mile away. He settled down to sleep but found he couldn't. He thought of Santee and of Colleen; he wondered what the morning would bring.

At dawn the woods were teeming with men. They

ate quickly, checked their guns and affixed their bayonets.

"Did you hear what General Johnston told his officers?" Saul asked. "He said that tonight we'll water our horses in the Tennessee River."

"Them that has horses might," Floyd said, "and then again, they might not."

All along the line, the men were ready. Captain Baird rode among them, encouraging and exhorting them. At last the word, long awaited, long feared, long hoped for, came.

"Forward."

They advanced through the woods with the sky lightening above them. Saul kept getting ahead of the others, at times almost breaking into a trot.

"Not so fast," Nelson cautioned him. "The Yankees aren't going anywhere. They'll wait on us."

"I mean to see the elephant," Saul said. "Today all of us will see the elephant."

They heard a scattering of shots off to their left, the sound far away. More firing came from ahead and to their right. Nelson peered through the trees but could see nothing. Captain Baird led them down a heavily timbered slope into dense underbrush. At the bottom of the hill they hesitated on the edge of a swamp thick with shrubs, saplings and vines.

"Damn." Nelson felt water go over the tops of his shoes. He slogged ahead, seeing the men in front of him split into two groups, one circling the swamp to the right and the other to the left. He heard the crack of shots ahead of him, the sound coming from a partially wooded hill.

Nelson struggled through the last of the swamp and onto solid ground. A steep slope rose ahead of him with a small log structure near the top.

"That's Shiloh Church," Floyd said.

"Shiloh. That means land of peace," Saul said.

The line of men left the shelter of the woods and advanced into an open field. Firing broke out far above them, the steady pop-pop-pop of small arms and the roar of cannon. As Nelson climbed the hill in the face of the fire, smoke rose above the crest. He had yet to see a Yankee.

The advance had started at a fast walk. Now the men began to trot. Some ran forward, gathering speed as they climbed. Everyone was yelling and shouting. Nelson heard himself call out, a Rebel yell. Little clouds of smoke appeared ahead of him and he heard the cracking of Federal rifles. A storm of bullets tore through the ranks on both sides of him.

Men fell to the ground, cut down by the shot and shell. Nelson saw a man who had been shot in the face groping ahead, blinded by either the blood in his eyes or his wound. A boy lay sprawled off to Nelson's right. He recognized him as a private he'd spoken to that morning. The boy's eyes were glazed by death.

Nelson fired, reloaded and fired again. He couldn't be sure of a target so he aimed for the crest of the hill. A man fell at his side. Cries for help and short sharp shrieks of pain mingled with the shouts of the attacking Confederates.

Nelson saw the gray line waver. Men turned and ran. Saul, who had been at his side, stopped, cried out in terror and bolted down the hill. He couldn't see Floyd. Was the older man hit and down? Nelson felt nothing, no fear, no elation. He was numbed by the shooting, by the dangerous climb up the hill, by the specter of death all around him.

He stopped and looked about him. The attack had failed to reach the Yankee line at the top of the hill. Nelson fired once more, turned, and hurried, crouched over, down the slope. Another volley of Federal fire raked the retreating line. Men screamed and fell. Nelson broke into a run.

He was at the edge of the trees. He pushed into the brush and threw himself to the ground before turning and looking up the hill. Bodies lay scattered on the field. One wounded man raised his hand; it fell lifeless to the ground. Nelson reloaded and fired, reloaded and fired again. Saul crawled up beside him.

"I broke and ran," the young Georgian said. "I peed in my pants up there on the hill."

Captain Baird rode behind the line, his horse crashing through the brush. "We're going after them!" he shouted. "On your feet! We're going after them!"

Saul pushed himself up and looked down at Nelson. Nelson stood and rammed a charge into his musket. The soldiers left the shelter of the woods for the second time, their ranks diminished. The men in gray, yelling and shrieking, climbed the hill. Musket fire from the crest raked their line, cannon roared, shells exploded around them.

A man ran in front of Nelson. Suddenly his head was gone, severed. His body went on for a few faltering steps, then collapsed to the ground. Nelson fired and reloaded automatically. He didn't know what he was doing; his every action seemed by instinct. Load, fire, climb; load, fire, climb. He smelled the acrid fumes of gunpowder and heard the cries of men in pain.

He was at the crest. The dead and wounded around him no longer all wore gray. Here many were dressed in blue. The Confederates charged over the top of the hill. Nelson expected to find trenches and barricades; there were none. He saw tents ahead of him; Union troops fired as they retreated through their camp. Nelson loaded, fired; loaded, fired. One of the Yankees clutched his stomach and fell.

A young boy in blue ran from a tent, holding a book. A Bible. Nearby, two Confederates closed on a wounded Yankee, bayoneting him as he lay on the ground. The man opened his mouth to cry out. The boy holding the Bible stopped to stare at the bayonet-wielders, then ran on. One of the Confederates fired after him but the boy disappeared into the woods.

They were beyond the camp now, at the edge of the trees. Firing came from both sides, then from the right only, then died out. Nelson saw a Union private on his back with a hole blown in his abdomen from which a long section of intestine hung out. Nelson knelt beside him, pressing the slippery mass back inside the man's body.

"Oh, dear God," the man whispered. "Dear God, dear God, dear God."

Nelson got to his feet and ran on. He met Confederates coming back from the woods.

"We've beaten them," one shouted. "We've licked them. They're running for the river."

All around him men in gray were foraging through the Yankee camp, emerging from the tents with food, letters, mementos. A man holding a sleeve scorched on a stove passed by him. "They were cooking breakfast within rods of the front line," he said. "We either surprised them this morning or they're blessed with the most daring cooks on record."

Nelson saw officers reforming the men into ranks. He came on Saul sitting with his back to a tree, holding his head in his hands.

"I broke and ran. I done it twice now." Saul looked up at Nelson with tears in his eyes. "I couldn't take no more of the shooting."

"We all ran," Nelson told him, offering him his hand. Saul took it and stood up, his shotgun at his side.

They pressed on into the far woods. The firing was on both sides of them, little coming from the front. They crossed a field and climbed a small knoll. Shooting came from behind them and the men stopped, puzzled.

"Get down! Get down!" Captain Baird shouted as he rode by. "It's our own men shooting at us, by God."

Nelson hurled himself down among logs. The captain rode back toward the crest of the hill, calling for the advancing men in gray to stop firing. Another volley crashed into the woods, wounding the captain's horse. The animal reared, throwing Baird to the ground, his foot tangling in the stirrup, the horse dragging him ahead until at last he freed himself and staggered to his feet. The firing from the rear lessened and stopped.

They were on their feet again. Nelson saw a road ahead of them, a sunken road overgrown with weeds. The Federals were firing down from the heights beyond. Cannonballs tore through the branches of the trees over their heads. The tents behind him were in flames, while off to his right lay horses writhing in agony.

They waited in the woods near the sunken road. Floyd was beside him. They both lay on their backs looking up through the branches of the trees at clouds scudding across the sky.

"Do like I do," Floyd said. "When the firing gets heavy find a good safe spot and take cover. No one will be the wiser as long as you make out like you're wounded."

"I didn't sign up to hide," Nelson said. "I came to fight."

"Then you're a damn fool," Floyd told him. "You got to live to fight another day. These bayonet charges with green troops against entrenched positions are madness."

"Why did you sign up?"

"I'll be goddamned if I know."

They were on their feet once more, moving ahead. Nelson could only see the men to his immediate right and left because of the trees, the ridges, and the concealing smoke. The men were dirty and sweaty, their uniforms torn and smeared with mud. The sun came from behind the clouds, a hot sun.

All about him Nelson saw dead and dying men. He passed shattered guns, abandoned limbers and caissons, dead horses, discarded Union knapsacks. The din of the thousands of muskets was deafening, never-ending; cannons roared and shells exploded while all around him men yelled and shouted as they charged past the wounded who moaned and cried for water.

Nelson was resting beneath a tree. Saul was sitting beside him.

"That's a regular hornet's nest up there," Saul said, nodding to the site of heavy firing. "A regular hornet's nest."

Men straggled back from the front line, some wounded, others not. Nelson and Saul were on their feet, going forward. An officer passed them, coming from the direction of the battle.

"Fill your canteens, boys," he said. "Some of you will be in hell before night and you'll need the water."

They charged a hill, fell back, charged again over

the corpses left from the first attack. In some places
bodies lay in piles, arms and legs at grotesque angles, some bodies cut in two. Wounded men crawled
back toward the Confederate lines.

Reinforcements came up from the rear and the
soldiers in gray swept over the hill. Nelson saw Union
soldiers raising their hands in surrender. The Confederates ran past them into a field and up another
hill, a volley thundering from the crest. As the fire
cut through the gray-clad troops their line seemed
to undulate like tall grain waving in the wind.

Nelson saw Saul go down clutching his side. The
Confederate line hesitated and gave way, the men
stumbling down the slope, Nelson with them. He
stopped. Through the stinking smoke he saw Saul
raise his hand, as though pleading for help. The boy
was twenty yards up the hill. Nelson ran back into
the drifting gunsmoke. A shell exploded behind him
and he pitched forward on his face. He levered himself from the ground, feeling his back with his hand.
His uniform was torn but he felt no blood.

He crawled ahead, trying to keep as close to the
ground as he could. When he saw puffs of smoke
rising from the crest, he imagined the volley was
meant for him. Bullets whirred over his head, a man
screamed behind him. He threw himself down at
Saul's side.

"I wasn't scared," Saul said. "I charged them damn
Yankees and I wasn't a bit scared."

Nelson lifted the youngster's hand from his side
and grimaced when he saw the ugly red wound.

"I'll carry you," he said. "You'll be all right."

He raised Saul to his shoulder, bending under the
boy's weight, and plodded down the hill. The trees
rose ahead of him, impossibly far ahead of him. Saul

groaned in his ear. Nelson heard the thud of bullets all around them. He tripped over a body and almost fell, recovered, stumbling into the shelter of the trees. He carried Saul behind the lines and laid him gently on the ground.

He heard a voice next to him say, "He's dead. You been toting a dead man."

Nelson looked down and saw that it was true. Saul was dead, a bullet had carried away the back of his head. Nelson drew in his breath. He felt like retching. Taking Saul's hands, he crossed them over his chest.

"He wasn't scared," Nelson said. Looking around he saw there was no one to hear him.

Nearby, men were singing and he recognized the song as "Cheer, Boys, Cheer," a favorite of the Kentuckians. Soldiers marched past him, singing as they went toward the lines. Nelson stared after them. Their uniforms were clean, their faces bright.

He was in the lines again. He hadn't been able to find his company nor his regiment. There seemed to be no organization. The men were fighting on their own, charging, retreating, charging again into the face of the devastating fire.

"We're almost out of ammunition," he heard a sergeant tell a colonel.

"You've got your bayonets," the colonel said.

A fire started in the woods near him, the woodsmoke mixing with the smoke from the powder. Saul's body was in that woods. Nelson searched for it until the flames raced toward him and he ran. He saw a horse galloping from the fire, snorting in terror, its entrails, soiled with dust, dragging along the ground behind him. He shot at it, but missed.

Exhausted, Nelson sank down beside a tree. All

around him men were dropping to the ground, played out, their eyes empty, hollow. He sniffed the air. That stench. What was it?

"Thats the bodies burning in the woods," someone said.

A colonel rode by. "On your feet, men!" he called. "We're whipping them. We have them. On your feet, men. As you value your honor, on your feet."

Nelson was going forward. Union troops were laying down their arms. A Confederate private ran up to a mounted Union officer and called for him to surrender. The officer put his pistol in the Confederate's face and pulled the trigger. A barrage of bullets struck the officer from the saddle and men ran to him, bayoneting him as he lay on the ground. A Confederate cavalryman held an Iowa regiment's banner aloft, then rode back and forth dragging the flag in the mud and water.

They charged across a field. Nelson thought he saw Floyd sprawled on the ground, pretending to be wounded, smiling up at him. He blinked. No, it wasn't Floyd. Besides, this man was dead. Far off to his right a shell ricocheted and landed on top of a soldier. The man, terrified, scrambled to get away. The shell exploded, tearing the man to pieces.

Another Federal defense line was ahead of them. The day was darkening. Was it that late? Nelson had eaten all his food, and his ammunition, already replenished twice, was nearly gone. Puffs of smoke rose from higher on the slope ahead of him. He felt a stab of pain in his leg, and he fell. There was a ravine nearby and he crawled in that direction. A shell exploded close to him and pain seared his side. He rolled onto his back, clutching his wound. Blackness enveloped him.

Nelson woke to a strange rustling sound. All around

him he heard the moans and the cries of the wounded. It was raining, he realized; he had been listening to the whisper of the rain. He crawled ahead, using his arms to pull the rest of his body forward. His side ached and his leg throbbed with pain. His hands, reaching ahead of him, touched cloth, then flesh. A dead man. He crawled around the body.

The night was dark. Nelson heard no firing and saw no signs of life. Was he already dead? He crawled on, the rain harder now, driven by a chill wind. When he reached the ravine he crawled down the slope, rolling the last few feet to the bottom, where he hunched against the bank to escape the worst of the rain.

Light flashed in the sky. Nelson shrank deeper into his shelter. Not a shell, he realized belatedly. Lightning. Thunder rolled across the battlefield, the sound seeming muted in comparison to the remembered roar of the guns. He heard a single cannon and, looking up, saw the trail of a red fuse light the starless night for a brief moment before the shell screamed down into the trees to explode some distance from him. Again the night was quiet.

Nelson lost consciousness. When he opened his eyes the sky was lighter. Firing began again, far away at first, then closer. He heard a man's voice call out. "Kill me," the voice said. "Kill me, please kill me."

A gray-clad soldier ran by along the top of the ravine, glancing down at the wounded men huddled below him. He looked quickly away. Nelson heard another voice. "Oh God, have mercy!" the man cried. "Oh God! Oh God!"

I have to get out of this ravine, Nelson told himself. He crawled a few feet with pain searing his leg, tears blinding him. He lost consciousness but came awake again to crawl a few more feet, before surrendering to blackness once more. I'm dying, he told himself. May the Lord have mercy on my soul.

The Negro walked stolidly about the battlefield, examining the corpses, each time shaking his head and going on.

Dead horses lay scattered among the dead and wounded men. Union soldiers hauled the horses away, covered the carcasses with brush and set the piles afire. They carried the wounded men from the field to the hospitals behind the lines.

"What are you doing?" a Union private challenged the Negro. The black man stared at the soldier for a moment and walked on. The private shrugged and let him go.

The bodies were turning black and bloating; the air was redolent with the stench of death. The burial details, masks covering their faces, worked quickly and quietly. They dug long trenches, dumped the bodies in, and covered them wtih dirt, at times, in their haste, shoveling less than a foot of soil onto the corpses.

The Negro went on, ignoring the burial details and the litter-bearers carrying the wounded to the rear. Where the fighting had been the fiercest, he saw that a man could walk across a field on the bodies without ever setting foot on the ground. He came to a pond where the dead were gathered around the water as though seeking a last drink. The water of the pond was blood red.

The Negro shook his head, awed by the savage madness of these white men.

He climbed into a ravine, examining each of the bodies in turn. One was a grizzled older man with a broken nose. Nearby he saw another gray-clad body, huddled as though in death. The Negro knelt beside the body, turned it over and stared down in surprise and recognition. He rose to his feet and looked around him as though seeking help. The Union soldiers ignored him as they cared for their own.

The Negro knelt again, grasping the soldier's arm and putting him across his shoulders, straining as he raised himself to his feet. Carrying the wounded man, he made his way out of the ravine and across a field. He gazed in horror as he saw an arm extended from a hastily covered grave, the unmoving clawlike fingers open and reaching heavenward.

A Federal soldier blocked his way.

"Where you going, nigger?" he asked.

"Home," Aaron said.

"Stay here with us and you'll be free."

Aaron, with Nelson's body across his shoulders, stood staring at the soldier.

The man shrugged and steped aside. "Some folks don't know when they're well off," he said.

Aaron walked on, heading south toward Corinth, away from the stench of Shiloh.

14

WHEN JETHRO DROVE up to Santee, he found Ida Vaughan waiting on the front piazza. He helped her into the carriage and urged the matched bays ahead.

"You're not bringing flowers?" he asked.

Ida shook her head and they drove in silence under the oaks to the burial ground beyond. After Jethro helped her from the carriage, they climbed the low hill together. At the crest Ida knelt on the grass, bowing her head in prayer, while Jethro stood behind her, staring down at the newly engraved headstone.

When Ida stood up, she said, "I don't know if I should pray or not. I wonder whether the Old Colonel would welcome prayers."

Jethro raised his eyebrows.

"Did I ever tell you how my father said grace?" she asked.

"You never did."

"He always said grace—but after meals, not before. It was his notion that we should know what we had received before offering thanks. Now I wonder how he'd feel about my praying for his immortal soul. If he's in heaven he might think the prayers weren't needed. If he's not in heaven, he probably wouldn't think they'd do him any good."

"We'll all miss the Old Colonel," Jethro said. "Still and all, perhaps the time had come for him to die. I doubt if he'd have wanted to live to see the changes this war will bring to the South."

"The *Mercury* said his death represented the passing of an era. I do believe they were right. For once."

They walked arm in arm away from the cemetery to a nearby knoll where they sat on the grass, the sun high over the cornfield below them. A butterfly flitted among the wildflowers, alighting for a moment and then dancing away again.

"When one reaches our age," Ida said, "life becomes a succession of losses, of departures. I'll miss my father. I remember years ago, how I used to waken in the early morning and hear him walking along the corridor to my mother's room. When I passed her door I could hear them talking while they drank their morning cups of tea. Later, after she died, I never heard my father in the early morning again, except once. I heard a sound as I was passing her room and I looked in and he was on his knees beside her bed, crying."

"Life doesn't have to be all pain and suffering," Jethro said. "I've always believed it's what we make of it, at least for the most part."

Ida opened her handbag and brought out a wrinkled newspaper clipping.

"'Although General Beauregard,'" she read,

" 'claimed victory after the first day's fighting at Shiloh Church, the Confederate Army vacated the field the following day after the death in action of General Johnston and retired to the south. Our special correspondent in Corinth estimates our losses at over 10,000 men killed, wounded and missing. Northern losses are reliably believed to be significantly higher.' "

"I take it there's still no word of Nelson."

"No, none at all. Colonel Chesnut has made inquiries in Richmond and with General Beauregard himself. Nelson's name is carried on their rosters as missing."

"He could well be a prisoner of the Yankees. I wouldn't lose heart, Ida. I have a feeling that Nelson is still alive."

She shook her head. When he saw tears glistening in her eyes he took her hand and pressed it tightly between his own. With her other hand she brought a handkerchief from her pocket and dabbed at her face.

"You're right," she said. "Perhaps it's just as well my father passed on when he did. After his first stroke he was never himself again."

"I can still hear him. 'Times are bad,' he'd say, 'and they'll get worse.' "

Ida stood up. "Yes, that was the Old Colonel. This war distressed him, he thought it a great mistake. When he was younger . . ." She smiled faintly. "If you can think of seventy as being younger," she said. "Twenty years ago he never would have permitted me to grieve over Nelson before I knew for certain what had happened to him."

She started down the hill toward the carriage. "Will Jared be home again soon?" she asked.

"I never know when to expect him. He's been stationed in Wilmington and Richmond. He has something to do wtih the ships running the Yankee blockade. Money-suckers, leeches, that's what they are."

"Surely not Jared."

"Not Jared, the blockade-runners. The captains and their crews and their owners. They buy our cotton at five cents a pound and sell it in Nassau for fifty. They bring back tea and coffee and sell it at auction in the city for exorbitant prices. They take their ungodly profits and squander them on liquor and whores in Nassau. Pardon my language, Ida, it's a subject I've strong feelings about."

"Jared doesn't appear to have profited from his association with those people."

"Jared's never been particularly interested in money."

"I asked after him because of a matter he should know about. I only found out myself this last week."

Jethro handed her into the carriage. "Shall we take a short drive?" he asked. When she nodded he flicked the reins and the bays trotted toward the river, the air around them redolent with the scent of magnolias and roses.

"What did you find out?" Jethro asked.

"Aaron was here at Santee two months ago. Only for a few days, I understand, and neither Mr. Brady nor myself was aware of it. I don't know what happened between Aaron and your son in Wilmington. I don't believe I want to know."

"The fault may well rest with both of them," Jethro said. "Jared has an overbearing way with slaves. And Aaron, if I may say so, was spoiled by your son. Where did Aaron go when he left Santee?"

"No one seems to know. Even Melinda claims not to know."

"Is Melinda the young woman who—" He stopped in embarrassment.

"Yes," Ida said abruptly. "I've always believed she and Aaron would eventually marry," she went on after a pause. "I suspect he's gone north to try to make his way through the lines."

"If he did, he's making a grievous mistake. I've traveled in the North many times and I know their view of Negroes is much harsher than ours. We understand blacks and know how to deal with them. The Yankees think they understand them, though in their heart of hearts they secretly wish they'd disappear from the face of the earth. If Mr. Lincoln and others of his ilk had their way all the Negroes in America would be returned to Africa from whence their own Yankee ancestors brought them." He drew a deep breath. "Forgive me again, Ida. Our peculiar institution is another subject I feel strongly about."

"What will become of Santee?" Ida nodded to the chimney-studded roof of the plantation house visible above the trees. "What will become of us all?"

"There'll have to be changes," Jethro said. "We'll win the war, of course, first. After Shiloh we're in danger of losing the Mississippi Valley, but General Lee will win in Virginia, make no mistake about that. The Yankees will soon tire of the war. They're not fighting for their homes and freedom as we are."

"I never believed the war would last as long as it has. More than a year now! How long can it go on?"

Jethro shrugged. "As long as the Yankees refuse to listen to reason. There's even talk in the city that Lincoln's considering issuing a proclamation purporting to emancipate the slaves. It would be a terrible mistake. If he's foolish enough to do that, he'll be opening a Pandora's box of trouble—not only for us but for the North as well."

They left the carriage and walked to the piazza on the west side of the Santee house. Melinda came and stood in the doorway. When Ida shook her head, the slave nodded and slipped away.

"She's well-favored," Jethro said.

"The best house servant I ever had. I thought there might be jealousy when I sold the town house and brought her here to Santee. There wasn't. She behaved beautifully and she's been accepted without a whisper of ill feeling." Ida glanced to a table near the doorway. "Would you like a sherry cobbler, Jethro?" she asked.

He shook his head. The last year had aged Jethro Hunter, Ida realized. He was grayer than ever and his pace, as he walked nervously back and forth in front of her, was slowed. Suddenly he thrust his hand into his pocket and came to stand before her.

"This is for you," he said, bringing out a small black case.

Taking the case, which was in the shape of a book, Ida turned it in her hands.

"Look inside," he said.

She undid the clasp and lifted the cover, gasping in surprise as she looked down at the diamonds sparkling on the dark velvet lining.

"It's a necklace," he said. "Let me put it on for you."

Ida shook her head. "No, I can't accept it," she told him. "I couldn't possibly."

"I've been meaning to give it to you every day for the last three months," he said. "The time's always seemed wrong. I know this isn't the right time either but I've done with waiting."

"They're lovely." Ida gazed down at the gems which, she saw, formed a heart. "It's much too valuable a gift for me to accept."

"It's not as valuable as you might think. I paid for the necklace months ago with Confederate bonds before their value went down. This is a time to own things, Ida, not money. At least not Confederate money." He sighed. "Damn it," he said, "you've distracted me. I don't mean to offer you only the gift of the necklace, I mean to offer myself as well."

Laying the jewel case on the table beside her, Ida rose and walked to the railing where she gazed across the lawn to the fields in the distance. The sun was at the zenith and a shimmer of heat rose from the ground. She heard Jethro clear his throat. This was the moment she had been expecting, dreading, looking forward to, ever since spring of the year before.

"I know this isn't the way to ask you to marry me," Jethro said. "I'm a bumbler where the fair sex is concerned. I was a bumbler years ago when I first knew you and I still am today, only worse. I know I should have waited for moonlight and the scent of roses from the garden. I should have but, damn it, I didn't. Ida, I want you to be my wife. It's something I've wished for as long as I can remember, at least since Alexander died. I believe I've been gathering my nerve to ask you for the last year. No, that's not true, it's not the nerve I lacked. I didn't want to risk your saying no to me. I thought the better you knew me, the better my chances would be."

"I've come to know you very well over the last year."

"I realize you don't love me," Jethro said, "at least not in the way I hoped you would. I'm no fool, I can see and accept that fact. Yet I believe you've come to care for me, at least a little. The rest can come later. I've known many happily married couples who were hardly acquainted with one another when they wed. I can name several and I suspect you can as well. We've known each other for years, Ida. I love you and I need you."

She turned to face him. "You don't have to say any

more than you have, Jethro," she said. "I accept your proposal of marriage."

"Knowing someone well, sharing the same . . ." He stopped in mid-sentence and stared at her. "You accept?" he asked in disbelief.

"I've suspected you might ask me," she said. "I made up my mind weeks ago what my answer would be. The answer is yes, Jethro."

He stepped to her and took her in his arms, cradling her head against his chest. When he looked down at her, he saw tears in her eyes.

"They're tears of happiness, Jethro," she said.

He leaned to her, kissing her gently on the lips. After a moment she stepped away.

"I can't promise you all you might hope for," she told him. "You'll have to allow me time. And privacy."

"You can have all you need of both. I know now why men say, 'You've made me the happiest man in the world.' You have, Ida, you have."

He went to the table near the door and poured two glasses of wine. After handing one to her, they touched glasses. "To us," Jethro said, "to Jethro and Ida Hunter."

They sipped their drinks in silence.

"We'll be married in two weeks' time," he told her. "A small wedding, here at Santee or at Hunter Hill if you'd prefer, and then we can go into Charleston for our wedding trip. I think a longer journey would be inappropriate in a time of war." He stopped. "In fact, I feel like a youngster of twenty again. I realize I should be asking you, not telling you. Is that all right with you, the wedding, the wedding trip?"

"I think that would be just fine," Ida said. "A year ago, after Alexander died, I decided to stop running from life and I don't intend to start again. No matter what happens to our slaves or to our plantations,

we'll make the best of it, you and I, Jethro. I think
you'll find I'm my father's daughter in many ways. You
may be getting more than you bargained for."

"If I am," he said, smiling, "so much the better."

"I have one request," she told him. "When we come
back from the city after our wedding trip, I want to
have a ball here at Santee, Jethro, war or no war. I
want to have one last party, the kind we had before
the fighting started. I want that, Jethro."

He raised his glass. "And you shall have it. It will be
my wedding gift to you."

They heard shouts from the far side of the house.

"Could your people have heard the news already?"
Jethro asked. "I didn't expect quite such an instant
and exuberant celebration."

Ida walked to the railing and leaned over, peering
in the direction of the shouting. "I can't see what it
is," she said. "We'll have to go through the house to
the front."

They hurried along the hallway. When Jethro
opened the door, they saw Negroes running from behind the house and along the driveway, calling out
and waving.

"It's Aaron," Ida said. "Aaron's come back."

Aaron, astride a mule, had ridden out of the trees to
the curve of the driveway leading to the house. Behind
him, on a decrepit horse, rode another man, ragged,
his hair and beard long. He was dressed in the uniform
of the Confederate Army. When he looked up and saw
the house he straightened in the saddle.

"Nelson!" Ida cried.

She ran down the steps and along the drive. Nelson
saw her, reined in slowly and painfully dismounted.
He stood beside his horse, waiting, and she threw herself into his arms. She was crying.

"Oh, thank God, thank God," Ida said.

* * *

"So much has changed since I left." Nelson and his mother were in the parlor at Santee. He had changed clothes and shaved off the beard and moustache.

Though the sun had set two hours before, the day was still hot and Ida fanned herself with a slow, steady rhythm. She watched her son pace back and forth in front of her, but said nothing.

"Colleen's dead," he went on, "and the Old Colonel. And now you're to be married in two weeks."

"Jethro and I can always postpone the wedding. There's no reason we have to be married so soon."

"I don't suppose it matters when you get married. It's the idea of it that troubles me. Father's been dead such a short time."

"More than a year," Ida said. "I know you don't get along with Jared Hunter, but I never thought you harbored ill feelings toward his father as well."

"I don't."

Nelson stopped pacing and sat in a chair, realizing, when he saw his mother's quick look, that it was the Old Colonel's favorite rocker. He started to get up, changed his mind and leaned back, crossing his legs. "I have nothing against Jethro Hunter. I imagine I expected you'd never marry again."

"I have my own life to lead, Nelson," she said quietly.

"You have every right to marry, I don't deny that." He stood and walked to the large window overlooking the rose garden. "It's this damn weather. We need a good rain. The heat has all of us on edge."

"I'm only thankful you're home safely. Nothing matters to me as much as that."

"It was Aaron's doing. I owe my life to him. He found me on the battlefield at Shiloh and carried me

off. He borrowed a mule and we rode to Corinth but
the city was a pesthole. It was filled with troops. There
weren't enough surgeons to care for the wounded, and
there was disease and filth everywhere. Aaron took me
to a plantation near Decatur, where an old colored
woman cared for me, using herbs and potions and God
knows what else on my wounds. They worked. I survived. That's all anyone could ask who was in the
fighting at Shiloh. I suspect that battle made men of
peace out of a lot of people, Yankees as well as Confederates."

"Do you want to tell me about it?"

Nelson shook his head. "Perhaps someday I'll be
able to, but not now. I don't even want to think of it
any more than I have to. I'm wearied of wars and
fighting, mother."

"You've done your share."

"I'll go again if I'm needed. I don't want to, I'll hate
it, but if the South needs me, I'll go. We have to beat
the Yankees if we're ever to be free."

"Jethro feels the same way. He was telling me only
last week that we should press north from Virginia
into Maryland and strike at Washington City. Jethro
says . . ." Ida let her voice trail off.

"Jethro." Nelson walked from the window and sat
down again in the Old Colonel's rocker. "There's no
reason to postpone the wedding on my account. Have
the wedding, have the ball here at Santee. I may
sound bitter, mother, but I don't mean to. I've
changed, I hope, from the man I was a year ago.
From the boy I was a year ago. I know it's your life
and you have to do what you believe is best."

"We'll go ahead with our plans then." She looked at
him closely. "You may believe in your heart that I'm
betraying your father. I'm not, Nelson. We were never

close, Alexander and I, not after the first few years. It was my fault as much as his, of course, but he wasn't blameless."

"I admit that when I was younger I always felt closer to him than to you."

"I understand that, Nelson. The fault was mine. I was selfish, I'm afraid."

"Now it's almost like getting to know you all over again."

"I feel the same about you, Nelson. You *have* changed."

"My thinking has, at least. We'll have to do something about the slaves, mother. It's not only because Aaron saved my life, though that's a part of it. He didn't have to come to Shiloh. He traveled hundreds of miles looking for me when he could have run off to the Yankees at Hilton Head or in the North. He didn't, though, he came to be with me, almost as though he knew I'd need him."

"You and he were very close when you were boys. There's a bond between you."

"He was like a brother to me, as much as a Negro and a white can be brothers. Aaron saved my life but even before that I had second thoughts about slavery. Mother, slavery is wrong." He hit the side of the chair with his palm. "It's wrong, wrong, wrong. One man shouldn't own another no matter what the color of their skins might be."

"Slavery's doomed, Nelson."

He looked at her in surprise. "Then you agree with me?"

"Of course I do. And most women in the South would agree with you, at least in part. I always hoped and prayed the institution would die a natural death by becoming unnecessary or unprofitable. That would have happened after many years. Now, with the war, slavery's dying before our very eyes."

"You mean to free our slaves?"

"When the war is over, yes. Not now, we couldn't now. Besides, what would they do? Where would they go? We haven't the money to pay them laborer's wages, it's all we can do to feed and clothe and house them as it is. I do intend to free one of them, though."

"Melinda? Aaron told me today they want to marry as soon as they can."

"Yes, Melinda's the one. I've talked to her about it. She knows my intentions."

"I'm surprised, mother. In fact, you're continually surprising me. First when you took over Santee after father died, then when I found out you planned to marry Jethro Hunter, now freeing Melinda. I always sensed you didn't like her."

"And I don't. I never liked her, though the fault's not hers."

"She does act strange at times. She's always been afraid of me, drawing away as though I might, well, might hurt her. Not that I ever did or ever wanted to."

"There's a good reason for her acting like that. It's the same reason I've never been able to like her."

"And that is?"

"She's your sister, Nelson. To be more precise, Melinda is your half-sister."

Nelson stared at his mother. "My half-sister! Then you mean that my father, that he—"

"Exactly. Alexander Vaughan was her natural father, though he never acknowledged her, of course. I knew the truth, knew it from the first. How could I help knowing? Harriet Beecher Stowe didn't tell the worst of what we endure. She didn't tell of the husbands who go to the slave quarters and the wives who see them come back to share their beds, all the while knowing where they've been."

"My father. I didn't know. I never realized."

"I said it would be the women of the South who'd agree with you about ending slavery. Not the men, the women. Do you know why? Because we understand what it's like to be slaves. Not all of us, and I know I may be exaggerating, but that's how it felt at times, as though I was a slave or little better. The Negroes of the South are at the bottom and the women are just above them—and not far above them at that."

Nelson looked at his mother as though she was a woman he'd never seen before.

All at once she got up and half-walked, half-ran from the room. Nelson stood gazing after her, shaking his head.

"I'm not afraid of Massa Jared or what he might do," Aaron told Nelson.

"I'm not speaking of being afraid of him. It's only common sense for you to leave Santee. Where you go is up to you. You know I'll help you in every way I can. I'll never be able to repay you for saving my life at Shiloh."

"I don't expect no repayment. I did what I had to do. When I was here at Santee two months ago I asked my mammy, 'Where's Massa Nelson?' and when she told me I knew what it was I had to do and so I did it."

"Whatever your reasons were, you saved my life and I'm beholden to you as much as one man can ever be to another."

Nelson walked to the fireplace of the office on the first floor of the main house where he stared for a moment at last winter's ashes still laying in the grate.

"It's not just here at Santee, Massa Nelson. It's everywhere. Things has plain gone to hell."

"All the more reason to leave here while you can. What *are* your plans?"

"Me and Melinda are getting married. Then we're heading south to Hilton Head where the Yankees are. All the niggers there are free. And when the war's over and done with, I'll be close to Santee so's I can come back if I want."

"That sounds as good a plan as any. I have friends I can trust down in Beaufort. I'll write them, have them help you if you need help."

"I'd be mighty obliged if you did that."

"So when do you expect to leave? I'll not let Jared harm you but you are his property and there's no telling when he might come back from Wilmington. You've never told me all that happened there. I only know there's bad blood between you."

"He hurt me," Aaron said. "After I hurt him. The reason's neither here nor there. He'll likely try to kill me if he sets eyes on me again." The black shrugged. "It don't matter what he tries to do to me. What's going to happen, will happen."

"He won't harm you, Aaron," Nelson said. "I'll see to that."

"When we're leaving Santee depends on Melinda. If it was just me we'd be setting out tomorrow or the next day, soon's we packed what little we got. Melinda's bound and determined to stay till the wedding's over and the Missus is settled in with Massa Jethro."

"There's no reason for her to wait that long. I'll talk to Melinda and see if I can get her to change her mind."

"No amount of talking's going to sway her. You know what women are once they get a damn fool notion into their heads. There's no reasoning with them."

"I can't understand why she wants to stay."

Aaron shifted his feet uncomfortably.

"I know about Melinda," Nelson said. "My mother told me she's my half-sister. You mean you've known all along? And never said a word to me?"

"I thought if the good Lord wanted you to know He'd find a way to tell you without my help. And He did. I didn't think it would help you none to know."

"Is that why she wants to stay? Does she feel beholden to my mother in some odd way because of what my father did so many years ago? That's plain damn foolishness."

"You knows it's foolishness and I knows it's foolishness but does Melinda know it's foolishness? That's the question, Massa Nelson, and the answer is no. There's no use you talking to her, she's made up her mind. She's bound and determined to stay for the wedding and the celebration they're planning."

Nelson shook his head. "I suspect it's this weather. The heat's making everyone act peculiar."

"I can't remember it being so hot for so long at a stretch. When it finally rains, it is going to *rain*."

The storm clouds began gathering early in the afternoon of Jethro Hunter and Ida Vaughan's wedding day.

"It's lucky I'm superstitious," Ida said to Nelson as she looked at the thunderheads piled high in the western sky. "This is one bride the sun won't shine on."

Lightning flickered in the distance; the air had been sultry all day.

"The rain may hold off," he said.

Late in the afternoon a breeze swept across Santee but no rain followed. The wind quieted and Nelson thought the storm might miss the plantation altogether. Despite the clouds and the breeze the day remained hot, the air heavy and muggy. Fans gave little or no relief.

The wedding party, the bride and groom, Nelson and Mr. Brady, gathered in the front parlor shortly before eight. The wind came up again, rattling windows, making lamps flicker, and Melinda hurried from room to room latching windows and closing doors. Outside, the sky darkened to a midnight blackness.

A loud crack of thunder was followed by large drops of rain splashing on the window panes. More drops followed, the wind rose, lightning flickered in the distance and thunder rumbled. A great flash of lightning lit the room with an eerie white glow and thunder, a crashing crescendo, sounded almost immediately as the storm swept down on Santee with rain gusting against the sides of the house and beating a tattoo on the roof.

The Reverend Williams took his place in front of the stone fireplace.

"Will the bride and groom come and stand before me?" he requested. Jethro and Ida stepped forward, Ida gowned in a hoopskirted green brocade, Jethro wearing a brown frock coat and vest.

The minister opened the book he held in his hand. "Dearly beloved," he began.

The hall door opened, swinging back and slamming against the wall. A man stood in the doorway with water dripping from the brim of his hat, his long gray cloak dark from the rain. Jared Hunter threw his hat on a chair. When he swept off his cloak, the lamplight glinted on the sword at his side. The white scar on his cheek was clearly visible.

"I trust I'm not too late for my father's wedding," he said.

15

W E'RE ALMOST THERE," Jared said as the carriage
left the wooden bridge and passed into the long
tunnel of oaks.

"It's so lovely," Margaret said: "The stars, the moon
rising, the scents of summer all around us."

"South Carolina's the grandest state in all the Confederacy. Is there any wonder we'd give our lives
for it if need be?" Jared began whistling a stirring
marching tune.

"What is it?" Margaret asked when he paused. "The
name of the song you were whistling."

"I'm surprised you haven't heard it. It's 'The Bonnie Blue Flag.' Let me sing you a verse. It's from
New Orleans, I've been told." He started to sing
in a strong, unmelodious tenor:

We are a band of brothers, and native to the soil,

*Fighting for the property we gained by honest
    toil;
And when our rights were threatened, the cry
    rose near and far;
Hurrah for the bonnie Blue Flag that bears a
    single star!
Hurrah! hurrah! for the bonnie Blue Flag
That bears a single star.*

Maggie clapped her hands when he finished. "That
was splendid," she said. "Just splendid."

"And here we are."

The carriage rounded the last curve of the drive
and ahead of them she saw the house. Torches flared
besides steps leading to the piazza. The entire building was ablaze with lights and in the garden along
the side of the main house Japanese lanterns of red,
orange and yellow had been looped between the
trees.

"Santee," Jared said. "It's a handsome pile. The Old
Colonel must have spent a fortune to build the place.
It's nothing like our place."

"Remember you promised to show me Hunter Hill."

"And I shall, Maggie, I shall."

Jared handed her out of the carriage. "You're beautiful," he said.

Margaret wore a hoopskirted ball gown with a
bodice of gold satin. Narrow white lace edged the
low scoop neckline that left her shoulders bare; her
short sleeves were of ruffled lace. The full, sheer over-
skirt of gold tulle draped across the white satin of the
skirt in shirred swags edged with lace trim. In her red
hair, parted in the middle with long curls behind her
ears, she wore a gold satin ribbon tied in a bow.

They climbed the steps and Margaret swept into
the hall. Scores of candles flickered in a chandelier

over her head and, to her left, a stair curved into the upper reaches of the house.

A tall graying man dressed in a frock coat approached them.

"Father," Jared said. "I'd like you to meet Margaret Boyd. I've mentioned her in my letters. She's nursing now in a Charleston hospital."

Jethro bowed and raised her hand to his lips. "My wife and I are pleased you could come, Miss Boyd." He turned to his son and said, "She's even more beautiful than you claimed."

"Now I know from whom Jared inherits his gallantry," Margaret said.

When more couples crowded into the hall behind them, Jared took Margaret's arm and led her into rooms cleared for dancing. A small orchestra was playing a waltz, the music rising and falling, and Margaret saw beautiful women in hoopskirts, handsome men, mostly in Confederate gray, whirling around and around in front of her.

Jared took her in his arms and they danced, dipping and gliding. As the room circled about her, she glimpsed gilt chairs, men standing near the richly papered walls dressed in black broadcloth with white ruffles and wearing satin ties, older women with white feathers in their hair fanning themselves as they talked.

"It's enchanting," Margaret murmured. "Like a scene from a fairy tale."

"Everyone is here." Jared nodded to a couple dancing by. "Those are the Buchanans." As they passed another dancing couple, he whispered in her ear, "The Rhettes." She hardly heard him, excited as she was by his nearness, by the lilt of the music, by the gaiety of the women and the admiring glances of the men.

"The Petigrus," Jared said. "The Hamptons . . . the Chesnuts . . . the Randolphs. They're all here. All of

Charleston and most of South Carolina must be at Santee tonight. This is how it used to be at the Cecilia balls in the city before the war."

"If only there had never been a war!" She suddenly thought of Peter, of Buck and Alex.

"I shouldn't have mentioned it. Tonight there is no war. This is a night for us, for you and me."

He led her to the punch bowl. "This wine has made me so lightheaded," Margaret said, "that I want to dance and sing. What is it?"

"Champagne from the Old Colonel's cellars. They were once the best in this part of the state." He held up his glass as though he meant to propose a toast, then hesitated. "I have a notion."

Jared found a chair and climbed onto it, raising his hands and calling for attention. The music stopped and slowly the excited hubbub of talk quieted.

"I have two toasts to propose," Jared said.

Margaret looked up at him in his gray uniform, the saber at his side, the gold sash about his waist. He looked handsome. Dashing. Like a cavalier.

"To the South!" Jared shouted. The men cheered and the women clapped. They drank.

"To the bride and groom!" Jared called out. Again there was cheering and clapping.

The orchestra struck up a Viennese waltz and the floor cleared. Jethro walked through the archway from the entry hall with Ida on his arm. When he reached the center of the room, he bowed to his wife, murmured a few words and took her in his arms. They waltzed, looking into each other's eyes. After their first circle of the room another couple began to dance and soon the floor was crowded with rustling hoopskirts.

"That was a wonderful gesture," Margaret told Jared. "So romantic."

He bowed to her, took her hand and raised it to his lips. When she felt his tongue trace the lifeline on her palm she drew in her breath, staring at him, her mind in a whirl. Jared leaned close to whisper in her ear.

"I must dance with my new mother." He escorted Margaret to a chair next to Mrs. Chesnut. "You're the loveliest woman here," he told her and was gone.

As she watched Jared thread his way through the crowd to seek out his father and Ida Hunter, she had the impression someone was watching her. Shrugging the notion away, she looked back to the dance floor, where she saw Jared waltzing with Ida while his father stood to one side, smiling and nodding at something a portly man was saying.

Someone *was* watching her. More than watching, he was studying her. She turned slowly and saw a brown-haired young man in a frock coat staring at her. His eyes were unusual, she noticed, with flecks of yellow amidst the brown. She was accustomed to men's glances but this stare was not one of admiration; the young man's look was puzzled, unsure and uneasy.

When she looked at him, he walked to her and bowed.

"Permit me to introduce myself," he said. "I'm Nelson Hunter Vaughan."

Jared had mentioned that Ida Vaughan had a son. If Ida was now Jared's mother, this young man must be . . .

"Then you're Jared's brother."

"Good God, no!"

When she looked at him in surprise, color suffused Nelson's face. "I beg your pardon," he said. "Yes, you're quite right, I imagine we're now stepbrothers. I hadn't thought of it that way before." He smiled— insincerely, she thought.

"May I have this dance?" he asked. "In my brother's' stead?"

"I'd be delighted."

Margaret had expected Nelson to be an indifferent dancer but she soon found he was lighter on his feet than Jared despite the stiffness in one of his legs. Jared danced aggressively, often having to say, "Pardon, sir," or "Pardon, madame," as he nearly collided with other couples. She and Nelson, on the other hand, danced as one.

"I'm sorry if I was staring at you," Nelson said. "You reminded me of someone."

"Of anyone in particular?"

"No one I ever met. A picture, perhaps, or a dream. You're very lovely, Miss—"

"I'm sorry. I'm Margaret"—she paused imperceptibly—"Boyd."

"From Virginia, I believe?"

"A small town near Harper's Ferry."

"You sound more northern than southern."

"I've been told that before, Mr. Vaughan. I believe Jared has mentioned the fact that I don't have the delightfully slow speech of the South. Perhaps I've been infected by my relatives in the North."

"I believe Jared said you were a widow."

Margaret stopped dancing and stood staring up at him. Nelson returned her stare. "Yes, I'm a widow, Mr. Vaughan. My husband died quite unexpectedly and I took my maiden name. Is there anything else you'd like to know? If I had dreamed you'd be so interested I would have prepared a written summary of my antecedents and my life to date."

"Forgive me if I appeared rude," Nelson said. He added, perfunctorily, "I didn't expect we'd have much time together, knowing Jared, so I thought it best to find out as much as I could about you while I had the opportunity. There, I see him coming for you already."

"You've met Nelson," Jared said to Margaret.

"She has," Nelson said. "I'm afraid I failed to impress her with the charm of my conversation."

"Shall we dance?" Jared asked Margaret, who nodded.

"Wait." Nelson put his hand on Jared's sleeve. Jared let his arm fall to his side so that Nelson's hand dropped from him. "Aaron?" Nelson asked.

"In honor of my father's wedding, I've decided to forgive and forget. I never want to see Aaron again but I'll do nothing to cause him harm."

"Do I have your word on that?" Nelson asked.

Jared led Margaret to the dance floor. "Yes," he said over his shoulder.

"I can't say I particularly care for your new brother," Margaret said once they were dancing.

"My brother? Oh, you mean Nelson." Jared laughed. "Which do you take him for? Cain or Abel?"

"I don't understand."

"It's nothing. I was thinking aloud. Someone once told me they thought of myself and Nelson as being like Cain and Abel and I'm afraid they cast me in the role of Cain. I can't say I understand Nelson. I always took him for a dandy, though they say he fought bravely enough at Shiloh. Battle's the true test of a man."

"No, I don't believe that."

"Pardon me, sir," Jared said as he brushed against another couple as he and Margaret left the floor.

"One more glass of punch," he said, "and then we'll sample the food on the buffet before I take you for a drive. I have something I want to show you."

"I'm not terribly hungry," Margaret said, sipping the champagne punch.

"The ham and the jellies will keep, then. Come with me. Bring your glass with you if you want."

Taking her arm, he led her from the house. At the stable a Negro boy held the horses while Jared helped her into the carriage and climbed in after her. He flicked the reins and urged the horses around the house and along the road leading from Santee. Margaret looked behind her at the brightly lighted house, hearing the fading sounds of music and laughter.

Soon they were among the trees, riding in silence. She felt lightheaded from the wine and the dancing and when Jared put his arm around her she rested her head on his shoulder. Overhead the stars shone brilliantly in the vast vault of the sky, like a sparkling diadem she thought, and through the trees she saw the full moon rising large and golden.

They passed a long row of cypresses dark against the sky. "Hunter Hill begins here," Jared said. She warmed to the pride in his voice. They rode on between fields of cotton silvered by the moonlight.

"The plantation's so large," she said. "I never dreamed there'd be so much land."

"Our property extends all the way to the river on the west and to Santee on the east. Hunter Hill will be mine when I marry; my father promised it to me as the elder son. Of course he'll still have the tobacco plantations in Virginia. That land has belonged to our family for over one hundred years."

As they drove up a long hill Margaret saw a group of dark buildings ahead of them. At least she thought they were a cluster of buildings, but when they drew nearer she realized it was all one building, a vast rambling structure that sprawled across the top of the hill.

"Welcome to Hunter Hill," Jared said.

When he stopped the carriage she realized that,

except for a single light in one of the wings, the house was dark. Jared sprang to the ground and helped her from the carriage.

"Hector's about somewhere," he said. "The others are all at Santee."

"The others?" Margaret asked.

"Our slaves. There's a party at the slave quarters at Santee to celebrate the marriage." He opened the front door and she went in ahead of him, curious yet strangely ill-at-ease. She wondered why she was here; surely not to further her work for Alan Pinkerton. Why then?

Jared escorted her down a long, dark hallway and opened another door. "Wait here," he told her. She heard him cross the room, saw a match flare, and watched as he returned with a lamp in his hand.

"I'll show you the house." His voice was husky, causing her unease to mount. He stood looking at her, making no attempt to take her arm to lead her from the room.

"The house," she repeated. She felt the pounding of her heart, could hear her breath, loud and rapid.

Jared put the lamp on a table next to him. "You're beautiful," he said.

She waited, her pulse racing, her head whirling. I should say something to break this spell. I don't want him to touch me, she told herself—knowing full well he meant to take her in his arms, to hold here, to kiss her.

"I want you," he said.

She seemed frozen, unable to move.

Jared stepped to her and enfolded her in his arms. His lips crushed down on hers and he kissed her and for an instant she returned his kiss, her hand going to the nape of his neck. His lips left her mouth, trailed along her cheeks and across her eyelids. His hands grasped her bare shoulders and his lips went to her neck, his tongue seeking the hollow of her throat.

She gasped. Suddenly she felt as though she was standing in a chill draft. She tried to push Jared away but he held her to him, his hands gripping her arms, his lips going to the full upper curve of her breast.

"No," she whispered. "No, no, no." Margaret put her hands to his chest and pushed him away. He stepped back, releasing her.

"What's wrong?" he asked.

"I can't," she said.

She turned and ran from the room and into the entry hall, throwing open the first door. She ran on, expecting to find herself outside but she was in a dark corridor. She thought of Peter. How could she have let Jared touch her? Yet she had wanted him to; at least, for a moment she had. She had wanted him to kiss her, nothing more. Why had he tried to force her?

She stopped, breathing heavily. She didn't know where she was, she was lost in the dark maze of Hunter Hill. With one hand, she felt in front of her, touched a door and opened it. Another corridor, moonlight filtering in through open doors on one side. She heard the sound of footsteps behind her. A door opened and closed.

Jared. He was looking for her, pursuing her. She had to get away. Margaret raced along the hallway to a short flight of stairs, ran up the steps and opened the door at the top. She faced a blank wall. Turning, she ran back to the hall.

"Maggie! Maggie!" Jared's voice was loud and insistent.

She opened another door to a room where moonlight lay across a four-poster bed like a pale coverlet. She shut the door, opened another and saw a dark corridor, the only light coming from behind her. She hurried along, her skirts rustling, came to a turning, went on, came to another turning, ran up a short flight of stairs to a door and opened it, half expecting to see a wall blocking her way, instead finding another long corridor with moonlight streaming through a window at the far end.

As she hurried along the corridor, she saw the moon above trees, felt a breeze on her bare flesh. When she looked down, she found that her bodice had been pulled low, revealing almost all of one of her breasts. She pulled her dress up. She stopped at the window, putting her hands on the frame and pushing up, but the window was nailed shut.

She looked around her, hearing the sound of her own breathing, nothing more. There was a door to her right, another to her left. She opened the right-hand door. A sitting room, a low-burning lamp on a table. Margaret stepped inside, intending to turn up the lamp and take it with her. She was at the table when a figure rose from the darkness beyond the circle of light; a man, dark-faced, loomed over her. She screamed, turned, and fled the room.

Arms grasped and held her. She looked up. Jared.

"Maggie," he said. "Maggie, there's nothing to fear."

"Don't touch me." His arms dropped to his sides. "In there," she whispered. "A man."

"Hector," he said. "It's only Hector."

"Hector," she repeated. She drew in a shuddering breath.

"I'm sorry, Maggie," he said. "I didn't realize what I was doing. I couldn't help myself. Here, take my arm. I'll see you to the carriage."

She hesitated a moment before putting her hand on his sleeve.

"Will you accept my apology?" Jared asked. "Please."

He sounded ill-at-ease, making her suspect Jared Hunter seldom if ever found himself apologizing to anyone for anything. Did she mean that much to him? Surely not.

"I accept your apology," she said.

"I lost my head. The champagne, being alone with you, wanting you so terribly . . ."

Confused, angry with herself for being afraid, she said nothing and, in silence, they left Hunter Hill and began to drive back to Santee.

"Massa Nelson!"

Nelson looked around him to see where the voice came from. The open window? When he saw a face in the darkness outside he walked to the door and into the warm night.

"It's me, Aaron."

"I thought I recognized your voice," Nelson said.

"We're ready to leave, me and Melinda. We're all packed up and the mule's hitched. Melinda's seen Miss Ida married and safe to home so we're leaving."

Nelson grasped the black man by the shoulders, then embraced him. "God go with you," he said. "If there's anything I can do, write me. Hear?"

"I will Massa Nelson." Aaron stepped away and the two men stood gripping each other's arms. From the house came the lilt of laughter and the sound of the orchestra playing a sprightly air.

"When the war's over," Nelson said, "you and Melinda are to come back to Santee. There'll always be a place for both of you here. As free men. I mean that."

"I know you do," Aaron said. "We might well be back. This is home to us. And I don't know if I'm going to cotton to freedom, Yankee style."

Aaron turned away and Nelson watched the other

man walk toward the stable across a lawn silvered by moonlight. With sigh, he went back to the dancing.

Minutes later, Aaron, with Melinda beside him, drove their wagon around the side of the house to the front driveway. He glanced right and left before clucking to the mule to urge him on. A carriage approached as they were entering the tunnel under the oaks. Guiding the mule into the darkness at the side of the road, Aaron watched the carriage go by, glimpsing Jared in the driver's seat and the red-haired woman at his side. He didn't think Jared had seen him.

As soon as he was back at Santee, Jared nodded to a man lounging near the library door. The man crossed the room and left the house.

Margaret looked inquiringly at Jared.

"A friend," he said.

He was about to excuse himself when Margaret said, "Will you excuse me for a time, Jared? I'd like to freshen up."

He smiled and she noticed that his hand went to the scar on his left cheek, his finger tracing the white line.

"Of course," he said.

Jared watched until she was out of sight, then hurried from a side door to stand waiting in the darkness. After a few minutes a rider approached leading a second horse.

"They're only five minutes ahead of us," Jared said as he swung into the saddle. "This will be easier than I thought."

The two men galloped along the drive, passed in front of the house and rode into the trees. When he saw the dark shape of the wagon ahead of them, Jared slowed.

"Aaron," he called when the wagon entered a patch of moonlight.

"Aaron," he called again, "I've come for you."

He saw a figure stand in the wagon. "I got a gun here, Massa Jared," Aaron said. "And I ain't afraid to shoot."

"There's to be no shooting," Jared said, easing a rifle from its saddle scabbard. He had been careful to stop in the shadows.

"Aren't you going to ask what I want?" he said to Aaron.

Aaron said nothing.

Jared fired. The shot knocked Aaron from the wagon and sent him sprawling to the ground. The mule brayed. Jared swung from his horse and approached the wagon slowly, cautiously. Aaron's shotgun was on the road beside the wagon; Aaron lay next to the front left wheel.

Jared knelt at the Negro's side. Aaron was breathing. Taking out his sword, Jared held it to the Negro's chest and pushed down hard. Aaron moaned once and was still. When Jared pulled the sword from Aaron's body, he thrust it into the damp earth to clean it.

"The woman ain't here," the man said from the other side of the wagon. "I don't see hide nor hair of her."

"Let her go, Harry," Jared said. "I've no quarrel with her. This is the bastard I meant to kill."

"She'll talk. She probably knows who we are."

"Aaron's mine to do with as I please and she knows it. A nigger runs away, he's brought back and flogged. He runs away again, he's hanged. We're better off without this bastard around."

Harry said nothing. "We could hunt for her," he said after a moment. "We can scare her good if you don't want to kill her."

"I reckon she's scared enough as it is. She'll keep her peace. I've had dealings with her before and she said nothing. Now I want you to drag this nigger into the woods and bury him deep enough so he'll never be found. Understand me? And I want you to take this mule and wagon and get rid of them. I don't care what you do with them, just don't leave a trail leading back to us. Understand me?"

"I understand, Colonel Hunter."

"Good."

Jared returned to his horse and swung into the saddle to ride back to Santee. As he neared the house he heard voices singing a stirring song. At first he hummed the tune, then began to sing:

> *Then I wish I was in Dixie—*
> *Hooray, hooray!*
> *In Dixie's land I'll take my stand*
> *To live and die in Dixie.*
> *Away, away,*
> *Away down south in Dixie.*
> *Away, away,*
> *Away down south in Dixie.*

He was still humming when he entered the house. Seeing Nelson coming toward him, Jared smiled, clapping his cousin on the shoulder.

He looks strange, Nelson thought. Flushed. Excited. As though he's been with a woman. He glanced behind Jared and saw Margaret Boyd descending the stairs. Her color was heightened so that she seemed lovelier than ever, alive and vital. Nelson looked from her to Jared.

"I haven't seen you for the last hour or so," Nelson said to his cousin.

"Maggie and I drove over to Hunter Hill," Jared told him. "I'd promised to show her the old pile."

Margaret came to stand beside Jared.

"And how did you like Hunter Hill, Miss Boyd?" Nelson asked.

Margaret seemed confused. Nelson could have sworn she looked guilty. He sighed. Why did he feel this pang of disappointment? he wondered.

"As a matter of fact," she said, "I saw very little of Hunter Hill. I was impressed with what I did see."

Nelson nodded, turned and walked off without another word.

"Have I displeased him in some way?" she asked Jared.

"Don't mind Nels, I suspect he's envious of me. Because of you. It's been like that ever since the two of us were boys. Shall we dance?"

"You don't have your sword," Margaret said.

"I left it in the carriage. The damn thing gets in my way on the dance floor."

He bowed, held out his arms to her, and she stepped to him. They waltzed onto the floor, dancing around and around, dipping and gliding. As they passed an older woman sitting in a gilt chair, Margaret couldn't help overhearing her say to her companion, "Don't they make a striking couple?"

It was after midnight. The last of the carriages had left Santee and the great house was dark. Clouds sweeping down from the north had covered the stars and moon, and thunder rumbled somewhere in the distance. Behind the big house the slave quarters were quiet, the celebration over long before.

A woman crouched in a thicket near the river, listening to the growl of the thunder and the soft lapping of the water against the bank. She didn't know what to do. She was afraid, yet filled with hate. Aaron was dead, she was certain of that. When the horsemen pursued them, Aaron had told her to run and she had. When she heard a shot she started back, heard white men's voices, one, she was certain, Jared Hunter's. Melinda buried her face in her hands and cried. . . .

The bedroom was dark. Jethro was asleep. Ida lay staring into the darkness, listening to the thunder in the distance. Had it been the champagne? she wondered. No, not only that. Jethro had come to her tonight for the first time and she, to her surprise, had responded to him, tentatively at first and then with a frenzy she didn't understand. She smiled. Was she in love? After all these years? At her age . . . ?

Jared lay waiting for sleep. All in all, he thought, a good night's work. Maggie would come his way in time, he was positive. Be patient, give her time. He pictured her, the mistress of Hunter Hill, descending the curving stairs, resplendent in white and gold, while he waited for her in the hallway. He sat up. Yes, this was the woman he wanted to marry. Margaret Boyd was the woman he *would* marry. . . .

Margaret tossed restlessly, oblivious to the thunder. She had thought she would never again be aroused by a man, and yet Jared Hunter had aroused her, however briefly. Jared Hunter! She shook her head. No, I don't even like him. She looked to the window and saw the flicker of lightning beyond the trees. . . .

Nelson Vaughan placed the lighted candle at the side of his desk and pulled out the bottom drawer. He took the gold locket from its hiding place and opened it, staring at the daguerreotype for many minutes. There could be no question about it. The dead Yankee soldier had carried Margaret Boyd's picture. Why? Who was she? Why was she here?

BOOK IV

Turning Point

SHARPSBURG

16

MELINDA RETURNED to Santee in the early morning hours of the following day. With no plan in mind, she acted more by instinct than reason, knowing she had nowhere else to go, nowhere else to turn. There was nothing left for her now that Aaron was dead except an abiding hatred of Jared Hunter.

As she crept from the woods to the back of the main house, she heard a horseman ride off to the east where the sky was lightening with the first hint of dawn. Paying no heed to the sound, she slipped inside, finding the great house asleep and quiet. She went directly to the stairs and, with the assurance of long habit, climbed to the hall on the second floor.

Melinda entered Ida's sitting room and crossed to the desk in the far corner. When she tried the center drawer she discovered, as she had expected, that it was locked, so she opened the lowest drawer on the right side of the desk, felt for and found a key, and used it to unlock the drawer. Her hand closed on the grip of Ida's pistol.

After carefully closing and locking the drawer and returning the key to its hiding place, she went back into the hallway carrying the pistol at her side. She made her way to her right, knowing that the last room along the corridor, the room known at Santee as the red guest room, was Jared Hunter's.

When Melinda came to the door she lifted the latch and swung the door open. The room was shadowed by the dim gray light of early morning, paling the two windows to her left. She saw the outline of the high curved footpiece of the bed directly in front of her. There was no sound in the room other than her own breathing.

She walked into the room, her motions trancelike, leaving the door open behind her. Going to the side of the bed, she raised the pistol, aiming at the dark mass of bedclothes. As she started to pull the trigger, she stopped, sensing that something was wrong. She put her hand on the bed and leaned closer, listening. She heard nothing. Her hand explored the rumpled sheet. The bed was empty.

She swung about, thinking that Jared might by lying in wait behind her. The window curtain shivered slightly in the early morning breeze. The room, though, was as deserted as the bed.

Melinda walked slowly into the corridor, closing the door to Jared's room behind her. Still holding the pistol at her side, she climbed the stairs leading to the quarters of the house slaves and the storage rooms under the eaves.

"Your father looks quite handsome in all of them," Margaret said. She handed the photographs to Jared, who was sitting beside her on the divan in the front parlor. "You should have *your* photograph taken."

"I don't believe I'd have the patience to sit for ten or fifteen minutes without moving a muscle. The photographer would be left with nothing but a blur."

"As you probably know, they have braces to hold you steady that don't show in the pictures."

"You're quite the expert." Jared stacked the cardboard-framed pictures of Jethro and his new bride and laid them on the table. "You've been photographed?"

"Only once. Almost a year ago."

"Sitting for photographs was all the rage in Charleston before the war. Even General Beauregard found time to have his taken. I'd certainly like to see yours if you have it with you."

Margaret clenched her hands in her lap. Why had they started talking about photographs? she asked herself. "It was—" She paused. "It was lost," she said. "And the picture was a daguerreotype so there are no copies."

"A great loss."

"A great loss?" a voice repeated.

Jared and Margaret looked up to see Nelson standing in the doorway.

"A daguerreotype of Miss Boyd," Jared said. "She was telling me that she had but one, and that one was lost. Have you seen these photographs of the newly married couple?" He stood and handed the pictures to Nelson.

"I'm not intruding?" Nelson asked.

"Not at all," Jared said stiffly. "Miss Boyd and I were just about to say our goodbyes before we left for the city. She's expected at her hospital in Charleston this evening."

"Then you've eaten breakfast?"

"Hours ago. As a matter of fact, I was up before dawn for a morning ride around the plantation."

Nelson heard the rustle of a dress behind him and when he turned he found Melinda standing in the doorway. He was about to say they didn't need her when he realized she shouldn't be at Santee at all.

"Melinda," Nelson said, walking to her. "What are you doing here? Where's Aaron?"

Melinda brushed past Nelson, her eyes fixed on Jared who turned to face her. Margaret, startled, looked up at the young black woman. For a moment the only sound in the room was the ticking of the Seth Thomas clock on the mantel. Melinda took her hand from the concealing folds of her dress; she held a pistol. Raising her right arm until it was fully extended in front of her, she aimed the weapon at Jared Hunter.

Jared stared at the gun, not moving, his mouth slightly open as though in surprise. Margaret gasped. Nelson leaped forward, grasped Melinda's arm and pulled it down. The pistol fired and pain seared Nelson's calf. He wrenched Melinda's wrist, causing the gun to fly across the room and thud onto the carpet.

Melinda stared down at the stain of blood on Nelson's trousers. "He killed him," she said in a low voice.

"Killed who?" Nelson pulled up the leg of his trousers to expose the tear made by the bullet, a red crease two inches long, bloody but not deep. He tied a handkerchief around his leg.

"He killed him," Melinda said again. "He killed him."

"She's lying," Jared said.

Nelson shook her savagely, Melinda's head bobbing

back and forth. She started to cry, the tears coursing down her cheeks.

"Leave her alone." Margaret took one of Nelson's hands but he shook her off.

"Tell me!" he shouted.

"Massa Jared killed Aaron," she sobbed. "Last night. Not more than a mile from here. He shot him."

"She's lying," Jared said.

Nelson released Melinda and the young woman buried her face in her hands.

"What happened?" Ida came into the room as house slaves crowded the doorway behind her. "I thought I heard a shot."

"There's been an accident," Nelson said.

"An accident?" Ida looked down at her son's leg. "You're hurt."

"Not seriously," Margaret said. "Have someone bring bandages and I'll bind his wound."

Ida nodded to the doorway. "Abby," she said, "bring sheets from the linen closet." Ida glanced from her son to Melinda and then to Jared. "Tell me what happened, Jared," she said.

She saw Nelson and Jared exchange glances.

"It seems that Aaron had an accident last night," Jared said. "Melinda came back to Santee, found the pistol you see there on the carpet and brought it to us. While Nelson was examining the gun it went off."

Ida looked at him in disbelief. Finally she said, "Melinda, you're to come with me." When the black woman didn't move, Ida took her by the hand and led her from the room.

Jared watched Margaret clean and bandage the flesh wound on Nelson's leg. No one spoke. At last, in exasperation, Margaret burst out, "Why did you lie to her about what happened, Jared? Why did you say it was an accident when Melinda meant to shoot you?"

"This isn't your concern," Jared said. His voice softened. "I'm sorry, Maggie, yet what I say is true. I regret you became involved, that you had to be here this morning, yet you were here and there's nothing to be done about it now. This is a family matter between the Hunters and the Vaughans."

"No," Nelson said, "it's between me and Jared." He looked at Margaret. "He's right, this isn't your concern. The two of us will settle the matter in due course."

"The girl's lying, you know," Jared said to Nelson. "I haven't the slightest notion what became of Aaron. As you remember, I was at the ball last night when I wasn't driving Maggie to Hunter Hill. Whatever befell Aaron was none of my doing. I wouldn't be surprised to learn he's run off again."

"I'm glad to hear it was none of your doing." Jethro Hunter stood in the doorway. "Jared," he said, "if you'll come with me, please. I want a word with you."

Jared followed his father from the room.

"Aaron," Margaret said. "I remember that name. Isn't he the slave that was with Jared in Wilmington and before that in Richmond?"

"He is."

"They fought and Aaron ran away. Did Jared harm him? Did he kill him as the young woman says?"

"That's none of your concern." Nelson stood up and walked a few experimental steps on his wounded leg. "I don't mean to be churlish after you bandaged my wound, Miss Boyd, but the matter *is* between my cousin and myself. It's not your concern."

Margaret sighed. "I wouldn't walk for a day or

two," she told him. "You don't want the wound to start bleeding again. Have it newly bandaged every day and keep it clean. Your only danger now is if putrefaction sets in."

Nelson nodded and Margaret turned from him and crossed the room. When she reached the door, he called after her. "Miss Boyd," he said, "go back to wherever you came from. Please. Don't ask me why. And don't tell me it's none of my business. Just go. Take the first train north from Charleston and forget us. You'll be the better for it, I promise you."

"I don't know what you mean," she said.

"There's a curse on all of us," Nelson said. "On the Vaughans, on the Hunters, on all those handsome couples you saw dancing here last night. I don't know what the curse is or what brought it about, I only know it's there and before too many more years we'll all be the worse for it."

"You're being very melodramatic, Mr. Vaughan. You remind me of stories I once wrote, tales of princes and magicians and potions and ancient curses. I don't believe in curses and I don't think you do either."

"Do as I say," Nelson told her. "Please."

She smiled tentatively, as though not certain he was serious. After leaving the room, she hesitated at the foot of the stairs, knowing she should make sure all her packing had been done. Yet something nagged at her, words Jared had spoken the night before. What were they? She started to climb the stairs, still pondering, and then she remembered.

Margaret retraced her steps to the hall and went out through the front door. She followed the drive around the side of the house, with the stable to her left and the slave quarters behind the grape arbors to the right. The carriage that had brought them from

Charleston was in front of the stable. As she neared it a black boy led a horse from the barn.

"I was just going to hitch him up like Massa Jared told me to," the boy said.

Margaret nodded, paying him no heed as she looked inside the open carriage. A blanket lay in a heap on the floor; she pulled it to one side to reveal Jared's sheathed saber on the carriage floor. She took the sword from the carriage and held it in front of her in both of her hands, undecided.

Making up her mind, she drew out the saber and stared down at the discolored metal. When she put her finger to one of the smears, she nodded, certain the stain was dried blood. Drawing in her breath, she let it out with a sigh. But wait. Hadn't Melinda said that Aaron had been shot?

"What are you doing?"

Margaret swung around to find Jared watching her. Holding the saber and sheath over her head, she threw them from her to the ground.

"I believe the sword's yours," she said.

"It's mine."

"Did you kill him? Did you kill Aaron?"

Jared looked steadily at her with a half-smile on his face. He did do it, she told herself. He doesn't deny it; he did kill him.

"I warned you," Jared said, "that this wasn't your concern. You're interfering in affairs you know nothing of. Why did you come out here? What right did you have to take my saber? Answer me, what right did you have?"

"You haven't answered my question," Margaret said. "Did you kill Aaron?"

"Aaron was mine, he belonged to me. My father bought him from the Vaughans and gave him to me. You know he attacked me in Wilmington without cause, broke my leg. You ought to know, by God! That was how I met you."

"Did you kill him?" she repeated.

"Is that all you can say? Is that all you care about, what happened to a nigger slave you've never even seen? Is it?"

"Did you kill him? You won't answer me, will you, Jared? You're afraid to answer me because it's true what that girl said, you did kill Aaron."

"She lied. I didn't kill him. Why should I?"

"I don't believe you, you're lying to me. You killed him because of what happened in Wilmington, because of the bad blood between you. Admit you killed him."

"You say I'm lying?" His face paled as he glared at her and she was suddenly afraid of him. "You take the word of a nigger over mine?" he asked. "Who are you that you believe a nigger and not me?"

He stepped forward and grasped her wrist, pulling her to him. She drew back, fearful, and for a moment neither of them moved, frozen as though in a tableau. Then he pulled her to him, kissing her, and she beat at his shoulders and back with her fists until he released her.

"I don't want you to touch me," she said.

"Don't be a fool. What's the matter with you, Maggie? Have you completely lost your senses?"

She stared at him for a moment, her breath coming in gasps, and then Jared swung on his heel and walked off toward the front of the house. Jared Hunter had killed Aaron, she was certain. She began to walk slowly to the house, then stopped.

How many men have *you* killed? she asked herself. How many men have you sent to their deaths with your messages to Alan Pinkerton and his agents?

She recalled that she had another assignation the following evening in Charleston. How many more men will die because of you?

That was different, she reassured herself, that was war. The Rebels had killed Peter and she was only avenging his death. Killing men in war wasn't the coldblooded slaying that Aaron's death must have been a man killed because he was a slave, killed because of bad blood between slave and master. But was the war that much different, after all? Was there any reason why thousands of men and boys, Northern as well as Southern, had died at Manassas, at Shiloh, in Missouri, in Kentucky, in Tennessee, on the Peninsula in Virginia? Couldn't the quarrel between North and South have been settled without both sides resorting to this slaughter?

If women had more power, Margaret told herself, if they could vote, for example, there would be no more war. A mother, knowing her son might die, would do all she possibly could to prevent nations from fighting one another.

Mr. Niles had been wrong. She wouldn't one day write a book about growing up in Virginia. When this terrible war was over she would write about it, tell the truth, make war as horrible as it truly was so that men would try every other means to solve their disputes before they took up arms again.

Margaret dressed carefully, wearing her bonnet with the navy blue bow and fastening her gold breastpin above her heart. The man she was to meet a short while after sunset would be hatless, would carry a walking stick, and would have a black ribbon affixed to his right lapel.

She left the boarding house early and for a time walked aimlessly along the palmetto-lined streets of

Charleston. The late afternoon was warm and damp, as though a miasma had risen from the swamps near the town and crept into the city, and soon her face was beaded with perspiration.

The houses sat comfortably behind wrought iron fences amidst gardens ablaze with color, just as they had for countless decades. A charming city, she thought, old and proud. And doomed? She remembered Nelson Vaughan's words. The Vaughans were cursed, he had said, as were the Hunters and the South.

Margaret turned a corner and stopped, gasping. Ahead of her were the charred ruins of block after block of shops and homes with their brick chimneys pointing accusing fingers skyward. Only after a moment did she realize that these were not recent ruins but older ones. Here and there, new wooden frames already rose from the rubble.

A woman came to stand beside her, a short woman whose head was covered by a black shawl and whose face was lined by age. "I lost everything I had," she said to Margaret. "Even after all these months I come back, hoping to find it was all a dream, a nightmare. There was no warning. One minute I was embroidering in front of the hearth and the next minute I heard the fire bells and then I heard the flames. I lost everything I had, everything."

"I'm sorry," Margaret said. "Was it the war?"

"The war? No, not the war. No one knows how the fire started, perhaps a stove or a lamp. It was like a judgment on me, the fiery judgment of God."

"You'll be able to start anew," Margaret said.

The old woman shook her head. "It's too late for me to do that," she said. "When I was your age, I could have. Now I lack the will. They're nice enough, my son and his wife, but they have three children with a fourth on the way. They don't want me with them, though they claim they do. But where else is there for me to go?"

"There must be somewhere," Margaret said. "Other relatives, friends."

Again the old woman shook her head. "It's too late," she said. "You wouldn't understand. You're so young, you don't believe you'll ever be old. You will be, my dear, and when you are, God help you."

Margaret put out her hand to touch the woman's sleeve but she had already stepped away and was shambling off.

"God help you, God help all of us," the old woman said and was gone.

Margaret shivered, as though from a cold breeze, though the day was still warm. The setting sun touched the rooftops so she turned from the burned buildings and hurried along the street leading to the park at the Battery. After a few minutes she looked behind her and saw palmettos along the street, old homes set in their gardens, and the blue sky overhead. There was no sign of the burned houses, none at all.

The sky darkened and a breeze sprang up from the direction of the harbor. As she walked, lights came on in the houses along the way. Through a window across the street she saw a woman arranging flowers in a vase. She lifted the vase and brought it to the window to place it on a table, smiling in satisfaction before disappearing from view. In another window a man sat rocking, an older man peering at a newspaper through his spectacles. As Margaret watched he took a wine glass from a table beside him, held it before him and then raised it to his lips.

She heard laughter from a garden and looked

through a fence and saw children at play, a boy and a girl. The boy, stocky and smiling, reminded her of Alex and she felt a pang of homesickness for her children, for her house in Fairfield, for all the familiar sights and sounds and smells of New England.

Margaret walked on. Ahead of her was the park with the harbor beyond. Though the sun no longer glinted from the waves, the sky was still light and so she knew she was early. She waited on the sidewalk until a cab clattered past and then, walking slowly, crossed the street.

In the west the rim of the sun was resting on the hills and as she watched the orange disc slowly disappeared. She drew in her breath and began walking along a path leading into the park, with the bandstand to her right and the waters of Charleston harbor ahead of her.

This will be the last time, she vowed. Never again will I come here, never again will I help one man kill another.

She smiled ruefully to herself. Alan Pinkerton had been right. He hadn't wanted to employ her, sensing she didn't have the stomach for the work, so she had forced him to hire her. And she had done her work well. This, though, was the end. She would pass on this last message—the information she had gleaned in the last two weeks was meager enough—and then she would leave Charleston for the North.

A man approached along the path, a tall, dark-haired, hatless man carrying a walking stick. She glanced at his lapel, his left lapel. He wore no black ribbon; he wasn't the man she had come to meet. Noticing her glance, he nodded to her as he passed while she looked straight ahead.

Should she keep this rendezvous? she asked herself. Perhaps she should leave now while she had the chance and take the cars north to Richmond and make her way from there to Washington City. She had been alarmed by the way Jared had looked at her when she left Santee the day before.

He had stood on the front piazza of the house, his gray hat in his hand, and watched as she climbed into the carriage. She nodded to him and he raised his hat in salute.

"We'll meet again, you and I," he said.

She met his eyes without answering and then the driver flicked his quirt and they rolled along the roadway and into the trees. She resisted the urge to look back, knowing she would see Jared watching her from the top of the steps, his hat raised above his head, the sardonic smile still on his face.

Jared wanted her, she knew, and he loved her in his way and meant to have her. He was a man who wasn't accustomed to being denied. When she had accused him of killing Aaron and of lying about it she sensed that, at that moment, he was close to striking her, hurting her, perhaps killing her as he had killed the slave, and only his rigid self-control—what Jared had often referred to as his discipline—had saved her.

Now she wondered if there had been more meaning to his words than she suspected when he asked who she was to accept Melinda's word rather than his. Had she revealed too much of herself when she reviled him for killing Aaron? Wouldn't any woman, Northern or Southern, have done the same? She didn't know.

She did know that Jared had betrayed the *Celeste*, had been responsible for the ship's destruction as surely as if he had loaded and fired the Yankee guns that sent her to the bottom. He had revealed the *Celeste's* strategy to her and sooner or later he would connect that revelation and the sinking of the ship. Unless his sense of his own infallibility, which she realized was great, prevented him from seeing his actions clearly.

No, she wouldn't forsake her mission. She wouldn't be able to live with herself afterward if she fled from danger. First she would meet this agent, a man she had never seen, and tell him that this was her last rendezvous, that she meant to leave for the North and would have to be replaced.

The hair on the nape of her neck prickled.

Surely she was being followed. Never before had she had this sensation, this sure knowledge of being watched. Clenching her fists tightly against her body, she resisted the impulse to look behind her. Ahead, the path crossed another and when she reached the intersection she turned sharply to the right, glancing from the corners of her eyes.

Had she seen a man slip into the shadow of a building across the street? She kept her eyes on the spot for a moment and then looked away. Someone had been there who was now gone and she had the impression that it had been a familiar figure, a man she knew. You're imagining things, she chided herself, you're seeing things that don't exist.

Again she turned abruptly so she was walking toward the harbor. Ahead of her, indistinct in the fast-dimming light, was the dark pile of Fort Sumter. Looking to her right, she imagined a beach not more than fifty miles to the south, pictured the white sand and palm trees of an island she had never seen, Hilton Head, where her husband had fallen victim to a Rebel bullet.

A man was approaching her. He was of medium height, neither good-looking nor homely, his face plain and undistinguished with features one wouldn't remember for more than two minutes after seeing him His clothes were dark and unexceptional. In fact he was, all in all, a quite unexceptional man.

Except, she realized with a shiver of excitement as he drew closer, for three items. He was bareheaded —his brown hair was parted in the middle—and he carried a walking stick and he wore a black ribbon in the left lapel of his jacket.

As he neared, he glanced at Margaret and then away, looking beyond her. Yes, there was no doubt that this was the man she was to meet. And then he did a remarkable thing. Instead of nodding to her and raising his cane in salute before passing by to sit on a bench overlooking the water, as she had been told he would, he reached up and unfastened the ribbon on his left lapel and, turning it over, transferred it to the right side.

What did he mean by that? she wondered.

The man walked past her without making another sign. Puzzled, Margaret went on until, coming to a bench beside the path, she sat down and pretended to gaze out over the water while actually glancing back the way she had come. The man was walking on, a bit faster than before, she thought, along the path skirting the harbor.

Three men appeared in front of him, all dressed in civilian clothes, all walking purposefully toward him, one from his right, one from directly in front, the third, between the others, closing in at an angle.

The man immediately in front of Pinkerton's agent stopped and Margaret saw his lips move though she couldn't hear his words. The agent turned and ran back the way he had come, toward Margaret. The three men ran after him, their arms waving, and she saw they were brandishing pistols.

As the agent began to outdistance his pursuers, shots cracked one after the other, one, two, three. The agent stumbled and she thought he would fall but he recovered and ran on. A woman screamed and Margaret heard shouts from behind her. Two more shots cracked and the agent stumbled again and pitched forward onto his face on the grass beside the path.

Margaret was on her feet. The wounded man was only twenty feet from her. She ran to him and knelt at his side. He lifted his head, looking up at her hat and breastpin.

"Tell McClellan," he whispered. He coughed and choked.

"What? What?" she asked. "Tell McClellan what?"

The men who had fired the shots ran along the path toward them.

"Trust Dickens," the agent said. He opened his mouth to say more, choked again, and his eyes closed and his head dropped to the grass. Her hand went to his pulse.

The first of the three men stopped next to her and looked down. He was panting. "What did he say?" he asked.

Margaret shook her head. "I'm a nurse," she told him. "He's dead; you've killed him."

"We're officers of the law," the man said. "What did he say?"

"Nothing," she told them. "He mumbled a few words but I couldn't make them out."

From his hiding place across the street, Nelson watched a crowd gather in the park.

"A Yankee spy!" a man shouted.

When Nelson saw Margaret slip from the crowd and hurry away in the direction of the city, he nodded to himself, crossed the street and joined the others standing around the dead man.

There was no longer any doubt in his mind. Margaret Boyd was a Northern agent.

17

THE SLAVES LEFT SANTEE in a long single file with Caesar in the lead. They were field hands, their clothing rough, their faces shielded from the sun by battered broad-brimmed hats. Each man carried a spade on his shoulder. When they reached the small clearing where, the day before, Melinda had shown Caesar the place Aaron's wagon had been halted and she had fled into the woods, they laid their spades on the ground and gathered in a semi-circle around Caesar.

He was a middle-aged man, his hair graying, but he stood tall and the others looked to him as though by being the Old Colonel's body servant for so many years, he had inherited some measure of the Old Colonel's authority.

Ida had often said of Caesar, "He walks like the Old Colonel and he talks like him. At times, I even believe he thinks like him."

Now, an officer directing his men, Caesar sent search parties out in a half-circle from the spot where they had discovered traces of blood on the grass.

What about the other side of the road? he was asked. Shouldn't they search there as well?

Caesar put his thumb and forefinger to his chin, as the Old Colonel had often done, and pondered the question.

"No," he said. "Only this side. They wouldn't cross the road to bury him." The reason he knew this wasn't clear to him, but he was certain that whoever carried off Aaron's body would not have taken it to the far side of the road—just as he was certain that the body was buried near this spot.

The men tramped through the underbrush in a widening arc, walking slowly, stooping now and again to study the ground before moving on. A man called out and the others rushed to his side, Caesar pushing his way through the crowd and kneeling on the ground. The man who had shouted pointed to a boot-print in the soft earth.

Caesar nodded. A white man's print in a woods where no white man was likely to go. The print was deep as though the man was unusually heavy. Or carried a burden. And the print was fresh, surely no more than three days old.

The men went on in the direction of the boot's pointing toe. They had gone only a few hundred feet when the man who had found the print raised his hand and knelt. Caesar walked forward to kneel beside him, the others gathering behind. The ground was covered with brush, unnaturally so, as though the sticks and branches had been hastily dragged here and thrown to the ground in a cross-hatched pile. Beneath the brush the earth was raw.

"Bring them spades," Caesar ordered.

The men hurried away, crashing through the under-brush in their haste, and returned with the spades. After clearing away the piled brush they stood at the edges of a newly turned earth, realizing they formed a rough rectangle six feet long and two feet wide. All at once they were hesitant, as though no one wanted to be the first to dig.

"Hand me that spade," Caesar said to the man next to him.

Thrusting the spade into the ground, Caesar threw the dirt to one side, causing the men standing there to scramble back out of the way. The others started to dig, crowding around the growing excavation, cursing as they got in each other's way. At the depth of three feet one of the spades uncovered what appeared to be a swatch of black cloth. The men stopped digging and Caesar climbed into the hole and scooped the earth away from the cloth.

He uncovered first the bloodied chest and then the neck and face of a black man.

A shiver passed through the group of men around the rude grave.

"It's him," one said, "it's old Aaron."

Caesar scrambled out of the excavation and stood on its lip, looking down at the dead man while the others watched him.

"Dig up the body," Caesar said, "so's we can have Aaron buried proper in the graveyard."

Still they looked at him as though they expected him to speak, to give them strength in this time of trouble, perhaps, or to pronounce a eulogy for the dead man or to lead them, as Moses had led the Israelites out of Egypt. Caesar shook his head. Aaron would have had the right words, he thought, would have known what to say. But Aaron was dead.

He said the first words that came to his mind. "Times are bad," he told them.

"I admit it's horrible, finding Aaron's body, knowing he was killed and buried in the grove." Ida stood talking to Caesar with her hands clasped in front of her, conscious of Jethro behind her gazing into the cold and empty grate.

"Yes, missus," Caesar said.

"You have no way of knowing for certain who killed him, do you?"

"No, missus," Caesar said. "Not for certain."

"And now that he's buried you wish my permission to go into Charleston?"

"Yes, missus, I does."

"Why do you want to travel to the city, Caesar?"

"To tell Massa Nelson about what was done to Aaron. He'd want to know."

"I'm not sure that's a good idea," Ida said. "There's been so much trouble and now this."

"Let him go, Ida," Jethro told her. She glanced at him but he continued to gaze into the grate. "Let him go," he said again.

"I'll write a pass for you," Ida said to Caesar. "See me when you're ready to go."

"Thank you, missus." Caesar nodded and left the room.

"Jared must leave this house at once," Ida said as soon as the slave was gone. "I won't have him here any longer. I realize he's your son, Jethro, and I know you love him, but I cannot have him at Santee."

"Jared's already left. No, not because of this—this killing. He received a telegram from Richmond. A rider brought it out from the city this morning. He's been ordered north to take command of a regiment in Lee's Army of Northern Virginia." Jethro shook his head. "I looked at the body. Aaron was shot in the chest and then killed with what appeared to be a saber thrust through the heart. I can't believe Jared would have done that."

"He killed Spartacus last year with less reason than he had to kill Aaron. He hanged Spartacus."

"Jared's my son, Ida, my firstborn. A man's proud of all his children, but his firstborn son is different from the others. All my hopes are centered on him, all my dreams. He's me in a special way. I even gave him the same initial as mine. Jethro. Jared."

"I understand."

Ida went to him and laid her head against his chest and he remembered the four small headstones in the Santee cemetery, the first four of Ida's children. He put his arms around her.

"My love," he said, "my wife," and they stood with their arms about each other, clinging together in the front parlor of the great house on the Santee plantation near the Ashley River in the state of South Carolina in the second year of the Confederacy.

Nelson watched from the waiting room as the train outside gathered steam. Caesar had ridden off a few moments before to return to Santee, leaving him with the certain knowledge that Aaron had been murdered and that Jared had already left for Richmond and the Army of Northern Virginia.

There was no doubt in Nelson's mind that Jared had killed Aaron. He meant to find his cousin, confront him with that knowledge, and . . . He didn't know what he intended to do. Aaron would be avenged, he vowed, and he was the one who must do it.

The bell on the locomotive began an insistent clamor. "Board!" the conductor shouted, expanding the word into three syllables—"Ba-orr-dah!" he called again. Jared waited, watching the black smoke pouring from the funnel-shaped stack on the locomotive and swirling back above the coal car and the brigade of five passenger cars. The wheels groaned into motion and the train lurched ahead, slowly at first, then gathering speed. Only then did Nelson leave the waiting room, hurry across the platform and climb up the steps of the last of the cars.

Inside, he stood for a moment at the end of the car, glancing at the aisle separating the two rows of back-to-back cushioned seats, the potbellied stove standing to one side, the oil lamps on the wall along the other side. Nelson found a vacant seat—the car was less than half full—and put his hat and valise on the overhead rack. The car was hot from standing in the summer sun. He debated opening the window but when he saw gusts of smoke and cinders swirl past him he decided not to.

Settling himself in the corner next to the window, he felt the train gather speed, leaving the railroad yard behind and passing between rows of two-story wooden houses which soon gave way to fields and woods and an occasional farm.

Margaret Boyd, he knew, was in the car two ahead of his own. Convinced that she was a Yankee agent who had meant to meet the man killed at the Battery the day before, he intended to discover why she was traveling north and then turn her over to the authorities.

Ruefully, he admitted to himself that he had other reasons for following her onto the Richmond-bound cars. Who was the man he had killed, the man who carried Margaret Boyd's picture, the man who, as he faced death, had opened the locket to see her face one last time?

And, Nelson conceded, he was intrigued by Margaret Boyd herself. He liked to look at her, true enough, but there was more to his fascination with her than that. He had known other beautiful women, but Margaret was different, though he couldn't pinpoint the reasons he thought so. She was an unknown, he decided, like the beautifully wrought cover of a book that promised a delightful story within.

He bided his time, waiting until they were well east of Florence before retrieving his hat and making his way through the swaying cars. He stopped at the rear of the third car. Yes, there she was, sitting alone staring straight ahead as though lost in thought, paying no heed to the passing North Carolina landscape. Nelson walked along the aisle toward her, forced to hold onto a seat back as the train rounded a curve. As he stood slightly behind her, he gazed down at her radiant red hair.

After a moment she glanced up at him, her mouth opening in surprise, her eyes narrowing with suspicion.

"May I join you?" Nelson slipped into the seat beside her before she had a chance to respond. Margaret turned her head and gazed from the window at the passing telegraph poles.

How will I find out what I need to know? he wondered. If only I were a phrenologist able to read the bumps on her head or a gypsy who could decipher the tea leaves at the bottom of a cup. He was neither, though, and he believed in neither.

"They found Aaron's body." He meant to startle her and her sudden gasp told him he'd succeeded. "He was murdered," he went on, "he was shot and then stabbed with a saber. Stabbed through the heart."

Margaret's face paled and Nelson felt a surge of sympathy for her. He had an irrational desire to comfort and protect her. She doesn't need protection, he warned himself; she's more than capable of looking after herself.

"Why do you tell me these things?" she asked in a low voice. She glanced at him and again he was struck by the loveliness of her hazel eyes.

"I expect Jared Hunter will want to know what became of his slave. Aaron was his, you know. When you meet Jared in Richmond you can tell him that Aaron's dead."

"Jared? In Richmond?" She sounded genuinely puzzled.

"Don't you plan to meet him there?"

"I didn't even know he'd left Charleston. I never want to see him again," she added vehemently.

Nelson looked at her in surprise, at the same time feeling a rush of elation. "You don't?" he asked, forgetting his intention of catching her off-guard. "Why?"

"That, Mr. Vaughan," she told him, "is none of your concern." Again she looked away from him.

"Jared's been recalled to a command in the Army of Northern Virginia," Nelson said.

Margaret said nothing.

"Aaron and I grew up together at Santee. We were like brothers. When I find out who killed him . . ." He left the sentence unfinished.

Margaret had closed her eyes.

"A Yankee agent was shot and killed yesterday in Charleston," he said. "The account of the incident is in today's *Mercury*."

She opened her eyes for a moment, then closed them again. After several minutes of silence Nelson stood in the aisle, removed his coat after taking a newspaper from its pocket, placed the coat in the rack, and sat down and opened the paper. He pretended to read, occasionally glancing at Margaret who, he decided, was shamming sleep.

At last, tired of holding the paper in front of him, he folded it and laid it on the facing seat. He put his feet on the paper, leaned back and closed his eyes, listening to the steady clack-clack-clack of the wheels. These damn trains, he thought. You can't relax in them, much less sleep.

When he opened his eyes, Margaret was eating a chicken sandwich. He shook his head to clear it.

"You looked so comfortable," she said, "that I didn't wake you when we stopped for dinner. Not dinner, actually. They sold sandwiches from a cart beside the station."

Nelson realized he was hungry and that his wounded leg had begun to throb. He shifted his leg and the pain lessened. He looked enviously at the sandwich in Margaret's hand.

"I would have wakened you," she said, "if I'd imagined you'd be hungry. A gentleman was kind enough to bring me something to eat, so I didn't have to disturb you. Are all Carolinians so courteous?"

"Most of them are."

"I had him bring an extra sandwich in case you were hungry when you woke up." Margaret reached into the carpetbag at her feet and handed him a sandwich she had wrapped in a handkerchief.

"I hope you're quite recovered," she said as she watched him eat.

"Recovered?"

"You seemed to be suffering from dyspepsia or some disease of that sort when you first sat down next to me. Although I'm truly sorry about what happened to Aaron. I didn't mean to imply I wasn't."

He finished the sandwich. "I feel much better now."

The train grated to a stop at a small country station. "We'll be in these cars for days at this rate," he said.

Margaret took a bound ledgerlike book from her bag, opened it and began to write. "I'm keeping a journal," she said, "describing what I see and hear, what people say and do."

He had an idea while waiting for her to finish writing and, when she put her pencil away, he spoke. "I remember a game we used to play at Santee. I think the Old Colonel, he was my grandfather, learned to play it at Princeton. He attended college there before the turn of the century."

"I've always liked games," she said.

"Fine. If you'd like to join me it might help us pass the time."

"I warn you," she said, "I don't like to lose."

"Oh, this isn't that kind of a game." He nodded at her journal. "It's more of a storytelling game. Can you use a sheet of paper from your ledger?"

"I imagine I could." She opened the journal and tore out the last page.

"Now," he said, "imagine you're going to write a story about yourself. All right?"

She looked at him with an expectant half-smile. "Yes," she said.

"First tell us the season of the year when your story takes place." He paused while she wrote a word on the paper in her lap.

"Am I supposed to tell you the season I chose?"

"Not now. You may tell me later, when you're finished, if you want to. Next choose the time of day when your story takes place." Again he waited while she wrote. "Now in this story," he told her, "you're to imagine you're walking in the countryside when you come to three paths leading away from a fork in the road. The middle path goes directly to your home, the path to the right climbs gently through fields and groves of trees and along a low hill, while the lefthand path leads into a woods so thick you can't make out what lies ahead. Now write down which path you choose."

He watched her as she wrote. My God, he thought, she is a beautiful woman. Her skin so clear, her hair so lustrous, her eyes . . .

"What next?" she asked, startling him into awareness.

"Oh, yes." Nelson felt his face redden. "As you walk along the path you decided to follow, you meet a bear. You're to write down the kind of a bear it is and what you do when you see him." He paused until she looked up. "After leaving the bear," he said, "you come to water. You're to describe it."

"It can be a birdbath or a puddle or a pond? Even an ocean?"

"Yes, whatever you imagine it to be."

For a moment she looked from the train at a passing grove of pines, then wrote a few sentences.

"Finally," he said, "you come to a wall. This wall is high, so high you can't see over it, and it stretches away on both sides of you as far as you can see. You're to describe the wall and say what you do when you come to it."

"Is that all?" she asked when she finished.

"Yes, the wall's the end," Nelson told her.

"I don't think I understand," she said.

"That's the end of the game unless you want to tell me what you wrote so I can try to interpret what your story means. Of course, this is all nonsense, but what your story supposedly reveals is your character. Just as the lines in your palm are said to do."

"Now I *am* curious," Margaret said. "There's nothing I've written that I couldn't read to anyone."

"Good. Tell me what you wrote and I, the Great

Nelson, will reveal the secrets of your life. To begin, what was the season of the year?"

"I chose spring."

"Ah, that means you see yourself as being young, as coming to life just as the Earth comes to life in the spring of the year. And the time of day?"

"Dawn."

"The meaning's the same. A beginning or a new beginning. Your entire day, your life, lies ahead of you. No matter what your age might be, you're young at heart. At least that's what the Old Colonel would have said."

"Even from the little I've heard about the Old Colonel, I know I would have liked him."

"You would have. He was a grand old man of a breed you don't find anymore, even in South Carolina. And he would have liked you. Even in his eighties he had an eye for a beautiful woman."

"You were telling me what my story meant," she said. "I chose the third path, the one leading into the dense forest."

"You're an adventurer, you enjoy the unknown, you like to take risks. Perhaps it means you're a romantic as well, I can't recall for certain. At least you're willing to dare the unknown. And on that path, I believe you met a bear."

"Mine was a grizzly standing on his hind legs."

"The bear, if I remember a-right, shows the troubles you see yourself facing. If you had chosen a small bear—perhaps even a toy one—your troubles, or how you see them, would be small ones. A grizzly, you say?"

"He was standing in the path blocking my way."

"The kind of b'ar Davy Crocket would have slain with his bare hands." His tone was light but he looked at her closely. "Your troubles, I'm sorry to

say, are horrendous ones and you see little chance
of escaping them. Except, perhaps, by running away."

"That's exactly what I imagined myself doing. Running from the bear."

"The water was next."

"I saw a great lake. Though it was in the spring
of the year, the water along the shore was still frozen.
Beyond the ice was open water beneath a blue sky.
Even though the day was clear, there were waves, so
high they were capable of capsizing a ship and sending her and all aboard her to their deaths."

"The water," Nelson said, "represents your life of
the senses, your physical life, not the spiritual. Yours
is turbulent, it's easy to see that, though I don't understand what the ice means or the high waves and
the sinking ship."

Margaret looked away from him to the window but
in the reflection in the glass her face appeared troubled. "And the wall?" she asked. "In my story I didn't
try to climb the wall. I was afraid of what I might
find on the other side."

"The wall is death. Your death, perhaps, or the
death of others. How you envision death. You're
afraid of it, especially of a watery death. I don't
know why, of course; only you can tell me that.
Can you tell me the reason, Margaret?"

She stared at him for a moment, her eyes wide.
Suddenly she stood up, her journal falling to the
floor of the car, and pushed past him to the aisle.

"No," she said, "I can't tell you. And I don't believe this was a game you learned from your grandfather. I think you concocted it, all of it, and in-
vented what my answers meant as well. I don't know
why you're here or what you want. I only know I
want no part of it or of you."

"Then the things I told you weren't true?" Nelson

asked. "You couldn't see yourself in the person I
described?"

"I never said that." Margaret's voice rose. "Did I
ever say that? I'm not accustomed to lying and I
don't mean to begin now. I want to . . ."

The train slowed suddenly, brakes squealing, and
lurched to a stop, throwing Nelson forward toward
the facing seat so he had to put up his hands to
stop himself from falling. Out of the corner of his
eye he saw Margaret hurled to the floor. Bags fell
from the overhead racks and all up and down the
car men and women shouted in panic.

Nelson leaned over Margaret, turning her onto her
back. Her face was pale and her eyes were closed
but she was breathing. "Margaret," he said. "Maggie, Maggie."

"Oh, Jared," Dyan said, "I loved the dinner and
the wine and the flowers you brought me. After you
left Richmond for Wilmington last February, I said
to myself, 'Dyan, you're never going to see that handsome Colonel Hunter again.' I knew about Colleen
Hughes, of course. I loved Colleen and when I heard
she had drowned when the *Celeste* went down I
cried my eyes out. Not only for her but for you as
well, knowing how you must have felt because you
loved her so."

"Here," Jared said, "let me take your hand and
help you from the carriage."

"Thank you, Jared. Do you know, you're one of
the most gallant gentlemen I know? I've met a great
many officers with gentlemanly pretensions, as of
course I would with my father being on General
Beauregard's staff and then on General Lee's, but the
men from South Carolina are the only true gentlemen in the Confederate Army."

"We'll go in through the back door. It's always so crowded in the lobby."

"You're a tragic figure, Jared, with your fiancée being drowned while sailing to Nassau in your stead on a secret mission after you were set upon by an ungrateful slave. No one blames you for what happened to her, not in the slightest."

"We have to be quiet in this hallway, Dyan. That's the door to the Chesnuts' rooms and you've probably heard what sticklers for propriety they are."

"Oh, fiddlesticks, Jared. What do I care what Mary Chesnut might think or say? I'm old enough to visit a man in his rooms. If she doesn't like it, you know what she can do."

"We go up these stairs. My room's the first door at the top."

"I must have had too much of that wine, Jared. I am decidedly lightheaded. Is this your room? Why, it's lovely. You have a much nicer view from here than they do from the rooms on the other side of the hotel. How do I know? Why, my father stayed there once, that's how. This is a good bed; here, feel, it's not too hard and not too soft."

"You're a lovely girl, Dyan."

"Do you really think so, Jared? My father says I've put on too much weight since I came to Richmond. And in all the wrong places, according to him. You don't think I have, do you, Jared? Oh, Jared, kiss me again. Just like that. Oh, Jared, that was so nice. It's been so long since we've been together. I've missed you, I really have. As they say, it's an ill wind that blows no good."

Jared sat on the bed beside her. "Turn around," he said.

"What do you mean to do, sir?" Dyan giggled. "I should have guessed you were going to undo those buttons. No, there's one more. Yes, that's all of them."

"Do you want me to turn off the lamp?"

"Leave it on. I want to see you. You don't believe I'm immodest for wanting to, do you?"

"No, I don't." He stood up beside the bed and began taking off his clothes. "Take off your gown, Dyan," he told her.

He heard her breathing quicken. She stepped from the dress, removed her petticoat and her camisole, and stood naked before him.

"I feel all fluttery inside," she said, crossing her arms over her breasts. She drew down the sheet, slid into bed and pulled the sheet up to her chin.

"Hurry, Jared," she said. "Please, please hurry."

He threw the last of his clothes to the floor, held the sheet aside and for a moment lay on the edge of the bed staring at her, his eyes roving from the lush paleness of her breasts with their pink nipples to the dark secret places below. She *was* plumper than she had been; her father was right. With a sigh mingling disappointment with desire, he took her in his arms and kissed her.

When at last she turned her head away, she said, "Tell me about the war."

"The war?"

"You remember. Like you did the last time I saw you. Tell me about the battle at Manassas."

He had, in fact, remembered, but he'd hoped she'd forgotten.

"The firing was fierce," he said, closing his eyes. "The men aligned themselves in battle formation and charged the Yankees as shot and shell tore through their ranks. Men fell to my right and to my left, bleeding, horribly wounded men, men dead with minié balls through their hearts . . ."

He described the heat of the day and the carnage,

the soldiers lying wounded and dying on the field, and as he talked her breasts rose and fell and her mouth opened and she kissed him deeply. He felt her fingers seek and find him, leading him to her and into her, and he pleasured her, still telling her of the battle and the fear and agony he had seen in men's eyes. As he talked her fingernails bit into his back until at last, her body slick with perspiration, her blonde hair bedraggled about her face, her legs wrapped about him, she trembled against him.

When it was over he lay beside her. He hated her, he decided. There was a sickness in Dyan, not of the body but of the mind. He wondered why he was here with her, why he had brought her to his bed. Was his luck, which had run so strong for so many years, changing for the worse? Colleen was dead, Maggie had spurned him, and here he was with Dyan Raleigh-Beckwith. He turned from her, cursing her, but she was asleep and didn't hear him.

18

A s OTHER PASSENGERS pushed past him, Nelson put his arms beneath Margaret's shoulders and knees and lifted her from the aisle of the train. He stood and carried her to the door at the end of the car. He hurried, fearing a fire, although he knew the chance of a conflagration was less in the summer because the fires weren't lit in the stoves.

He climbed awkwardly from the car and stood in the gravel beside the track. Looking over the heads of the men and women milling around him, he saw the locomotive sitting atilt as though it had left the track. He made his way forward along the sides of the cars, holding Margaret close to him, breathing in the delicious fragrance of her, the scent of flowers.

"Damn roadbed's been washed out," he heard a man say as he neared the crowd gaping at the disabled locomotive. Smoke still drifted up from the funnel-shaped stack and steam eddied around the wheels and boiler. The engineer stood to one side, gazing disconsolately at the damage.

"A doctor," Nelson said loudly. "Is there a doctor on the train? This lady's been hurt."

Men and women turned to look at him, shaking their heads.

"A concussion, more than like," an older man with bushy sidewhiskers said. "All she needs is rest."

"There's a doctor in the village over yonder," a boy told Nelson, pointing across a field.

"Yes," an older man, evidently the boy's father, said. "Dr. . ." He searched his memory. "Dr. Garwood, I believe his name it. We're from the next town over," he added. "We boarded the cars at the last stop."

Nelson looked in the direction the boy had pointed and, past a fringe of trees, saw the roofs of houses.

"If I was you," the man said, "I'd take my wife to that doctor. There's no telling how long we'll be stranded here. This goddamn railroad."

"She's not my wife," Nelson began, but the man had already turned from him to listen to the engineer.

"At least till morning," the trainman was saying. "They'll have to bring a crew from Weldon to repair the track and the roadbed."

"Tomorrow morning," someone groaned.

"You're welcome to make yourselves comfortable in the cars," the conductor told them.

Nelson looked around. No one else appeared to be injured and no doctor had volunteered his services. Well, he thought, at least the village isn't far, a mile at the most. Returning to the cars, he laid Margaret on the grass beside the train, retrieved her carpetbag and his own valise and, holding her awkwardly in his arms while carrying the bags in one hand, he set off across the field in the direction of the village.

The sun, lowering in the west, was still hot and he sweated as he trudged along a rutted lane. Corn grew as high as his head in the field beside him and a crow cawed overhead. The village was farther away than he'd thought.

He glanced down at Margaret and found that she was breathing regularly, her breasts rising and falling, her mouth partly open, her eyes closed. He was certain she was all right; he willed her to be all right. He felt responsible for her. After all, he had been the one who had goaded her to leave her seat just before the train came to its sudden halt.

He followed a path through the woods, crossed a small creek by stepping from rock to rock, and found the continuation of the path on the far side. The sun shone through the branches of the trees, dappling the ground ahead of him, and he remembered another day when, near a church called Shiloh, he had carried a young boy from Alabama across a battlefield only to discover that the boy was dead.

He remembered opening his eyes later near the same battlefield to find himself across Aaron's shoulders, remembered being lifted to the back of a mule and riding mile after mile away from the stench of the dead and the dying. Aaron was now dead; Jared had killed him. Nelson sighed, pushing the memory away. Trying unsuccessfully to push the memory away. He'd never forget the swaying of the mule and the pain from the wounds in his back and leg.

His leg ached now. He should have changed the bandage before this; he'd ask the doctor to look at his wound once he was sure Margaret was all right. He stopped walking, lowered her to the ground, and rested. As soon as he regained his wind, he gathered her into his arms again, picked up the bags, and limped on.

His face felt flushed and hot from the heat of the day. Or perhaps he was feverish. Melinda, while intending to shoot Jared, had wounded him instead. Through chance, yes, but he believed there was a meaning in what had happened. Melinda was not meant to kill Jared. Nelson Hunter Vaughan was, and his wound was a reminder of that fact, a reminder that Aaron had saved his life, a reminder that as an indirect result of Aaron's bringing him home to Santee, the slave was now dead.

You *are* feverish, Nelson told himself. You're finding meanings where there are none, seeing portents where none exist. But the fact remained that he was beholden to Aaron. Ever since Aaron's death he had put off thinking of what he must do to avenge him. Now he knew, without doubt and without reservation.

He must seek out Jared Hunter and kill him.

Nelson shrank from the thought. Kill a blood relation over the death of a Negro? There had been so much killing already. The casualty lists in the newspapers grew longer with every passing week. Death followed death, Northern and Southern, deaths without end. And yet there must be one more. Jared Hunter's.

Nelson was nearing the first house, an unpainted one-story building on a dirt road that came to a dead end at the field he had crossed. Finding a break in the stake fence bordering the field, he approached the house along a weed-grown path as chickens scattered from under his feet and a dog barked in the rear of the house.

A thin woman with wispy brown hair opened the

front door. "Land of Goshen!" she said. "What on earth—"

"The locomotive derailed," Nelson told her. "This lady was hurt. Is there a doctor in the village?"

"Dr. Garwood, yes." She nodded along the road. "You go around the bend and then turn left at the next street and it's the second house past the livery stable on the left. Garwood's place is the big white house, you can't miss it. Is there anything I can do?"

"No, no," Nelson said. "I'll carry her to the doctor's."

The woman came down the steps to the path. "Your wife's such a pretty woman," she said. "It would be a shame if anything happened to her." She walked beside Nelson to the road. "I recall the time George Worthington fell from the roof of his barn. He wasn't even unconscious though they saw blood coming out of his ear. He got up and went about his work as if nothing had happened and an hour later he fell over dead."

Nelson increased his pace. "I'm certain she'll be all right," he said. "And thank you."

"I'll pray for her." The woman stopped at a row of trees bordering her property. "What's her name?"

"Margaret," Nelson told her.

He met no one else along the way, although he saw men lounging behind the livery. The doctor's house, a large two-storied wooden building, sat on a low knoll surrounded by trees. The house had once been white but now the paint was faded and peeling.

As Nelson climbed the steps to the piazza, a young man on crutches hobbled around the corner of the house. The two men stared at each other and then the injured man swung clumsily about and disappeared to the rear.

Nelson pulled the bell handle and heard a clang

on the other side of the door. He waited. When there was no answering sound from inside, he rang again. The door swung open almost at once and an old woman, small and hunchbacked, looked up at him and his burden.

"You'll be wanting to see the doctor." She stepped aside and he thought she was nodding to him before he realized the motion of her head never stopped. She led Nelson down a dark corridor to a small sitting room. "If you'll lay her there." Margaret's eyes opened as Nelson laid her on the couch to the right of the door.

"Trust Dickens," she whispered.

Nelson leaned closer. "What?" he asked.

"Trust Dickens," she said again, and then her eyes closed.

"Bring her into my office."

Nelson looked over his shoulder to see a querulous-looking older man with a graying beard and unkempt gray hair. His dark suit was badly rumpled. Nelson left the two bags on the floor and took Margaret in his arms once again to follow the doctor into a cluttered office. He laid her on a raised examining table.

"I'm Dr. Garwood," the bearded man said. "What's the trouble here?" His fingers held Margaret's wrist to take her pulse.

Nelson described the accident and Margaret's fall.

"That damn rail line," Dr. Garwood said. "If we've had one wreck we've had a hundred and one. Three men were killed only last month when the bridge over Otter Creek gave way. Where did she strike her head?"

"I'm not certain," Nelson said.

Dr. Garwood gave him a scornful glance. Lifting Margaret's hair, which had come loose from her chignon, he began probing her head.

"Here we are," he said. "She has a nasty swelling." Margaret shifted on the table, moaning softly. "A mild concussion, I suspect," the doctor said.

He went to a cabinet behind his desk and returned with a small-necked brown bottle. Uncorking the bottle near Margaret's nose, he waved it back and forth. Nelson caught a whiff of the penetrating odor.

"Spirits of ammonia," the doctor said.

Margaret opened her eyes.

"There, you see," the doctor said, "there's nothing to be alarmed about. Where were you and your wife bound?"

"Richmond," he said. "And she's . . ."

"You're an able-bodied young man," Dr. Garwood interrupted. "I'm surprised you're not fighting for your country."

Nelson started to say he *had* fought, but stopped. Somehow, without reason, he didn't want to have to defend himself to this man. And then he changed his mind again.

"I was at Shiloh," he said evenly. "I was wounded and sent home on an injury furlough." And he added words that surprised him. "I'm heading north now to join Lee's army in northern Virginia."

Jared was on his way there, he knew, and somehow, somewhere, he would find him.

"It weren't any of my damn business in the first place," Dr. Garwood said. "My son was wounded in the fighting around Richmond. He's home. I don't expect he'll ever walk again, at least not walk right. He took a minié ball in the knee."

"I saw him when I came in," Nelson said.

The doctor looked down at his patient. "And how are you feeling, young lady?" he asked.

Margaret put her hand to her forehead. "Joining the army," she said, repeating Nelson's words.

"She's still a mite dazed," the doctor said to Nelson, "and her head probably hurts like the blue blazes. How are you?" he asked Margaret again.

"Head . . . hurts," she said slowly.

"You'll have to apply damp compresses for a time," the doctor told Nelson. "She'll be perfectly all right. She's young and healthy. A little fall shouldn't bother her."

"I'm not taking her back to that train today," Nelson said. "They'll probably not leave until tomorrow anyway, or so they said. Is there a hotel in the village?"

"Tomorrow? It'll more likely be the day after, if then. If I ran my practice like they run their rail line, there'd be no room left in the cemetery."

"The cemetery," Margaret said, trying to sit up.

Dr. Garwood held her by the shoulders and gently pushed her down on the table. "No, no, don't try to get up. After a night's sleep you'll be as good as new. No need to rush it." He looked at Nelson. "I shouldn't have mentioned cemeteries. We doctors forget how much patients hear of what we say and how they always believe we're talking about them. If you mention the word death they believe they're dying and if you say the word cancer they believe they have one. A hotel? No, there's no hotel here in the village. Mrs. Addison over on Cypress Street used to take in a few boarders but she died last January."

"There must be somewhere we can go," Nelson said.

"Of course there is. Both of you can stay here for the night. I've little to offer. My wife passed away in the typhoid epidemic last year and Agnes isn't the cook and housekeeper she once was. Denton does nothing, absolutely nothing, hardly has a civil word to say and hasn't since he hobbled home from the North on his crutches. As you can tell, I'm not the most civil of hosts. And why should I be with men intent on killing each other off the way they are? Isn't it bad enough to have to die of disease and pestilence without shooting one another with minié balls?"

"I thank you most kindly for your offer of a place to stay," Nelson said, "and we'll accept it."

He went to stand beside Margaret.

"You've got a limp," the doctor said. "I missed seeing that before. From Shiloh?"

"No, an accident. As a matter of fact, the leg's bothering me some. I'm afraid the dressing needs changing."

"Sit in the chair there and I'll take a look."

Dr. Garwood began peeling off the strips of linen binding Nelson's wound. Nelso winced as the badage came unstuck, sarrying away a fragment of dead flesh. A trickle of dark blood ran down his leg.

"Seems a trifle putrid," Dr. Garwood said. "I'll wash it out with aloe water and bind it up again."

When the doctor finished wrapping strips of muslin around Nelson's leg, he stood, wiping his fingers on a hand towel laying on the examining table near Margaret's feet.

"I'll show you to your room," Dr. Garwood said. "Agnes can't manage the stair, not with her arthritis as bad as it's gotten the last year or two. Besides having the palsy. Can you carry the young lady? Of course you can, that's how you brought her here. I'm Denton Garwood," he said. "My son's Denton, I'm Denton, and my father was Denton."

"I'm Nelson Hunter Vaughan. And this is Margaret." The hell with it, he thought, he wasn't going to explain their relationship now.

Dr. Garwood opened his office door and Nelson took

Margaret in his arms and followed him up steep stairs to the gloomy second floor of the house. The doctor showed him to a room and watched as he laid Margaret on the bed.

"Cool moist applications," he said. "You can get the water from the kitchen pump. I should apologize for the dust in this room but I won't."

As soon as the doctor left, Nelson knelt beside the bed. "Are you all right?" he asked Margaret. "I'll bring water for you to drink. Are you hungry? Would you like something to eat?"

"No, nothing to eat," she said. "I am thirsty. I'm all right. My head hurts."

"I'll bring the water and a cloth to put on your forehead. I'll be back presently."

"Thank you, Peter," she said. When he stopped to stare at her, she said, "How foolish of me. Nelson. Thank you, Nelson."

She watched him leave the room. Something must have jarred her memory, she thought, made her forgetful. Of course he was Nelson, Nelson Vaughan. He had accosted her on the train. Despite his rudeness, she told herself, she liked him. He seemed a gentle man, quiet, even unsure of himself at times. He needed a woman who could give him encouragement, self-confidence. Ah, she thought, you're remaking his life to fit a plot of your own devising. You can't even plan your own life; don't attempt to steer another's course.

From the window she saw the day dying in a golden sunset. The curtains billowed inward, catching the last of the light, but she could no longer make out the floral pattern on the wallpaper because of the darkness gathering in the room. The house reminded her of home, not of Fairfield but of the house with the seven door, the doors that she had always believed led to opportunities, to new possibilities.

Peter—no, it was Nelson—had carried her up the stairs and laid her here on the bed as she remembered her father carrying her upstairs in that old house in Virginia when she was recuperating. She had been ill, yet well enough to be allowed downstairs in the evenings. As the lamps were lit, her father gathered her into his arms and mounted the stairs, whistling a tune. As soon as she was under the covers he turned up the lamp on the bedside table and read to her, tales of knights and maidens and dragons, of ships and storms at sea. Closing the book, he leaned over her and kissed her forehead.

"Don't forget to say your prayers," her father said, turning off the light and leaving the room.

"Now I lay me down to sleep," Margaret said. "I pray the Lord my soul to keep. If I should die before I wake, I pray the Lord my soul to take. And this I ask for Jesus' sake. Amen."

How long had it been since last she prayed? Many months. The last time was before she came south from Washington City. Not once in all that time had she asked God to forgive her sins. She had felt she was no longer entitled to ask.

She imagined herself coming to a wall. When she climbed to the top she looked out across a raging sea. A ship foundered in the distance and she heard a steady thump-thump-thump but whether from waves breaking on the shore or from gunfire she did not know. A woman screamed. Men shouted for help.

Margaret blinked her eyes. Why had she thought of a ship in distress? Of a wall? Of course, the game Nelson Vaughan had enticed her into playing on the train. She remembered it all clearly now, Nelson following her onto the train, telling her of the agent killed in Charleston the day before.

"Tell McClellan," the agent had said. "Trust Dickens," he had said. And then he had died.

"McClellan" must be General George McClellan, commander of the Union Army of the Potomac. "Trust Dickens." Who Dickens was, she had no idea. Charles Dickens, the English novelist? Surely not.

She raised herself onto one elbow. She had to leave here as soon as possible and make her way to Richmond and to the house on Libby Street where she could pass the message on. An important message, she was sure, otherwise the man in the park wouldn't have sacrificed his life to pass it on. Why was she no longer on the train? Vaguely, she remembered a growling of brakes, the lurch of the car, her fall to the floor. And then Peter had carried her here to the doctor's house, the house so much like her own home in Virginia. Of course she remembered.

"Here, drink this." Nelson leaned over the bed, raising her head with his hand and putting a glass to her lips.

After she drank, Margaret lay back on the pillow. Why did she keep thinking Nelson was Peter? She felt a cooling sensation and realized he had laid a damp cloth on her forehead. A name swam into her consciousness, the name of the woman she had seen briefly in the hospital in Wilmington and then had heard mentioned during the ball at Santee by that caustic-tongued woman, Mrs. Chesnut.

"Colleen," she said. "Who was Colleen?"

"You should rest now," Nelson told her. "The doctor said sleep will do you a world of good."

"Who was she? Tell me."

Nelson sighed. "Colleen Hughes was a young woman I knew in Charleston before the war. Once we were engaged to be married. It seems ages ago, though it's been little more than a year."

"And then she was with Jared?"

"She was with Jared before she sailed for the Bahamas. Her ship was sunk and she was drowned at sea."

"The fault was mine," she said.

"It was no one's fault. Her ship was attacked by Yankee gunboats. They're to blame, no one else. You're to try to sleep. You'll feel better when you wake."

"Yes," Margaret said. She began to pray. "Dear God," she said. Her voice trailed off, becoming inaudible so only she knew she prayed for Colleen Hughes and for Aaron and for all the men drowned at sea because of her; for Peter, shot to death on a beach in South Carolina; and for all the men dead and mutilated on the battlefields of the war at Manassas, at Shiloh, at Second Manassas, in the attack on Richmond. And before she finished her litany of death, she fell asleep.

When she wakened the room was dark. She sat up, wondering where she was. Peter had carried her here, she told herself; Peter, who was leaving soon to join the army. And it was her fault. She had accused him of cowardice and he was enlisting to prove her wrong. So much seemed to be her fault.

She felt a damp cloth on the bed beside her and, picking it up, she remembered that she was not in Fairfield but somewhere north of Charleston, making her way to Richmond and from there to Washington City. After she delivered her message at the house on Libby Street.

"Are you awake?"

Peter? No, of course not. It was Nelson.

"Yes," she said softly, "I'm awake."

"How do you feel?"

"Much better. My headache's gone."

Unable to see him in the darkness, she heard him walk across the room to the bed and kneel at her side.

"You're to sleep," he said. "It's the middle of the night."

"I must go to Richmond," she told him.

"The train won't leave until noon at the earliest. I made inquiries while you were asleep. I'll see that you're awake in time."

"Goodnight, Nelson," she said. She knew he wasn't Peter and didn't understand why she had confused him with her husband other than that Nelson, too, was leaving for war.

Impulsively, Nelson leaned over her and she felt his lips on her cheek, felt him kiss her forehead. Thinking of her father, she wanted to cry. She reached up to him, touched his hair and drew his head down to her.

All at once he was kissing her mouth, his hands holding her head up from the pillow, his lips meeting hers. She turned away but his lips followed, insistent, and she shook her head, sobbing, feeling the tears staining her cheeks.

"I'm sorry," he said. "I forgot myself."

She heard him get up and cross the room, pictured him standing at the window, though she saw him outlined there, but the room was so dark she couldn't be sure.

"Nelson," she said softly. She heard him turn and draw in his breath.

"Nelson," she said again, wanting to comfort him, wanting comfort herself.

"Margaret." His voice was so close to her she realized he must be only a few feet away.

"Hold me," she said.

He lay on the bed and took her in his arms, drawing her close to him while he kissed her, his lips warm on her mouth. Margaret kissed him in return, clinging to him as one survivor might cling to another, and for a long time they lay on the bed with the sheet separating them, holding each other in their arms.

When at last he moved from her, pulling the sheet down, her hands moved along her own body to discover that her gown had been removed and that she was dressed only in her camisole and under-petticoat. She trembled, afraid, and closed her eyes, imagining herself at sea, where she had never been in her life, with the deck of a ship tossing beneath her.

A hand touched her arm and she realized Nelson lay at her side, near her though not touching her except where his fingers lay on the flesh of her forearm. With a sigh she went to him and he came to her and they joined like the gentle meeting of surf and sand, slowly, as the waves lap on the beach, and they clung to each other, holding to one another as their bodies pulsed together, their senses rising until they seemed to burst in a shower of reds and yellows and oranges; subsiding slowly, his head, unseen, beside hers, her hair cascading over the pillow, her body, naked now, cradled in his arms as his lips met hers, kissed her mouth, her eyelids, and trailed lowed to her breasts to kiss each in turn. She held his head between her breasts, comforting him and herself with his nearness, holding him close to her as she felt the passion rise in him once more.

Margaret reached for him, found his sex and caressed him, led him into her, feeling a great warmth envelop her. He held her tightly, their arms and legs entwining, and they joined in ecstasy.

When the tide of their passion ebbed, she lay back, at peace with him and the world. And with herself. She wished that she could lie there forever with this gentleman at her side, could sleep and dream and reawaken to find him wanting and needing her as Peter had needed her long ago, so she could go to him and give herself to him. Not take, but give, and then be able to sleep in peace again.

She imagined a storm in the night outside, though she knew the sky was clear; a winter storm with the two of them isolated, alone together in a house of many doors, many possibilities, and yet she would open none of the doors, choosing instead to stay where she was, with Nelson, forever. She wished this for only a fleeting instant, imagined it while realizing her dream was impossible, that the morning would come and she must journey to Richmond and the North while he joined the armies fighting along the Potomac, going from there, if he lived, to wherever his destiny led him. There was no peace for him, no safe place.

She grieved for Nelson and for herself, drawing in her breath and letting it out in a sigh. Her hand fondled his hair, curling strands around her finger until, groggily, he came awake.

"Margaret," he whispered.

And they made love in the early hours of the morning.

When next she awakened daylight was paling the windows. Nelson lay sleeping beside her, the sheet drawn up over him except for one bare arm lying on its top. She smiled, slipping from the far side of the bed.

Using water from the pitcher on the stand, she bathed before dressing. Seeing Nelson's clothes scattered on the floor, she picked up his shirt, smoothing it before she draped it over the back of a chair. Taking his pants, she folded them over her arm, intending to lay them on the back of the chair as well.

She heard a thud and looked down to see that an object had fallen from his pocket to the floor. A gold watch, was her first thought. She placed his pants on the chair and knelt to pick up the fallen object. No, it wasn't a watch, it was smaller. A golden locket on a chain of gold.

With pounding heart, she opened the locket and saw, as she knew she would, her own picture and her initials entwined with Peter's. She glanced at the bed to find Nelson looking at her.

"This is my locket," she said numbly, "my husband's locket."

"Yes," he said, "I know."

From the despair in his voice and the look of hopeless resignation on his face, she knew without being told that he had found the locket on the body of a Yankee soldier on a beach at Hilton Head, knew how Nelson had come to be there and what he had done.

As Margaret let the locket fall to the floor, she felt a stab of pain in her heart. She crossed her hands over her breasts and lowered her head.

"Oh, my God," she murmured. "Oh, my God."

19

Margaret Boyd paused on Libby Street in front of an innocent-appearing shop. Atkinson's Drapers was printed in gilt on the glass on both sides of the entrance and bolts of cloth were arranged attractively in the display windows. She pushed open the door, heard a bell tinkle, and went in.

The interior of the shop was darker than she'd expected. Although there were several women customers in the aisles, the cloth on display, in contrast to that in the window, was meager in quantity and appeared poor in quality. The Union blockade was having its effect, Margaret decided.

"May I help you?" The draper's assistant smiled up at her. She was a young girl, no more than fifteen, with brown hair pulled severely back from her freckled face.

"I'd like three-and-a-half yards of serge," Margaret said as calmly as she could.

The girl blinked. "Exactly three-and-a-half?" she asked after a pause.

"Exactly."

The girl glanced at the other customers. "I don't know if we have any serge," she said. "If you'll wait a moment, I'll fetch my mother from the back."

The girl disappeared into the rear of the shop while Margaret waited with her fingers gripping the counter edge, her knuckles white. She drew in her breath and let it out slowly, rubbing her hands together.

"May I help you?" A short graying woman looked at her over narrow metal-rimmed spectacles. "You asked for three-and-a-half yards of serge, I believe."

"Serge?" Margaret repeated. "I've changed my mind. I'd like dimity."

"I see. The same yardage?"

"Yes."

"If you'll come with me, please. We received a shipment from Wilmington yesterday and I believe there were several rolls of dimity."

After holding a swinging waist-high door open for Margaret, she ushered her through curtains and along a narrow hall to a door at the far end. When Margaret stepped inside she found herself in a sitting room. Walking to a lace-covered table near the window, she turned to face the shopkeeper.

"I'm Isabella Atkinson," the woman said.

Margaret nodded.

"You have a message for me?" the woman asked.

"I do. It's intended for . . ." Margaret paused, wondering whether she should say McClellan's name.

"The general?" Isabella Atkinson suggested.

"Yes. The message is 'Trust Dickens.' "

"And that's all?"

"There may have been more. If there was, our friend

didn't have time to pass it along. He was killed in Charleston."

Mrs. Atkinson put her hand on Margaret's sleeve. "You were very brave to come here," she said. "I know what happened to the man you talked to in Charleston. Not only is he dead but he left records that were discovered by the Confederates. Your name may have been among them. You must hide until you can make your way north."

"I intended to leave for the North in any event."

"There's no time to lose. I'll do all I can to help but we must make haste. You're in great danger."

"Colonel Raleigh-Beckwith will see you now, Colonel Hunter."

Nodding to the aide, Jared walked into the command tent. Beckwith stood leafing through a sheaf of papers with his back to Jared. When he turned, he smiled wanly.

"Being on General Lee's staff is a demanding assignment," Beckwith said. "He's a stern taskmaster."

"So I've heard."

"I didn't summon you here, however, to discuss the Army of Northern Virginia or our campaign into Maryland. I had quite another matter in mind, no less important. Sit down, Hunter, sit down."

Jared sat stiffly erect in a camp chair. The bastard, he thought, noticing that Beckwith intended to remain standing so he could look down at Jared while they talked.

"Is it about your daughter, Dyan?" Jared asked. Two could play this game, he thought.

"My daughter?"

Jared couldn't read the other man's expression. Besides the surprise in Beckwith's voice he thought he detected a hint of fear.

"Yes. I happened to meet Dyan in Richmond last month on my way here. I thought you might have heard and sent for me to find out at first hand how she is. I can assure you she's never been better. I believe Richmond agrees with her."

"No, I did *not* ask you here to discuss my daughter." Beckwith looked at Jared uncertainly, as though he couldn't decide whether to show offense. For a moment a suspicion flared in Jared's mind. Beckwith and Dyan? Had he taken advantage of his own voluptuous daughter? What had Dyan told him about her father? He couldn't remember. No, the whole idea was preposterous, though he wouldn't put it past the man.

"The matter does concern a woman, however." Beckwith paused. "What do you know of a Margaret Boyd?"

Jared forced himself to remain impassive. "I don't believe my private life concerns you, Colonel," he said.

"It wouldn't normally. It does when the woman in question is an agent of the United States government."

"Margaret? An agent?" Jared's voice showed his disbelief and rising anger.

Beckwith backed away. "We have no reason to question your loyalty to the cause, Colonel Hunter," he said hastily. "None at all. There's no doubt, however, that the lady in question is one of Mr. Alan Pinkerton's agents who was sent to the South specifically to report on the movements of blockade-runners operating out of Wilmington and Charleston."

Jared recalled a disheveled Captain Hendricks pounding on the door of his hotel room in Wilmington. "I bring distressing news," the captain had said. Jared recalled the *Celeste*. And Colleen. Had he told Margaret details concerning the ship's plans to run the blockade? No, he hadn't told her anything of importance.

"I can see you're surprised by my news," Beckwith said. "We discovered the truth when another of Pinkerton's agents, a man, was shot and killed in Charleston last month. Miss Boyd is now being sought. Do you have any idea of her present whereabouts, Colonel?"

"No, sir, I don't," Jared said. "I saw her last at Santee plantation near Charleston more than a month ago. We parted under less than auspicious circumstances, you might say. I haven't seen or heard from her since."

"Do you expect to?"

"I do not. I have no notion where she went or where she might be."

Beckwith nodded. "I'm satisfied, Colonel," he said.

Jared stood and saluted. Beckwith returned the salute. As Jared was about to leave the tent, Beckwith said, "There's no question of your own loyalty, none at all."

Jared said nothing. As he walked from the headquarters tent, though, he swore under his breath. The stain on his loyalty, however slight, was there and would be as long as he held a command position in the army. He had observed other officers tainted in similar ways, heard the talk, the whispers, the innuendos, and watched as they were passed over for promotion time and time again.

He cursed Beckwith, cursed the powers-that-be, cursed Margaret Boyd, and cursed himself, knowing his oaths would avail him nothing. For perhaps the first time in his life he looked into the future with a feeling akin to despair.

"General," the aide said, "this is the intercepted Rebel message."

George Brinton McClellan unfolded the document. "Special Orders No. 191," he read. He glanced at the closing words of the dispatch—"By command of General R.E. Lee. R.H. Chilton, Assistant Adjutant General."

"The handwriting is Chilton's," the aide said. "I've served with him and there's not a vestige of a doubt in my mind."

McClellan nodded. "This could still be a hoax intended to lead us astray," he said.

General McClellan was a cautious man, too cautious, his critics had long maintained. He was young, still in his thirties, a short man with a barrel chest and a handsome face. He had dark hair and a black moustache. His men would follow him anywhere, for he had the gift of being able to inspire respect and devotion and they cheered him as he rode among them.

He saw himself as misunderstood by Lincoln and his cabinet, a martyr to the mismanagement of lesser men motivated by jealousy. He was overly deliberate—careful, he would have called it—slow to set his arm in motion and, once underway, hesitant to seize whatever advantages fate offered.

He read the orders General Lee had sent to his Confederate commanders: "The army will resume its march tomorrow, taking the Hagerstown road, General Jackson's command will form the advance, and, after passing Middletown, with such portions as he may select, take the route toward Sharpsburg . . ."

When McClellan finished reading he laid the orders on top of a map spread on the table in front of him. "You say two of our infantrymen found these orders?" he asked the aide.

"Yes, sir. Now we not only know where Lee is but where he intends to be tomorrow and on the days after that. He can't hide his movements behind the mountains any longer. He's been delivered into our hands."

"*If* this message is authentic." McClellan drummed

his fingers on the paper. Noticing a word on the reverse side of the orders, he picked them up again. "Dickens" had been printed on the paper in small block letters.

"Dickens," McClellan said. He recalled the information he had received and dismissed as gibberish only the day before. "Trust Dickens," he had been told by a man who had never failed him. By Alan Pinkerton himself.

"I'm confident the message is authentic," the aide said.

"As am I," McClellan said. "We'll advance over the mountains through Turner's Gap and Crampton's Gap. Lee has made a great mistake coming north into Maryland and he will be severely punished for it."

Nelson Hunter Vaughan's company retreated south along the Hagerstown Pike, finally taking up a position near a church north of the village of Sharpsburg.

"They calls it the Dunker Church," a soldier sitting beside him said, "'cause of the way they baptize people by dunking them."

The men, dirty and bedraggled, lounged on the slope in front of the church. Straggling had been heavy in the Maryland campaign as men left the army in the night to make their way back across the Potomac and south into Virginia.

"We signed on to defend the South," one of the stragglers had told Nelson, "not to invade the North."

Lee must have expected the citizens of Maryland to rally to the Southern banner, Nelson reasoned, once the army had crossed the river. They had not. Instead, they met the Confederates with hostile stares, with fear, or with indifference.

Nelson couldn't blame them, not completely. The army gave the appearance of an organized group of ragamuffins. His own uniform consisted of a torn pair of trousers, a stained and dirty jacket, and a slouch hat with a brim pinned up by a thorn. He carried a dirty blanket over one shoulder, a stained haversack full of apples and corn foraged from fields and orchards along the way, a musket and a full cartridge box. His shoes were well worn, with holes in both soles. He considered himself lucky to have shoes at all since many of the men were barefooted.

Still, he told himself, these were fighting men. The slackers were gone, had deserted long ago. Those who were left would give a damn good account of themselves. And Robert E. Lee was their commander, a man who wasn't afraid to risk all in order to gain all.

After a sleepless night, they moved north from the church shortly after dawn on September 17, 1862. Ahead of him, Nelson heard the pounding of the cannon and the whir of shells. Soon he heard a more ominous noise, the rattle of musketry.

He noticed an occasional soldier leave the column and sit on the side of the road with his head in his hands. Usually, the man would push himself to his feet after a time and rejoin the march. No one spoke as they doggedly advanced toward the developing battle. he men's lips were tight, their teeth clenched. The sound of the firing grew louder, punctuated with single shots or ragged volleys.

They left the road and entered the woods, the firing coming from ahead and to their right. In front of them, on the other side of the Hagerstown Pike, Nelson saw a field where corn grew taller than a man's head. The stalks waved as though swept by a wind but there was no wind and he realized the shooting and men advancing through the field created the wavelike motion.

As he watched, men in blue ran from the cornfield toward the Confederate line, climbing over a zig-zag rail fence along the pike. Confederates on the other side of the road, in advance of Nelson's company's position, were loading and firing. Union soldiers fell, sprawling on top of the fence or toppling into the road. Still the Yankees came on, with one wave of men following another.

The roar of the batteries was deafening, greater than any he had ever heard. The gray line near the road broke, the men running, stopping to load and fire with grim determination as the Union troops rushed forward, shouting and laughing hysterically. Acrid powder smoke lay over the field, covering the movements of the troops, swirling away for an instant to reveal fleeing men, a horse pitching forward, a flag shredded by musket fire.

The captain rode in front of their line. "After them, boys!" he shouted and Nelson ran forward with soldiers on both sides of him. The Confederates retreating in front of them ran back through their line. Nelson stopped, fired, ran forward, stopped and fired again. He saw blue-clad soldiers falling. A horse lay sprawled on the ground in front of him and he ran around it. The Union troops held for a moment and then their line wavered and they ran, the Confederates sweeping them north along the pike and back into the cornfield.

The Confederate advance reached the far side of the road, where the men stopped behind the rail fence. The noise all around them was deafening, the air acrid. When Nelson slumped to the ground behind the open railings, he was trembling. Remembering Shiloh, he was afraid. Not of death—at least not of a clean, quick death from a minié ball he wouldn't even hear—but of being wounded and left between the lines, crying out in pain, calling for water to ease his thirst.

The Union troops counter-attacked from the cornfield, charging toward the fence. The men around Nelson fired, Nelson fired, and the Union line fell almost as one man. A few Yankees turned and fled once more into the corn.

Officers rode up and down behind the Confederate line, urging the men out of the shelter of the fence. No one moved. Nelson, dazed, his vision blurred, pushed himself to his feet and climbed up on the rails. At the top of the fence he rolled over and dropped to land on his feet on the far side. Raising his musket, he gave a long Rebel yell, motioning the men behind the fence to follow him. Without waiting to see if they did, he ran ahead into the corn with the stalks rasping around him.

After a moment he looked over his shoulder and saw other men climbing the fence. One paused at the top, his musket fell to the ground and the man's arms reached high over his head. For an instant he stood poised on the fence before toppling backward out of sight. The rest of Nelson's company was in the corn now, thrashing ahead, and as they broke into the open on the far side of the field they saw the Union troops fleeing into the shelter of the woods.

Union artillery raked the open field in front of them, stopping their advance. The firing gradually lessened and in the lull two Confederate officers, both unknown to Nelson, rode up.

"What's your name, soldier?" the first asked.

"Private Nelson Hunter Vaughan, sir," he told him.

As they cantered off, Nelson heard the officer who had asked his name say, "That man's a born leader. He shouldn't be in the ranks."

Jared Hunter's regiment joined the main body of the Confederate Army of Northern Virginia on the evening before the battle. Jared was put under the command of General Robert Toombs on the right wing of the line defending Sharpsburg, where the regiment took up positions on the crest of a hill overlooking a stone bridge crossing Antietam Creek.

On the morning of the seventeenth, Jared rode along the line. He nodded with satisfaction as he inspected their defensive alignment on a high wooded bluff pockmarked by rifle pits dug the day before. A stone wall ran along the crest among oak trees whose branches concealed a host of Confederate snipers.

Jared was still rankled by an incident that had happened the day before. Nearing Sharpsburg, his men had paused at a farm to fill their canteens only to discover that the Maryland farmer had fled after removing the handle of his pump and uprooting the pump itself. And they had counted on the Marylanders welcoming them with open arms!

To the north, Jared heard the thunder of the guns as the battle began. Shortly after dawn General Toombs rode up on his white gelding.

"No sign of the damn Yankees?" he asked Jared.

"No, sir, it's all quiet here."

"The Yankees on the other side of the creek must be West Pointers," Toombs said. "If only all West Pointers had been on the Union side in the beginning, we'd be in Washington by now."

"Yes, sir." Jared smiled, and thought of his brother, Fremont, who was at West Point. He'd heard of Toombs's feelings about the Academy but was still surprised the Georgian made no effort to hide them.

"You're not an Academy man, are you?" the general asked.

"No, sir. The Citadel, sir."

"Good. Carry on."

Jared rode back to his men, who were lying in wait along the top of the ridge. Through his field glasses he saw Union troops massing beyond the creek, yet they didn't attack. Not until ten in the morning did the Yankees make their first attempt to cross Antietam Creek.

The Union soldiers, with skirmishers in advance of the lines of regulars, left the shelter of a woods and crossed a low open field toward the bridge. The Confederates, Georgians for the most part, waited until the blue-clad troops were in the middle of the field before they opened fire with volley after volley Yankees fell screaming in the field but others came on, a handful reaching the creek under a hail of fire from the ridge above them, a few managing to cross and hold a short section of the west bank for a few minutes before being forced back across the creek. Their attack broken, the Yankees fled in disarray into the cover of the trees.

"Good work," Jared shouted as he rode along the line on the ridge.

Soon the thunder of Union artillery increased and shells whistled over and into the Confederate lines. At noon the Federals attacked again and once more they were turned back at the creek.

"Yankees are marching downstream to outflank you," a courier reported to Jared.

"Tell the general our ammunition's running low," Jared said. "We only have two or three rounds left a man."

No ammunition was forthcoming; the artillery barrage continued and Confederate casualties mounted. At one in the afternoon the Yankees attacked for the third time, running across the open ground with their bayonets fixed, meeting a storm of fire from the ridge, men in blue dropping every step of the

way. After a few minutes the first of the attackers
reached a stone wall extending from the bridge on
the east bank.

The Confederates on the hill poured fire down on
the Yankee position. The Federals returned the fire,
loading, shooting, loading, shooting. The Confederate fire slackened. Six Union soldiers followed an
officer onto the bridge. When all crossed safely, others ran across to the west side and soon the Yankees
were charging up the hill.

"We're out of ammunition," a third lieutenant reported to Jared.

"Give the order to withdraw," Jared told him.

His men began pulling back, in good order at first
and then fleeing to escape the Yankees. Confederate
snipers slid down the trunks of oaks or dropped from
low overhanging branches. Some surrendered by
raising their hands. Others stuck newspapers on the
ends of their ramrods and waved them in the air.

The bulk of Jared's regiment retreated to another
ridge where they were protected by the main Confederate army. The Federals reached the crest of
the hill over the creek and halted, waiting for reinforcements to cross the bridge.

"Stay in your present position," Jared was ordered,
"until you're relieved. General Hill is on his way
from Harper's Ferry by forced march."

As they waited with the Harper's Ferry Road at
their backs and Sharpsburg a half mile to their left,
the men received ammunition and fresh water. The
Union troops moved out from the cover of the woods
above Antietam Creek, charging in the face of heavy
fire across the open field to Jared's left in the direction of General Longstreet's Confederates.

As the Union soldiers advanced, Yankees falling
amid the smoke obscuring the field, their line swung

away from Jared's regiment and he saw his chance.

"At them," he ordered and his men charged into the open field toward the Yankee left flank. The Union line nearest them broke, the men in blue taking shelter behind haystacks or fastening white handkerchiefs to their muskets and bayonets.

Jared's men swept past the surrendering Yankees in the direction of other Union troops sheltering behind a stone wall. The Confederates fired, advanced, fired. Again their ammunition ran low. At the same time, more Federal soldiers came into the line behind the wall.

"Go back! Go back!" Jared ordered.

His men retreated slowly, reloading and shooting as they went. All at once firing broke out behind them, and Jared turned and realized that the Yankees who had surrendered, now in their rear, had regrouped to form a skirmish line on the far side of a lane. Breaking into a run, the Confederates fled past the Yankee position, returning to their original line at the road from Harper's Ferry, leaving their dead and wounded scattered on the field.

As Jared galloped along the road he felt a pull at his shoulder. Reaching up, he found a jagged tear in his uniform that bared his skin, but he was uninjured. He swore. He might have been better off if the bullet had found its mark, he thought, wondering what General Toombs would say about the loss of life in the charge. The tactic had seemed so right at its inception, but it had turned into a costly retreat.

Late in the afternoon, General Hill's men arrived from Harper's Ferry and the Yankee thrust from Antietam Creek was halted. Jared marched his men to the rear for ammunition and, after an hour's rest, brought them back into the lines in support of Hill.

As the setting sun touched the treetops behind the Confederates, the firing lessened and then died out. Exhausted and ravaged by their losses, both Northern and Southern soldiers bivouacked on the battlefield.

The night was rent by the cries of the wounded calling for water and for an end to their agony. General McClellan's Union forces held the cornfield in the north, a sunken road near the center of the line where savage fighting had taken place during the day, and the bridges crossing Antietam Creek. General Lee occupied an unbroken line in front of Sharpsburg and, more importantly, held the ford across the Potomac leading back into Virginia. However, he had lost perhaps a fourth of his troops and was outnumbered by more than two to one.

Jared Hunter rode among his men on the following morning, encouraging them, preparing them for the withdrawal he knew would soon begin. The day was warm, with scattered clouds hinting at the possibility of rain. There was scattered firing, though neither army attacked the other in strength. The invasion of Maryland was over, Lee had been checked and his Army of Northern Virginia would soon retreat beyond the Potomac.

Jared, thirsty, dismounted at a springhouse, a roofless building on the side of a hill with whitewashed walls as high as a man's head. He picketed his horse and strode inside, where he knelt beside water spouting from a pipe, taking off his gloves and cupping his hands to drink. He was tired, wearier than he had ever been before. The water was clear and cold and he drank for many minutes. While filling his canteen, he thought he heard his name.

"Jared!"

Yes, someone was calling him. A familiar voice.

"Jared!"

The cry was closer and he stood, his hand going to the pistol in the holster on his belt.

Nelson Hunter Vaughan, a musket under his arm, stepped into the entrance to the springhouse. He was dirty and unshaven, his clothes were ragged.

"I thought it was you," Nelson said, "when I saw you ride by."

"As you can see, it is."

A sense of fatality settled over Jared. It was as though he was standing off to one side watching himself and Nelson, their figures distorted, their voices sounding far away as they enacted a scene that seemed eerily familiar, as it had happened before.

"You killed Aaron," Nelson said. "You hunted him down and murdered him."

"I don't deny it," Jared said. After the bastard tried to kill me in Wilmington, he thought.

"I've followed you here to kill you," Nelson said.

Jared smiled faintly. "You won't kill me, Nelson. You don't have the nerve. You never did have nerve, not when we were boys at Santee and at Hunter Hill, and not now."

Nelson raised the musket. Jared stood his ground, making no move to defend himself, still smiling slightly. He looked at the black muzzle of the gun aimed at his heart. Slowly Nelson lowered the musket.

"You see," Jared said, "I always was the better man and we've both always known it. Maggie has ten times more spirit than you do."

"Maggie?"

"Margaret Boyd, the woman I brought to Santee after my father's marriage." Jared bowed. "When you became my brother," he said.

"What about Margaret Boyd?"

"She's one of Pinkerton's agents. Works for the

North. She's a spy. They found her out when another agent was killed in Charleston. I only heard the day before yesterday that she's been apprehended and is being held at Manassas Junction. At least they believe it's Maggie. After this campaign's over I'm going there to identify her."

"And you would? You'd turn her in?"

"Of course. She's betrayed the cause. Now stand aside, Brother Nelson, and let me return to my men."

As Jared stepped forward, Nelson raised his musket and fired. The shot hurled Jared back and he reached out to steady himself, but he slid down the white-washed wall to the ground. A red stain spread slowly on the gray front of his jacket.

Jared heard the faint sound of hooves, and after a time became aware of a gray-clad officer looking down at him. "I heard a shot," the man said.

"Not from here," Jared told him. "A stray Yankee bullet. I was looking for water. This is my cousin. Came to help me."

The officer nodded. "I'll fetch bearers." He ran from the springhouse.

Jared smiled up at Nelson. "You see," he whispered. "Even now I'm the better man."

From a distance he thought he heard the roll of drums and the echoing call of a bugle. "We were in the right," he said.

"The right?" Nelson asked. "About what?"

Jared struggled to speak. About everything, he thought. Bombarding Fort Sumter, the war, everything. He tried to speak but found he could not. The darkness closed in upon him and he died.

20

FOLLOW ME, SERGEANT," Lieutenant Moyers told Nelson Hunter Vaughan. He led him along the dusty Manassas street toward the hotel.

"We had very little information to go on," the lieutenant said. He was short and blond and about the same age as Nelson. "She might be the woman they want in Richmond and she might not. Her first name's Margaret and she's as tall as this woman is supposed to be, but when we stopped her on her way north we found nothing to suggest she wasn't all she said she was."

"And what does she claim to be, sir?"

"A housewife from Connecticut who's been searching for relatives in Virginia. She hadn't heard from them in months, she claims, and feared they had been killed in the fighting."

"She calls herself Margaret DeWitt?"

"That's correct. I wouldn't think she'd keep the same first name if she actually was the Federal agent we're seeking, but one never knows. I've seen some strange sights and heard a few unusual tales since this war began."

"We all have," Nelson said.

"As you know, it was your cousin who was supposed to identify the woman. Colonel Hunter. I regret your loss."

A muscle twitched in Nelson's cheek. "Jared was a good officer," he said. "The Confederacy will miss him."

"Did you know this Miss Boyd well?" the lieutenant asked.

"No. She was more my cousin's friend than she was mine. He brought her to Santee—that's my home in South Carolina—and I met her there. I'd know her again, though, without a doubt."

"Good." The two men climbed the steps to the hotel porch and went inside. The lieutenant directed Nelson to a small sitting room off the front hall. "If you'll wait here," he told him, "I'll bring the lady down from her room."

Nelson crossed to a ladder-backed chair that faced the door, then shook his head. He was too tense to sit down. He heard steps on the stairs and the lieutenant appeared in the doorway, his arm extended as he ushered a woman into the room. Margaret Boyd stopped just inside the door and stared at Nelson. He drew in his breath.

Her hair, coiled on the back of her head in a chignon, was black. Her modest magenta dress was plainly cut and buttoned to the neck. But he hadn't drawn in his breath in surprise at the change in the color of her hair or the severity of her costume; he had been struck, as he always was, by her beauty. He took a step toward her, paused, then took another.

This was the woman who had worked for the enemy,

he told himself, who had endangered the lives of his comrades, who undoubtedly detested all he believed in. And yet this was the woman he loved.

Nelson turned from Margaret to the lieutenant. "I've never seen this woman before in my life, sir," he said. "I'd be willing to swear that she isn't Margaret Boyd."

"I'm sure that won't be necessary, Sergeant," Lieutenant Moyers said. "Your word's good enough for me."

When the two men were alone a short time later, the lieutenant said, "I was certain she wasn't the woman they wanted. I don't know how I knew, but I did."

"What will become of her?"

"She'll be permitted to continue on her way north. In fact, she intends to leave on the next train. May I buy you a drink, Sergeant? You've saved me a great deal of botheration and filling out of forms by coming here."

Nelson hesitated. "Andy Jackson used to say, 'I'm overly fond of liquor so I never touch it.' That's been my motto this last year and more. But today, sir, I'll make an exception and join you in a glass."

After he left the lieutenant outside the grogshop, Nelson walked through the village to the depot. Margaret stood alone on the platform, her carpetbag at her feet, her bonnet hiding her dyed hair. The sun was setting behind her and the cool evening breeze from the north brought with it the chill of autumn.

Nelson took off his hat and bowed stiffly. He couldn't find the words to express what he wanted to say.

"Nelson," she said softly. "How difficult it must have been for you to deny knowing me."

"I liked your hair much better when it was red," he told her.

"You don't want to talk about what you did. I understand."

"I love you," he said.

"Oh, Nelson." She put out her hand, meaning to touch him, then drew back. "You don't love me," she said, "not really. How could you? You know next to nothing about me. I'm not at all the woman you imagine me to be."

"Does that matter? If I'd known you all my life I couldn't love you more than I do. I think I loved you from the moment I first saw you—the night Jared brought you to the ball at Santee."

"I was told that Jared was killed."

"Yes, at Sharpsburg. I was—I was with him when he died." She thought Nelson meant to go on but he shook his head and was silent.

"I can never thank you enough," she said, "for what you did at the hotel a few minutes ago."

"You *are* going north? The lieutenant told me you were."

"Yes, you need have no fears about that. I'm going home to Connecticut."

Margaret thought of the men in the hospitals, brave men, cowardly men, Southerners for the most part, a few Northerners, each with his own hopes and fears and dreams. She thought of the killing and the maiming on the battlefields. She had served her country, had done her share. Haven't I, Peter? she asked silently. Haven't I done enough to avenge you?

"You have a family there?"

"Two boys, Alex and Curtis. Though Curtis insists I call him Buck."

"You never told me you had children."

"You never asked. I intend to go home to be with my boys and to write. I've written stories for magazines and had them published. A Mr. Niles came to see me just before the war. He's a publisher in Boston. I plan to see him about an idea I have for a novel about the war."

"You told me you wrote stories. I had no idea you'd had them published."

"There's so much about me you don't know. I'm an independent woman, though you may have guessed that, and a difficult woman, or so I've been told. We were together for a few days and you thought you'd learned all there was to know about me and yet you hadn't. You have a dream of me. Jared had a dream of me, a different one, I'm sure, yet neither dream was me. They were what you wanted me to be, what you expected me to be, not what I really am."

"Don't all men dream of the women they love?"

"I suppose they do, Nelson, just as women have dreams of the men they love—or think they love. Just as we all have a dream of the country we love. Mine's of the North, the Union, yours is of the Confederacy."

"I want to know what your dreams are. You're right, there's a great deal I don't know about you. I want you you to tell me everything about yourself, Margaret. What your hopes are, your dreams, what you like, what you don't like. I want to know you completely— though I realize I never will."

"What do you intend to do?" She looked at his new stripes. "Sergeant?"

Nelson nodded. "Yes, sergeant. For a week now. I'm a soldier, Margaret, and a soldier fights. I'll fight for the Confederacy until we win the war."

"And you truly believe you will win?"

"I do. We may not invade the North again and we may never take Washington City, that's true enough. I thought the people of Maryland would rally around our flag when we crossed the Potomac. They didn't. We'll fight on because we're fighting for our freedom. The North will tire of the killing and eventually they'll let us go our way in peace."

"And the slaves? Like Melinda?"

"She's already free. My mother promised me Melinda will always have a home at Santee if she wants it. The others will be freed when the war ends, if not before. I can even imagine Jefferson Davis freeing the slaves so they can fight for the Confederacy."

"If he does, won't that mean this whole war has been fought for nothing?"

"No, the war's been fought for more than slavery. We're fighting to be allowed to choose our own course. Isn't that what the Revolution was for?" He frowned. "Why are we talking of North and South, Margaret, when we have so little time left?"

"I'll always remember you, Nelson."

He shook his head. "That's not what I want, to be remembered. I want you."

"How can you possibly expect that? After what happened? After what happened to my husband?"

"Can you ever forgive me?"

"Forgive you? I forgave you long ago. I wouldn't be talking to you now if I hadn't. I can forgive you, Nelson, but I can't forget what happened on Hilton Head. I'll never be able to forget. Never."

He heard the conductor giving the last call to board the lone passenger car at the front of the waiting freight train. Nelson took her hand in his.

"Someday?" he asked. "After this war is over?"

"No." She shook her head and he could see she was fighting to hold back her tears. "No, not even then. I don't think I'll ever be able to forget Peter—and what you did—for as long as I live. I'm sorry, Nelson."

She drew her hand from his, touched his cheek with her fingers, then turned and hurried to the steps leading into the car.

"Margaret!" he called after her as he saw her disappear inside. He ran along the platform, calling her name. The train inched forward, its wheels grinding, steam and smoke billowing around him. Nelson ran beside the car until he saw her inside. "Margaret!" he shouted.

As she looked down at him, she pitied him, realizing all he had lost, the Old Colonel, his boyhood friend Aaron, his mother through marriage to Jethro Hunter. Even Jared, a man he had hated but to whom he was bound in a way she didn't understand. And now he was losing her. She remembered their night together on the way north to Richmond and she felt a tenderness for him, a thankfulness, for he had given her a great gift, re-awakening her to a part of life she had thought was dead forever.

And she felt love for him. She couldn't explain her love or defend it to herself, but it was there, in her heart. Love, she thought, needs no reason.

She wanted to tell him how she felt, so she reached to open the window. Though she pulled and pushed, the window refused to budge. She saw Nelson running beside the car, could see his lips move as he called her name, though she couldn't hear him. And then the car was beyond the platform and he was gone. . . .

Nelson walked slowly back to the station. In the pane of the depot window he saw his reflection and paused to look at the gray uniform, with its new sergeant stripes, and at his face, older than he remembered it. He recalled looking at himself in another mirror long ago, though it had been only a year and a half, and accusing himself of being a coward.

He shook his head. No, he wasn't a coward. He had been afraid—and he would be afraid again—but he had done what he had to do. He had survived. At great cost. He had killed Jared and the guilt would haunt him for the rest of his days.

The Nelson Hunter Vaughan he had seen in the

mirror in the Charleston town house before the war had been a different man. Before the war. Yes, that was what had changed everything for better or for worse. The war. From now on, at least in the South, all time would be divided into two eras, before the war and after the war.

He had lost Margaret, as he had known in his heart he would. She had gone, though he would remember her always and love her always. He sighed for what might have been if the world had been a different place. It wasn't, the world wouldn't change, so he must make the best of it and somehow he knew he would.

In the distance he heard the lonely wail of the train whistle and he looked up. Above the hills to the west he saw the first star, as bright as a promise, in the evening sky. And he felt a sudden urge to head toward that star, to travel west, to make a new life for himself in a new land.

After the final battle, when the guns were silent again, he promised himself. Yes, after the war.

EPILOGUE

T HE BATTLE OF SHARPSBURG, resulting in Lee's withdrawal south of the Potomac, was one of the turning points in the war between the states.

England and France, who had long considered recognizing the Confederacy or even intervening on its side, drew back. And on September 22, 1862, President Abraham Lincoln, using this battle as his backdrop, issued the Emancipation Proclamation. The war would no longer be fought only to preserve the Union. It would now involve a large, more emotional, more fundamental issue—freedom.

If a copy of Lee's Special Orders Number 191 had not been lost, a loss never adequately explained, General Lee might have won a decisive victory at Sharpsburg. If he had, England and France might have intervened on the Confederate side and Lincoln might have indefinitely postponed issuing the Emancipation Proclamation.

These are might-have-beens. The fact is that after Sharpsburg the initiative shifted, slowly at first and then with gathering momentum, as the tides of battle turned from the South to the North.

THE END